DAY

Also Edited by
Ellen Datlow

After (with Terri Windling)

Alien Sex

The Beastly Bride: Tales of the Animal People (with Terri Windling)

The Best Horror of the Year: Volumes One through *Seventeen*

Black Feathers: Dark Avian Tales

Black Heart, Ivory Bones (with Terri Windling)

Black Swan, White Raven (with Terri Windling)

Black Thorn, White Rose (with Terri Windling)

Blood and Other Cravings

Blood Is Not Enough: 17 Stories of Vampirism

Body Shocks: Extreme Tales of Body Horror

Children of Lovecraft

Christmas and Other Horrors

The Coyote Road: Trickster Tales (with Terri Windling)

The Cutting Room: Dark Reflections of the Silver Screen

Darkness: Two Decades of Modern Horror

The Dark: New Ghost Stories

The Del Rey Book of Science Fiction and Fantasy

The Devil and the Deep: Horror Stories of the Sea

Digital Domains: A Decade of Science Fiction & Fantasy

The Doll Collection

Echoes: The Saga Anthology of Ghost Stories

The Faery Reel: Tales from the Twilight Realm (with Terri Windling)

Fearful Symmetries

Fears: Tales of Psychological Horror

Final Cuts: New Tales of Hollywood Horror and Other Spectacles

The Green Man: Tales from the Mythic Forest (with Terri Windling)

Haunted Legends (with Nick Mamatas)

Haunted Nights (with Lisa Morton)

Hauntings

Inferno: New Tales of Terror and the Supernatural

Lethal Kisses

Little Deaths

Lovecraft Unbound

Lovecraft's Monsters

Mad Hatters and March Hares

The Monstrous

Naked City: Tales of Urban Fantasy

Nebula Awards Showcase 2009

Nightmare Carnival

Nightmares: A New Decade of Modern Horror

Off Limits: Tales of Alien Sex

Omni Best Science Fiction: Volumes One through *Three*

The Omni Books of Science Fiction: Volumes One through *Seven*

Omni Visions One and *Two*

Poe: 19 New Tales Inspired by Edgar Allan Poe

Queen Victoria's Book of Spells (with Terri Windling)

Ruby Slippers, Golden Tears (with Terri Windling)

Salon Fantastique: Fifteen Original Tales of Fantasy (with Terri Windling)

Screams from the Dark: 29 Tales of Monsters and the Monstrous

Silver Birch, Blood Moon (with Terri Windling)

Sirens and Other Daemon Lovers (with Terri Windling)

Snow White, Blood Red (with Terri Windling)

Supernatural Noir

Swan Sister (with Terri Windling)

Tails of Wonder and Imagination: Cat Stories

Teeth: Vampire Tales (with Terri Windling)

Telling Tales: The Clarion West 30th Anniversary Anthology

Troll's-Eye View: A Book of Villainous Tales (with Terri Windling)

Twists of the Tale

Vanishing Acts

When Things Get Dark: Stories Inspired by Shirley Jackson

A Whisper of Blood

A Wolf at the Door and Other Retold Fairy Tales (with Terri Windling)

The Year's Best Fantasy and Horror: Volumes One through *Sixteen* (with Terri Windling)

The Year's Best Fantasy and Horror: Volumes Seventeen through *Twenty-One* (with Kelly Link and Gavin J. Grant)

Merciless Sun: Tales of Daylight Horror

Edited by

Ellen Datlow

LONDON **NEW YORK** TORONTO
AMSTERDAM/ANTWERP NEW DELHI SYDNEY/MELBOURNE

1230 AVENUE OF THE AMERICAS, NEW YORK, NEW YORK 10020

First Saga Press trade paperback edition September 2025

SAGA PRESS and colophon are trademarks of Simon & Schuster, LLC

Simon & Schuster strongly believes in freedom of expression and stands against censorship in all its forms. For more information, visit BooksBelong.com.

For information about special discounts for bulk purchases, please contact Simon & Schuster Special Sales at 1-866-506-1949 or business@simonandschuster.com.

The Simon & Schuster Speakers Bureau can bring authors to your live event. For more information or to book an event, contact the Simon & Schuster Speakers Bureau at 1-866-248-3049 or visit our website at www.simonspeakers.com.

Interior design by Lewelin Polanco

Manufactured in the United States of America

10 9 8 7 6 5 4 3 2 1

Library of Congress Control Number: 2025939768

ISBN 978-1-6680-8000-9
ISBN 978-1-6680-8001-6 (ebook)

Contents

Preface

An interesting thing about horror that takes place during the day is that it upends our expectations. We've been led to believe that light is good and dark is evil, and violating that belief suggests that something has gone wrong with our understanding of the natural order.

In addition, sunlight gives us a false sense of security because with 100 percent visibility, we *must* be safe, right? Evil is banished in the light of the day, right? After all, vampires sleep during the day. We're fooled into thinking nothing can harm us if we can *see* it. The dissonance is starkly revealed when horror takes place in the light and that light illuminates the ugliness and gore in shocking detail and clarity.

We're used to seeing monsters come out at night, but what if there is something inherent in the day that brings those monsters out then, in full daylight?

DAY

THE BRIGHT DAY

PRIYA SHARMA

The air was still cool from the night but it wouldn't last. Mel finished putting the chickens away in the shed and locked the door. When she turned, she saw the figures moving high on the slope beyond the electric fence.

"Andy!" She ran for the house, up the steps, and through the open door.

Andy heard the alarm in her voice and was already pulling on his boots. He took a rifle from the rack.

"What is it?"

"There are people out there. I think one of them is a child."

Mel grabbed the goggles from the hook by the door. She'd need them when the sun came up.

There were three of them outside the perimeter. A man carrying a child and a woman who trailed after them. The wiry man eyed the fence. He put the limp boy, who must have been about ten, down at his feet. Then he picked up a stone and threw it at the fence. It sparked.

"Hey, mate," the man called. "My name's Eddie. We need your help. We've been walking all night."

Andy didn't move.

"A group of us camped out by the next town, back that way. Do you know it? We were attacked. We had to split up and run. My son was hurt."

The boy groaned.

Mel looked to Andy. The nearest town was a long way off, a place where sand filled up the rooms. They must have walked all night.

"Please. You can't leave us out here." The man pointed to the sky. "The sun's coming up."

Mel put a hand on Andy's arm. It had been such a long time since they'd seen a child. Another life, when she was a teacher. It had been a long time since they'd seen anyone at all, in fact. Andy tried to keep Mel away when people came, begging to be let in. He didn't look at Mel, but he could still hear her crying.

He'd stopped clearing the sun-scorched bodies away at sunset, letting her see them. *That would be us if we let everyone in. I'm only doing this to protect us.*

This was different. There was a child.

"Andy."

The man seized his name. "Andy, mate, come on. Please. Your wife, she's kind. So are you. We won't be any bother and we'll leave at sunset. Please, Andy, for my boy. His name's Josh."

"Who attacked you?" Andy didn't move.

The man looked up at the sky. They could see his features more clearly now in the grey dawn. The woman had come closer. She was tall and large-boned. Her dazed, blank face bore an old scar that ran down her left cheek to her chin. Her arms dangled uselessly by her sides.

"Sunbathers." A comical name for the Sun Cultists who exposed themselves in brief bursts to their deity. They bore the stigmata of their worship. Leathered bronze skin, marked by tattoos and melanomas. "They took everything we had when they realised that none of us was their Messiah. They said if we converted, they'd let us live."

The Messiah. A being who embodied the Sun itself.

"So why didn't you?" Andy asked.

Sunlight was creeping down the dry, cracked earth of the slope. The scrub had burnt up long ago. The sand lizards would be out soon, their blood excited by the heat.

"Because this is Britain, and we are free."

"This *was* Britain."

"They'd make us slaves. You've got solar stills. I can see them. Just a little water and shade. That's all we want."

Andy started to walk back to the house.

"Please." It was the woman. "Please. My son."

"Andy." Mel ran after him. "Please."

They had rules. The rules were why they were still alive.

She gripped his forearm. He shoved her hard with a flat hand, high up on her chest, and she landed in the dust, shocked. His touch had never been anything but gentle before.

"He's just a boy. He'll die. They'll all die."

Mel couldn't see the man she'd fallen in love with. His gentle expansiveness had died when he shot the dog. He was terrified. It had crystallised into something hard and cold. Mel couldn't keep her fear of him from her face.

Andy put out a hand to help her up. She took it, not wanting to argue or cry while Eddie was watching them.

"Just until sunset. Then they'll be on their way."

● ○

Mel reactivated the fence once they were inside. Andy kept the rifle trained on the family as they walked up to the house.

"Thank you, mate. Thank you, Andy," Eddie kept saying.

Andy motioned with the rifle for Eddie to sit in the corner. The boy, Josh, was on his knee. The woman stood apart from them. Something was wrong with her besides thirst and fatigue. Her eyes were glassy.

"You're making me nervous, Andy, mate."

"I'm not your mate."

Mel filled a cup with water and slid it towards Eddie, stepping back out of his range. He gulped it down. Eddie put down the empty cup and pushed it back to Mel. Once refilled, he trickled some onto Josh's lips. The child moaned and sat up. Mel filled another cup and passed it to the woman.

It would soon be time to lower the blinds. The light was rising. The woman's face was slack, her lips dry and cracked.

"Could my son have a bed?" Eddie asked. "He needs to sleep. Maybe some food later. You have food. You look well-fed."

"Shut up." Andy kept the gun pointing at Eddie. "Put him on the table and then sit back down."

The man complied.

"I'll put him on the couch next door." Mel picked him up. He was a feather in her arms. She turned to the woman. "Is that okay?"

The woman nodded and made to move but Andy said, "You stay right there."

"He'll be safe, I promise. He'll just be in the next room."

Mel took him through and covered him with a light blanket. Before she lowered the blackout blind to protect him, she saw the line of light hit the compound, a relentless tide.

She missed the temperate sun. They'd worked abroad in their younger years, Andy in engineering and her teaching, in

Thailand, Hong Kong, and Japan. She missed children, humidity, and other people.

Mel went back to the kitchen. The woman had taken a seat beside Eddie. He'd finished another cup of water and was talking.

"Is it just the two of you here? It must be lonely." He couldn't keep the avarice from his voice.

"We like it."

"That's not very friendly, is it? You have an embarrassment of riches. You could spare some."

"I'm not your friend." Andy was impassive in a way that meant his hackles were up. Mel could tell that he was regretting letting them in. Better to leave them out to fry, or to the lizards.

The sun was hitting the windows, the glare unbearable. Mel turned on the lights and closed the kitchen blinds. "We should eat," she said, to no one in particular.

"Feed them first. No cutlery. We'll eat later."

"Did you make this?" Eddie asked as she passed him a thick slice of bread and butter. He took a bite. "It's good."

"Would you like some?" Mel willed the woman to speak. She longed to hear another woman's voice. "I'm Melanie."

The woman held out her hand.

"What's your name?" Melanie asked.

"Olwen." It came out as a whisper.

"I'll get you some." Mel crossed the room, back towards the countertop by the door.

"You're quite cosy here, aren't you?" Eddie's gaze landed on the closed blind, as if he could see through it.

Andy opened a slat to look out, the rifle still pointed towards the far corner where Eddie and Olwen sat. Then he darted across the room, ushering Mel out ahead of him. "Outside, now!" Then he backed out after her.

Andy dropped to one knee on the veranda and aimed at

Josh's back, but it was too late. The boy was beyond the gun's reach and had already thrown the switch for the fence and was letting the other men in.

● ○

There was no time. The baying men were closing the ground between them and the house. Mel could hear laughter from the kitchen. They ran, although they weren't dressed for daytime. They ran, even though they had no water. The men shouted and whooped.

Andy ran fast, pulling her along. They paused between the small complex of outbuildings.

"I'll draw them. Double back around the chicken shed and run up to the gate."

And then?

"Not without you."

"I have the rifle. Go!" He gave her a push. There was no time. Not for anything. "I'll follow you."

From the cover of the barn he picked off the man at the back. Then the one headed in their direction. He fired a few shots, trying to herd them towards the house, to give Mel a better chance.

"I'm staying."

"They'll kill me and they'll rape you. They'll never let you leave. Go!"

Mel ran uphill to the gate, not daring to look back. A dust cloud rose around her. One of the men turned and saw her. He gave chase, but Andy's shot rang out. He dodged it by throwing himself to the ground. It was enough for Mel. The power to the fence was still off. She was through the gate and headed up the side of the hill. More shots rang out. It wasn't supposed to be like this. They were supposed to die together from old age in their sleep, holding hands.

It was over when Andy ran out of bullets. There were too many to fight off. When they finished giving him a beating they dragged him, wrists bound, onto the veranda. He sat quietly after that, gathering himself. The front door screen banged, followed by slow deliberate footsteps. Andy looked up.

"You."

"Yes." Olwen. She sat on her haunches before him. "Me."

Olwen's men stripped those that Andy had killed. There was a skirmish over a shirt. The two dead men lay naked in the dust. The boy, Josh, poked at their staring eyes with a fork until he was chased away. The ground was too hard for digging graves, so they were set on fire.

Olwen had found Andy's wide-brimmed hat and had stuffed a large kitchen knife into her belt. It was a point of bright promise in the shade. She had grown in stature, transformed from the dull, cowed creature in the kitchen. Her gaze was as sharp as the knife.

"Andy, I'm going to take you out to where Mel can see you, and you're going to shout to her. Tell her everything is going to be okay and that she needs to get out of the sun. She won't have long out there. I reckon she'll be dead by noon. You don't want that now, do you?"

"She's long gone. You won't catch her. We've got gear hidden out there."

Andy wished it were true. All his preparation, and he hadn't prepared for this.

Olwen tilted her head. Close up, Andy could see the variegated moles on her face. It didn't matter. Despite skin cancer, she'd still outlive Andy.

"That might well be true, but she's tenderhearted, your wife. She'll stay, as long as you're alive."

"You already have something more valuable than her."

"What?"

"Look at this place. Solar panels, stills, hydroponic sheds. Chickens. Me. I maintain all this tech. It'll keep you fed and watered all your life."

"I would really like you to be one of my boys but I think you'll be much more obliging with your wife tucked up here, all snug." Olwen pulled the knife from her belt and started to clean her nails.

Then she got up and pulled Andy out into the sunshine and tied him to the post in the yard. She cut off his clothes with the kitchen knife. Andy's skin was pale, unaccustomed to the light. Some of Olwen's boys watched, sly looks passing between them. They had seen this before.

"This is your chance to save her. Go on, give her a shout."

"No."

Olwen went into the house and came out with a poker.

"I'm going to leave you out here to have a think about things."

She wrote in large letters in the dirt: COME DOWN OR HE DIES. Then she went back into the shade.

Eddie came out and picked up the poker and turned it over in his hands, testing its weight. Then he prodded Andy with it.

"Stop it."

Eddie ignored him. He hit Andy's shins with it. An experimental blow, not hard enough to break bone. Pain shot up and down his legs and bright lights burst in his vision.

Eddie hadn't finished. His gaze lingered on Andy. He used the tip of the poker to lift Andy's genitals, inspecting them and letting them drop. Andy closed his eyes, humiliated.

"Hey, get out of the sun, you daft sod," Olwen called.

Eddie, surprised as he'd not noticed Olwen on the veranda,

dropped the poker as he darted away. It landed in the dust with a thud.

● ○

The rocks at the crest of the hill were bleached white as bone. They gave Mel cover from the house below, but not shade. She could see anyone coming after her and would have time to run. Not that there was anywhere to run to. Or that she'd be able to run for long in the heat. When she looked out, all she could see was the plateau of stones and skeletons.

She had one thing to be thankful for. She had left the goggles hanging around her neck. She put them on and switched them to day mode. It was nearly 8:00 a.m. and the sun was blazing.

Mel lay on her front. As a child she'd sunbathed, lying on a blanket beside her mother, both of them plastered in copious amounts of factor 50. The heat soaked her, and her stomach clenched with the pleasure of it. She remembered the long grass of the field. The green of her dreams. Or she thinks she remembers it. When does memory get mixed up with imagination? Sand and scavengers were all that remained of England.

● ○

Andy had been brought back to the safety of the porch. He was dumped before Olwen. His skin was red and sore. It hurt to move. After he vomited, Olwen gave him water. She helped him, holding the cup to his lips. He was grateful. It was pure and sweet.

"Can we kill some chickens?" Eddie asked Olwen.

"How many are there?"

"About twenty."

"Only two then. But not the cockerel."

He went to turn, but then stopped. "Which one is that?"

"The one with the flapping red thing on its head."

"Okay."

She sighed as he went off. "He's keen but his education is sorely lacking."

"Why do they follow you?"

She leant forward in the chair.

"Because I keep them alive. And I've picked my boys for a reason. You see, I was like you once. Before all this I had a husband and a son. A job. Then afterwards I was, what's the right term? A sex slave."

Andy's skin was on fire. He wanted to writhe on the floor and rub it all off. He didn't care about what happened to Olwen. There was a time when he would have, but not now. He tried to conjure that other Andy.

"I'm sorry, Olwen. I wouldn't wish that on anyone. How did you escape?"

"Divide and conquer, using everything I had. Sex, lies, manipulation. Eddie was one of my captors. You don't have to wield the knife when the time comes. You just need to put it in the right hands and say the right words. Not that I haven't killed lots of men myself. Anyone that I couldn't bend to my will."

"I can be useful to you. I can keep this place running."

"What makes you think that we can't? Shout to Mel. Tell her to come home."

Andy would do anything to stay in the shade, but not that.

"She's gone."

"No, she's somewhere around here. Close, but not close enough for us to find her in daylight. She won't last long. Which is a shame because women are as precious as water." She stood up. "I'm putting you back out. This is your last chance to save yourself. Remember, Andy, you're just a man, and I have plenty of those."

● ○

Mel wasn't wearing a watch. Time escaped her. The only way she could mark it was from Andy's lengthening shadow. She'd dialled up the tint on the goggles but by noon it would be too bright to see anything, even with them. Not that it mattered. She'd be dead by then.

Andy's skin, which was pale under her hands, was now florid. It had started to burn and blister in places. He'd kept his eyes shut. That they kept pulling him back onto the veranda for shade and water intermittently gave her hope.

The exposed parts of her burnt in sympathy with him. What had started as a stinging sensation was now a forest fire. She was dimly aware of the onset of heatstroke as the sun climbed higher. It glowed white in the sky.

Her tongue stuck to the roof of her mouth. She was nauseous and dizzy. Her head pounded. The heat shimmered in waves on the land.

I should go down, she thought, but couldn't move.

The men were dragging Andy back to the post. He was going to die. The reprieves were only prolonging his suffering. Her earlier kindness was killing him. Her *weakness* was killing him, but still she couldn't move. What was the worst they could do to her?

● ○

The sand lizard was dancing for Mel. It raised one foreleg and the opposite hind one, then swapped over. When the sand got too hot even for this, it would burrow. Then she would be in trouble.

The sand lizards had thrived in this environment, mutated by solar rays and their blood energized in the heat. They'd swelled in size and were omnivorous.

A wild dog had followed Mel and Andy at a distance on their

journey to the compound. Andy had tried to befriend it with water and scraps of food but the mangy animal growled if he got too close. It trailed them across the biblical landscape of wildfires and dust storms. Even the rocks were beaten into submission.

They'd been woken one morning after only a few hours sleep by the sound of barking and then whimpers. When they'd opened the tent flap the dog was lying on its side, panting. The sand lizards nestled against its abdomen in a mockery of suckling. There were at least half a dozen of them, with more snapping and jostling for a share. They fled when Andy fired the gun. The dog's abdomen spilled its intestines. Andy put the next bullet in the dog's head. Mel put a hand on his arm, knowing what that cost him, but he turned away.

The sand lizard eyed Mel. Its flanks were vivid green. At least one thing in the world was that colour, even if it was temporary. That was good for her. It meant mating season. They were no longer hunting comrades but mating rivals. A large pack of them would kill her.

The lizard's tongue darted in and out, tasting the air. Mel lay still, ignoring the dust in her throat and nostrils. She stifled the urge to cough. It inched closer. Its reptilian scales repulsed her. Those claws that would find her soft underbelly. Her throat raged with thirst. She wished she'd taken a last drink of water when she gave some to the boy and the woman. Soon she wouldn't just be playing dead.

The lizard advanced. Its forked tongue flicked at her forefinger. She willed herself to be still. She'd only have one chance.

Bold, funny, dancing lizard. When it came close, she snatched at it, grasping its leg, not caring that it tried to bite her. It became a length of pure muscle. The strength in its twisting, thrashing body was equalled only by Mel's desperation. She flipped it onto its back and flung herself onto it.

A pause would undo her, so she didn't allow herself the luxury. She sank her teeth into its throat. The animal went wild, bucking under her, but she bit down. Pulsing, hot blood flooded her mouth. She kept drinking long after the lizard lay still.

● ○

Olwen licked her forefinger and held it up. The rising wind made her coat flap. The sky had changed, waves of green and purple.

"Best get inside, Andy."

She took a handful of his hair and raised his head. His face was a violent shade of red, his body worse. Some of his extensive blisters had burst. Olwen put her ear close to his mouth and listened. No breath. She let his head drop. No matter. It was a shame about the woman, though.

● ○

Mel crawled on her belly to where she had a better view of the compound. She wiped the goggles with her sleeve. All the men had gone inside, leaving Andy stripped and tied to the post. He wasn't moving. His skin was livid and blistered. Raw. She couldn't see his face, as his chin was on his chest.

She should've gone down there when she saw the message in the sand. Why hadn't she? She should have submitted. They might both have survived.

The meter in the goggles' peripheral vision was flashing a warning of an incoming solar storm, not that she needed it. Mel could see the sand lizards digging for their lives, burrowing to wait it out below ground. Maybe she should be following their example, but it was too late for that.

The storm had arrived. The sky was alive with it, a glory of colour. Mel had never seen such a show. No wonder ancient races fell to their knees in awe.

Closing her eyes and drifting into a wakeless sleep wasn't an option. She would be scoured by the sun itself. To end like this enraged her.

The storm blew out the transformers. A fire started at the back of the house, which contained the machinery of their survival. The electric fence fizzled with light and then died. Mel's goggles went blank, their circuits disrupted. She threw them away when they sparked.

The colours were falling to earth and she was whipped by the wind. Blinding light penetrated her closed eyelids. The storm lifted her. Particles of sun hit her in waves. The pain was searing. It filled her. Every atom buzzed. Her molecules realigned. Her cells illuminated.

The storm dropped her back onto the sand and moved on. It left a stillness in which she was aware that she was shaking and panting. She raised her arms before her. They were blistered and raw. She was bright. As bright as the sky. Mel was remade of light.

The desperation and resignation were gone. Blazing fury remained. She sat up. The sand lizards had come out, the enmity of the mating season forgotten. One of them came close and snapped at her. She put out a hand and the air between them rippled and sprang. The lizard was flung into the air and exploded. Its meat landed heavily to be devoured by its comrades.

Mel strode down the hill. The fence wasn't an impediment. She wouldn't have to scale it. Even still electrified, it wouldn't have mattered. She tore a hole in it at a distance with the flick of her fingers. The edges of it glowed white-hot, but that didn't trouble her. She stepped through. The sand lizards followed, hoping for more carrion in the wake of this greater predator.

Mel stopped in the yard to look at her husband. Andy would've cried if he'd been alive to see her. She was golden and glorious. She was as merciless as the sun.

The fire had been extinguished and black smoke bellowed from it. Mel heard raised voices from inside. She put out both hands and the front of the house collapsed. She picked off anyone who ran. Then she set to work on those hiding within.

It was 10:00 a.m. and the sun was still climbing. It was going to be a bright day.

FAIRE

RACHEL HARRISON

The sun rises over the castle gate, hovering between the turrets, a bright tyrant, the true king. A bead of sweat tickles the back of my neck. It's going to be a hot one, and I'm dressed in velvet. I know what lies ahead of me. Humidity. Perspiration. Old English.

"Good morrow, lords and ladies!"

"Oh, Christ," I whisper to Gabby, clutching her arm.

She bats me away. "It's going to be a long day if that's your attitude."

She's right, as per usual. I lean over the stroller to peek at Leah, who appears vaguely amused by the pageantry. At two, she's in the early days of a princess obsession. I'm trying to be a supportive honorary auntie, but dating postdivorce has turned me into a wicked cynic and it's proven difficult to read her fairytale bedtime stories without rolling my eyes so hard they fall out of my head. I can't even pretend to take it seriously.

When Gabby invited me to come along on their family trip to the Merrywood Renaissance Faire, I originally declined.

"It'll be like immersion therapy," she'd said. "Let go of all the bullshit of the last few years and let yourself play along. Not every fantasy is a trap."

"You sure about that?" I'd asked.

Unfortunately, the reason I decided to come today is further proof that there's no such thing as a happily ever after. I look over at Sean, and he's looking back at me. Gabby's not paying attention. She suspects nothing.

"'Tis a pleasure to welcome you to our kingdom," bellows the middle-aged man in the town crier getup, an excess of feathers sticking out of his already ridiculous hat.

"Now I know where all the drama-club kids are put out to pasture," I say.

"Everything's a joke to you," Gabby says, swatting at me again. But Sean laughs. Of course he laughs.

"This is why you asked me to come, Gabs. I'm a good time. *The* good time."

"Yeah, yeah. Alright."

"I'm being a good sport. Doing the dance, playing along. I put together the most medieval ensemble I could find in my closet. I'm wearing *velvet* in *July*."

"You are," she says, giving me the up-and-down. She opens her mouth, and I anticipate a crack about my outfit because it's Gabby and ever since she moved to the suburbs and had Leah, she's become a bit of a pearl clutcher. I'm on the precipice of a witty retort when she pulls out a map of the fairgrounds and changes lanes. "Where should we start? Are we hungry? There's a donut stand . . ."

"Ye olde donuts," I say. "What do you think, Leah? You want some ye olde donuts?"

"Yeah!" she cheers, waving her cute little toddler fist.

"Here, we say huzzah," Gabby says. "It means hooray."

"Huzzah," Leah says sheepishly. Trying it on.

"Huzzah!" Sean says, lifting Leah out of the stroller. He tosses her up in the air. "Huzzah!"

She giggles like crazy. He catches her and she settles into his arms, nestles her face into his chest. Watching them together does something to me, sets off a chemical reaction—baking soda and vinegar, frothing up my insides. It could be guilt, *should* be guilt, but I really don't think it is.

"Okay," Gabby says. "So, we're going to make a right up here onto Forrest Lane."

I look over her shoulder at the map. "This place is huge. I had no idea."

"It's the biggest Ren faire in the Northeast," she says in a tone that implies that this is common knowledge. "Sean, are you good to carry her? It's early."

"I'm fine," he says.

"Fine," Gabby says, tucking the map into her back pocket. She pushes the empty stroller across a patch of grass. "This way."

We follow Gabby onto a dirt pathway. It's early, but it's already crowded. Everyone's in costume. There are knights and maidens, wizards and witches, pirates and pixies. I spot a Tinker Bell, which . . . to each their own. A lot of flower crowns, corsets, cloaks, chain mail, wings. It's difficult to make the distinction between who works here and who's just an enthusiastic guest. It's like a very specific Halloween parade. Sarcasm aside, I admire the dedication.

And I'm impressed by the production value of the place. It's not Disneyland, but the facades are incredibly detailed. We pass a stone pub with actual vines growing up the side. An entire row of Tudor-style shops. I'm beginning to understand the price of admission.

"Captain Chocolate's cheesecake on a stick," Sean says. "Just like they had back in the olden days."

I snicker. Gabby huffs.

"You make fun of it all you want; by noon you'll both be gnawing on turkey legs and speaking the King's English."

"Hear ye, hear ye," I say. I turn to Leah; her mouth and eyes are wide in awe. "What do you think so far? Do you like the Renaissance faire?"

She nods, sticking her fingers in her mouth like she does when she gets overwhelmed.

"What do you want to do today, Lee? See a show? A joust? That's when two knights ram each other with sticks," I say. I elbow Gabby. "That sounded a little more salacious than intended."

"Sure," she says. "Sure."

We've been friends since we were Leah's age; she knows me better than anyone. She could read my mind if she wanted, if she weren't so distracted trying to find donuts. If she were to turn around and look at me now, really look, she'd know. *Did you meet someone? Did something happen? Spill.*

A tiny finger taps my shoulder.

"Yes, Miss Leah?"

"I want dat," she says, pointing to a conical hat with ribbons flowing from the top.

"Ask your mom and dad," I say. "If they say yes, I'll get it for you."

"You don't need to do that," Sean says.

"You spoil her," Gabby says.

"Well, I'm not having kids. Leah is my only hope to make sure I'm not getting abused in the home when I'm old," I say. "This is an investment."

"Get her the hat, then," Gabby says.

I look to Sean. He smiles at me. Nods.

"Okay, then. Huzzah," I say, taking Leah from his arms and approaching the stand selling the hats. "Which one?" I ask Leah.

"The pink one!" she says, clapping.

"Ah, a marvelous choice, young princess," says the seller. He's dressed sort of like Robin Hood, which is appropriate because he's about to rob me. The hat is sixty dollars. I pay, and it's worth every penny to see Leah's face light up when I place it atop her tiny head. Sean snaps pictures of her, takes a video. Leah then insists on watching the video, tittering in delight as Gabby and Sean bicker about screen time.

We find the donuts. We get a box and some apple cider, eat at a picnic table under the shade of a giant oak tree. Still, the sunlight bleeds through the leaves, patches illuminating stains on the table, ants crawling around seeking crumbs, a rogue thirsty wasp that has Leah on edge. Sean assures her it's fine.

"Just ignore it," he tells her, so sweet and reassuring.

Practical advice. Impossible advice.

Just ignore it.

Alone in the kitchen last night, after too much wine at dinner.

Just ignore it.

Hot breath whispering promises of it staying between us. Is it foolish to think that I can keep this secret? That he can, too? If Gabby were to find out, I'd want it to be from me. But I don't want her to find out.

"I'm going to find a bathroom," I say, standing. "Be right back."

"Here," Gabby says. "Take the map."

"I'll manage," I say.

She raises an eyebrow and clicks her tongue. "You're about to get lost, babe."

"Me? Lost? Nah." I give her a wink before turning my back.

There's another bug, maybe another wasp, hovering at my ear. I can feel it, a small, pesky presence. A light touch. I walk faster. Faster. I can see it my peripheral vision. A little dark smear at the corner of my eye. Faster, into a crowd. Let it bother someone else. Sting someone else.

I shimmy my way through a group of teenage girls in matching fairy outfits. One of them steps on my foot, looks up at me, but doesn't apologize. I limp forward, cursing under my breath.

"Thou art a fucking bitch."

There are signs everywhere. Too many signs—for the Market Village, for Storybook Theatre, for Tournament Field, for Pirate's Bay. I can't orient myself. There are too many people. Too many voices tangled in different conversations, too many conflicting scents, too many fabrics, textures streaking past—velvet, satin, lace, leather, polyester. Everyone wanders haphazardly, disturbing the flow of traffic. There's too much to look at, buildings emulating fairy-tale cartoons, colorful and exaggerated and oddly shaped, too narrow or too wide. It's all so garish and overstimulating. I spin around looking for restrooms, which better not be porta-potties.

Finally, I spot a sign for Royal Flushing's Privies.

I experience a moment of relief, followed by a sudden, gut-plummeting feeling.

I'm lost. I have no idea where I am or how to get back to Gabby and Leah. And Sean.

And . . .

There's a court jester standing ahead of me, in the middle of a strange split in the crowd. It's like the sea parted for him, but no one acknowledges him. They pass right by chattering away.

He wears that distinct jester hat, with those two dangling hornlike protrusions, bells on the ends. His costume is gold and black, diamond patterned, but the colors are faded, and it has holes in it, like it's been worn and reworn for far too long. Or like it's been kept in a cardboard box in a basement, abandoned as moth food, totally forgotten about until today.

He has on black gloves, but the fingers are extended and pointed at the tips. His face is painted white. He wears red contact lenses, and there's black makeup around his eyes in diamond patterns that match his costume. His lips are also painted black, embellished, pulled wide to give the appearance of a dark smile that stretches ear to ear.

He carries a staff with a spiked gold ball at the end, almost like a mace. He lifts it slowly and points it toward me. I know it's real metal by the way it catches the light.

His head jerks to the side, and with the sudden movement the bells on his hat start to ring. This sharp, earsplitting chime.

It's deeply unsettling. Sweat pours down my back. I blink and he's still there, still pointing his weapon at me. He knows he's scaring me. He's doing it on purpose.

Just past the fear is annoyance. There are kids here. This isn't a late-night haunted house. It's a Renaissance faire. It's 10:30 a.m. Fuck this guy.

Everyone else seems to be ignoring him, which is maybe some part of Ren faire culture that I'm unaware of. They can't stone him in the town center, can't send him to the gallows or guillotine or have him drawn and quartered, but they can ice him out. Pretend he doesn't exist, to signal to him that he's unwelcome in this kingdom.

I take a left, push through the crowd to make my way to the bathroom. The privies, which aren't porta-potties but aren't much better. After, I adjust myself in the mirror. I bought this dress the day my divorce was final, to wear out on dates. A deep scarlet, real velvet, sweetheart neckline, short but not too short, not an invitation. The white balloon-sleeve blouse I layered underneath to make it more medieval sort of ruins it.

I dig into my purse for my lipstick. Pop the top off, twist it up. Lean closer to the mirror to reapply.

It takes me a second to register, to understand what I'm seeing. The lipstick is black. It goes on black. Thick. It's sticky. And it smells like rancid trash. I gag, clutch the sink. The donut threatens to come back up. I throw myself at the paper towel dispenser, yank out as many as I can, hold them under the faucet, then aggressively rub them against my lips. I pull the wet paper towels away, check my reflection.

It's still there.

It's not coming off.

My mouth is a wide black smear.

Like that jester.

The sinking feeling is back, the one I had when I first saw him standing there in the crowd. And now, now I hear his laughter. It's in my head, I know it is. But I hear it like it's behind me. Like he's standing at my back, hunched over, laughing directly into my ear. A laugh like a machine gun—quick and loud and ugly, dizzying in its viciousness. A laugh with no mercy.

And along with it, the ringing of bells.

I get more paper towels. I scrub harder. Harder. I reach up and use my fingernails, peel it off. Keep going until it's gone. Until my lips are raw. Until they start to bleed. Until my cheeks are pink and irritated. Until there's no trace of black.

I look puffy and sweaty and insane—like I had an allergic reaction. Which, maybe I did? I look down at the lipstick, and it doesn't look black. It looks like the shade of berry pink it's meant to be. So, what the fuck?

The cap goes back on, and I toss it into the garbage. I get out my concealer and get to work, but it only goes so far in covering the damage.

I don't know how much time has passed. Too much. I imagine

them waiting for me at the picnic table, Leah getting anxious because Gabby is getting anxious. She has a full day of activities planned. She didn't used to be so regimented, but that's what happens when you become a mother.

Sean doesn't like this new version. I know he doesn't. He tried to leave last year, but she begged him to stay.

He stayed for Leah, not for Gabby.

"What's most important is that my family is together," she'd said to me at the time.

And they are. They are still together. But I'm here with them. I don't want to break them up.

I don't know what I want.

Whatever I had last night in the kitchen with Sean.

I walk out of the bathroom and take a deep breath. The humidity is so intense that breathing feels like drowning, and it's so hot, the heat coiling around me. It's heavy. It's all heavy. The sun has climbed higher, and everyone squints, not wanting to wear sunglasses and ruin their costumes, ruin the illusion.

But the illusion *is* ruined because it always is. I spot someone in jeans.

He's drinking beer out of a stein. It's not even noon. It's . . .

The jester stands a few feet from me, leaning against a tree. He tosses his staff from one hand to the other. He waves.

I flip him off.

He better fucking not be following me.

I turn and walk in the opposite direction. I pass the shop where I bought Leah her princess hat, and make a right, keep going until I spot the picnic tables.

They're not there anymore.

They're gone.

There are other families swarming the tables now, but none of them are *my* family. Rather, the family I'm here with.

I check my phone.

A message from Gabby. "We left to make the eleven a.m. show at the Storybook Theatre. Meet us there."

"Got it," I reply. I slip my phone back into my bag and take a moment under the big tree, hoping the shade will help me cool down. Calm down. A kid screams nearby. Full-on tantrum. Parents argue. Birds sing. Music emits from invisible speakers—irritating, erratic harpsichord. More teen girls in fairy wings frolic around, break into fits of shrill giggles.

A woman dressed in an elaborate queen costume walks by, waving at us commoners. A man walks behind her, holding her train. I wonder what those power dynamics are like outside of the faire.

It smells like frying oil and body odor. I'm not the only one out here sweating.

There's no cloud cover. The sky is blue and empty. Not even a vapor trail or fugitive balloon. The sun is all alone up there.

My lips are cracked and sore, my throat dry in the heat. I find a stand selling lemonade. It stings to drink. Citrus and cuts. A dumb choice. I go back and buy a water, drain the bottle, throw it into the nearest bin. When it hits the rim, it makes a sound. A sound it shouldn't make. Like the chime of a bell.

The bottle bounces into the bin, disappearing into the void. But it's still making that noise. That ringing.

I whip around, wondering if I'm wrong, if the sound is actually behind me. It isn't. It is *definitely* coming from the trash. And I could, I should, walk away, but it's so loud, and it's getting louder. And it *is* bells. It's the sound of bells.

I approach the bin. I plant my feet, ignore the reek of sun-fried garbage, and crane my neck, peer down.

Inside is the hat. The jester's hat.

The bells rattle on their own.

Until they don't. Until the hat jolts, begins to shake, like there's a vibrating head inside it. It stops as suddenly as it started. In the stillness, I try to justify it. The man threw his hat away. He got the hint that his costume was egregious. And now it's being worn by a chipmunk or . . .

The hat shifts, angles back, revealing a single red eye in a black diamond on a pale white face.

My throat goes dry again, my scream dying in the desert.

I stumble backward to the sound of the bells, and to that hideous laughter. It's not in my head this time. I swear, it's not in my head.

"M'lady?" There's a man standing beside me, this guy in his early twenties dressed like a duke or something, wearing a hat like a pillow. He drops the shtick. "Are you okay?"

"Ye . . . Yeah. I'm f . . ." It hurts to speak, my lips split, my throat burning. "I'm fine. Thanks."

My phone buzzes in my bag, breaking me out of the spell of my fear.

It's Gabby. I answer.

"Where are you? The show's about to start. Are you lost?"

"I'm . . . No. I'm not lost."

"Sean offered to go find you," she says. Maybe there's a hint of suspicion in her voice, or maybe I'm losing it, maybe I'm having a heatstroke. Confused. Panicked. Fucking hallucinating.

"That's . . ." I consider. A moment with him could save me from this feeling. Distract me from this bizarre anxiety, from these visions of that creepy jester. Sean's voice could exorcise the belligerent chime of bells, banish the echoes of that horrible laughter. But if I say yes, and she *is* suspicious, what then? "No. Not necessary. I'm coming now. See you soon."

Inhale. Exhale.

I ask the friar running the lemonade stand where the theatre is, and he points me in the right direction. Straight down Midsummer Lane, a right at the wishing well onto Wizard's Walk. Theatre will be on my left.

I weave through the crowds, trying to dismiss a claustrophobic itch.

For a second, I think I see them. Sean, a head taller than everyone else at six-five. A curly-haired toddler in his arms. And Gabby, walking beside them, her jet-black hair pulled back into a high bun. But it can't be them because they're at the Storybook Theatre.

I get to the wishing well, but there's no Wizard's Walk. There's no right to take. It's just more Tudor-style shops selling flower crowns and crystals. Selling palm readings and jewelry.

"Step right up, common folk! Make a wish! Thy fortune could change!"

There's a man in a stockade next to the well, and he's collecting dollar bills in exchange for giant silver coins. The coins get tossed into the well, along with wishes. If they come true, people will swear it was money well spent. If they don't, they won't miss the dollar. Or the next one. Or the one after that. Hope is cheap until it isn't.

"Thy luck could change!" the man repeats, grinning up at the line of customers. He wears a set of fake, rotted teeth.

I know it's meant to be ironic, to be silly. A man in a stockade selling wishes. But I find it a little grim. A little off-putting.

This entire place is off-putting. There's something about everyone doubling down on playing pretend, on being so committed to the fantasy. It's like a giant shared delusion.

Not every fantasy is a trap, Gabby had said.

She's so wrong.

I get my phone out to call her, but it's dead. I could have sworn I'd charged it this morning.

There's a giant clock tower not too far ahead. I hurry toward it so I can see what time it is, but get stuck behind a group of college dudes in peasant clothes eating kettle corn and drinking out of flasks.

"Jousting is so gnarly," one of them says.

"It's legit violent, dude."

I'm surprised that not even Ren faires are safe from bros. I push past them and get to the clock tower.

It says it's one forty-five.

That's not possible. It was ten thirty when I left to go to the bathroom. That was half an hour ago, at most.

I turn to the woman next to me, who's dressed like an elf. Fake ears and everything. "Is that right? What time is it?"

She blinks at me.

"What time is it?"

She bows her head. "Forgive me. Do you come from a foreign land? You have such a peculiar way of speaking."

"Are you fucking kidding? Can you please just tell me what time it is?"

Her head snaps up and she gives me the nastiest look.

"Bat-fowling bog wench," she snarls, before stomping off.

"That's it. I hate it here," I say, throwing my hands up and turning back toward the wishing well.

I think I see Sean again. He's alone. Maybe he came to find me, after all. But he's walking in the opposite direction, walking away.

I set off following.

"Sean?"

He doesn't turn around.

"Sean!"

He can't hear me. It's too loud here.

I'm getting closer.

I'm so close, I can almost touch him.

Until I can't move.

Because I hear them.

The bells.

It's those damn bells again. I can't tell which direction the sound is coming from. I scan the crowd, and there's a flash of black and gold, gone before my eyes can focus, can confirm the sighting. I'd be quick to dismiss it if I couldn't still hear the bells, and a surge of that awful laughter, somehow louder than the roar of the faire.

I take a cautious step back and reach up to cover my ears and—

"Ah!"

There's a hand on my wrist. Green, wrinkly old fingers pressing down. A woman in a witch costume, face hidden under the brim of her pointy hat.

"You're a rotten creature, aren't you?" she asks, her voice hoarse. It's not that classic witch voice. It's worse.

"Get off me!" I attempt to pull my arm away, but her grip is too tight.

"Beware, beware," she says. "Thy fate is sealed. Thy wicked nature shall be revealed."

"I'm not into this shit. Let *go*. Now."

She cackles as she releases me. Carries on while I rush off.

I don't know where Sean went. If it even was Sean in the first place.

I close my eyes for a second, and I'm back in the kitchen last night, sitting on the counter, my legs spread, him standing between them. His hands on my knees traveling up to my hips, pulling me toward him. We were so quiet. We had to be. Gabby and Leah were asleep upstairs.

That witch is still cackling.

I open my eyes, look down at my wrist where she grabbed me. My skin there is discolored. It's grey. It's shriveled. It looks like dried mud.

"What the fuck . . ."

I search for another bathroom so I can wash my wrist. Among all the signs naming whimsical attractions and shops and streets, there's a set unlike the others. They're the same shape, white arrows, stacked one on top of the other, but instead of that classic gothic font, these letters are bold. Written in fresh, dripping red paint.

The one sign says A FOOL THOUGH I MAY BE.

The other, YOU ARE NOT FOOLING ME.

I can't be seeing what I think I'm seeing. I take off running, but it doesn't matter.

The jester waits at the fork in the road, standing in the middle of a rose garden, next to an enormous sundial. He lifts his staff up over his head. Lowers it. Lifts it. Like he's leading a marching band.

"I see you again and I'm going to security, asshole," I say as I walk past, going left.

It's the bells that let me know. He's behind me. He's my shadow.

I'm being stalked in broad daylight. I should stop and confront him, make a real scene. I should scream. But would anyone hear me over the crowd, over the harpsichord music, over the birdsong, over the pop and hiss of food frying? Would anyone notice if this jester beat me to death with his staff right here on this dirt path? Would they assume it's part of the faire? Would I bleed out while everyone gathered around clapping, marveling at how real it all looked?

The worst part is, I'm not sure I could blame them. It's so blurry here, so hard to separate fantasy and reality.

But the reality is that jester doesn't know anything because it can't. And that witch . . . I'm projecting. Maybe I do have some suppressed guilt over what happened last night. It's my subconscious. No. It's this place. It's just this fucking place. I need out of here.

I dart over into a shop so I can ask about the nearest exit, but it's packed, too full of people, and I get pushed back onto the street and swept into the crowd. The bells. The bells. And the laughter.

"I mean it. Stop following me," I say. "I carry a gun."

A lie. But I made a comment on the way in about how I thought the security was a little lacking.

"What if someone brings a gun?" I'd asked.

"No one's bringing guns. They're bringing swords," Sean said.

I realize in this moment that it's totally possible the jester's staff is a legitimate weapon.

My chest is tight, my blouse soaked through with sweat, my hair matted to my forehead and the nape of my neck. The sun is so bright I can barely keep my eyes open. I'm seeing orange spots. I'm exhausted. I might pass out.

I stop short. He takes the opportunity to step around me. To step in front of me. To face me.

"This isn't funny."

He stares. Slowly cocks his head.

"What do you *want*?"

He starts to laugh. He raises his staff, and instinct takes over. I turn to run.

It's a gloved hand over my mouth, stifling my scream. My knees give out, and I'm being dragged back. I flail, but I'm so weak I can't inflict any harm, can't break free of his grasp. I bite down on his hand, but the gloves are too thick. A taste floods my mouth—the tang of rot. He pulls me around a tree and pins me there with his staff across my neck.

"Please," I tell him. "Stop. Someone will see you."

He shakes his head side to side. He smiles, his wide lips parting to reveal rows of fake pointed teeth. Only, there are far too many of them. They couldn't possibly fit in a mouth. It's not normal. It's wrong. Something's wrong. His mouth is too big. It's too big. It's too big.

My jaw unhinges, preparing for a scream, but then the jester takes a step back, releases the staff from my throat. He hands it to me, laughing, laughing, laughing, laughing. Wild laughter. Brutal laughter. Mad laughter. Uncanny, inhuman laughter.

And he starts to dance, tall knees and swift elbows, jagged movements, angling his chin up, every one of his many, many, many teeth glinting in the daylight.

The shock of it, the horror of it all freezes me in place. Keeps me still when the jester abruptly stops his little jig, reaches up to his head, and removes his hat. He uses both hands, lifts it high up toward the sky, toward that bright, blazing sun. Then he brings it down. Then he places it on my head.

Then comes the darkness.

● ○

The sun sets over the castle gate. I watch from the inside, through my new red eyes.

TRICK OF THE LIGHT

BRIAN EVENSON

1

It began when she was young, only nine or ten. There was no warning, no signs of—and here she made finger quotes in the air—"disturbance." In the years since, no therapist had managed to ferret out a cause—some buried trauma, something untoward inflicted on her that would explain it. *That is not to say there isn't anything,* she was careful to tell me. *There may well be. But if there is, nobody has managed to discover it.* The implication being I wouldn't discover it, either, no matter how well I got to know her, and that I shouldn't try.

I nodded politely and didn't say anything. This is what I tend to do in such situations, simply listen and wait for the person to go on, to get in their own time to what they really want to say.

She took a few slow sips of her water, and so I took a sip of my water, as well. We were in a café in the afternoon, a number on the table beside us, waiting for pastries to be delivered. The light was, at this point, mellow, the sun not shining through the windows yet. I did not know her well. We'd talked online, but this was the first time we'd ever met in person.

She checked her watch.

"I'm going to set a timer," she said.

I found this a strange thing to say on a first date, but again I nodded. *Perhaps,* I thought, *she already knows she doesn't want to meet again.*

"Nine," she said, once she was done fiddling with her watch. "I'm pretty sure I was nine." She looked up, a little confused. "I don't know why I'm telling you this," she said.

I did. People often feel compelled to tell me things. I have that kind of face.

"Can I trust you?" she asked.

Before I could answer, our pastries arrived. I had thought it a little strange to order pastries when, properly speaking, it was lunchtime, but when she ordered one, I did, too.

We ate for a moment in silence, her tearing pieces off her Danish and nibbling them out of existence, me unrolling my morning bun and slowly circling my way toward its center. Before I had finished eating, she'd pushed her plate away, most of the shredded Danish still on it. That was when she really began to speak:

2

I was nine. Or ten. But I'm pretty sure it was nine, the first time it happened. My mother and I had just moved. My father had lost his job in Los Angeles and couldn't find another, so my mother called in some favors and got her cousin Sean to hire her to work in the day care he managed. From one day to the next, my mother and I packed and were moving to Flagstaff. Dad would stay in L.A., sleeping on a friend's couch, and try to find something new.

The house we rented was something my mom's cousin found before we arrived. *Good place,* he claimed, *lots of space, safe, furnished. Close to the day care. Also, cheap? Did we want it?* The price was right—next to L.A. prices how could it not be?—and so my mom said yes.

For me, it was an adventure, at least at first. Being an only child, I spent more time with my parents than with other kids. Sure, I had a few school friends I missed when we left, but I wasn't distraught. Besides, my parents told me that as soon as my father found another job we'd move back to L.A. So it felt more like a vacation than anything permanent.

We packed a couple of suitcases and threw them into the trunk of the car. Dad had rented a storage unit, and after we left he and Dennis—this was the name of the friend whose couch he was borrowing—would move what was left into it. I don't think I realized Dad wouldn't be driving us to Flagstaff until we were saying goodbye.

I don't remember much about the drive, just that despite being from L.A. I'd never really seen the desert before. You probably think I'm going to say we got to the house and it looked ominous or haunted or some such bullshit, but truth be told it seemed a perfectly ordinary house. It was part of a seventies split-level development: brick walls, asphalt-shingle roof. I didn't take it all in at the time, mind you, but a few years ago I went back and took a good long look to see if it brought any buried memories back. It still didn't give me a bad feeling, didn't stand out from any of the other houses in the neighborhood.

We arrived nearly a month before school began, but my mother had to start working right away. Her cousin didn't care if I tagged along to the day care, even though I was at least four years older than any of the other children there. The more, the merrier, he said. And so in the morning I'd go in with my mom and help her and the others out. Or I'd bring a book and sit in the corner and read. Either way, after a few hours, I was bored.

Each afternoon, around one, my mom took a thirty-minute break for lunch. Since the house was only a few blocks away, she'd drive me home, make us both a quick sandwich, and then drive back. The first few days I drove back with her, but by the third or fourth day she could tell I didn't want to return. So she said I could stay at home if I wanted.

It was not the first time I'd been left on my own. I'd often been alone for an hour or two in the apartment in Los Angeles, but my mom knew our neighbors there, and I knew if anything went wrong I could run down the hall and pound on their door. In Flagstaff, though, we didn't know anybody except for Cousin Sean. If there was a problem while Mom was gone, I'd have to handle it on my own. Still, I understand why my mother let me stay alone: She was being nice, she knew I was bored. She probably thought, *It's the middle of the day. What could possibly go wrong?*

She stopped talking, just stared at the surface of the café table. Then, suddenly anxious, she checked her watch.

I've got to hurry, *she said, but still didn't continue. I prodded her gently. "Did someone come to the door?" I asked.*

She shook her head.

Nobody came to the door. I already told you there wasn't a cause they could find. Weren't you listening?

She shook her head again.

Sorry. I always get anxious in the afternoon. The sunnier it is, the worse I get. I really should move to Seattle or something. Somewhere where I don't have to always be worried about the sun. If I ever have the money, I will.

The first time was the worst because I didn't know it was coming. There I was, in a new house, all alone. It was bright outside, and pretty bright inside, too—my mother hadn't gotten around to hanging any curtains. The sun had passed its zenith and had begun its descent, but darkness was still hours away. And where it was in the sky meant now it was shining through the inset panel of the front door.

I haven't told you about that panel yet. I probably should have before now. It was a long rectangle made up of irregular interlocking sections of colored glass, a strip of putty between each section. It was supposed to look like a stained glass panel, but it wasn't stained glass per se, just two panes of glass with a colored sheet of plastic between, and the pattern it formed was abstract. At least I thought so at the time.

I was bored. I'd been bored at the day care and now I was bored alone at home. I was idly watching motes of dust float in the sunlight, waiting basically for time to pass and my mom to come home, when I felt my gaze drawn to the door. Not the door itself, but the inset panel.

Something seemed off. What was it? I didn't know, couldn't quite put a finger on it. I furrowed my brow and stared, and when I did, when it *felt* my attention, it became palpable, became sharper. At first I told myself it was a trick of the light, just the sunlight shining through the sections of colored glass in exactly the right way to create an unusual effect, something that combined the colors in such a way as to give the illusion of a three-dimensional shape. But as I continued to look, I became more and more convinced there was more to it than that. It kept turning and shifting, and growing, too, the motes of dust in the air swirling and slowly cohering into a vague, almost humanoid form—if humans had shimmering, flapping membranes in lieu of legs. If I stared at it just right, squinting a little, I began to see in the pattern and play of light something that looked, loosely, like a face, albeit with far too many eyes, and the wrong sort of eyes, too.

At this stage, I wasn't scared. More than anything, I was curious, interested in how a play of sunlight through colored glass could trick me into thinking something was there.

And then that shimmering, insubstantial form turned all its eyes on me.

I sucked in my breath, I think—made a noise at least. At that, the attention of the figure in the air sharpened. It opened what I suppose could be described, just barely, as a mouth. An orifice anyway.

"Hello," it whispered. Its voice, I remember feeling at the time, was the color of nothing at all. I know how strange this sounds, and it's hard to explain what I meant by it at the time, but the phrasing still feels right to me. "And what sort of name do they call you?" it whispered.

I didn't answer. The figure moved away from the colored glass of the door and came a little closer, but stopped before reaching me. Because of the time of day and the angle of the sun, the couch I was sitting on hadn't yet been touched by the light. And the figure seemed either reluctant or unable to cross into shadow.

"Care to come over here and be my friend?" it whispered.

I shook my head.

"No matter," it whispered. "I can wait."

We stayed there, the sunlight advancing slowly across the floor and toward me. As it did, the figure shuffled closer little by little. Eventually I lifted my feet off the floor and sat cross-legged on the couch. When the light began to creep up the couch's body, I stood on the cushions.

"Not long now," it whispered.

Its orifice widened and revealed something like teeth, only black and jagged. That was the moment I became afraid. I felt

I had to leave right away, before the sunlight struck me and the figure reached me. I pulled myself up onto the top edge of the couch back and, balancing one hand against the wall, began sidling closer to the doorway leading to the kitchen.

It followed me, staying as close as it could.

There was a stretch of light between the couch and the kitchen, high enough that I knew I couldn't leap over it. The figure went and stood there and held out its arms, all of them, as if preparing to catch me.

"Don't be afraid," it whispered. But how could I not be afraid?

I waited as long as I possibly could, until the light had nearly reached the top edge of the couch back, and then I leaped.

The figure darted forward hissing as I did so, its limbs passing through my legs in a great burst of pain. I landed on the kitchen floor and sprawled for a moment before scurrying as far away from the light as I could get. The figure stayed there, pacing along the line of shadow. I was throbbing with pain where it had touched me, and when I glanced down I saw red welts already rising on my skin.

"Soon the whole kitchen will be flooded with joy," it whispered, "and then we'll be friends forever."

I looked around. The figure was right, I knew: Sunlight would flood the kitchen soon. And so, not knowing what else to do, I opened the cupboard doors beneath the sink and crawled inside. I pulled them shut after me and stayed there listening, waiting, in the dark where it was safe.

It talked to me from the other side of the door, even managed at one point to knock. It did its best to coax me out. When I refused to come out and even refused to speak, it became angry. It began berating and threatening me. And then, abruptly, it fell silent.

I didn't come out right away. I was afraid it might be a trick. I waited a little longer until I was sure the sun had really gone down and it was no longer there. When I was sure I was safe, I crawled out and dusted myself off. A few minutes later, my mom arrived.

I pretended nothing had happened. The welts, impossibly, were already nearly gone, the pain fading with them. Maybe they were never as bad as they had initially appeared to me. By the next day I had almost convinced myself I had imagined it. Still, for the next three or four days when Mom offered to let me stay home while she went back to the day care, I opted to go with her. But after those few days, the memory faded enough that I no longer believed in it. And so, on the fourth or fifth day, I let her leave me at home again.

At first it seemed fine, but then the sun slipped down a little and I saw the figure begin to form. This time I rushed right away to the kitchen and stayed under the sink in the safety of the darkness, covering my ears with my palms as it tried to coax me out, paying no heed to the knocking on the cabinet door, until at last the light faded and I heard my mom come in. I had just enough time to pull myself out, brush myself off, and pretend like nothing had happened.

It might have ended there. School was on the verge of starting, and since I would be riding the bus and our street was one of the last stops, I wouldn't be home when light was streaming through the panel. Until school, I could go to the day care with my mom. Since my mom was working six days a week and we attended an afternoon worship service on Sundays, it felt like I could simply wait it out.

But then, three days before I started school, my mother told me my father was coming to visit. Wouldn't it be nice to see him? It would be. She said I would go with her to work as usual, then on her break she would bring me home. My dad, she claimed, would already be there, waiting.

Except he was not there waiting. Perhaps he was running late—since this was before cell phones were common, and he didn't have one, there was no way of knowing. My mother hemmed and hawed, but in the end, her break almost over, she decided to leave me alone at the house to wait for my father. He would, she reminded me, be there any second. I made the mistake of agreeing.

Her watch beeped. She silenced it.

Not much time left. Suffice it to say my father did not show up any second. In fact, he had had car trouble and so did not show up until the following morning, which meant I was left there, waiting, when the light began to creep through the panel.

The shimmering figure began to form, but this time I felt like I couldn't simply run. I had to do something. My father could come at any moment, and the last thing I wanted was for him to walk in to have the figure take him. I was not sure what *taking him* would mean, exactly, but I was sure it wouldn't be good. For a moment I hesitated, and then before the figure had fully formed I leaped up from the couch, rushed to the front door, and punched repeatedly through the ersatz stained glass panel.

I cut myself rather badly. When my mother came home, she found me lying on the floor, a towel wrapped around my arm to stanch the bleeding. She bundled me up and rushed me to the hospital. I needed fifty-six stitches*, she told me, and showed me the scarring all down one arm.*

I just nodded.

You might think that was the end*, she said.* It was not, because even though I'd broken the glass panel I hadn't destroyed the figure. I had, instead, released it. Afterward, every day at exactly the same time, if there is enough light, it tries to take me.

Her watch beeped again. Excuse me, *she said, and walked to the back of the café, slipping into one of the bathrooms.*

I sat there, one hand resting atop the other, waiting for her to return.

3

After a while the server came over and asked me if I needed more coffee. I hadn't had coffee, I told her, just water. Well then, she wanted to know, did I need more water?

When I said no, she turned to leave. But then she hesitated and turned back.

"Are you waiting for her?" she asked, and gestured back at the bathrooms. And when I indicated I was, she shook her head.

"She'll be in there at least an hour," she said. "Every day at this time she goes into one of the bathrooms, locks herself in, turns out the light, and waits. She says she feels safer that way."

I made a noncommittal grunt and after a moment glanced away. I looked instead into the light now streaming through the windows. I quickly turned back to the server.

"Thank you for telling me," I somehow managed to say.

I left the café shortly thereafter. I have not seen the woman since. I hope she is okay, that the only reason she is not returning my calls is because she's embarrassed about how much she told me. But, more than that, I hope I never ever see anything like what I was just beginning to glimpse in the light pouring relentlessly in through the café window.

ONE DAY

JEFFREY FORD

Geena was sitting at the front window in her living room, staring out at the sun and the blue sky. Occasionally a breeze shook the branches, and yellow leaves fell through her gaze. She was thinking about how much she hated her job—teaching composition online to freshman college students. The previous night, she'd marked twenty essays, and after the typos, the missing paragraphs, the shifting tenses, the faulty pronoun reference, the tributes to abstraction, she was on the ropes. She'd been a fool, trying to expose the students' use of ChatGPT. It was clear that the world didn't give a fuck. They were just as happy to have AI do the thinking for them. The job was what her mother would have referred to as "shoveling shit against the tide."

She finished her coffee and put the cup down on the table to her side. The morning was so quiet in the neighborhood. After the bustle of folks going out to work and the kids catching the bus, the day dropped into a serene silence. One of the better things about working at home; a brief respite from the perpetual motion of six- and eight-year-old boys—and Craig's moods and mansplaining. She told herself she would only sit there and enjoy it until she saw the young woman from up the street come by, pushing the baby carriage. It was a sweet scene, like clockwork every morning—a young mother, taking the new babe for a spin through the bright autumn day. She wondered where her own sweetness had leached off to. "Snap out of it," she said, laughed aloud, and started through a checklist of things she had to get done before class started at four.

Her head was filled with a vision of a trip to the grocery store, but her eyes continued to gaze out across the porch, under the trees dotting the lawn, to the street. She was picturing an inevitable encounter with the store manager she'd bitched out over the fact that no matter how many people were in line, the store only ever had one register open, when a flash of brightness momentarily blinded her. Adrenaline kicked in and she jerked forward and cleared her eyes to see what had happened. It was like the blast from a bomb, but there was no sound and no destruction. Her heart pounded.

Maybe just a transformer blowing on the telephone pole, she thought, but then saw that there was some kind of disturbance in the air out on the street. It whirled and rippled like water then split open, and a four-legged creature the size of a very large dog leaped through. It crawled unsteadily to the edge of her lawn and fell over onto the grass. It wasn't a dog, but she couldn't really place what it was. It had a head like a small horse and was shaggy with pale blue fur. "What the fuck?" she said aloud, but should have saved her words because when she focused again, the thing had stood up in the shape of a man. Even though the features were impossible to discern, it seemed to have the bearing of a male—wide shoulders, a height of over six foot two, a big head.

No matter how hard she tried to concentrate and fix the stranger's looks, his face shimmered like the sun in a pond. She realized his whole form was rippling. He staggered up next to the biggest tree in the yard and appeared to be hiding behind its trunk. It came to her that he didn't know she was watching, and she pushed her chair back so she was behind the curtain, barely peering around it.

That's when the young mother came into view, pushing a baby carriage. Geena wanted to move, go to the door and call out to the girl to run. She wanted to catch her breath. She did neither, but watched as the stranger approached her neighbor, swift as a thought and, with one arm, swept the carriage out of the mother's grip to the lawn on the opposite side of the street. It rolled over twice before coming to rest. The young woman opened her mouth to scream, and a huge gray tongue shot out of the attacker's mouth and stuffed hers, no sound escaping.

He lifted his left hand, with long fingers that tapered into something like the ends of branches, to grab her by the throat. Even from where Geena hid, she could see the beautiful smooth skin of the girl's neck and face suddenly erupting with boils and welts and bursting, blood spitting and dripping from the wounds onto the street. With his other hand, he reached up and shoved the long, sharp index and middle fingers into her eyes. Geena thought she heard them popping but couldn't have. A yellowish ichor burst from the sockets as his hand pulled free. Her body rotted in a gory mess and fell away with the speed of a time-lapse video. A large hole opened in his whirlpool of a face, and he consumed, like a snack, the dripping orbs.

Geena, hands clasped to her mouth, fell forward out of the chair onto her knees. She cried, and there was a buzzing in her head that meant she was leaning toward unconsciousness. A directive shot through the static in her mind and told her she had to get up quickly and lock the doors. She took three huge breaths and blew each out slowly, deliberately, trying to regain control. Putting her fingertips to the floor, she took off from a sprinter's stance. She wore no shoes, only socks, and slid on the polished wooden floor as she rounded the corner of the hall, heading for the front door. There in a blink, she attached the bolt and the chain and was off toward the side porch door in the kitchen, and the sliding glass doors in the back. The whole operation took less than a minute. She threw herself into one of the kitchen chairs and worked at catching her breath. As soon as she could speak, she took her cell phone out of the pocket of her sweatpants and dialed her neighbor across the street. Her first thought was to call the police, but she could barely believe what happened and *she'd witnessed it.* She was hoping her neighbor Ron might have seen something to corroborate she wasn't crazy.

Three rings and Ron picked up. "Did you see that?" she yelled.

"See what? That thing crawling out of thin air and murdering that girl with the baby carriage? Yeah, I saw it. Jesus Christ."

"I'm calling the cops," said Geena.

"I'm just loading up to go out there and get the baby," said Ron. "If you hear a gunshot, that'll be me blowing a hole in that thing. Did you see where it went last?"

"No, I'm in the kitchen. I ran and locked the doors."

"Good. I'll call you back when I get the kid."

He hung up, and she tried to imagine a sixty-eight-year-old going up against Mirage, an apt name for the entity whose form was elusive. Ron had a good sense of humor, but a bad back, a bad hip, and shaky hands. He was great at a cookout, or when she and Craig had him over on holidays for dinner, but against whatever that thing was, it seemed unlikely he'd come out on top. She ran upstairs to the second-floor bedroom in order to get a wider perspective on the scene. Sitting on the edge of her bed, she peered down through the trees. Enough leaves had fallen by then for a fairly clear view. She admonished herself for not thinking of the baby in the carriage. She wondered if it could still be alive. Phone in hand, she was about to dial 911, when Ron's front door opened, and he stepped out onto the porch followed by his old white Lab, Mike.

The old man had a pistol in his left hand and a billy club in his right. He eased down the steps sideways, favoring his bad knee, and she wished he might move a little faster. Crouching slightly and turning every way to watch for the killer, he sidled over to where the baby carriage lay upside down by his flower beds. He'd attached the club to a hook on his belt and bent over to flip the carriage. From out of nowhere, the stranger zipped up in a blur to within twenty feet of Ron. The dog, who was usually laid-back and weary, charged in between his master and the killer, barking like mad. Ron got the carriage righted, and Mirage backed away from Mike.

Seeing he had the advantage for a moment, the old man reached in and grabbed the baby, thoroughly bundled in a blue blanket. As Ron stood straight, Mike charged closer to danger and growled so loud Geena could clearly hear him across the street and upstairs. The stranger lifted his arms above his wavering head, and they appeared to be attached by a membrane to his body like bat wings. From within their folds, a squall of small black creatures flew. They swarmed straight to the dog and attached themselves to his body so that little of his white fur was visible. Mike howled and in seconds was reduced to a puddle of blood and fur and guts. Ron yelled something, took aim, and fired three shots into the stranger, who spiraled down to near darkness like a TV in a thunderstorm. The black creatures on Mike puffed out of existence in tiny clouds of smoke.

Ron took off, not inside his own house, but across the street toward Geena and Craig's place. Before she dashed out of the room, she saw the killer swirl back into existence and re-form. Geena made it down the stairs to the front door before Ron. She opened it, and he staggered in, clutching the baby. The door slammed shut and the dead bolt and chain were applied. She helped him into the living room and put him in a chair. Then she took up the blue bundle and pulled the cloth back from the baby's face. Its green eyes looked back at her and it smiled. "Oh my God. The kid is alive." Ron nodded and tried to catch his breath. With his free hand he gave her a thumbs-up. "I need a serious drink," he said.

"Let's get to the kitchen. I'll make us both one."

A bourbon on ice with a shot of seltzer sat before each of them at the kitchen table. Ron's pistol lay next to his. He spilled some as he brought it to his lips. The baby was in the dry sink with a cover and chair pillow beneath it, gurgling and baby talking. Geena took her cell phone back out and dialed 911. Sipping her drink, she waited for a voice to come on. Eventually, she closed the call and laid the phone next to her drink.

"They didn't answer?" asked Ron.

"The line is dead."

"Oh, honey, excuse my language, but we are fucked."

"No need to apologize," said Geena. "There's no other word for it."

"What are we gonna do?" he said.

"My first inclination is to run, but that thing is superfast. Didn't seem the bullets did much but for a minute or so."

"Maybe, maybe, it'll leave us alone and go up the block."

"And what, bubble up a few neighbors, eat their eyes, and eviscerate their dogs?"

"Don't think less of me, Geena, but if eyes are going to be eaten, I'd rather they not be mine."

"I know exactly what you mean," she said. "Do you know this kid at all? I never talked to the mom. I just waved from the porch when she'd go by."

"I know a little. A few times I was out in front raking leaves when she passed. I forget the mom's name, but the baby is a girl, and her name is Renata or Rebecca, I can't remember which."

Geena went to the sink and looked down at the now-sleeping infant, a vague smile on its face. Satisfied the baby was fine, she returned to the table and took up her phone to dial Craig. At first the line seemed dead again but in an instant sparked to life and there was ringing at the other end. Craig answered, and the suddenness of it scared her.

"Babe, what's up?" he said.

"Don't talk, just listen," she told him. "There's a killer in the neighborhood. I don't know how else to put it but he *melted* the young mom who walks by in the morning and also killed Ron's dog."

"What?"

"Don't talk. Call 911 and have them send the cops over here. Then pick up the kids after school and take them to your mother's place. Stay away from here. I can't talk more. We have to hide. Ron is here and he has his gun. He saved the girl's baby. Love you." She didn't want to give Craig a chance to carry on with a storm of questions and so hung up. A second later, he called back, but she didn't answer. She put the phone in her pocket. Back at the sink, she lifted the baby and its blanket with both arms. She rocked the girl back and forth and watched her sleep, which reminded her for an instant of the serene morning before it had all fallen apart.

"This is some kind of alien shit, I'd say," said Ron. "Maybe a visitor from another dimension? A demon escaped from hell? What do you think?"

"Like a nightmare," she said, and as soon as the words left her, there was a terrible banging sound at the kitchen-porch door. It was clear from the din that the wood of the frame was giving way against the force. Geena didn't turn around to look, but holding the baby close, she dashed to the entrance of the hallway. There, she stopped and turned. Mirage's face was in the glass panes of the upper part of the door. She wondered at the fact that the thing appeared so amorphous within its features but was so physical, slamming the door each time like a sledgehammer.

Ron, shuddering, slowly got to his feet and grabbed the gun. The door took another massive hit and then opened, ripping through the dead bolt and sending chips of wood in all directions. The only thing that prevented it from bursting wide was the chain lock, which would not hold for long. "Ron, let's go," she yelled, but he again took wobbling aim and fired three times. The first shot was off. It hit the molding and splintered it. The next two broke glass and both hit the stranger, who was pushed back and turned to static. The old man dropped the gun and followed Geena down the hallway.

She slid to a stop by the stairs, and said in a frantic burst, "Basement or upstairs?"

"Up," he said. "Don't wait for me."

She took the stairs in a few bounds and heard Ron clumping slowly along behind her. They both reached the landing when the chain lock snapping echoed through the house. "In here," she said and led the way into the bedroom. "Lock the door." He did. She laid the baby in the middle of the bed and went to a huge cherrywood armoire that was to the right of the doorway. Putting her shoulder to it, she tried with all her strength to budge it, without effect. Ron, gasping for air and hobbling, slipped in between Geena and the wall and threw his body against the massive furniture. It inched toward the door. They ended up slamming into the thing to move it, the way their pursuer attacked the porch entrance. In less than a minute, they had the locked door blocked by it. Ron staggered to the bed and sat on the edge.

"Where's the gun?" said Geena.

"No more bullets," he said, and reached to his side to unhook the billy club from his belt. "This is it."

"We've got one more way out," she said, going to the corner and grabbing the arms of a chair. She dragged it into the middle of the room and was about to step up on it when she heard the siren. She hopped down and ran to the window to see a police car turn into the driveway. Ron joined her. After all their pounding against the armoire, the noise of the siren woke Renata or Rebecca, and she wailed. Geena lifted her up and bounced her gently in her arms. They watched the police get out of the car.

"Push up the window," she said to Ron. He did as she requested. "The screen, too." He did and it opened with a screech, the sound drawing the attention of the cops. Geena stuck her head out and yelled, "He's got us trapped up here." One of the officer's waved and called, "We're coming." There was so much more she needed to tell them, but then Mirage was already there. She wished against it, but she knew what was coming. *What did I expect?* she thought as the cop yelled, "Halt! Stay where you are!" Even after he'd already been touched, began decomposing, and had lost his eyes, he managed to fire one wild shot.

Mirage took out the other officer with a swarm of the flying black dots. The poor fellow was turned to a pile of bloody entrails, hat nestled neatly on top. Each of the vicious little things that had devoured him turned to smoke and disappeared. The stranger licked his fingers and then looked up at Geena with his shifting, sparkling face.

Ron, who was resting on the bed again, said, "Thing's done with them already?"

"I shouldn't have called them."

"In another minute, the ambulance will be here, maybe SWAT, fire guys. If those two cops were any indication, there's gonna be a lot of eyeballs à la carte."

She put the baby down on the bed, shut the window, and returned to the chair she'd placed in the middle of the room. It was a sturdy wooden type, and she stepped up onto it. Reaching with both hands over her head, she found the latch to the attic, a ring set into a panel that only became obvious when she tugged it open. She pulled it down to reveal a set of folded wooden stairs. Getting down off the chair, she opened the contraption to its full length.

"A scuttle," said Ron, and smiled. "You get up there with the kid. I'm gonna stay down here. I'll seal you in and move the chair. When he comes, he may not notice it."

"Get up there," she said to him.

He shook his head. "I'm not climbing one more fucking set of stairs. Besides, how are you going to close that thing from up there in order to hide? I'll take my chances with the armoire and the club. There's no other way."

She wanted to have a good argument for him, but her mind was blank. She went to the bed, picked up the baby, and took it to the steps. Looking back, she wanted to say something but didn't. Ron pointed the way with the end of the club. When she reached the attic, he got up on the chair, folded the steps, and let the panel spring back.

It was warm up there and smelled of mildew and mice. Dust motes danced in the bright sunlight streaming in from a window at the front of the house. Because of the slanted ceilings of the attic dormer on either side, Geena could only stand upright in the center aisle of it. Luckily the baby had stopped crying and fallen back to sleep. They stood in the stillness surrounded by the flotsam and jetsam of Geena and Craig's life—the ridiculous oil paintings she'd done, Craig's hockey equipment, her grandmother's tea caddy she didn't have the heart to toss, two stacks comprising the entire works of Charles Dickens—maroon covers and threadbare bindings—and all manner of other debris that had gathered in the wake of their days together. Most of it was neatly stacked, but some had fallen or leaned into time. She thought of sadness but didn't feel sad. The unreality, the impossibility of it, blocked her from feeling anything but a dreadful awe.

When the pounding started at the bedroom door, she pictured the inevitability of Ron's death. It was only a matter of time. The noise was incessant, and she felt every blow in the rattling of the boards beneath her feet. She looked down at the trapdoor panel and saw a sliver of light. Kneeling, she leaned forward and saw that when the attic hatch had shut it did so off-kilter and there was enough of an opening for her to peek through and see Ron. She lay the baby carefully next to her on the floor, surprised none of the hammering shocks had woken her.

The old man sat on the edge of the bed, club lying next to him, his arms folded. In between crashes, he yelled out, "Fuck you." The door broke open and the scarred body of the armoire fell forward into the room, its glass doors shattering on the carpet. She saw Ron stand up, club now in hand. The stranger approached him and wrapped that long-fingered hand halfway round his throat. The old man reared back with his club hand to strike, but that arm and the side of his head went soft as candle wax in a flame and flopped into a rain of pus and blood. With his last strength, bellowing in agony, Ron threw a punch into the unstable face of his attacker, and the flesh of his fist burst into flame. The removal of his eyes was an off switch to his screaming. She watched what was left of him hit the floor and roll to a stop, his partially intact head staring directly up at her with dark, empty sockets. She lifted the baby, held tight, and turned away.

That death scream of Ron's had startled Renata or Rebecca, and Geena felt the baby's little body jolt to it. She knew crying was on the way but it came slowly, having to work through the shock of the death din. At the exact moment the baby gave a full-throated peal, the sirens sounded outside. *The fire guys and SWAT, maybe the National Guard, might be out there,* thought Geena. *And they have a lot more than six bullets.* She walked to the back of the attic and then through a small opening to a shallow storage space where the Christmas decorations were kept. She huddled in there, in the pitch dark, cross-legged, her back against the wall between two large boxes, and tried to shush the baby.

Two minutes later, gunfire and screaming erupted out in the driveway. Geena shut her eyes tight and sang a song she'd sung to her sons when they were small—"Under a Blanket of Blue." She dove deep into her thoughts, trying to hide from the horror that had seized the day. She pictured Craig and Matt and Eric, saw the boys grow up, saw her husband grow calmer, paunchier, his jokes become less funny. She loved them all and all their good and bad. In the dark part of her mind, it came to her that if she escaped the harrowing danger of Mirage, she would never forget how inconceivable change, impossible change, could step out of nothing in an instant and invade her life. The sweat dried on her forehead, her legs hurt from all the running and stair climbing, but her nerves finally got a chance to rest. Incredibly, she fell asleep there in the dark, surrounded by the aromas of Christmas past.

She awoke suddenly to the sound of the scuttle hatch to the attic groaning open. For a moment, she didn't know where she was, and thought the horror had merely been a dream. Then she felt the squirming baby in her arms and reality swamped her. She let out a gasp and Renata or Rebecca began to cry. She heard the wooden stairs to the attic being unfolded and the clomping of whoever or whatever was ascending. Looking out from the dark hiding place, she realized there was no more din of guns or sirens outside and she knew it would be Mirage even before that sparkling, rippling head came into view above the floorboards. She frantically rocked the baby to quiet it, but it was too late. The full figure of the stranger stood free of the steps and turned to face where she was hiding.

"This is it," she said into the baby's blanket, trying not to think about coming apart, boiling down to a mess, having her eyes skewered and torn out, or worse, any of that happening to the baby. Tears fell as the figure slowly approached them. She fiercely clutched the crying infant to her and closed her eyes. When she opened them, Mirage was right outside their sanctuary. Now that he was close, she heard his ambient sound of static and smelled a scent of sulfur or burning wood, like in the aftermath of a tornado. Pushing back so hard against the wall, she wanted to push through it, but it was as substantial as his form appeared shifting and fluid. He knelt and reached for them. She couldn't help but scream, seeing for certain she was within his grasp.

The long fingers like sharpened tree roots were inches from her when the hand began to fizz, and smoke came off it. Right in front of her face, Mirage's weird flesh disintegrated, turning to dust and falling away. The stranger let loose a scream of many voices—like a hundred coyotes in the spring out in the cornfields—and quickly pulled back his arm, which had vanished up to the elbow. His whole figure turned a stone gray, and he fled so rapidly, it was a blur. The next she knew, she and the baby were alone in the attic. Mirage's anguish echoed through the house, and then seemed to trail away out into the yard. She was stunned, unable to move, but when her senses returned, she crawled out of the storage den and gingerly got to her feet. From the dim window at the other end of the attic, she saw the day was dwindling.

With one hand holding the baby, she descended, grabbing ahold of each rung above until she stood in the bedroom. Ron's remains lay, still smoking and bubbling, at her feet. The armoire was blasted to pieces, the debris of which she quickly stepped over on her way to the hall. Ever aware and expecting an attack, powered by adrenaline, she decided without ever actually deciding that it was the only chance they might have to run. Down the stairs to the kitchen, they moved through the darkening house. On the counter, she found her car keys. Running, sliding on the wooden floor, she reached the door of the utility room that led to the garage. She passed through and locked it behind her. Her heart was pounding, and her mouth was dry.

The big, black SUV never seemed so flimsy, but she got in the driver's side and set the baby in the seat next to her. Pulling up the belt, she tried as best she could to secure the bundle. "Okay, Renata," she said in a whisper. "Let's go." The car started with too loud a roar, and she pressed the button to open the garage door. As it rose, her heart sank at the realization that there might be too many rescue vehicles and bodies in the driveway for her to get to the road.

It didn't matter, though, for standing right in front of the lifting door was Mirage, pointing his partially disintegrated arm at her as if in a fury of revenge. Behind him the last rays of twilight were being smothered by the gathering dark. He raised his arms, revealing those bat-like membranes in order to release the black swarm. Then, another change. As swiftly as bodies toppled from his touch, night suddenly fell, and the stranger's shimmering form let off streamers of smoke that turned to plumes. The autumn breeze whisked away the dust. She put the car in gear and hit the gas, ramming into the vanishing form and sending embers flying toward the stars. She hit the brakes before slamming into a rescue vehicle in the driveway and killing the engine.

When nothing happened for several minutes, and she'd caught her breath, she got out of the car, carrying the baby, and left the driveway awash with blood and melting remains. On the lawn, she could see the road, and under the streetlight on the other side, parked by the curb, was Craig's empty car. She staggered back to her front steps and sat down. The night was as still and serene as those mornings she'd once loved.

THE WANTING

A. T. GREENBLATT

It was morning and everything was calm, practically back to normal, and the bus was empty—aside from the driver and Don. Dread did not pool in Felicia's stomach, as it often did these days, and she paid her fare. Her only thought was *I hope Bennie got off his unemployed ass and made breakfast.*

It was numbingly cold and she bundled her shapeless down coat close as she took her usual seat in the middle of the bus, halfway between the driver and Don. The young daylight took the edge off the worst of the mess outside, and she leaned her head against the scratched-up double-pane window, soaking up the sun. She closed her eyes. God, her feet hurt, and this bus smelled like ass.

The driver lingered for a minute or two longer than he needed—like always—a small and unexpected kindness to any warehouse stragglers. In the three months of working in the warehouse, Felicia's coworkers changed routinely, but the bus driver had stayed consistent: a big doughy man with life lines on his face and good-natured eyes. She didn't know his name. She never asked. They did not have that type of relationship.

Anyway, it was only a twenty-minute trip to her apartment. *Freya better have cleaned up the living room*, Felicia thought. *Or at least vacuumed.*

Finally, the bus released its brakes, closed its door, and began to trundle its way down Turner Boulevard. Though traffic was light, the driver took it slow. There was plenty of debris in the road, trash, broken glass everywhere, and other undefinable objects littered about, some of them stretched beyond recognition like old taffy. Shapeless lumps of people twitched under blankets on the sidewalks.

"I think it's getting worse," said Don, his voice way too close. Felicia jerked away from the window. She turned and saw he'd moved to the seat behind her and there was this ridiculous grin on his face. Don was the type of person who believed they were handsome, and he would have been with his lean-muscled body, beautiful hands, and smooth skin, if he didn't think so. She could smell the tuna sandwich he'd eaten at break on his breath. "Mind if I sit here?" he said.

"Do what you want, man," she said, turning back and looking out the window. Though he had only been working with her in the warehouse for a few weeks, he wasn't the pushy type. He'd tried once, but had gotten the hint.

They passed Walnut Street, where a delivery truck had overturned, Styrofoam spilling out from boxes that had been torn into, torn apart. Little pink packing peanuts drifted down the street like cherry blossom petals in the spring.

"Looks like it was a rough night," continued Don sagely, like he wasn't uttering the obvious.

"It's the middle of winter, Don," she replied. "They're all rough nights." Everything started going to hell at dusk and winter nights were the worst, when the sun set at 4:00 p.m. and didn't bother appearing again until 8:00 a.m. Felicia used to stay awake listening to the screaming and howls that overtook the streets. The pleading and crying in the alley of her apartment building. The stop, just stop, please, God, please. In the worst moments, it was like she was with them, those trapped people, scrambling to get away from the wants of others.

No, that wasn't true. The worst moments were when she wondered if—when—she would become like them at dusk fall.

The morning sunlight was glorious as it refracted off the windows of tall buildings and shattered storefronts as the lingering people on the corners blinked up at the sky, dazed, as if they'd just awakened. Felicia wondered if Bennie and Freya had gotten out of bed yet. She wondered if they'd managed to get a good night's sleep and envied them either way.

Just make some eggs or waffles or something, she'd said to them earlier that week. *This job is fucking tiring.*

You're not the only one who's exhausted, replied Bennie. Which was fair—the walls of their apartment were thin and the windows leaked, and the nights turned them into something else entirely, but she was the one working her ass off in this relationship to make rent while her partners spiraled.

She almost missed those summer evenings in the beginning, when the nights weren't so bad, when she and Bennie and Freya used to bat around theories of why certain people swelled up like balloons and lost their minds at sundown over a discounted six-pack and a freshly packed bowl. *Being outside. Secondhand smoke. Plastic in the water. Proximity to other people. The phases of the moon. Masturbation. Not enough masturbation.* God, they used to laugh about this shit.

The bus halted suddenly, jolting Felicia and Don forward in their seats.

"Sorry," the bus driver murmured, glancing up into the large rearview mirror as a man in a nice wool coat stepped off the sidewalk in front of the bus, lurching across the street. Though it was unforgivingly cold out, his head was bare and his wispy hair was disheveled. His face was upturned toward the sun, like it was his comfort blanket or saving grace. His skin hung in folds around his naked hands and around his thirtysomething face, like it belonged to someone a size up. He looked distraught and utterly spent.

"They say it's wanting something that swells you up," said Don, watching the man as the bus rolled past. "Sun goes down, lights go out, and bam, we become all id."

Jesus Christ. They had both worked sixteen-hour shifts. How the fuck was this man still in the mood for small talk?

"People say lots of shit," she said to the window instead of turning around and smacking him.

"Hey, Joe?" Don called up to the bus driver. "What's your theory on all of this?" He gestured out the window at the general mess.

"As long as I can drive away, I don't care about the whats and the whys," said Joe with a shrug that rolled off his large shoulders, and Felicia wondered when Don had learned the driver's name. They didn't seem like they had that type of relationship.

"Can't argue with that, man," Don said.

Felicia clenched her teeth, and there was a sharp stab of pain in the back tooth she'd been meaning to see a dentist about, but had been dreading, too.

What if the craziness starts lasting longer and longer? Bennie asked one late morning as they passed a joint back and forth on the living room couch. *I mean, this used to only happen, like, once a month, during witching hour on a harvest moon or some shit like that.*

It won't, she said. *It's only a night thing.*

But what if it isn't?

What strain is this? she said, holding up the joint. *It's getting you paranoid, babe. You're annoying when you're paranoid.*

And yet, Bennie's stoned ramblings haunted Felicia. What would she do if it got worse? Maybe that was why she stuck with this warehouse job, when most people gave up after a week or two. Though it involved long hours on her feet and was boring as shit, the warehouse was large, locked from the inside, soundproof, and understaffed enough that she could dream she was alone. She got overtime for it, too.

If any of her coworkers changed during the night, she had yet to witness it, and when she pinched the skin around her face, around her hips and ass in the bathroom during her breaks, testing it, it continued to cling tight.

God, the sink is probably still full of dishes, Felicia thought. She closed her eyes and imagined what it would be like to live alone.

"Oh shit," Don said loudly. "I used to drink there." Felicia opened her eyes. He was pointing at a busted-up sports bar across the street. "Best half-price beer and wings on Tuesdays."

"Not as cheap as drinking at home," replied Felicia. There were a handful of disoriented people on the curb outside the bar, a few with bloody hands, dirty mouths, and loose skin that hung around their necks like extra scarves.

"C'mon, don't you miss nightlife?"

"No."

But it wasn't true. Next door to the ruined bar was once a great dance club and she ached for the nights that were just normal nights with normal hungers and she would go clubbing and lose time. Lose herself in music that was more like a deafening heartbeat and in the heat and stink of strangers' bodies, where occasionally a hand would run down her body, but she would take as much as was taken and it wasn't personal. That was the part she loved the most.

She hadn't been clubbing in months. Going during the day like Freya did sometimes felt unnatural, like living in a photo negative.

"What are you doing today, hon?" Don's breath tickled her ear.

"Sleeping." Her voice was sharper and louder than she expected. The driver looked in the rearview mirror at her, concern creasing his brow. God, she wished everyone would stop trying to get in her space and leave her the fuck alone.

"Alright, alright," Don said, leaning back and finally, mercifully, shutting up.

If you're this selfish now, Felicia, I'd hate to see what you turn into at night, muttered Freya after a particularly bad fight last week.

The bus continued down Walnut, passing more vandalized trucks and stretched-out people. Some of them still had slightly swollen arms or kneecaps or noses, throwing their centers of mass off-balance. But then again, the morning was still young, the sunlight was still chasing the night terrors away. The bus paused at a stop where a white standard poodle on a leash wandered around lost. It reminded Felicia of Bennie.

We used to care for each other, he said, yesterday, right before she left for her shift. Freya was also standing in their kitchenette, which was too small for all three of them, but where they ended up having all serious conversations and arguments anyway. *What the fuck happened to us?*

And Felicia looked at the dangling skin around her partners' faces, their knuckles and bony, bare knees, dread roiling in her stomach, and said: *We've changed, I guess.*

You haven't, said Freya, and where there once would have been venom in the words, there was only tiredness.

It was true, though. Felicia had never experienced the distortion or the wanting at night. Unlike everyone else, it seemed, she had no baggy skin to regret. Yet.

The bus turned down Union Street, the last stretch before home.

"Oh hell," said the driver and eased the bus to a stop, the engaged brakes squealing. There, in the road, was an overturned dumpster and some of the contents of an arcade had been pulled into the street. There were people here, too. A woman in a blue parka stared at a gumball machine like it was a riddle to be solved.

"It's getting worse," Don said, breaking the silence by stating the absolute obvious again.

"Are we stuck here?" Felicia called up to the driver with more fierceness than she expected. And then added, conciliatory: "Joe."

"Maybe?" the bus driver said, and the large man began to shake.

She couldn't blame him; her grip on the seat in front of her was white-knuckled and her stomach clenched. This couldn't be happening, not now, not with the morning sun shining down on everyone, showing the ruined world so clearly.

Before Felicia took the warehouse job, some nights she would lie wide-awake listening to the terrible mayhem outside. Those became the good nights. On the bad ones, she would listen to noises that Bennie and Freya made as they tapped on her locked bedroom door and rattled the knob with their swollen hands, stumbling over come-ons with swollen tongues.

The woman in the blue parka began rattling the gumball machine, trying to make something come out.

"All that want," Don said sadly.

Fuck, should she make a break for home? It might be better than sitting on a stalled bus, dread boiling in her stomach, feeling her powerlessness like a cornered animal.

The woman in the blue parka's hands began to balloon. Growing and stretching until they were as large as her head. With an expression of utter delight, she drove them into the dome of the gumball machine. Bright candies went scattering across the road as the woman cackled joyfully, as she popped gumballs into her mouth, one after the other.

"Oh my God," said Felicia. This shouldn't be happening. The sun was out, she could feel it on her face. *The sun was out.*

"Enough," said the bus driver. He stood up and Felicia saw that the large man had grown larger still. His chest had become a barrel for his neck and head to sink into like a turtle. His legs had become longer. Which served him well as he opened the bus doors and sprinted.

"Shit," Felicia breathed, the dread in her stomach transforming into uncut terror. *Please just leave me alone,* she prayed as she watched the growing chaos outside. So far, no one noticed or wanted the bus.

She felt a hot sigh on the back of her neck. The tuna on his breath had become rank.

"You're really pretty, you know," said Don.

"Back off, Don," she said, turning and then going very still. "I'm already in enough relationships."

"Sure there's not room for one more?" he asked and reached out to touch her hair.

Felicia shoved his hand away. And that was when she felt how unnaturally long his once-beautiful fingers had become.

"*Back off,*" she repeated.

"I don't want to," he said, grinning.

Then, he leaned forward and bit her ear.

It wasn't a hard bite. Just enough for her to feel his teeth's indents as she wrenched away and touched her ear.

"What the *fuck*?" she said, staggering into the aisle. Don's smile widened. He stood up as his fingers grew even longer, reaching for her, and the bulge in his pants grew, too.

He lunged at her.

She had taken self-defense classes, of course she had, she wasn't going to be caught in an alley helpless. So, when Don threw an arm around her neck and tried to bring his head close, she responded by swinging her own arm to strike him right under the nose, hitting the pressure point just so. His head snapped back.

With a fluid motion she spun. She used the momentum to trap his neck and head in a deadlock. He screamed in frustration, his stretched and distended fingers straining to find purchase, but she had him.

The morning's sunlight was growing brighter. Even in this adrenaline-soaked moment, Felicia could see his unnatural fingers deflating, his skin beginning to bunch around his nails and knuckles. She knew this would be over soon.

She could have thrown Don against the seats and pinned him there. Waited for everything to settle and shrink, return to itself. Watch realization and guilt seep into Don's eyes, like it always did the next morning for Bennie and Freya.

But Felicia was tired of waiting. For the mornings. For her partners. For the world to right itself again.

Now she just wanted to be left the fuck alone.

Don strained against her as she angled her body toward the open doors of the bus and put all her strength into the throw. He flew down the steps, skidding down them until the back of his skull connected loudly, wetly with the pavement. She didn't stop to listen to what he tried to say through wheezes or the thumps of his legs as they spasmed against the bottom steps of the bus. She didn't pause to consider the fresh smell of blood and piss, or watch his extremities deflate down to their usual size. Instead, Felicia pushed his legs out of the bus and shut the door.

It was only when she was alone in the bus, heart pounding, gasping, the clear morning sun warming her face, that she considered the wreckage of her actions. The damage she had caused. The person she had probably killed. She wondered which parts of her anatomy had swollen beyond recognition.

Why did you fall in love with me? she'd asked Freya and Bennie once, years ago, when nights were just nights.

You're consistent. Don't like to change much, Bennie said promptly.

You're not afraid to go after what you want, said Freya after a moment and with a shy smile.

Felicia turned to the bus's wide rearview mirror and braced herself, expecting to see her eyes or her chest or her head swollen to an ungodly size.

But there she was. Herself, as always, unchanged.

HOLD US IN THE LIGHT

A. C. WISE

Jules watched the light move across the cabin floor. Jagged and splintery where it seeped around the gaps in the curtains, hungry and determined in its slow march. Sunlight, but also teeth that would hollow her out if she let them.

The summer she'd turned twelve, the summer their mother left them, light had haunted her dreams. It had poured itself into the space behind her eyelids every night until she'd thrown the fucking carving she and Tristan had found in the quarry into the lake.

And now, the same carving lay there, just past her feet, and the same light, a bright, wavering line, inched toward it.

In those unwanted dreams, Jules had known without knowing how, the light could and had stripped flesh from bone, bleached color from those same bones and turned them as fragile as glass. It followed her through a terrible city, dragging sharp-edged shadows away from twisted structures too big to house anything human. The angles and architecture made her head hurt. Whatever had built and abandoned the city leaned up against the skin separating the world she could see from the one she could not, pressing like a hand or a face against a gauzy curtain. At any moment those terrible ghosts might break through.

A constant susurrus like a lonely wind. Voices murmuring just on the edge of hearing that today would be the day she finally lay down on the dust-grit streets of powdered bone and glittering salt and gave up. How sweet it would be. Oh, oh, oh, how the light would savor her and make her last.

Jules remembered reaching her arm back as far as she could, throwing, then watching the carving arc end over end before dropping into the water. It sank, taking the horrid light and the city with it, but it didn't fix everything else their mother had broken. She didn't come back, their lives frayed at the edges, and by the time Jules let herself see it, it was already too late.

Her spine ached, pressed against the bedroom wall, her knees drawn against her chest and her arms wrapped around them. The line of light finally reached the carving. Touched it, crept across the wood. Jules braced herself, and nothing happened at all.

The shaky breath she exhaled might have been laughter or a sob.

What had she expected? Some monstrous anatomy to unfold? Mouths to open in the idol's vague suggestion of a face, ringed with endless rows of teeth?

Whether the dreams came from somewhere real, whether the story Tristan had told her was actual truth, didn't matter. At the end of the day, it was Jules's fault. She crawled forward, picked up the idol. It didn't bite, didn't buzz or hum or do anything. It remained wood, pale and almost weightless as if hollow inside. A scant oval of a face, with no visible features, just a suggestion of a halo or a crown, which increasingly looked to Jules like a head engulfed in flames. A robe, sketched in rough knife cuts, but were those marks truly meant to represent folds of cloth, or were they wings, or hundreds of arms, tucked tight against the body?

She held the idol the way she should have held Tristan. Instead, she'd deflected, placated, avoided confrontation, telling herself he wouldn't possibly be so stupid. Jules's breath caught; she gripped the carving tighter. He was, and she was, as well. Her go-to strategy of dealing with her brother had never once achieved anything other than enabling every terrible decision he'd ever made. She'd always been there to pick him up when he fell, lending him money, giving him a place to crash, bailing him out of jail. She was supposed to look out for him, but she'd let him turn out just like their mother.

Always dreaming, always with some wild plan that was going to change everything, always leaving someone else to clean up the mess left behind. And now, like her, Tristan was gone.

Jules stood, grabbed her rucksack, retrieved a flashlight from one of the kitchen drawers, though she wasn't sure she would need it. She took Tristan's damned map, and stuffed the idol into the bag, as well. If she didn't go now, she never would. For all she knew, she was already too late.

● ○

Jules hefted a stack of magazines, warped and water-stained and—she imagined—entirely unread. She tried not to think of mold rubbing against her skin, tried not to think of her father filling the spaces her mother left behind and turning the cabin into a hoarder's paradise. She could tell herself she hadn't known it had gotten so bad, but the truth was, she hadn't wanted to know. He didn't have a problem, he just needed to tidy up a little; she'd made every excuse, letting the junk and her father's loneliness accumulate, telling herself there was still time to fix everything. Until there wasn't.

Her eyes prickled. Dust. Another excuse. Jules turned to carry the magazines to the trash, and stopped. The idol lay on the coffee table, revealed by the pile in her arms. Everything in her went still and cold. It couldn't be, but it was. Her knees wanted to buckle under the weight of its eyeless attention. As if someone had dropped a clear glass slide into the space behind her eyes, Jules saw the cabin suddenly overwritten by vast ragged and crumbling towers, washed in terrible, merciless light.

"Tris? Where did you find this?"

Jules set the magazines down. Her arms ached. She edged toward the coffee table, reached out one finger, but stopped just short of touching the wood.

Tristan stuck his head out from the kitchen and, seeing where Jules's attention was fixed, grinned.

"Would you believe I found it jammed up into the chimney? The flue was stuck, and when I reached in to see what was blocking it, there it was. It has to be the same one, right?"

"Did you—" Jules stopped, words sticking in her throat.

She'd been about to ask if Tristan had pulled it out of the lake, years ago, and hidden it. Why would he? She'd never told him about the dreams, and he'd had no reason to doubt what she'd told him back then—that she didn't know what happened to the treasure they'd found in the quarry, but surely it would turn up sooner or later. And now it had.

"Never mind." Jules shook her head.

"I was going to surprise you with it," Tristan said.

He emerged fully from the kitchen, wiping his hands on a towel slung over his shoulder. He'd arrived at the cabin at least three days before her—the benefits of not having a full-time job to leave behind. But she couldn't fault the work he'd already done, excavating the place and getting it ready for sale.

"You'll never believe what else I found. Why don't we take a break. I'll order pizza, and I'll show you."

Jules glanced toward the window, surprised to see the sun already well on its way to setting. Tristan picked up the idol. He turned it, even as an objection died on Jules's tongue. The tips of her fingers tingled, almost an ache, like she was the one holding the thing, tracing the words scratched into the wood like thin white scars.

Hold Us in the Light.

A prayer, a wish, a hope.

They'd wondered over it as kids, suggested countless meanings, spun ever more fantastical tales about its origins, and searched the area all around the quarry for more buried treasure just like it. They'd never found anything. No bootlegger stashes, no secret hidden caves, no more mysterious artifacts, and certainly no gold. Likely the carving had been made by a bored camper, accidentally dropped on a hike, and lodged between two rocks for Jules to one day trip over it.

But the way Tristan's eyes had shone, suggesting wilder and wilder theories as they roamed all through the woods that summer—what was the harm in indulging his imagination? They had both needed the distraction, after all.

Tristan set the idol back on the coffee table, wiped his hands again, and pulled out his phone. Numbness replaced the tingling sensation in Jules's hands, crawling up her arms and spreading to the rest of her body. She imagined Tristan—or even her father—inexplicably wading into the lake, emerging dripping with the carving clutched in their hands. She imagined it coming back on its own, looking for her after all these years. It was stupid, but those dreams had felt so real, and seeing the carving made her feel twelve years old again. Lost, with the weight of all those unseen eyes and whispers pressing against her, with the weight of the world and her crumbling family on her shoulders, as well.

"There." Tristan slid his phone back into his pocket. "I added a stop so the driver is going to bring us beer and ice cream, too."

"You're a good brother," Jules said.

The words fell from her lips automatically. She might have even meant them if her body wasn't so locked up with sudden, irrational fear. She deliberately put her back to the carving, planning to clear the table so they could eat, keeping her hands busy in an attempt to ignore the itch growing between her shoulder blades.

"I found the whole history, Jules. Mystery finally solved." Tristan intercepted her, his grin returning.

He steered her down the hall toward the two bedrooms at the back of the house. The smaller one had held bunk beds once upon a time; she and Tristan had shared the space for nearly twelve summers. When Jules had arrived, it had been filled floor to ceiling with junk. They'd managed to clear half the space, stacking things they might want to sell or keep in the other half. The bigger bedroom across the hall had been their parents' room. After their mother left, their father replaced the queen bed with a single and turned the other half of the room into a kind of office.

They'd stopped coming to the cabin as a family, but their father had kept up solo trips—shipping them off to camp, or foisting them on grandparents and friends. Fishing and hunting, he'd claimed, but in reality he'd spent his time scouring flea markets, garage sales, antique stores, and even dumpster diving, filling the space with broken electronics and furniture and old newspapers—a compulsion he couldn't help, but felt the need to hide.

Tristan had cleared this room before she got here and he led her to the desk against the wall. A small lamp threw a pool of illumination over what looked like a survey map, unrolled and pinned at the corners by various weights.

"I found this in Dad's things." Tristan bounced lightly on his toes, peering over her shoulder. "I'm not even sure he knew he had it, but Mom was right after all."

"Right?" Jules stiffened, but Tristan directed her attention back to the map.

"What am I even looking at?"

"Okay, so, remember how Mom used to say there were gold mines all over the hills around here and that we were going to go panning and strike it rich?"

He leaned into her eyeline, memory lighting his face.

"Tris—"

"I know, I know." He waved her objections away. "All bullshit, but there were coal mines."

"So?"

"That's where the idol came from, the mines, and the mines connect up to real actual caves, just like the ones we searched for as kids."

Tristan practically vibrated with energy, the same Jules remembered buzzing from their mother's skin as she'd expounded on her latest scheme—they would move to Alaska and make a fortune on the ice roads, they'd buy up land somewhere in Texas and strike oil, they'd drive to Las Vegas, she'd hit the jackpot, and they'd never have to worry about money again.

Only the last wild promise had ever been realized, but their mother had gone alone, and whether she'd ever struck it rich or lost everything, Jules would never know. A postcard had arrived a week after she'd left, the neon glow of the strip on one side and the back signed with a row of *X*s and *O*s and her name. No goodbye, no way for them to reach her, and they'd never heard from her again.

"I started doing research and—" The doorbell rang, their food arriving and interrupting him.

Her first chance to throw the brakes on whatever was building slipped away. Jules trailed after her brother. Dusk had fallen, darkening the space between the trees. He gathered the pizza, beer, and ice cream, stowing the container in the freezer and laying out the rest on the kitchen table. Once they were seated, he picked up the thread, talking between bites.

"I found out a company called Circle Mining used to own all this land," Tristan said. "Long before anyone built vacation cabins and rental homes around the lake."

Jules noted the dirt worked into the creases of Tristan's knuckles, no doubt from digging and sifting through piles of their father's crap, even though she'd seen him wash his hands before they sat down. She wasn't the only one mourning. This excitement firing him was simply his way of processing grief, of distracting himself. No different from what they'd done as kids, only they were grown up now. Was it healthy to go on believing in fairy tales?

"The owners of the company were cheap assholes." Tristan paused for a swallow of beer. "They charged the workers for every single piece of equipment they used, tallied it up at the end of the day, and took it out of their pay."

Jules tried to picture Tristan rifling through the stacks in the local library, falling down an internet rabbit hole. She recognized their mother's cadences, the dreaming light in her eyes. Had he really found this story, or was he making it up on the spot? Their mother had always made a game of it, inviting Jules and Tristan to chime in with the first thing they wanted to eat to celebrate their fortune, the first extravagant thing they wanted to buy, encouraging them to be less practical, more ridiculous. A hot-air balloon. A whole extra house, just to keep their shoes. If she could make them part of it, they wouldn't ask questions or poke holes.

"The workers would go into the mines sometimes with one lantern or headlamp among them, doing most of their work in the dark," Tristan said.

Jules pushed her plate away, cheese congealing on the last half slice. She pulled her beer closer, cradling the sweating bottle. She tried to imagine miners working in the pitch-black, but what her mind conjured instead was brutal light, printing the miners' shadows on the tunnel walls. Even sitting on the coffee table in the other room, she couldn't shed the awareness of the idol, shake the feeling it was listening and watching them.

"The workers started telling each other stories, down in the dark. They started hearing whispers, like the tunnels were haunted."

Voices like a cold, lonely wind, telling the miners to give up and lie down.

Jules startled, nearly knocking over her beer. The idol and the dreams had always been tied inextricably in her mind, impossible to separate. And now, without even knowing about the dreams, Tristan was telling her the connection was real?

"So they started praying."

"Hold us in the light," Jules said.

She hadn't meant to say it aloud; the excitement firing Tristan's expression when she did was almost unbearable.

A reasonable prayer for men trapped down in the dark. The light would seem like salvation, but it was hungry, and if it could convince the workers to feed it willingly with their faith, with their very selves . . .

Jules closed her eyes. They hurt. Even the kitchen light with its soft amber glow felt intrusive, bruising. The carved idol felt imprinted against her eyelids, even though she'd last looked at it almost an hour ago—the unformed face, hidden features just waiting to rise, waiting to press through the skin. Hands had carved it in absolute darkness, by feel alone. How often did the knife slip, nick skin and feed the wood with blood?

Her eyes snapped open.

"Tris—" Jules tried to cut him off, deliver a warning.

Tristan wasn't looking at her, his gaze fixed on some inner landscape.

"They found something, or they called something, who knows? It answered their prayers, brought them light. They kept digging, and eventually the tunnels connected up with the natural cave system."

She wanted to tell him it was impossible. But it wasn't impossible. She'd been there, in the place the light came from, long before it ever found its way here. She wanted to push the thought away, couldn't.

"Circle Mining's owners," Tristan said, "figured out something was going on and decided to go down and see for themselves."

"What did they find?" Jules couldn't help asking.

Did she want to know what the faces of the things in the ancient, light-washed city looked like, even second- or thirdhand? Tristan reached for another beer, cracked it open.

"A god? A great power? Whatever it was, they believed in it as fervently as the miners, and they wanted it for themselves." Tristan made a grim face, his excitement tempered, but the shine only partially dimmed from his eyes. Did it matter where he'd found the story? He believed it, and so help her, Jules did, too. The problem was how to convince him that truth was a lie.

"The men from Circle Mining believed in exceptionalism: Having wealth and power meant you deserved wealth and power. If you were poor, it was your fault, and you would never be anything but," Tristan said.

Bitterness colored his tone. Jules forced herself to breathe.

Let the story run its course, and then she could work on redirecting him. It had only been three months since their father's death. This was the same as the summer they'd spent hunting for treasure. As long as they never stayed still a moment, they would never have to face up to their mother being gone.

"They collapsed the mine on purpose," Tristan said. "They left the workers to die."

They fed them to the light. Jules let the thought roll through her mind like a stone. Tiny crystals of salt coated her tongue, and she took a desperate sip of beer to wash them away.

"Once they were sure it had been long enough that nothing could be alive down there, they moved back in, extended the remaining tunnels into the cave system, and built a whole church underground. They began referring to themselves as just the Circle, convinced their new god would grant them endless money, power, and eternal life."

All things the light would happily promise, and maybe even grant, as long as it was fed.

Tristan set his bottle down, glass against wood, a sound with finality tucked inside it. He traced his finger through the condensation, voice a hush now, but words landing like a blow.

"What if it's all still down there, Jules, the church, everything?" He raised his head and Jules flinched, her heart flipping over. "What if there's treasure in these hills after all?"

Her brother's face was a mask, ill fitting, his mouth slightly agape, a hollowness around his eyes. And leaking through and all around the edges and gaps, a fever brightness; it had gotten inside Tristan, under his skin, emptied him out and made itself a home. What had it promised him, what had it whispered to him? If he followed it underground, what did he think he would find?

"Tristan."

A scant few inches separated their hands on the table. Jules made herself close the distance, cover her brother's hand. He flinched from the touch as if burned. Jules swallowed and tried again.

"You know it's just a story, right? None of it can be real."

The lie hurt. Tristan would see it, radiating from her, the hungry light was inside her, too.

"I thought we could go together," he said. "Like old times."

A wounded, little-boy plea, cracking at her heart. How many times had she picked Tristan up over the years? Righting his bike when he was learning to ride, swabbing blood from his knees and covering the scrapes with bandages. Even before their mother left, it had been her job. The transition from that to late-night phone calls in college, the request to crash on her couch, could she lend him just a little cash to tide him over, was a smooth one.

"The map, the carving," Tristan said. "It's all for a reason. The idol wanted to be found."

She stood, putting her hand on Tristan's shoulder. The look he gave her was forlorn.

"I'm not saying no." Jules let out a breath, chickening out, the look in Tristan's eyes digging at her like always. "Let's sleep on it, okay? We can talk about it more tomorrow, but for now, we're both exhausted, and we should get some rest."

Tristan nodded. She pulled him forward for a hug, and a measure of the tension coiled around Jules's spine unwound.

"You're a good brother." She wanted to mean it, said it like a prayer. *Hold us in the light.* "Now go take a shower. You stink. I'll clean up here."

She watched him leave the kitchen. An impulse. A passing fancy. She'd keep Tristan busy helping her clean out and sell the house, and eventually he would get distracted, something else would catch his attention. Maybe it would be another stupid scheme, but she'd be ready by then. She'd do right by him, and she wouldn't let him get lost. She'd protect him like a big sister should.

• ○

Jules dreamed of the light. Pale and syrupy slow, an inevitable tide, rising. The ruined city, as always, emptied of everything and everyone, but a presence remained—behind her, above her, below her, hidden inside the light. She climbed vast, spiraling stairs, each tread almost too big for her, white as stripped bone. The light lapped at her heels. Her legs ached when she reached the top of the ragged tower, a broken tooth glittering with crystals of salt. A sandcastle ready to crumble under her touch.

The light oozed up the tower's sides, still reaching for her. It would never ever stop.

She woke, a gasp stopped in her throat, eyes aching, knowing she was alone.

She'd fallen asleep on the too-short couch in front of the fireplace, bundled into her sleeping bag. Tristan had cleared their father's room; it seemed only fair he take the bed.

Now the cabin yawned around her, the feeling the same as the morning she'd woken and learned their mother was gone. The cabin too quiet, despite Tristan slumbering in the lower bunk. She'd crept past him, into the kitchen, and found it empty. Their father stood on the front step, just beyond the screen door, staring at the driveway where their car no longer sat. Jules remembered him clutching his coffee mug, the only thing anchoring him to the world. He hadn't turned when the door creaked open, when she came to stand beside him and lean into his side.

"She's finally gone" was all he said.

Jules wondered if it was relief, no longer having the eventuality of her leaving hanging over him.

She felt no relief now as she kicked free of the sleeping bag.

Even if she'd known, deep down, it was inevitable that Tristan would follow in their mother's footsteps. Down the hall to the bedroom just in case she was wrong. She wrenched the door open. The covers rumpled across the bed; Tristan had at least laid down last night and tried to sleep, but it hadn't lasted long.

He'd left the desk light on, illuminating the map, a spot circled with the idol lying atop it, as if there were any doubt where he'd gone.

Jules snatched up the carving. It weighed nothing in her hand. She hurled it at the wall. She'd tried to throw it away once before, and it had come back to her then, too.

The carving bounced and hit the floor, landing face up, accusing. Jules let her back slide down the wall until she sat, pulled her knees up against her chest, too hurt and hollow to cry, and waited for the sun to rise.

● ○

Jules might have missed the spot, even though she was looking for it—a slight depression in the ground, hastily covered with brush. A flat stone had been set out in front of the pile, roughly scratched with her name.

Tristan had left her a marker, one that looked uncomfortably like a tombstone. Then he'd wormed his way into the tunnel she assumed must lie beyond the brush, burying himself alive.

She knelt, yanked the branches aside. Sweat stuck her shirt to the small of her back under the rucksack. The hole revealed could have been left by un uprooted tree, a fox, a badger. She thought of the dirt in the seams of Tristan's knuckles. How long had he been planning this? How long ago had he actually arrived at the cabin? He'd only been waiting for her, hoping she would follow him willingly, knowing she would do so reluctantly when he went on his own. It was never a question of if, just when and how.

She slung the rucksack off and shoved it into the hole, ignoring the pebbles digging into her skin as she lay flat on her stomach. She tried not to think of mouths and being swallowed. It might have been more practical to back into the hole the way Tristan clearly had, but she couldn't bear the idea of not being able to see ahead.

And she could see—more clearly than should be possible, light seeping toward her from somewhere up ahead. Roots and more pebbles bit into her forearms as she pulled herself painfully forward, inch by inch. Stop, shove the bag, crawl. Repeat—her shoulders, back, and neck screaming.

All at once, the dirt gave way, spilling her forward. Panic flailed at her, but the fall was short, more of an awkward slide, cushioned by earth. The surface she landed on was smooth, and she could stand, which she did, brushing herself off. The fabric of her pant leg had torn, a thin line of blood showing through.

Jules stood on a path, winding between natural stone formations. She remembered a family trip, but not the name of the caverns they'd visited. She'd been maybe four years old, clinging to her mother's hand, Tristan young enough that their father had carried him on his hip the whole time. Jules had been afraid of the sound of dripping water, unsettled by hearing something she couldn't see.

Those caverns, naturally formed, had been tamed and turned into a tourist attraction. This cave was the same—shaped to a purpose—but it wasn't a space meant for anyone and everyone, only a select few—the Circle.

She lifted the rucksack back onto her shoulder, not bothering with the flashlight, and walked toward where it seemed brighter. Haunted. The feeling clung to her as she followed the path. It was like the city she'd dreamed of, the ruins. The people who'd inhabited it once were no longer there, but they weren't gone, either. She just couldn't see them. Yet.

Everything in her screamed to turn around and run. Claw her way back up the tunnel, like unburying herself from a grave.

But Tristan was down here somewhere. He needed her. And she couldn't leave him behind.

Jules ducked through an arch in the stone like a door and stopped, her breath catching. The church spread before her, below her, a house of worship flipped upside down, and driven deep into the ground.

Stairs carved into the stone curled along a wall circled with narrow ledges, studded with alcoves. The light made the shadows in the alcoves deeper, an impenetrable black. Velvet curtains, and the longer Jules looked, the more certain she was that someone—something—stood just on the other side of each one.

The floor of the church—she couldn't think of it any other way—was a maze, broken up by columns of stone like melted wax. She couldn't tell if they were naturally formed or carved. Or both. Some looked like altars, places to sit, statues. The Circle hadn't literally filled their church with gold, but power and promise thrummed in the air, a physical presence seething and writhing and making her skin crawl.

Jules reached the bottom of the stairs, stepped around a column, and stifled a startled shout. A human figure reached up toward her, like it was asking to be pulled free. A few shallow steps down—some kind of natural depression, carved into a basin, and the man—had it been a man once?—had died in the act of crawling out.

Or, not died. Something else.

She put her hands over her mouth, unable to look away. The figure looked both eroded and burned. If someone had carved it, they'd made something awful. Because Jules couldn't shake the feeling it had once been alive. Like the bodies at Pompeii. Like mummies unearthed from a bog, so transformed it was almost impossible to believe they'd ever been living, breathing humans.

Lowering her hands, she edged away from it while keeping her eyes on the figure. Looking away would be worse. The moment she did, it would move. Not dead. Not frozen. Behaving like the light itself, fractions of motion happening too slowly for the eye to see. Those crumbling fingers that looked like they'd spent eons being worn away by a hard rain would close on her ankle and—

The tension snapped and Jules darted forward, hiding herself behind the nearest pillar of stone. Maybe if the eyeless thing couldn't see her . . . But surely it would hear her breath, her blood, the slamming beat of her heart.

She wrapped her fingers around the straps of the rucksack, something to hold on to like her father gripping his coffee mug and waiting for the world to right itself. No sounds came from behind her, nothing running after her. Nothing crawling slowly, either.

Pushing away from the column, she rolled her shoulders back and then squared them. Another archway stood across from her, and beyond it, the source of the light—the ugly alien light from her dreams, from another world. Called here by the miners in their need, or already here, just waiting for their want to feed it.

Jules made herself keep walking, clinging to the straps of the rucksack. Tristan was somewhere up ahead. He had to be, and he had to be okay.

There were other figures scattered around the cave. Some sitting, some standing, some lying down. On plinths and tucked into alcoves. Some, like the figure in the basin, crawling like they were trying to get away.

Were they the remnants of the miners, or the Circle? Or both? Faceless and hollowed. Like the idol in her bag, blank ovals for heads that still somehow suggested features, buried and waiting to rise. She could see them wrapped in arms and wings, waiting to unfold, heads crowned—horrible saints about to burst into flame.

Jules stepped through the arch and into the light. Her hands went up instinctively, shielding her eyes, but she could still see—just enough—through the gaps between her fingers, and the breath went out of her.

Tristan stood, slack, face-to-face with the god.

All of it—her dreams, his story, all of it real. Whatever he'd hoped to find, riches or occult knowledge to sell off in his latest get-rich-quick scheme, there was only this.

Fingers. Hands. Thousands of them. Emerging from the rock, or part of the rock. She couldn't quite tell, didn't truly want to know. They were still, but she had the sense of them grasping, like they could touch her or Tristan anytime they chose.

They used to draw the sun with dozens of reaching arms in the temples of ancient Egypt. The thought tumbled uselessly through her head.

Not just hands, but mouths, or just one vast and endless mouth, ringed with teeth. With wings.

Part of the stone. Not part of the stone.

Like something pouring itself down the wall of the cave while also rising out of it. She thought again of crumbling sandcastles. But also melted wax. Of figures carved on the outside of a church, all but worn away by the rain. Face and hands pressed up against the thin skin between worlds, just waiting to break through.

She couldn't make sense of it and didn't want to. It was too bright. It had eaten everything in the ancient city and left behind a ruin.

Tears seeped between her fingers from the sharpness of the

light. Jules squinted behind her hands, lashes touching, but not closing her eyes all the way. She couldn't. Tristan was still there. She turned her head, as if it would help, as if she could escape the light.

But it was everywhere. Everywhere.

From this angle what she saw was—not worse. As bad. It was all terrible.

Tristan's arms hung loose at his sides, hands ceaselessly opening and closing, head tipped back, mouth open. She couldn't see his eyes, but she imagined them glassy, emptied. He'd already been hollowed out, the light taking up residence.

Yet she swore he swayed slightly, evidence of life. Or something like it.

His shadow stretched behind him on the cavern floor, pulled thin and ragged in a way that looked painful, painted or burned there. If he moved—if he ever moved again—the shadow would remain.

Behind him, other figures knelt in rows of worship. Rings of them, like the god was a dropped stone and they were the ripples echoing out from it. How long had they been down here? Stone, but not. Living, yet dead. Eroded faces and heads, hands resting on their folded knees, facing the light, on the verge of crumbling.

Except unlike the figures in the other room, these had mouths and eyes. Or at least the suggestion of them—depressions like thumbs pressed down into wet clay. Each head had the worn nubs of ears, as well, so they could hear their god. Its endless whispers. And answer with a terrible song.

Or maybe it was the light itself, humming like struck crystal, and the open mouths weren't singing at all, only crying out for release from their pain. The Circle had found their immortality after all.

Her own throat was too dry to call out, even if she'd wanted to speak Tristan's name. The light had sucked all the moisture from her. It would do the same to her blood, her sweat, her tears if she stayed.

A rough, bitter laugh dragged free, a sandpaper sound abrading her throat and leaving the taste of blood behind.

Jules shut her eyes, lowered her hands. It didn't matter. The light burned against her lids anyway. When, if, she ever tried to open them again, would there still be eyes behind them, or just endless black holes? She slung the bag from her shoulder, fumbled inside until she found the idol.

Did it twitch in her hands? Buzz? The wings, the hands and arms wrapped around it finally unfurling? She held it, maybe for too long, dropping the rucksack to her feet. She held it tightly enough that the thin lines of the prayer etched into its side dug into her hand.

Hold Us in the Light.

She could understand why the miners had wanted such a thing.

But now she needed the fucking light to let go.

Jules's lids snapped up like the motion would shatter them. Just long enough to be sure of where Tristan stood. Then she threw the idol as hard as she could.

It was her fault. She'd let it get this bad. She'd always been there for Tristan, but she'd never done him any good. If she could save both of them, she would, and if not, she would save herself.

Jules screamed and everything screamed with her as the carved wood arced and turned end over end. She needed it to hit Tristan, to wake him up from his trance so he would turn and run with her.

But she couldn't stay long enough to see if he did.

She ran, not daring to look back to see if her brother, or the light, followed.

DISMAYING CREATURES

ROBERT SHEARMAN

She looked at her husband and considered, as she so often did these dry, hot days, how much he resembled a frog. Ever since they'd been formally introduced she'd been trying to put her finger on it, but it was only on her wedding day that the perfect rightness of the comparison had struck her. *He's like a frog stuffed into a suit,* she thought, and she'd had to stifle the urge to laugh because she knew that wouldn't have been proper. A frog, yes—now she couldn't unsee it—his head seemed to erupt right out of the starched collar, and there was no neck, no hint of a neck at all, and there was something about the slippery smoothness of his skin, its slightly greenish pallor. As he'd joined her at the altar he'd affected to give her a slight, tight smile, and then he'd looked away, looked upwards, over the vicar's head, over the head of the stained glass Christ himself, staring hard, as if he'd just popped his head out from a lily pond and was hunting for flies.

In that moment she'd known she was going to be married to a frog, forever and ever more, and she wouldn't be happy, but at least she needn't ever be frightened. Because why would anyone be frightened of a frog? She felt the slightest stirrings of affection for him—not love, of course not, but something more tolerant, something that wasn't contempt.

She was under no illusions she was any sort of catch, either. That was why she'd suffered the indignity of watching as her younger sisters were married before her—and all to men with charm, and all to men with necks. She could only imagine the relief her parents must have felt when Froggy came a-courting! "But don't you see the way her teeth jut out?" her father might have said, fairly. Her mother chipping in, "They make her face bulge out in weird directions, like a rodent's!" But he'd agreed to marry her anyway—she had sufficed—and he had money, and some hope of a title, and he was the right side of fifty-four, she could certainly have done worse. *But what an ugly couple we must make!* she'd thought as the vicar pronounced them man and wife, and she'd leaned in for that first kiss, her buck teeth grazing at him all lipless and dry. The frog and the rat. *What dreadful creatures, how dismaying!*

That had been a month ago, maybe six weeks. She had lost interest in counting the days. Ever since they had been travelling—there had been trains, and two different ships, and now they were in a carriage, and though the window was open she couldn't seem to catch the breeze, the horses were going too slow, and it was miserably hot. She had no way to amuse herself. Looking across at her husband and considering the ways he looked like a frog could only distract her for so long. And then, it seemed to her without warning, the carriage came to a stop.

"Here we are, my dear. Here we are at last." He hadn't spoken to her for nearly three days. She'd have thought he was sulking, but there didn't seem to be any aggression to it, he had simply run out of things to say. But now he was talking again, and yes, even smiling, and there was a little gruff warmth to both. "I hope," he said, "that you'll be happy here."

He helped her down from the carriage. He had taken such pains to not so much as brush against her in the cramped interior that the touch of his skin now felt curious. Before her was another hotel, there had been so many of them. White marble, grand windows, pillars—too many pillars for practical use, surely. The lawns were vast and neat and so green, in spite of the stifling heat they were kept as watered as any garden in Kent or Surrey. And a Union Jack was flying from the flagpole. She didn't know which country they were in by now—still, no matter where they rested the night, there the Union Jack would fly, and whatever the colour of their skin all the staff spoke impeccable English. Three such staff were scurrying towards them now, picking up their luggage. Behind, walking with measured poise, a figure she supposed to be the manager.

It had been a long honeymoon, and she didn't know how much longer it was supposed to continue. Was this new hotel their destination, or just another stop along the way?

In his black dress suit she was surprised the heat didn't make the manager buckle over, but he withstood it quite admirably. "Welcome, Colonel. Madam. We hope you have had a pleasant journey."

Her husband nodded at this. "Is the hotel busy?"

"The hotel is *always* busy, sir, even out of season. But I shall see to it that you are not disturbed. There are some Italians in residence, but I have had them placed in another wing. The bridal suite is prepared. May I show you the way? And may I congratulate you. Your wife, sir, is quite the peach."

She didn't know quite how to react to this. Was it impertinence, or foreign courtesy? She looked at her husband for guidance, and it was clear he didn't know how to react, either. He just grunted, and nodded again, and so she decided it would be best to smile. The manager echoed her smile, displayed how many teeth he had. Then he turned on his heel, and began to march away. They followed him.

"The gardens are not at their finest at the moment," the manager explained. "You would need to stay until the spring. But there are jacarandas and bougainvillea, and you can pick the avocados right off the tree. Everywhere you can smell the jasmine. You are, naturally, invited to explore the gardens at your leisure, but do be aware that the grounds are vast and some of the wilder areas on the estate periphery may require caution." She took a sniff and thought that she could smell the jasmine, but she couldn't be sure—the manager was wearing a scent, it could well have been that. He led their way into the hotel, presenting it to them with pride as if he were not merely in employ but he himself owned the place. The veranda upon which evening tea was served, the restaurant that seemed ablaze with crystal glass and polished silver. A smoking room for the men, a billiard room for the men, a reading room that could be enjoyed by women if accompanied. Up the central staircase as grand as any she had seen on her travels, and then from the first-floor landing up another staircase that was grander still and made the first staircase paltry in comparison. "The bridal suite," said the manager, "is at the top of this third staircase here, exclusive to your own use," and it was the grandest staircase of them all.

As staff unpacked the luggage, the manager took her and the frog out onto the balcony, and prepared some tea. As he poured, there was the sound of a shriek from the gardens beneath them. She thought at first it was a baby—then the shriek came again, louder this time, and it was clearly feral, the cry of a wild animal.

"What is that?" she said.

"It is nothing to be worried about, madam," said the manager smoothly. "My men are dealing with it. I hope you enjoy the tea. In this wet heat some travellers are tempted to drink iced liquids. It is a mistake. It is better to let the body adjust with something mild and temperate, as we hope, sir, as we hope, madam, you shall find your stay at the hotel always mild and only temperate."

They sipped at the tea. She found it somewhat tart, but not unpleasant. Another shriek from the garden startled them, her husband even spilled his tea slightly. "How much longer is that to go on?"

The manager sighed. "It is a dismaying creature, sir." He shook his head with a sad smile, as if that in itself was explanation enough. "But I repeat, the matter is in hand, and I have my best man attending to it, and I am fully confident that it will be dead by nightfall."

"Is it dangerous?" she asked. And she couldn't help it, she felt a gentle thrill of excitement.

"Not in the normal way, madam," the manager said. "The dismaying creature is a cowardly thing. It will hide out there, in the bushes and in the scrub, and it will scream. It will scream for all it is worth. The only way one can stop the screaming, I am afraid, is to hunt it down, and to kill it, and to cut off its head, and to drink its blood. But I have an expert tracker on-site as a matter of course, and he knows the ways of the dismaying creature, and how to beat it to its lair."

As if on cue, there came the scream again, and it was louder still, and this time it seemed more protracted, she wondered it didn't run out of breath. "As soon as you can, please," her husband said. "I don't like the noise of it, frankly. So long as it's quiet by sundown. I don't fancy trying to sleep through that racket."

"Oh, there will be no sundown until the creature is found," said the manager. "Our legends say that in its dismay the creature eats the very darkness whole. Or that it screams so much that darkness hides itself from the world and refuses to come out."

"What rot."

"Rot as you say, sir. But one thing is quite certain. The sun will not set until the creature is killed. The day will go on and on and on and on, and the night will never come."

"Mumbo jumbo! Ha! You'll tell us you worship the wretched thing next!"

The manager did his best to mask his offence. "Sir, I am at heart a proper English Christian man. We are not savages here. But I tell you the truth. We have not found that creature yet, and it has been sixty hours of daylight. But I'm sure I shall soon have news it has been hunted down. Please enjoy your tea. If you require more, we drink upon the veranda."

And then they were on their own again, and it was as if the room had lost a little bit of oxygen. He turned to her, and opened his mouth, and he cleared his throat. And she wondered what he was going to say—make a comment upon the luxury of the hotel, perhaps, or the quality of the tea? Or the curiously strident screams of the creature outside, they seemed more urgent now, not in pain, but in desperation that was somehow worse than pain, as if it were imperative that something should understand what it had to say and yet nobody could, nobody could in the whole wide world, and what would that feel like, how appalling would that be, how *cruel,* forced to be screaming out your entire self to a world that didn't have the wit to care? No, he wasn't going to comment on that, but he was going to say *something,* she could practically see the words bubble up his throat. "I think I should try to impregnate you again." He looked dolefully at the bed, and then back at her, as if hoping she would refuse.

But of course she couldn't. "If that's what you think you should do."

"I haven't, since last Thursday. Not tried it in the light before, perhaps that would help. We could get it out of the way, then enjoy the evening."

"Very well."

She got undressed, and took position upon the bed. The sheets felt soft and clean and, for the moment, cool. Her husband undressed, too. He took off his trousers, and the smooth rolls of flesh around his midriff that had been held fast were set loose. He seemed to glisten—his undershirt was damp with sweat, his underwear damp, his socks damp. He at least took off the underwear, dried it cursorily with the back of his hand. And his member just lay there between the legs, heat drunk and shrunken. It looked as if it would never stir again. It looked dead. And then, as ever, her husband produced his usual magic. He gritted his teeth tight, he looked away from her, he looked away into some special private place. And then he began to hum the national anthem. In spite of herself she watched in fascination as the member began to stir and swell with pride, and as he raised his hand to his temple in salute his entire manhood heard the call of duty and hoisted itself to attention.

And now erect, he gave her a boyish smile of triumph, which rather spoiled the effect of a colonel on parade—but made her like him more regardless.

He lay on top of her, spread-eagled. It seemed to her, not for the first time, that this was not going to work—their bodies simply didn't fit. They were two different species of creature entirely, they weren't designed to be plugged together like this. She would have tried to help guide him in, or at least towards the right general direction, but there wasn't room for her rat paws to find purchase beneath his amphibian bulk—and besides, whenever she appeared to offer him any help, he grunted at her irritably, as if this were something a man should achieve on his own without reinforcements. He found a particular angle he wanted to thrust at, and she let him get on with it, no matter the strategy didn't work, he wasn't going to change his plan of campaign now—and his damp socks kicked against her thighs a bit, and his damp undershirt chafed at her breasts, but otherwise it wasn't all that uncomfortable, not really. *Just think of him as a frog,* she thought. *No one can be frightened of a silly old frog.* She closed her eyes tight. She wondered whether she might even be able to doze off. She knew, intuitively, that this would be impolite.

And then, out of the corner of her eye, she saw it. On the balcony, climbing upon the table where the tea had been set.

It was not a creature she had ever seen before. About the size of a weasel, maybe, or a large domestic cat. It was covered in dark brown fur. Nosing around the teacups, giving the contents a sniff.

She held her breath. She didn't want to disturb it. Which was ridiculous because her husband was grunting and gasping and his thrusts were now causing the bed to squeak. She knew somehow that the creature didn't care about any of that, it was all just noise and comedy—but if she so much as coughed it would take fright and scamper away.

It seemed to approve of what it discovered in the teacup. And out of its mouth extended a tongue, ever outwards, four, five, six inches. The tongue was soon longer than its own body, how could that be? She supposed it must be curled up inside it in a loop. It licked at one of the cups, and then without needing to change position, extended the tongue even farther so it reached the cup on the other side of the table, as well.

And then it froze. It had seen her. It turned its head directly towards her.

And she could see that between its black, inquisitive little eyes—eyes that were now staring right at her—there was a curved horn. No fur on it. Just bone. It looked sharp. It looked like ivory.

Still it stared. As if daring her to challenge it. Daring her to bring it to the attention of the frog pumping away on top of her.

She held its gaze the best that she could.

And then it gave her a wink. Deliberately so—it tilted its head, closed one eye slowly. There was something coy about it, too, almost salacious. And she thought, *Is this impertinence? Or some foreign courtesy?*

Then it turned its attention back to the tea. It tucked its horn into the teapot handle, swung the whole pot over its head, and poured the remaining dregs down its throat.

It was like a circus act, and she thought it was showing off to her, look at me, allez-oop! She wanted to give it a round of applause.

"Nearly, nearly," her husband muttered, "don't give in now," and then she heard him hum the national anthem once more and something jammed against her thigh twitched and stiffened.

The tea was all drunk now, every last drop. The creature lowered the teapot back to the table, gently, gently. It didn't make a sound. There was nothing left for it to feed on. But it was in no hurry to leave. It sat on the table squarely, its paws raised in what looked like greeting, gazing at her without fear. She dared give it a smile. She hoped it understood.

And it was then that a new scream came from the garden. The loudest yet—and this time there *was* pain to it because what else could that be? Something so full of misery and despair—"Damn it!" shouted her husband—the creature took fright, it was off the table, off the balcony—"Damn it all to hell!" Her husband was pulling away, and she could hear a dull sucking sound as their bodies came apart, and now he was storming around the suite, his belly wobbling from side to side and his member wholly spent. She had never seen him angry before. She hadn't even known he was capable of anger.

"It's difficult enough!" he panted. "Doing it in the dark. Where I can't see you. Doing it in the quiet. Where I can't hear. I'm just a man, aren't I? I'm just a man, it's difficult enough!" And he slammed his fist down upon the table, and all the empty crockery jumped to attention. "I need the dark," he said, more quietly. "I need the quiet. I need the creature dead."

He said nothing more to her. He pulled on his clothes, folded up the sweaty mass of him, and stuffed it inside his trousers and his tunic. And then he left the room.

She lay there on the bed for a little while. But it wasn't comfortable any longer. The sheets were askew and the mattress was wet. She got up. She dressed. She went onto the balcony. She stared out at the garden, into the unrelenting daylight of it all. Once in a while she heard a shriek, but no trace of any creature could be seen.

● ○

She stayed in the room alone for several hours, she did not know how long. She would at times think to sleep, but the light was too bright, and it seemed to be getting even brighter—and even if she drowsed she would be interrupted by new shrieks from the dismaying creature outside. She realised she didn't mind the shrieks. They felt to her like a sort of conversation, she only wished she knew what to shriek back in return—she'd have been on the balcony shrieking away to it in solidarity. She didn't even mind the light—it burned away beneath her eyelids and it hurt, but it was a hurt she could adapt to.

There was a knock at the door. Guarded, polite. She wondered if her husband had come back to apologise. She wondered if he were the sort of man who did apologise.

It was not her husband.

"I'm afraid the colonel isn't here."

The hotel manager nodded. “The colonel is in the smoking room, madam. He has been there for quite some time, and is of a mind to stay there a while longer.”

“Well, then.”

“I hope I might enlist your help to persuade him otherwise? He has been drinking and is in some distemper.”

“I barely know my husband, and I am quite sure whatever his distemper, I have very little power to influence it one way or another.”

“He has punched an Italian. It is no great matter, but even so, there is a level of decorum we expect.”

“Won’t you come in?” she said. “If there must be talk of my husband’s decorum, I would sooner it were not in a corridor.”

“I had better not, madam. Your husband is not present.”

“Quite so, my husband is in the smoking room. Please. Come in.”

The manager bowed his head, and entered. She smelled his scent once more. Was it jasmine? No, something stronger. She walked out onto the balcony, took a seat. He followed, studiously refusing to look at the dishevelled state of the bed, and sat down opposite her.

“I suppose,” she said, “I should apologise for my husband’s behaviour, but the truth is, I don’t feel remotely responsible for it. Isn’t that awful?”

“There is no apology necessary. The heat, the light. Even when you live here, it is not something you ever quite get used to. It brings out high emotions in men. Even sometimes madness.”

“How do you manage it?” she asked. *How can you live like this?* He looked so cool, his skin was so cool. Not a trace of sweat upon it.

“The unending days. The heat trapped, with no darkness to escape to. We learn to enjoy the times when the dismaying creatures are silent, we relish the dark because we know sooner or later it shall be taken from us yet again." Cool skin, she thought running her fingers over it would be like drinking a refreshing glass of iced water.

He said, "I knew a time when the darkness vanished for two whole months. How did we manage, you ask? We didn't manage. How could we manage? My father went mad. My father . . . who was kind . . . who only ever showed me love, and taught me to respect my betters in only the gentlest of ways. He cried for the darkness to return. He beat me. He beat my mother, quite bad. And then he stripped bare, and said he was going to find the dismaying creatures, and kill them, every last one of them, and bring their heads home in a sack. And we watched him walk away naked across the parched plains of the savannah, until he was too small to spy any longer, and we never saw him again. But sometimes I thought I could hear him. When the dismaying creatures shrieked, I thought I heard him shrieking along with them. I became a man that day. I was twelve. But all has been well. For, look, I have a hotel, and it is the finest hotel in the country. And soon the dismaying creature will be found, and its shriek will be stopped dead, and there will be night again, and peace, and the chill of the dark." He lifted the cup off the table idly, thought to look inside. He frowned. "Madam," he said gently, "you must take care with which beasts you choose to share your tea."

And then he stood up, nodded, and she saw she was about to lose him.

"What is your name?" she blurted out.

He hesitated. "You would not be able to pronounce it."

"Well. Do you want to know my name? Maybe you won't be able to pronounce *that*."

"I can pronounce your name."

"You can't be sure."

"All the people who come to my hotel. Do you think you're

the first to occupy my bridal suite? Men dragging their young wives all across their empire, so vast the sun never sets upon it. And all of them are the same. You are all the same. And I can always pronounce your names. I can pronounce every single one."

"Why did you call me a peach?" she asked.

"Because you *are* a peach. Will you come talk to your husband?"

"Yes," she said. "Yes, I'll come down."

"Thank you, madam," he said, and at that, at last, he rewarded her with a smile.

Her husband was sitting in a corner of the smoking room, all the rage had burned out of him. He was sipping at a glass of whisky, his body lolling as if it had forgotten how to support itself—and in that instant she thought he no longer looked like a frog, just a sad pathetic old man.

She sat down beside him. He looked up, and she saw his dull eyes widen in bemusement, he didn't seem to remember who she was. But he said gently, "Oh, it's you. Hello. Hello, my dear." She didn't know what to do. She put her hand upon his. He stared at it for a full half minute before speaking.

"I wish," he said, "that you'd known me when I was younger. I was quite something. Where were you in '68?"

"I was a baby."

"I like babies," he insisted. "I'll be good with our baby. I'll put a baby inside you, I promise." And his voice began to rise. "But I cannot do it in all the heat! And the light! Even when I close my eyes, I can't find any darkness in my head! I cannot be expected to perform under these appalling conditions!"

There was a commotion at the window. Everyone was hurrying out onto the veranda. They watched as a lone man emerged from the canopy of the distant jacaranda trees and onto the green lawn towards them. As he got closer it was clear that he was staggering. Closer still, they could see that his hotel uniform had been ripped apart, and there was blood. He carried a sack in his hand, limp, empty.

With a sudden roar the manager ran to meet him. He appeared to give comfort; the man collapsed into his arms.

"Is this your man?" called her husband. "Has he killed the creature?"

"Make way, make way," shouted the manager as he led the man into the hotel. "Fetch him some tea!"

"Bugger his tea! When are we going to get our sunset?"

The man babbled at the manager, who nodded, and then held a cup to his lips so he could drink. The manager said, "The creature is still alive. It was too savage. It took a wound, but the head is intact. There will be no sunset!"

At this there was a groan of dismay; her husband smashed his whisky glass to the floor.

"I don't understand," said the manager. "The dismaying creatures are timid. They hide from death like we all do, but when we track them down, they always seem grateful. They never fight back. This never happens!"

"I shall not let this day go on any longer!" shouted the husband. "Not a single hour! If your man cannot best this creature, then I shall do it. I shall be proud to do it!"

"It is not our way," said the manager. "It takes a lifetime of practice, the dismaying creatures are not yours to be slaughtered."

"I was an officer of the British Army, sir! And I have faced down Russkies and Hindoos, whole battalions of them! And I shall not be put off by some wounded creature crying like a baby!" He addressed the room. "I want all able-bodied men to come forward and serve with me now. All the Englishmen. All your kitchen coolies. Yes, even the Italians. We shall march together and defeat this thing. And restore a bit of order to the world!"

She thought he would be laughed at. This stupid frog-faced man, his cheeks now beetroot rather than their usual green. His words of pomp slurred with drunkenness. And there were a good few seconds of embarrassed silence when it seemed the room might indeed laugh. And then one man cheered. She didn't see which one. And then another, and another, until cheering was easy. Some of the hotel staff even, and the manager looked about him with shame.

"Then I shall come with you," said the manager. "I at least might know how to find it."

"Of course you're coming with us!" said the husband, and he clapped his hand on the man's back in something that may have been intended as camaraderie. "You're able-bodied, aren't you? Consider yourself under my command!"

It did not take long for the squadron to assemble. The men gathered on the veranda, each of them with some makeshift weapon: billiard cues, whisky bottles, cooking utensils taken from the kitchen. Her husband had his old service revolver, she hadn't even known he was carrying it. This ragtag scrap of soldiers—white faces, black, some young, most old—and all of them seemed to burn with a certain frenzy, they could hardly keep still with excitement. Some of the wives kissed their men goodbye—one or two even got flowers to wear. "Will you kiss me?" her husband asked, and she said yes, it was the very least she could do—and ablaze with martial fire he slipped his tongue into her mouth.

They marched on, then—up the lawn, out towards the trees, and towards the wild areas of the hotel grounds they had been warned about. She would have liked to have said goodbye to the manager; she couldn't find him, he was such a little man, he was lost in the crowd. She watched them walk into the distance waving their sticks and their soup ladles, and she thought they'd even begun to sing. It was hard to tell, the shrieks from the dismaying creature drowned it out, rather. And then, when they were gone, she went back into the hotel and up to the suite.

• ◦

There was a fresh pot of tea waiting for her. She didn't know who could have put it there. She went out onto the balcony and poured herself a cup. She drank it straight down. She poured herself another, and sipped at it, and it was only then that she turned back to the bed and its new occupant. "I really don't think you're supposed to be in here," she said.

The creature with its thick brown fur and its single bone horn cocked its head, seeming to contemplate this. It gave a little chirrup which seemed to offer neither explanation nor apology.

She stripped off again. Her bare skin baked in the thick heat. She went to the bed, and sat down upon it. She thought the creature might flee, but all it did instead was shuffle across slightly so she would have room to lie down beside it. So she did.

They lay there together for a while in silence, but it was a companionable silence. Neither had anything to prove to the other. *This is nice,* she thought.

There came another shriek from the beast in the garden, and she wondered whether it was because her husband had found it and was butchering it. Probably not. Not yet. The little creature took a deep puff, shook its fur with the effort. And then it let out a shriek of its own in imitation. It was more a mew than a roar, but it seemed quite pleased with the effect, and preened. She couldn't help but laugh.

She sat up, offered it some tea from her cup. It looked at it doubtfully, then turned away.

She took a mouthful of it herself. She didn't swallow. She lay back down. And then the creature put one paw upon her chest, tentatively, then another. Judging that the terrain was firm, it climbed upon her fully and, angling itself upon her breasts, stared down at her face.

She gazed up at it. It gave her a wink, and this time, she was quite sure, it was indeed impertinent, and she didn't care. She opened her mouth so it could see all the delicious tea pooling around inside it. It did not bend its head closer. But keeping its eyes on her, never looking away, it unfurled its tongue. She watched as the tongue slowly descended towards her—six inches long, longer—and then it was in her mouth, it was inside her, lapping up the tea.

It was in no hurry. She thought it was rather a relaxing sensation, feeling the rough tongue flick against her cheeks and her gums, extracting every last drop of tea that it could. And then the creature was thrusting harder, and the tongue seemed to swell and thicken. She wanted to shoo it away, enough was enough—for the tongue now filled her mouth, there was no room for her own tongue in there, as well, it struggled to find room and entwined itself around the intruder, licking away at it, and it tasted of tea and it tasted of meat—and now it was down her throat, the tongue was pushing deep within her, it was going to find every drop of tea it could. She couldn't breathe. But she wouldn't choke, she *refused* to choke, and she was happy, and she thought that if this was how she died then so be it, all her nerves burning, every piece of her suddenly alive.

Then it was over. She was gasping for breath, and the creature on top of her was looking very smug and pleased with itself. It gave another shriek, a proper one this time, a cry of celebration. She smiled and reached up her hand to stroke its head. It nuzzled into her. She fingered the horn, it was so wonderfully sharp—and then she took hold of it in her palm, tight. The creature blinked at her. Gave a nod. And so she wrenched it off. It broke away from the skull very easily, like old timber.

It was sharper than any knife. The creature laid its head down beside her, offered its neck.

The horn cut through the skin more easily than she could have imagined, just three hard tugs and that was it, the head was clean off.

She thought there would be blood, but there was no blood. And out from the neck popped out another smaller head, and then another—and she thought it was growing its head back, what a remarkable thing!—but no, inside the creature there were babies waiting, and wasn't that just as remarkable, really? She pulled the neck hole wider and tipped the dead creature upside down and three little cubs spilled out onto the bed. Already half the size of their mother and growing fast, she wondered how they could have ever fitted inside! They bounced about on the mattress playfully, and made funny little shrieks of their own, and she was laughing as she tried to catch them all together, shepherding them into her grasp and then chopping off their heads, too, one by one. And from their dead bodies came babies that were smaller still, and from those babies multiplied other babies, and pretty soon it was a fine game, they were all jumping about and falling over and squealing as she chopped away, they were so tiny she could no longer see if it were their heads she was cutting off, but it was such *fun*, this burst of exercise in the stifling heat, she was so tired when at last there was no movement and no more shrieking and the bed was still, and the crisp white sheets had been stained ink black as dark as night.

She put her finger into the black. It was cold. It numbed her finger wonderfully. She scooped some into her palm, and licked at it. It didn't taste of anything, but it filled her up and was so refreshing.

And she could hear the shriek again, but it was inside her own head. Filling every little crevice of it—and at last she could understand what the shrieking meant, and it was no great revelation, it was such a simple thing really. It was as loud as the world, but she didn't mind. *I could live like this,* she thought. *I can live within the shriek.*

She lay back on the pillow and closed her eyes and lost herself within it, and let it lull her to sleep.

● ○

When she woke up the shrieking was painfully absent, and instead her husband was babbling at her, he was standing over her, and his face was streaked with blood, and his eyes were wild.

"I couldn't save my men. I couldn't save a single one of them." And he sat beside her on the bed, he didn't seem to notice it was dripping with the black of night. He reached out his arms for her, and when she didn't move he got to his feet, began chattering again.

"It wasn't just one creature, you see. It was all of them. It was everything. Birds and, and mammals, and crawly things, and they were all screaming, I didn't know what to do. They wanted to fight. I did my best. I killed a few. I have no reason to be ashamed, I . . . But their heads wouldn't come off clean, and their blood was hard to drink."

He put his head in his hands. He was crying. She looked down at the sack by his feet. It had listed over, and some of its heads had spilled out onto the carpet. A fox, a stoat, what looked like a bear cub. The hotel manager, his eyes rolled tight into his skull.

She got up. She went out onto the balcony, and she poured a cup of tea. He was surprised when she gave it to him, he drank it down with a gulp.

"I made it back. I made it back, to you. I wanted to prove myself to you. And when I was out there facing death, it's you I thought of, and the future we might have. I'm sorry. I wish you had known me before. I think these last few years I have lost myself. I want to love you. And win your love for me, I hope. I can change. I can be the man I used to be. I can be anyone you want me to be. For you, and for our children." He tried to smile at her. He handed her his cup. "Would you fetch me some more tea, my dear?"

She went back onto the balcony, and she put down the teacup, and she picked up the horn dagger, and when she returned she plunged it deep into her husband's heart. She aimed for the heart anyway, it was hard to make out where it might be beneath those thick layers of frog fat—and he looked so surprised, he gave a wheezing grunt and opened his mouth and he looked as if he might speak, but she put a finger to his lips—*don't spoil the moment*. She wondered whether there would be any blood, whether he, too, was just empty inside and composed of nothing but night and dark space, but no, the blood blossomed across his tunic, it looked so rich and so real. She lowered him onto the bed, so gently, so sweetly, and watched him as he died.

She remembered a fairy tale in which at death the ugly frog turned into a handsome prince, and she waited to see if it would happen, and it didn't.

And she went back to the balcony. Stared out at her world beneath her, the burning bright, the unending day. She listened for the shriek within her, but nothing—she would just have to be patient. And she opened her arms out wide, and waited for the sunset, waited for the darkness to come down and envelop her once and for all.

BITTER SKIN

KAARON WARREN

Hilary and I were the opposite of vampires. Sunbaked brown, daylight dreamers, scared of the night because who was out there? *What* was out there?

We called ourselves the sun sisters, Hilary and I. On the bus to the beach every day we weren't working in the dress shop her aunt owned. Slathering ourselves with oil, pretending it was sunscreen so no one told us off. Dipping in the ocean when we got too hot, showing off our tanned bikini bodies.

Our favourite beach was Wilson's Bay, half an hour away on the bus, because it was popular and full of cute guys. This was a pickup beach; girls who went there were hot to trot. Was that us? Kind of. We were sixteen and pretty innocent, in retrospect.

We didn't know this would be our last time at the beach together.

Hilary had a new bikini and I had a hot-pink towel I'd bought myself. Half our towels at home were bloodstained, pale pink splotches that wouldn't go away, and I didn't want anyone asking about that. We lay there baking, one eye out for good-looking guys, all our secrets under the skin.

It was *hot*. At around four o'clock most people headed for the beer garden at the pub. No one asked for ID. The last bus for us was 6:00 p.m., so this way we could get in a few beers before heading home.

After we'd bought our beers (not before; they didn't want to be buying) two guys came up to us. As was always the case, they'd already decided who was talking to who. The good-looking one always gets to choose and he chose Hilary. They never chose me. "He looks a bit like your dad," she whispered, as if it was a good thing. I didn't see it. Sure, Dad was tall and knew how to smile. He could be charming. Flattering. He let us drink beer if Mum wasn't home. I knew the real man, the one on the inside, even if Hilary didn't. This guy was tall and solid, in a muscle shirt, his hair blond tipped. He smelled of coconut oil and beer. He was funny and his smile was infectious.

Everyone in the place glowed red with sunburn.

Mine was short and he clearly hadn't bathed. He was angry. I guess he liked Hilary better than me. When I told him straight up I wasn't interested his eyes narrowed. And his skin puckered and dimpled like lemon skin. My dad's skin looked the same at times. I called it his bitter skin.

I saw Dad shed this bitter skin (this *mean* skin) for the first time soon after my brother was born. I was five, so I shouldn't remember. A long time ago. But my dad and I had been having a nice time together while Mum was in the hospital. Cooking pizza and watching TV. When Mum and my brother came back home, everything changed. She didn't pay any attention to either of us. I hated having to share, but loved my brother the minute I saw him. I kissed him, giving him a lick to see what he tasted like. But Dad? "All I want," he said. "All I want is a little respect."

There's a hole in the wall where he punched so hard. He was always stronger when he drank. I watched him shudder, shrug his shoulders, looking like he was about to throw up, which he did sometimes. Instead, his skin shed, slipping off him like a sheet of almost-set gelatine. He didn't notice; shrugged again, stood taller. The skin dropped to the floor where he kicked it under the kitchen table without seeing it. Then he was calm, looking after Mum because he loved her, and carrying my brother around to get him to sleep. I eyed his skin under the table for a day or two until I gathered it up. It felt dry, brittle, and smelled faintly of citrus. I kept it folded under my bed.

● ○

Everybody has this bitter skin, to one degree or another. I can only see it during the day. At night the skins are disguised. Mum sees them, too. She told me everything once I turned fourteen and the boys started looking at me. "I only ever saw your dad at night for the longest time. We were both working hard during the day and we'd see each other at night. Until it was too late. I was pregnant with you."

She'd never told me I was a mistake.

"Make sure you see them in the daytime." We went to the open-air mall to window-shop and stop at a café for donuts and coffee. Girls' Day Out, she said. We walked slowly because she was limping. Her face thick with makeup. I didn't want to look at her.

She told me we all had these skins. Most of us keep them thin through acts of kindness, or a smile, or enjoyment of a beautiful day. Others will shed them with a sharp word, or in an act of violence.

You had to learn to see them; most people never learned. And you had to learn to feel it on yourself. She told me anyone could see them if they tried hard enough. Mum said most people don't even notice dropping the skins. They *could* notice, if they looked hard, but they don't. They knew they felt better after losing their temper. They felt lighter. Sometimes they couldn't remember what had happened. Dad would act innocent: Did I? he'd say, shaking his head. I told her I'd collected Dad's skin and she physically recoiled. She said collecting the skins was a bad idea. She couldn't say why because she didn't know, and I told her they were better gathered up so people didn't trip over them. Truly I didn't care about that; I was fascinated by the skins and wanted to understand them.

We practiced, there in the mall, until I could see the skin on every person we passed, thin or thick.

● ○

Hilary's guy bought her a beer. Mine offered grudgingly and I said no thanks. I didn't want to be under obligation. And the last bus would be coming soon. My phone rang. Mum.

"Your father is getting angry, Beverly. You should be home by now."

"I said I'd be home in time for dinner."

"Well . . ." She didn't have to finish a sentence. I'd seen his skin in the morning; I should have known he was on a knife's edge.

"We better get going," I told Hilary, but she wasn't going anywhere. "You'll miss the bus," I said. She'd be out after dark.

"She'll be alright," her man said.

"One more beer," Hilary said. She went to be bathroom and I looked hard at her guy.

Sometimes there are loose edges on the bitter skin. His was very fine, barely there, and I thought if I lifted it off, she'd be okay. Most people don't ever notice or feel their own skin. Maybe an itch, an increased irritation. Then a shudder as they shake it off. You have to be taught to even *see* your own. He put his arm around me as I worked at his skin, thinking I was flirting. I got the soft edge under my fingernail and lifted, like picking a scab when you've been swimming. It was thin, and satisfying to play with.

I'd tried to tell Hilary and our friends what to look out for, but none of them would listen. "Too many rules!" Hilary said when I told her she could only see the bitter skin in daylight, with the sun shining through. "And your mum is a bit off the planet, sorry!"

She came back from the bathroom to find his arm around me, caught me picking at the loose end of his bitter skin, and him not complaining, him not noticing. I'm the one she was pissed off with. "Leave him," she said. "Why are you always so jealous?" She couldn't see what I saw and I figured in this case it didn't matter. He wasn't a violent man.

So I left her. I told her to text me every hour and she laughed but nodded.

She didn't text once.

● ○

The little guy had already left. I saw him with a rock, smashing the headlights of a car. His bitter skin dropped off and I waited until he stumbled away. It was clammy to the touch, with the citrus scent familiar to me, and I folded it into my beach bag. Collecting the skins was a habit I couldn't break. I knew I'd use them one way or another.

I ran for the bus, jumping on with seconds to spare. A message from my brother. "Where are you?" I could hear how small his voice was. "It's still light, Benny?" I texted. "Still daytime."

"Hurry," he said. "He's in a postman mood." I couldn't get home any faster and wished I hadn't gone out at all. I needed to be there to protect Benny. "Postman mood" meant Dad was accusing Mum of things she hadn't done, and his skin was thick. I hoped she was locked in her bathroom.

The postman:

This was years ago. I remember standing on the front veranda, hoping my dad would come home quiet and kind, bringing fish and chips for dinner and we could all sit together, maybe in the backyard on one of the old blankets.

I sank so far into the fantasy that I went inside to find the blanket and spread it out ready for me and my parents and Benny.

Benny was four but he acted two. He was so annoying.

My mother stood on the front steps, her hand shielding her eyes as she looked up the street. I know now what she was looking for: a glimpse of Dad walking towards us, to assess how thick his skin was. If it was thin, he'd shed it if we were nice to him, and we'd be okay. If it was thick, opaque, starting to bag, better watch out.

"Dad'll be home soon. He's bringing fish and chips." My mother blinked. Later, I understood how much she wanted this to be true. She walked to the front gate, staring at him as he appeared at the end of the street. I stood beside her.

My mother grabbed my arm. "Beverly," she hissed. "You and Benny go to the playground. Quick."

"Are you going out with Auntie Jenny?" Dad had been shouting about that in the morning. She shook her head.

"Go on," she said. "Go to the playground."

Benny took my hand and tugged. "Come on, Bev," he said. "I want to go on the swings."

"You come too, Mum," I said, suddenly adult and desperate. "Dad'll go to sleep if you're not here."

"I can't, Bev. He'll only lay into someone else if it isn't me. Here." She pressed some money at me. "Go get something from the shops. Get ice cream."

I loved Mum, but I didn't want a beating, either, and I didn't want it for my brother. *She* didn't want us taking the blows.

We walked past the local park. Benny pulled in close to me, frightened by the shadows in there. We heard a bellow, like a cow in pain.

It was just the old drunks who hung out in the park all day. Sometimes I sat near them because they smelled like Dad but they weren't as frightening. These men didn't have the energy to do anything except talk quietly, laugh, drink.

We finished our ice creams and headed home. There was Dad, foot on the stairs, fists clenched, heading up to talk to Mum. Then distracted by the postman, a tall, ginger-moustached sleazebag. He didn't care if the mail was late, although usually he'd finish his route and then pop back with forgotten items. "Above and beyond the call of duty," I heard him say more than once, and the neighbours laughed about how he'd deliver to the door as if doing them a favour, all the while wanting a glimpse of something.

The postman knocked at our front door, unaware Dad was home.

Dad's skin reached for him.

The postman pulled back, dropping our mail on the front doormat. Dad picked it up. A postcard from his brother, and I could see Dad's bitter skin split and pus oozing out through the gaps.

Mum was locked in the toilet. She'd run there after Dad had got her a good one.

Dad threw down the postcard. "You're fucking my wife," he said. I'd never heard him swear before. He used his meaty fists to poleax the postman, who dropped to the ground like a sack of potatoes.

Dad threw the guy, literally, off our property. Dragged him to the gate, slammed it against his head. Threw him onto the street.

Dad straightened, raising his arms high and wide, rolled his head around. I saw his skin split further, drop off him. It was heavy, so it fell to the ground in a pile, like a wet towel. I called out, "Can we have fish and chips for dinner?" and he said yes, we could. His face was shiny, calm, and he clapped his hands, *who wants double chips*, as if his wife wasn't in the bathroom mopping up the blood.

His skin grew back, though, even thicker. His bitter skin.

● ○

As my bus pulled in, Mum texted, "Don't come home yet."

That's Mum for you. Always protecting. I climbed off the bus. Didn't respond to her. I was coming home, at least to distract him. I didn't plan what happened next. Hadn't thought about it. Until I saw one of the park drunks, slumped in the gutter. He mumbled obscenities, his hands clawing for the empty bottle at his fingertips. He was covered in cuts and bruises; didn't seem to be feeling a thing, didn't notice a thing. I stepped on his fingers to test this; nothing.

I rolled him up against the wall. "Thanks, mate," he said, slurring, bleary. "I mean it. Now go and wash your hands." He laughed, an awful squealing noise like a dying mouse. He held out a palm. "Any spare change? I only need enough for a bottle. Take it to the fellas."

Even the dregs of society have a hierarchy.

A woman more attractive (and one who stands by them, says the wife deserved it).

A stronger man.

In the park they were all violent men. Dad would hang out with them sometimes, king of the park, lord of all he surveyed. He reckoned they never judged him but of course they did. They judged him king.

"I got a bottle at my place you can have," I said. I didn't plan this; the words came out of my mouth unbidden.

I had the little man's skin folded in my beach bag. I laid this over the drunk to see what would happen, and he stood up. Rolled his shoulders. Then he followed me like a dog. A zombie.

"Do you want to come to my house? My mum can make you something to eat."

"Oh," he said.

"You can have a bath, too," I said, and he nodded.

"Sorry about the stink."

"Mum won't mind. Come on." I tried to hurry him along and he bounced on his feet, putting on a brave face, trying to make conversation. He'd long since forgotten how, so we walked the short distance to my house in silence. The sounds of the day went with us; doors slamming, birds chirping, children playing, lawn mowers.

When we got to my house the front door was open. I listened for noise; silence would mean I was too late.

There; a bang and a whimper.

"Go on," I said to the drunk. "You go in first. Mum is round the back. I'll get her." I guided the confused man in, and he stood in the entrance way. I plucked at the bitter skin I'd laid on him, tugging it away. "Help!" I called out.

I ran around to the shed, where Benny waited. At eleven, he was big for his age and tried to be brave. "It's okay," I said.

We heard "Who the fuck are you?" and the familiar wet sound of fists meeting skin.

We'd set up beanbags and comic books in the shed. A place

of refuge. Our mother came and joined us and we snuggled quietly until the noise in the house stopped.

"Who was he?" she asked me.

"He's no one." I went out to collect Dad's bitter skin. He'd fallen asleep on the floor, exhausted. The drunk was nowhere to be found; he'd crawled off somewhere. If he died in the gutter that was nothing to do with me. I called out to Mum and Benny to come in, I was making sandwiches. Benny sidled up to Dad and licked his arm. He couldn't see the bitter skin but could taste it.

"Oh my god, Beverly, you are so sunburned. You need to be more careful. That's gonna hurt later," my mum said. And as the sun set, it did. Sunburn always burns worse at sundown.

• ○

Hilary didn't text me. And we didn't get the news for two days. Her guy had driven with his headlights smashed (yep, the little fucker had damaged his friend's car). Maybe he didn't notice. Maybe he didn't care. I know Hilary wouldn't have noticed. It was a head-on crash, and they called it road rage.

You see why I'm a day girl?

• ○

The morning of her funeral, I was awake as the sun came up. I didn't want to go. I wanted to sit on the couch and watch action movies, watch violence, and know it was a lie.

I pulled on the black-clothes skin of someone grieving. I heard a banging noise downstairs. My dad slamming out the front door, carrying a six-pack in one hand, a bottle of something in the other. I couldn't see his skin. I didn't know his mood. He headed to the park, *lovely day for it,* he called out. I reminded him about the funeral; I wanted him there, big shoulder to cry on, and he gave me a thumbs-up as he walked onto the footpath. Mum and Benny stood on either side of me at the graveside, leaning in, holding me up. I felt numb, dead on the inside. I couldn't speak, had nothing to say. All I could do was throw some sand instead of dirt because she loved the beach.

Dad apparently collected Hilary's dad and the two of them showed up blind drunk. At least they were in a good mood.

• ○

I hadn't intended to go back to Wilson's Bay. My last memory of Hilary and what I should have done was too strong. How I wish I'd made her come home with me. How I wish I'd pulled harder on her man's bitter skin. But still; the good-looking guys went there. And the little angry guy? I let him know I knew what he'd done. I made him buy me drinks, introduce me to his friends. Anything to take my mind off Hilary and how bad it was at home.

Hilary's aunt changed the name of the dress shop to Hilary's. We sold beachwear. Day wear. We opened early to catch the morning crowd. I quit school and worked there every hour she'd give me, saving as much as I could. The beach didn't cost much, and if I let the ugly ones buy me drinks and food (never the bitter-skinned ones) I'd save money there. Bit by bit, putting it aside so Mum, Benny, and I could get away.

I was eighteen before I saved enough.

"Benny, come see our new house," I said. I hadn't told him the plan until now. He was an innocent, trusting. Even our father's violence was in the moment for him. Once it was done it was done.

He came with us to the small house I'd put a rental deposit on and he stayed for a few days, then back to Dad. Dad had no interest in finding us. Too much effort, and he had other women on the go.

So Benny went to and from, back and forth, and each time

he came home I pinched his skin, I licked him, but never found a sign of the bitter skin forming.

• ◦

I love the morning shift in the shop. Everything is fresh, as if a street cleaner has been through the whole place, outside and in. All day I'm fitting clothes on people like new skin, watching their moods change when something looks good.

Mum was late for work but I didn't give her a hard time. I'd hired her the minute Hilary's aunt made me manager, and she was so good with our older ladies. She arrived with pastries, enough for the early customers, which did make me cross.

"Greasy fingers on my clothes!" I said, but she pulled out a pack of baby wipes, so everyone was happy. I stepped into my workroom to put the last stitches into a dress for commission. The customer would be in around ten and I wanted the dress ready, laid out, for her to see. It was for a work function where, in the past, she'd been groped, propositioned, almost fired. It was Mum who'd had the idea to sew small strips of bitter skin into the hems of some of the clothing, and into the straps of bikinis. She said, *You might as well make good with them, Beverly*.

I stitched in strips of skin from a pair of street fighters, gave the dress a last iron, and took it out onto the shop floor.

The customer tried it on and didn't take it off again. She walked out clothed powerful, and I knew she'd be left alone at the function. Left alone to have conversations that didn't involve sex and how she could get ahead if she dressed in the right way.

I like to wear the skin of someone else, myself, as protection. A suit or a cloak. To look safe, no threat. No one wanted to touch me when I wore it. I could dance in front of a serial killer and he'd leave me alone.

I swept out the change rooms, finding traces of bitter skin, the lifting of a mood evident. I'm doing good work, one skin at a time. I'm weaving it into clothing I sell, refurbished clothing to make my customers brave.

I'm adding lace, I'm adding ribbon, I'm adding bitter skins.

Try it on and you can see the don't-give-me-shit look straightaway. The I-can-stand-up-for-myself look. This is what I'm giving my customers.

Most people don't notice bitter skin, although once they know, they know. A customer came in, on her own, "loitering," Mum whispered. I never wanted to judge if someone was going to buy or not. She did loiter, flicking through the dresses. She wore a tight white top, cutoff jeans, her blond hair high in a ponytail, makeup perfect. She kept glancing outside. A man out there, leaning against our window, talking on his phone, laughing.

"I want something to make him pay me attention," she said. "Make him notice me."

He laughed and the sun hit him just right so I saw his bitter skin, quite thick, almost pretty because he was so pretty.

"Watch this," I said. "Watch his skin."

I stuck my head out the door and said, "You can't lean there."

Without stopping his conversation he pointed at me, such fury on his face and the skin reaching out for me.

Then he turned away.

I went back inside.

The customer had seen it; she was horrified. She waited until he got bored and walked away.

She told me where he worked. I wanted his skin. So pretty. I followed and watched and there it was: after-work drinks, kicking one of his coworkers to shit.

When Benny saw me wearing that bitter skin it made him cry. To say, where's my sister? Give her back!

It shattered over time, turned to crumbs like old plastic bags do.

There were always more. Some of them, their bitter skin so thick it is like a suit of armour, tarnished and battle-scarred. Sometimes I'll step in a puddle of bitter skin shed, and I'll feel a moment of fury. A loss of temper, a frustration at something unimportant.

I keep them all in a trunk in my bedroom. A blanket box, my grandmother would call it. They shatter over time, leaving flakes like dry skin behind. Sometimes I'll wear the good ones like blankets, if I need courage to go out. If I'm in the skin, no violence comes my way. I kept a bowl of dried orange skins on top of the box to hide the smell. Not that it was strong, or even awful. The orange peel justified the citrus odor, if anyone else came into my room.

● ○

Three days before Benny's twenty-first birthday, I had three more designs to finish, and went out into our courtyard to think. Warmth is important to me. The burn of the sun. I closed my eyes, happy for a moment. I love the sun for its warmth, and because that way I can see the skins.

Then my brother came into the shop.

I would have pretended my dad didn't exist, left him to his shit, to his boss-of-tiny-world, violence-on-loser shit, but Benny still lived with him. Over the last ten years Dad had progressively downsized his homes as he lost his looks and his charm, moving farther and farther away. Always wanting Benny with him, never caring that Benny would be better off elsewhere. My brother was such a gentle giant he was unaffected. No bitter skin on him. He joined me in the shop courtyard, morning sun bright and clear, and his skin as smooth as ever. He winced as he sat down, though, pain twisting his face.

"Benny?" I said. He wasn't stupid. He knew I knew. He lifted his shirt to show me dark bruises across his chest and stomach, along his side. My skin itched; I could feel it thickening in anger. "Jesus, Benny. You can't let him do that. You're big enough to stop him."

He turned his head from me. I knew he was crying, could tell by the shake of his shoulders.

"I can't," he said. "He'll kill me, and then he'll come for you and Mum." I realised he'd been protecting us all this time, he'd made a deal with the devil.

Benny living with him as a bribe to stop him hurting us had gone on too long.

"I'm not strong enough," he said. His skin so pale I could almost see his bones, his veins. "Will you help me be strong?" We'd talked about the bitter skin. He could see it in the daylight, once I taught him to, and this kept him out of the clutches of violence many times. Except where Dad was concerned.

I told Mum we were going to the beach. It was such a gorgeous day. The shop was busy rather than frantic, and she was in her element, laughing and chatting and helping people. I loved seeing her this way.

Benny and I went home, and I opened my trunk of skins. I had him lie on the bed, and skin by skin I built him up. I remembered every one, remembered how the sun felt, the brightness of the day showing me the skins I collected.

The skins thick on the ground at the pubs and clubs, early morning.

The skins from the park, my father king of the hoop strutting about, committing his acts of violence and no one caring. I collected their skins and no one noticed. They want to rise, these men, sink into the grass (beer wet, piss soaked), then rise like balloons, out of themselves, free spirits. One is a vodka man, the rest are rum because rum you know you're drinking it, there is no doubt of the flavour. Like the skin of a broad bean. The slippery outer skin is tough and bitter, inside it is sweet. The old men are almost all tough outer skin. You can pinch it, thick and scaly, between thumb and forefinger.

I layered these on Benny.

This skin: He can't remember what his mother looked like. She was a pale woman, so pale her features blurred together so you couldn't tell if she was smiling.

This skin: A house full of shed skins, and an old man sitting in the middle of them, stripped naked, defying anyone to move him.

This skin: The young man's pelt felt like velvet in parts, sandpaper in others, and the smell of it made me gag, the citrus somehow stronger, caustic. This one was light as a balloon when I took it and shoved it into my backpack.

This skin: Inside the house the lights are off. A woman and three children huddle. She'd run to turn off the lights, hurting herself in her haste; banging a shin against the table, bending back a finger against the door, desperately turning off the TV, hoping if they are all quiet and in the dark her husband would forget they existed after three days away, leave them alone.

She puts the children to bed and she curls up on the bed, naked. If he finds her ready for his foul, sweaty ten thrusts, he'll fall asleep, collapsed on his side of the bed.

That's what she hopes.

She has a tube of lubricant ready because otherwise she'll tear. This is less painful.

She remembers, then; leave the hall light on so he can see or else nothing will stop his fury.

Oh, he's bright and cheery, kind, he kisses her cheek. He's always like this if he's had sex with another woman, paid or unpaid, and she can see his fists lightly bruised and blood underneath the fingernails. If she's quiet, acquiescent, if she doesn't ask questions, laughs at his jokes, it'll be days before his fury builds up again. He licks her bitter skin and it is her skin, she's angry at last and she kills him before he kills her.

This skin: An estranged wife. Living high in an apartment block, moving so many times, no one, not even her best friend, knows where she is. He found her.

This skin: Private school students, five on one. Five skins in one go.

● ○

I dressed Benny carefully. He took a lick and grimaced.

"To keep you safe," I said. "He won't touch you like this. I wish I'd thought of it before."

Dad's skin would be smooth right now. He'd beaten someone to a pulp, Benny said, come home happy and glowing. I hated the way Benny smelled. The citrus scent so strong it made my eyes water. "You show him who's boss today. He'll leave you alone from now on. Us, too."

He nodded. The suit sat loosely on him, shifting and blurring, all the violence I'd collected running together.

He headed down the path and I went back to Hilary's, where Mum was sharing champagne with women wanting informal fabulous for a wedding. They offered me a glass, lively friends enjoying themselves. Mum always managed the weddings. For me, it was too stark a reminder I had no one. And of how much I missed Hilary, my last true friend.

● ○

Breakfast the next day I hadn't heard from Benny, but I always made a just-in-case extra serving. I sat on the front veranda, reading the newspapers, picking out the violence by habit, knowing where I could head to collect more skins given I'd made them all into his suit, when he came stumbling in. The bitter-skin suit was in remnants around him and I tore at it until he stopped me.

"I added Dad's to it," he said, then, "I need to lie down."

"Your room is always ready." We saved it for the day he moved away from Dad.

He laid down on the bed. He groaned, crossed his arms over his midriff, still in pain from the beating Dad had inflicted previously, before I'd thought to protect him with the skins. His face was splattered with dark droplets and I went to wipe them off, but he turned his head away. The remnants of the suit were wrapped around him like a blanket.

"Sleep well," I said. "There's plenty of food in the fridge."

● ○

That's something I'll regret for the rest of my life. Going to work rather than staying with him. Mum and I arrived home together, carrying bags of shopping. We'd had a good day and we were going to treat ourselves with quiche and chocolate mousse and something good to watch.

"We're here!" I called up the stairs. I felt a chill in my bones. I hadn't thought of him all day. My fault. Sure, I was busy. Sure, I had clothes to make. No excuse for taking my attention off Benny. Mum felt it, too, and she was up the stairs before me, pushing me out of the way, screaming his name before she even opened the bedroom door and saw him. Strangled by my father's bitter skin.

Both of us on our knees, holding his hands to our faces, making so much noise, such a cacophony of grief, the next-door neighbour came and found us. In our old place the neighbours never responded, they let things be. But this noise, they said later. It was so heartbreaking they had to come see.

• ○

The official report said he died of internal injuries because of the bleeding, from the hard beating Dad had handed him. I gave them graphic details. Police tried to find Dad but he'd done a runner. Was nowhere to be seen. They'd knocked on his front door and no answer. They assumed Benny was a drug addict, so didn't really care. The skins affected the tests they did on him.

We wanted Benny buried in his favourite clothes, a double-breasted suit he'd bought for himself and saved for special, so I skinned myself up and headed over to Dad's house. I carried a knife with me, even though the police said he wasn't there, and I knew he'd be meeker after his recent violence. I wanted to be careful.

The house was small, and the outside walls damaged, needing repair. Mum and I would not be tempted to move in. We had our own place. This was way out woop woop, no one wanted to live there. The yard was all dirt; he'd killed the grass on purpose because he hated mowing the lawn. There were stacks of metal storage boxes, all of them empty. Dad's old car was parked out the front. Strange he didn't take it with him when he ran, but he always had buddies who'd drive him places. And he never drove drunk.

I had on a suit of bitter skin. Dank and slimy and stinking of bitterness and bile, with that citrus scent overall. Like putting on a wet bathing suit. Or wet jeans. I could barely breathe, the bitter skin tightening as it dried around me. I had to tear a gap or I'd suffocate.

The door was locked but I had Benny's keys. It occurred to me I should give them to the police to investigate, so they could find and charge my father with murder. Otherwise they'd forget. They'd happily put Benny in the unsolved/considered closed pile.

I unlocked the door. The place was very tidy for all its collapse. Benny liked order, as much as he could control. There were stacks of books on every surface and bowls of snacks.

The place smelled like citrus fruit gone mouldy. I checked the kitchen and nothing but packets of noodles and frozen food. Not really food.

● ○

I went to Benny's room. He was always very neat. The suit we wanted to bury him in would be clean and ironed. His wardrobe was closed, with black tape around the edges. The citrus smell was stronger here, coating my throat and filling my lungs. Clothes were piled high in front of the wardrobe door. I knew his good suit would be inside, so I dragged the pile away, pulled off the tape.

Inside nothing was hanging. All the clothes were piled on the floor. Dad did it in anger probably, fury at his own son's style and class.

Why did I look? Why did I? I was focused on the burial suit, wanting to find it, not thinking. The pile was damp. The smell rose. I pulled it all aside, and there were skins mixed in, and beneath it all was my father. Curled up. Beaten to a pulp. His eyes open wide, his tongue protruding, no breath in him.

My first reaction was to pile everything back onto him and I did it skins first, without thinking.

The pile moved.

Dad moved. He tried to rise. His hand lifted as he tried to stretch his foul fingers towards me. He wriggled in there, not enough skin to bring him totally back to life. I tripped backwards, fell over, staggered out of the room.

He didn't come after me.

I left the cupboard door open to let the sunlight in. It would disintegrate the skins eventually and he could die in peace. An act of mercy. He was my father, after all.

• ○

I cleaned out the fridge. Turned off the electricity. Locked the doors. He had automatic payments set up, so it would be years before anyone noticed. I went home. Showered. We bought Benny a new suit, and we had our boy cremated, my mother and I weeping alone as he turned to ash.

• ○

I needed the beach, the sun, I needed clean air, the sand, the water. I thought of Hilary, and how she was the one who drew the cute ones in. I felt stronger in myself, and strangely lighter. I lay in my own skin, feeling the sun warm me, burn me. I lay there until a shadow fell over me; a tall guy, not the worst-looking man who'd ever cast shade.

"You alone?" he asked me. I looked at the hint of bitter skin around his neck, and wondered how it would feel to wear him.

COLD IRON

SOPHIE WHITE

NOTE: The word "Sídhe" in this instance is pronounced "SHEE-jeh."

Based on true events.

We all saw Mammy die. In a variety of ways and at many different times. She only ever died in the full glare of daylight—a light so probing that any bewildered uncertainty at what we'd just witnessed was always instantly snuffed out. She was dead. Again and again and again, she was dead. She always murdered herself during the bald hours of daytime. This meant that the contours of the violence were razor-sharp, glinting—every colour dialled right up, and let me tell you the palette of a daylight death is Technicolour. Every hue of red and pinky flesh glistens when caught in the glare of a sunbeam. The usual murkiness of forming bruises is instead a confluence of almost-pleasing bright blues and greens.

She died in the kitchen, she died in the bedrooms, she died in the bathroom. Perhaps most memorably, she died when she stepped almost casually off the roof of the house one day in

January. In the frigid dawn, the vapour that poured from her mouth with each desperate exhale gave the whole thing a gothic slant, even though the setting undermined this somewhat. She was, after all, not diving from a cliff into churning ocean or the turret of a castle but a semidetached council house in Ballybrack in the 1970s not the 1700s. Once on the ground, face down, palms of her hands and soles of her feet up, a last couple of pearlescent breaths escaped from the sides of her buried face and then nothing more.

Diving from the roof was her most public death. The tendrils of smoke that had risen from her hot mouth had given the proceedings an undeniable glamour. My siblings and I (I should say my surviving siblings, I suppose) probably talked about this death the most. In part because it was the only one we witnessed together and so was irrefutable proof of our unusual childhood, and in part because, as I said, the drama of it! Of course, all murder is drama! All murder is spectacle!

The roof step was also the only murder in the garden. For the rest, she confined her demises to within the cinder-block walls of our house. The housing department of Dublin City Council seemed intent on making the accommodations they provided for families like mine as close to prison cells as possible. Punishment for being poor. My brother said the purpose of the unyielding cinder-block walls was to prevent us, the useless citizens, from making any permanent mark on the place so that when our unwanted lineage died off, the houses were unchanged by our presence. We couldn't even hang pictures on the walls. And it wasn't just decoration that the cinder blocks rejected. Even practical things like additional shelves were impossible to install in the denseness of those walls.

Of course, Mammy, who over the years must have utilised every means available to her, eventually took advantage of the cinder blocks to serve her project, pulling a ferociously ugly floor-to-ceiling oak cabinet that couldn't be secured to the wall down on top of her. That particular effort left a stain on the TV-room floor from where her skull and its pulpy contents had been mashed into the bald carpet. The next day she rose like she always did, appearing in the kitchen nonplussed and intact. The cleanup was up to her. First she had to scrape off the mucusy coils of brain matter and shards of skull. Then she scrubbed and scrubbed but to no avail. The garish stain was there forever now, like a bloody gash in the carpet. Our father, his face set with disapproval, homed a ratty beanbag over the dark rust shadow of death for the next time a council representative came for an inspection.

My siblings and I knew not to talk about the deaths with anyone but ourselves. This knowledge was implicit in the one modification our father made to our house. Dead bolts on the exteriors of the back and front doors. He put them in place shortly after she'd died in the garden. It was handy that the front door had a small porch area on the outside with a sliding glass door where we kids kicked off our trainers and dumped schoolbags, footballs, and hurling sticks. This porch meant the dead bolts could not be seen by neighbours unless they managed to breach the sliding porch door, which they never did. Of course, some of the neighbours—the men of the area—had an inkling of what went on in our house. After all they'd had something of a hand in it. Our father kept the postman at bay by tying a small steel post-box on the low garden gate out front. The neighbours who knew some things but not everything (they didn't, for example, know that Mammy died from time to time) didn't think it was odd that our mother was only ever seen as a stooped shadow beyond net curtains. After a tragedy like ours descends, a family will wear it always, a shroud of misery that few people want to lift.

From all this, we knew that the goings-on in the house were

to be contained. Mammy was to be contained, her activities contained, the gaseous desperation of her building behind the doors each day. We had to be careful not to breathe it in if we were to escape that childhood uninfected. The instatement of the dead bolts, that directly defied the council's regulations, was a measure so drastic that we knew the seriousness of them. Our father kept polyfill and paint that matched the doors on hand for when he had to remove and conceal the holes made by his screws from the visiting council reps.

And so with dead bolts on the outside of the house, we trooped out each morning. We closed the door and slid the bolt home to intern our mother and her proclivities for the next six to eight hours depending on what day of the week it was and what after-school activities were on. We left after our father each morning and usually returned before him. He didn't work but he was active in the community, especially in the local Men's Shed—an initiative in underprivileged areas to promote mental health among men and boys who were unemployed and, as the council saw it, prone to antisocial behaviours like addiction and gambling. A condescending presumption, but the men did seem to like their Men's Shed. It was actually a Portakabin rather than a shed, hunched under a row of Scots pine trees on the grounds of the Catholic church. Beside the Men's Shed was a vegetable patch from which our father brought home lumpen carrots and dirty spuds and sacks of soil. He'd come home and slam these offerings down in front of our mammy when he was annoyed with her. She would obediently put the vegetables into the dinner and leave the soil by the back door—for every death required a burial.

He wasn't always annoyed with her. Only really when she had one of her outbursts, which is what he called her deaths. Feelings in a family are catching, if one person is hated in a family—or *scapegoated* as a later therapist described it to me (ugh, the therapists never quite got me—how could they? They didn't have all the facts, what a waste of money) often the rest of the family will turn on them also. It's a sort of survival instinct; in order to not become the hated one, the others must join the war on the hated one. So we children would also become annoyed with her following an outburst. The reason for our irritation, apart from survival, was largely because her routine of dying impinged on our own routines. We could never bring friends home after school because even if the dead bolt didn't arouse their curiosity, the potentially dead mother inside certainly would. On any given day, we could be walking in on the aftermath of her death. As much as she had the routine of killing herself, we had the routine of encountering her dead. We never moved the body. We stepped over and around it, however cumbersome, because our father's routine was the removal. And it was always Mammy's job to scrub and clean the next day. You'd think having to deal with the filth of murdering herself would put her off doing it but it never did. She kept going.

It didn't matter where her corpse lay, we had to get on with things. I remember sitting on the toilet, knickers at my knees, my elbows resting on top looking across to the corner where she sat propped. It was a recent kill. Thick blood pulsed down her arms. It formed pools in her cupped hands and slicked the tiles beneath. I squeezed to try and hurry the urine out of me so that I could get done before the advancing blood reached me and I'd have to clean my shoes. When the murders were that fresh, there was always an accompanying heat and a tang of iron. The mugginess of it mingled with the air in the room. Blood freed from veins creates a sort of humidity, it stifles you. I suppose you could say our whole childhood was a bit stifling.

Because I was the oldest of the three living siblings, I remembered our life before her continual messy dying. There were babies and then there weren't. My first two siblings exist in my mind like shadows now. They were fleeting blurs on the landscape of my early years. I remember their names even though those names were never spoken afterwards. Banba and Eiru. They had a sour smell that I can still recall. They were soft as kittens. Banba was born first and then died in her cot. I came into the room before Mammy or Daddy. I was five and curious about my baby sister. It was morning. The day streamed through the curtains, glad and bright, but the room had a curious emptiness about it. It didn't just feel deserted but as though it contained less than nothing, there was a weight to the nothing. The source of the heavy nothing was Banba's cot, where she was still and hard when I reached in to pet the bundle.

Mammy wouldn't let them bury Banba. She held tight to that rigid baby for days in the TV room staring at something we couldn't see. There was a problem I was too young to understand. I only knew about the problem because one night Daddy's men from the Men's Shed came to help with the problem. They stood around my mother—she was the problem. And Banba left unburied would soon join her in being a problem. Mammy screamed a scream that, if I want, I can still call up. All these years later, I still contain that jagged shriek of agony. Then Banba was gone. Two men had gripped Mammy's upper arms while a third had extracted the baby. They put Banba in a crate to take her from the house. And so Banba was gone.

I was ten and sitting in fourth class when I realised that there'd been another problem with my baby sister. Banba hadn't been baptised. Our teacher was teaching us about purgatory and limbo and hell and the wonderful Catholic church that presided over our country. She told us that many churches didn't accept the babies who had died before baptism into the normal graveyard.

I had never thought to wonder where Banba had gone. Where did they put her? I suppose I never asked because it wasn't long before another baby lay in my mother's arms. Eiru. Eiru is less of a shadow in my mind. She lived to nearly a year old, long enough to make smiles and babble with excitement when you'd walk into the room. Until the silent morning came, of course.

Two babies dead eighteen months apart from cot death. The neighbours skirted my mammy's devastation. Whispers threaded through the rooms of the houses around us. One death is a tragedy, but two . . .

No one ever finished the sentence, but they didn't need to.

"You look different," Daddy accused Mammy as she moved about the house with frozen features and empty searching hands that never found, would never again find, any peace. It was hard to understand what he was getting at at first.

Looking at the two of them from my perch well beyond their interest, it seemed they each existed in separate realms layered over one another. My mother moved achingly slowly, bowed by the gravity of grief. She reacted in a delayed fashion to everything that was said to her. In the mornings I asked for breakfast, trying not to plead, and by nightfall, she might say, "You must be hungry."

My father on the other hand began to move and speak much faster. He whipped through the house at speed. He pulled books off shelves and ripped sheets from the mattresses convinced some rot was the cause of two healthy babies dying. Soon we were living in a blizzard of his obsessions.

One day it was the water—he slapped a cup out of my hands and knocked my head against the wall for being "so foolish." The next it was surely the type of gum the council used for the woodchip wallpaper. "Probably lead, they wouldn't waste better on the likes of us."

Then it was the religious relics my mammy kept around the house. He dragged the crucifixes from the walls.

"The church hated our babies, wouldn't put them in their precious blessed ground." The older harsher ideology of this island, one rooted much deeper than the church, had begun to creep into his mind.

"It's not like that, Seamey, the unbaptised just have a different place." My mammy's attempts at reason were like frail leaves in a gale.

Then his obsession was just my mammy. "*You* were the one feeding them," he muttered.

Glimpses of this paranoid season flare in my mind like matches in the dark: I look up at her as she rears back, his hand dug into her hair. "*You* were the one with them." He spoke slowly, each word bitten, clenched in his teeth. I can see her crawling towards me while he rises up behind her.

"*You* were the one." We sat at the too-small table for tea. My daddy beside me and Mammy opposite.

"*You* were the one," he sang as he pressed his palms to the table and pulled the waxy tablecloth, drawing her plate away from her.

"*You* were the one." He paid no attention to the plates and cups falling to the floor around us.

"*You* were the one." He flew to his feet and banged out the back door. Several minutes passed before Mammy seemed to notice and then crouched to clear the mess.

During this time, incredibly he still lay with her and pushed himself inside her. I knew because soon she was growing again. At first it was just a bud of a belly, but by the spring she had been completely taken over. I remember this pregnancy better than the others. By then, I was nearly eight and very wary. Of babies and birth, all I'd known was disaster. I'd seen the horror mask of grief fastened to my mammy's head for years. And dragging life forth, only for it to still and die, had turned my daddy half mad.

Her belly pinned her to the couch and I solemnly brought her tea and the oranges that I laboriously peeled for her. Daddy circled endlessly, watching. His grip on those wayward notions tightened. Over those iron-cold March days, he watched for signs of those malevolent forces he was convinced governed our land. He watched his wife so intensely that his eyes seemed to gouge at her, seemed to invade her. The pregnancy felt like a test, an extended ritual she must complete to banish once and for all the terrible question mark of her dead children. Neighbours and extended family came by for a look, their appetite for salacious talk seemingly having ebbed. Somewhat.

In pregnancy, my mammy's face was alive again. Her eyes looked like they were seeing once more. But I could feel that she was still nervous. Her hands fluttered under mine when I tried to capture them, trying to lock myself to her, in my child mind thinking that would make me safe.

Daddy was in and out of our house all day and all night. Up to the Men's Shed and home, back and forth like some kind of extended pacing, consulting with the older men there. He fixated on prospective tragedies. Mammy went from rarely leaving the house to being forbidden to leave. No one could visit if he wasn't there. In his myopic state, he turned against the hospital when they said the babies should be delivered by caesarean, as it was policy in cases of twins. He told the consultant they were switching to a new hospital so no one would come looking for my mammy when she stopped attending.

In the claustrophobia of the Men's Shed an idea germinated and spread through the men there, eventually taking root in my father. Could his wife be trusted? Could his wife have been lured by the Sídhe? And a changeling returned in her place? Could it be that the changeling murdered the other babies? Had my father lain with a changeling? The questions crowded in on my daddy, pulling at his reason.

I knew what Daddy was thinking because he told me. He told me to watch my mammy any time he wasn't there. "The Sídhe may have taken her." His hands locked on my shoulders.

"The changeling will do strange things when it thinks no one is watching." I nodded because what else can you do when you are eight and they are tall and they are your whole world?

When the pregnancy began dragging Mammy from sleep and she took to making tea and baking scones in the early dawn, Daddy gripped me, his fingers digging into my neck. "You see, don't you? The changeling has nocturnal tendencies. It must be watched."

From behind the door, I watched Mammy's eyes in the half-light. Why did they gleam in the near darkness of early morning? They shone out of the gloom, no pinprick of a pupil that I could see. Just two silver coins in her head. They rotated to find me and I fled.

I didn't want to lose my mammy and believing his stories meant I had already lost her. But . . . but . . . but. Ideas can be catching. A changeling. My child's unformed reasoning turned the word over and over. "Changeling, changeling, changeling." It sounded both beautiful and terrifying. My mammy had changed. Her wooden face gone and now a raw feverishness there instead and what about the rippling across her belly skin, the undulations of the creatures inside her?

I was afraid to ask Daddy about the Sídhe but I knew the word somehow. There was the song she used to sing to Banba and Eiru. I only remembered some of it, but I was certain she'd never sung it in front of Daddy.

See the Sídhe,
Vile mouths feed
And up they come and up they come.

Sink it down
And pound and pound
And up they come and up they come.

Bring them gifts
So revenge is swift
And up they come and up they come.

I'd given the words only the most passing attention. It hadn't seemed like anything strange especially compared with the other lullabies where cradles crashed to the ground in "Rock-a-bye Baby" and the old woman in "Weila Weila Waile" was strung up by the neck.

Now the vile mouths of the Sídhe needed feeding in my dreams, and every night, I begged in the darkness of my room for this whispering to stop. Every day, I felt like I was at the edge of a hole, teetering. Somehow I was both scared of my mammy and scared *for* my mammy.

In daytime, when she stood in the light beaming down at me over the rise of her belly and the sun poured through her, I thought I saw something in her face. A sudden tightening and shifting of her features as though another being was crowded in with her under her skin. The lips peeling back tightly to reveal a bone-white jaw, then resettling in an idle smile.

See the Sídhe
Vile mouths feed
And up they come and up they come.

In darkness, bad things can hide, but sometimes in daylight, in the glare of certainty, we can be even more easily deceived.

Finally the last, uneasy weeks of Mammy's pregnancy gave way to Saturday, May 18, and the quaking pains that drove her to the bed. Almost immediately the begging began. She wanted a midwife. She wanted to go to hospital. She wanted it to stop, oh god make it stop. She wanted to die.

The way my daddy stood watching her desperation, as pitiless as a priest, scared me more than the rabid woman on the bed.

Looking back, my mind sees the birth in violent snatches. Blink and she is impossibly arched, an inhuman angle. Blink and she is pressed so deep in the bed there must be some unseen thing bearing down on her. Blink and all I see is a stretched, glistening mass of red with a whorl of dark hair at the centre.

See the Sídhe
Vile mouths feed
And up they come and up they come.

The men from the Men's Shed began to appear. They stayed back against the bedroom wall, occasionally exchanging words.

"It doesn't seem right, does it?" said one.

"No," one shook his head.

"But have you seen one before? Maybe this is the way," a third offered.

Even now, I still can't decide if they were talking about a changeling or the brutal uproar of birth in general. At that time, in that place, men were never present at their children's births.

As the awful day drew to a close, with no letup in the garish mayhem, I remember that I began to plead with Daddy. Not even to help her, but to let me out of that room. I think it was then that I finally grasped that I couldn't help anyone and I needed to survive these people. I needed to survive our blighted family.

Daddy didn't answer. He had barely moved in hours. Finally he began to speak, though not to me.

"You think I don't know what you are, but this birth will purge you from our household. You will return my wife. And you will stop killing my children," he thundered.

The bed banged the floor under my mother and thin cloudy liquid spilled out the side of her mouth, but at that stage she seemed barely conscious. She was life beaten and weakened, at the mercy of my daddy and his friends and the very babies she had grown.

Sink it down
And pound and pound
And up they come and up they come.

I wondered if she was leaving us, after all how much longer could she withstand this? Then a last fearsome spasm flushed my entwined siblings out of her body. She bucked a few more times and a gargantuan slab of veined meat followed, roped to each baby. Then she lay still, though spent tears leaked from her closed eyes suggesting that she was still alive.

The men seemed to hesitate before coming closer and looking at the babies. They were smeared with cream but otherwise were surprisingly unbloodied by the ordeal. They didn't make any noise and their eyes were shut, but twitchy movements told that they were living. The men shunted the hollowed carcass of my mammy farther up the bed so that they could examine the twins as they unfurled. Daddy used the bedsheet to wipe them. The oldest man produced a stubby pocketknife and used it to lift the fleshy ropes. The men conferred quietly. They didn't seem to know a thing about what they were doing and this gave me a queasy swoop in my tummy as though I was inching closer to some inner precipice.

Some resolution was reached and one of the younger men—I recognised him from the street, he only lived a few houses over—hurried out.

From where I stood, I couldn't see if the babies had eyes. Their features were so small, folds of skin obscured all but their mouths, which soon asserted themselves. Petulant lips rimmed two tiny black caves and perched inside each cave was a flexed expectant tongue.

From the head of the bed, the pile of bones and rags that was my mammy spoke.

"Let me see them. They need to feed." The pile shifted and a head of misery lifted stiffly. Mammy stared at the men with exhausted defiance. "Give me my babies."

Daddy bent low over the babies. "I've seen you for what you are, thing."

"Seamey, please. This is madness. Please." She closed her eyes.

"Shut up. We'll be done with you soon."

The young man returned with an older lady, his mother, in tow and I felt a shimmer of hope. She would calm the men down surely.

"They let ye out of the shed, I see," she chuckled, looking around. "What do we have?" She elbowed through to the babies. "Terrible day to be born. Whitsun. A baby born on the seventh Sunday after Easter will be a murderer, don't ye know."

"Don't be stirring, Ma, sure it's Saturday." Her son shook his head.

"It's after midnight," she replied tersely as she briskly began fixing pegs to the babies' cords. She pinched the short gap between two pegs. "Wait 'til this bit is white to cut. The rest will come off by itself in a few days. And wrap them up! They're not livestock."

"Áine." Mammy spoke through a curtain of stringy hair. "Áine, please."

The woman shifted her eyes down. "Mind them with her," she muttered to Daddy. "We don't want any more *accidents*."

As the door closed behind Áine, Daddy walked to my mammy and picked up a length of her hair and slowly, slowly wound it up in his fist until it lifted her head and stretched out her neck. "Cunt Sídhe," he whispered.

"Seamey," one of the men spoke. "Maybe don't . . . Don't handle it . . . too rough I mean. The Sídhe . . . You . . . It . . . It could bring more of them on you. On all of us here, too. It's already cursed these babies."

Daddy continued to stare at the ruin of my mammy but he let her head go. "Sídhe, you won't hurt any more of my children." He turned suddenly and left the room.

My mammy, the heap of bones and hair and teeth, began to heave panicky sobs, while at the other end of the bed the hands of the twins curled and unfurled, grasping delicately at the sheet, at themselves and each other.

"They haven't cried yet," one of the men said nervously.

"We'll get finished and they'll be fine. Cold iron, fellas." The men nodded. This meant something to them. It even sounded familiar to me for some reason. A few fumbled in their pockets.

Daddy came back holding out a cupped hand ahead of him.

"So *glic*, so sly, Sídhe. To give me babies born on Whitsun. As if I'm a fool." He turned his cupped hand over and two tiny eggs fell onto the sheet. He sang softly: "Unlucky babies born Whitsun, bound by fate to kill someone."

He placed the tiny eggs in the left hand of each baby. He must have taken them from the robin's nest, they always came to our hedgerow in spring, I had made a project about the little bird families for school.

He closed the babies' hands around the eggs and squeezed. The babies began to cry at the first pain of their lives. My mammy cried out weakly and tried to get up but the fight was nearly gone out of her. Daddy's hands went white with the squeezing until a muted crunch came and something wet and veined with threads of blood oozed from the babies' fists.

"Now"—he wiped his hands on his trousers leaving a glistening slick—"they've made their kill, Sídhe, that cancels your curse. Nothing more you can do but return my wife."

He hummed a little and started to tuck the sheet around my brother and sister, ignoring the fact that they were now getting the shell and mangled bits of the baby birds all around their mouths as they sucked at their hands. Next he reached into his pocket and brought out a clump of nails and dropped them around the babies. The other men began to step forward with similar offerings: bolts and screws and small battered tools. I remember it was then that the last verse of mammy's song came to me.

To get Sídhe gone
Cold iron, cold iron.
And away they go and away they go.

Mammy mewled and tried with desperate clawing to push the shards of iron away from the helpless skin of her babies.

"You'll hurt them, Seamey, they'll swallow something. I need to feed them, please stop this."

"You, Sídhe, need to swallow something. Cold iron, my Sídhe."

I made myself as small as possible as the men took up their

positions. It looked practised. They each pressed down on a different part of my mammy. I told myself: *Don't look, don't look, don't look.* And then: *I have to look, I have to know, or else no one will ever know.*

The men stood shoulder to shoulder so all I could see were her pale feet, now stretched down and almost touching one baby. He swung a little arm blindly and grazed her toes. Her feet began to flex and kick and shake. The sounds were dreadful, huffing and strangled retching. And heaving and heaving and heaving until, after forever, the feet stopped.

They put Mammy in a hole in the garden. She lay on her back facing the sky where daylight was overtaking night. In the ruthless light of morning, it looked like she was down there screaming, but that was just what they'd done to her. They had packed her mouth tight with all the nails and rusted crap from their pockets.

"Our real mammy will be back now." Daddy swayed the two babies. They were small enough to share his arms.

She didn't come. Of course she didn't. She was in the garden under dirt, gagged with nails. Days and days passed and the babies' cries began to sound fainter, their eyes dimming.

Then one morning she was there, sitting in the kitchen smiling with a stretched raw mouth and dirty feet. Daddy was jubilant. He gave her the babies and left for his Men's Shed to report the news of their triumph. Over the next months, Mammy nursed the babies until they were round and brimming with health. She moved around the house doing everything, as was expected of her. Daddy was high on his own righteousness.

"I saved you, I saved you. I saved us," he told her over and over, never noticing that she didn't answer.

On the twins' first birthday, kneeling in the nursery, she took a knife to her throat and bled out all over the pristine laundry she'd been folding. The twins in the cots babbled until we came up. Daddy floundered. Reeling, he held his head and repeated beseechingly, "But I saved us."

In a panic, he didn't even wait 'til dark to hook an arm around her waist and drag her down through the house and out to her old grave. From the window of the nursery, with the iron taste of her blood in my mouth, I watched him stare into the old hole he'd uncovered. I've no idea what he saw, but a moment later he'd tipped her in with his foot and began packing the earth back down on top of her.

I understood better than my daddy what was happening. I sang softly to my siblings.

Sink it down
And pound and pound
And up they come and up they come.

The next morning she was there in the kitchen leaving dirty footprints but otherwise unchanged. The unchanged changeling.

So it goes, on and on. I visit them very infrequently now. The house of routine death is so unappealing and I don't want my children in the way of Mammy or Daddy—a changeling and a murderer are not exactly ideal grandparent material. Plus when it comes to the Sídhe, it's best to give a wide berth. Respectful distance is your safest option.

The thing is I get the Sídhe's logic. He wanted Mammy dead and now she will never stop dying. Maybe she'll finally stay dead when he dies. Either way, you have to give it to them, the Sídhe have a wicked sense of humour.

● ○

As stated at the beginning, this story is based (okay, loosely!) on true events, the death of Bridget Cleary in Tipperary, Ireland, in 1895.

Her husband and eight others were charged with her murder. The group believed that she had been abducted by fairies and replaced with a changeling. After days of a violent exorcism of sorts by her husband and others attempting to get rid of the changeling, Bridget was either burned alive or her body was set on fire immediately after her death. All the superstitious elements in this story, such as Whitsun and having the baby "murder" a creature to negate the curse, are true customs of old, though the songs and chants are made up.

A note on the word "Sídhe"—I took some creative licence by using it. There're a lot of names for fairies in Ireland, including Síog, Fae, Fairies, the Fair Folk. I used the word "Sídhe," which is used for fairies but only on certain grammatical occasions, as it felt like the right option—I didn't want non-Irish readers to think "fairy" and picture something Disneyish. In Ireland fairies are a malevolent force. So much so that after completing this story, on the advice of a wise friend, I left out a saucer of milk to make good with them.

*Still, using the word "Sídhe" in this story has come with some angst as, to quote the same wise friend, "*Gaeilge *(Irish) is slippery for writing and repels explanation." Some sources say "Aos Sí" (pronounced "eees shee") for the supernatural Irish race that is our equivalent of fairies. "Aes Sídhe" is the older version of this. There's also suggestion that "banshee" derives from "*bean sídhe*." Yeats, in 1908, referred to the fairies as "the sídhe," which sets something of a precedent—who's going to argue with Yeats? . . . A lot of people actually! I had much debate among friends and friends of friends from various parts of Ireland on both the pronunciation and the grammatical wisdom of using "Sídhe," all of which is far too involved and complicated to unpack here. Let's just say it's the word that felt right and to those who are* líofa*, please forgive me my linguistic sins. I know it's the Tuiseal Ginideach, okay?!*

About the Authors

Brian Evenson has published two dozen books, most recently *Good Night, Sleep Tight* (Coffee House Press, 2024). His collection *Song for the Unraveling of the World* won the Shirley Jackson Award and the World Fantasy Award and was a finalist for the *Los Angeles Times*'s Ray Bradbury Prize. His novel *Last Days* won the American Library Association's RUSA award for Best Horror Novel. *The Wavering Knife* won the International Horror Guild Award for best collection. He is the recipient of three O. Henry Prizes, an NEA Fellowship, and a Guggenheim Fellowship. He lives in Los Angeles and teaches at CalArts.

Jeffrey Ford is the author of the novels *The Physiognomy, Memoranda, The Beyond, The Portrait of Mrs. Charbuque, The Girl in the Glass, The Cosmology of the Wider World, The Shadow Year, The Twilight Pariah, Ahab's Return,* and *Out of Body.* His short story collections are *The Fantasy Writer's Assistant, The Empire of Ice Cream, The Drowned Life, Crackpot Palace, A Natural History of Hell, The Best of Jeffrey Ford,* and *Big Dark Hole.* Ford's fiction has appeared in numerous magazines and anthologies from *Reactor* to *The Magazine of Fantasy & Science Fiction* to *The Oxford Book of American Short Stories.*

A. T. Greenblatt is a Nebula Award–winning writer and mechanical engineer. She lives in New York City, where she's known to frequently subject her friends to various cooking and home-brewing experiments. Her work has been nominated for Hugo, Locus, World Fantasy, and Sturgeon awards, has been in multiple Year's Best anthologies, and has appeared in *Reactor, Uncanny, Beneath Ceaseless Skies, Nightmare,* and *Clarkesworld,* as well as other fine publications. You can find her online at atgreenblatt.com and on Bluesky at @atgreenblatt.bsky.social.

Rachel Harrison is the *USA Today* bestselling author of *Play Nice, So Thirsty, Black Sheep, Such Sharp Teeth, Cackle,* and *The Return,* which was nominated for a Bram Stoker Award for Superior Achievement in a First Novel. Her short fiction has appeared in *Guernica* and *Electric Literature*'s Recommended Reading, as an Audible Original, and in her debut story collection, *Bad Dolls.*

Priya Sharma writes short stories and novellas. She is the recipient of several British Fantasy Awards and Shirley Jackson Awards, as well as a World Fantasy Award. She is a Locus Award and a Grand Prix de l'Imaginaire finalist. Her work has appeared in venues such as *Reactor, Interzone, Black Static,* and *Weird Tales.* She lives in the UK, where she works as a medical doctor. More information can be found at www.priyasharmafiction.wordpress.com.

Robert Shearman has written six short story collections, and between them they have won the World Fantasy Award, the Shirley Jackson Award, the Edge Hill Readers Prize, and five British Fantasy Awards. He began his career in the theatre, and his plays have won the *Sunday Times* Playwriting Award, the World Drama Trust Award, and the Guinness Award for Ingenuity in association with the Royal National Theatre. But he is probably best known for his work on television, bringing back the Daleks for the BAFTA-winning first series of *Doctor Who,* and most recently as script consultant for *Constellation* on Apple TV+.

Kaaron Warren, a Shirley Jackson Award winner, published her first short story in 1993 and has had fiction in print every year since. She has lived in Melbourne, Sydney, Canberra, and Fiji, drawing inspiration from every place. She has published six multi-award-winning novels: *Slights, Walking the Tree, Mistification, The Grief Hole, Tide of Stone,* and *The Underhistory,* and eight short story collections, including the most recent, *Calvaria Fell,* with Cat Sparks. Her stories have appeared in both Ellen Datlow's and Paula Guran's Year's Best anthologies.

Her latest novel, *The Underhistory,* from Viper Books, was described in *The Guardian* as "a beautifully constructed, suspenseful gothic tale."

Sophie White is a novelist, essayist, and podcaster from Ireland. Her sixth novel, *Where I End,* won the Shirley Jackson Award for best novel in 2022. It was released in the United States in 2023. Her work has been described as "brilliantly visceral" by *The Guardian* and "exquisite and disturbing . . . brutish and beautifully crafted" by *The Irish Times.* She cohosts the chart-topping comedy-horror podcast *The Creep Dive* and she lives in Dublin.

A. C. Wise's most recent publications are the novellas *Out of the Drowning Deep* (Titan, 2024) and *Grackle* (PS Publishing, 2024). A new novel, *Ballad of the Bone Road* (Titan), is forthcoming in January 2026. Her work has won the Sunburst Award and been a finalist for the Nebula, Bram Stoker, World Fantasy, Locus, and Shirley Jackson awards, among others. In addition to her fiction, she contributes regular review columns to *Locus* and *Apex Magazine.* For more info visit www.acwise.net.

About the Editor

Ellen Datlow has been editing science fiction, fantasy, and horror short fiction for more than thirty years as fiction editor of *Omni* magazine and editor of *Event Horizon* and *SciFiction*. She currently acquires short stories for *Reactor* and novellas for Tor.com. In addition, she has edited more than fifty science fiction, fantasy, and horror anthologies, including the annual *Best Horror of the Year* series, and most recently *Echoes: The Saga Anthology of Ghost Stories, Final Cuts: New Tales of Hollywood Horror and Other Spectacles, Body Shocks: Extreme Tales of Body Horror*, and *When Things Get Dark: Stories Inspired by Shirley Jackson*.

She's won multiple World Fantasy Awards, Locus Awards, Hugo Awards, Bram Stoker Awards, International Horror Guild Awards, Shirley Jackson Awards, the Splatterpunk Award, and the 2012 Il Posto Nero Black Spot Award for Excellence as Best Foreign Editor. Datlow was the recipient of the 2007 Karl Edward Wagner Award, given at the British Fantasy Society convention for outstanding contribution to the genre; was honored with the Lifetime Achievement Award by the Horror Writers Association in acknowledgment of superior achievement over an entire career; and was honored with the World Fantasy Award for Life Achievement at the 2014 World Fantasy Convention.

She lives in New York and cohosts the monthly Fantastic Fiction reading series at KGB Bar. More information can be found at www.datlow.com and on Facebook and Twitter @EllenDatlow. She's owned by two cats.

Contents

NIGHT

NIGHT

NIGHT

Preface

Traditionally, midnight is the witching hour, the time when some believe there is the most supernatural activity and the veil between the living and dead is the thinnest.

Darkness is typically considered the period of time humans most fear, when we believe we are the most vulnerable. This results from thousands of years needing to be more alert at night, and our relatively poor eyesight. We want to believe we're safe in our beds, in our houses, asleep. Yet, are we? Evil lurks and we can't see it. It might be under the bed or just around the corner.

TRASH NIGHT

CLAY McLEOD CHAPMAN

T*hat's a baby's foot.* I'm staring at an infant's tender leg sprouting out from this split-open garbage bag.

There's a streetlamp directly over my head, a sodium-bulb spotlight shining down on the compactor's belly. This kid's skin is all blue. Got a robin's egg complexion, cracked and covered in yolk. Still some baby fat clinging to its thigh. A paste of coffee grounds clings to its shin, like coal-black sand.

What I wouldn't give to be in the Rockaways right now. Anywhere but here.

Mt. Trashmore. Three a.m. on a fucking Tuesday night.

Trash Night.

We're gathering garbage from the apartment complex at DeKalb and Washington. You know the building. Everybody does. Seven floors of eyesore. Hundred units, easy. Maybe more.

We're talking a metric shit ton of garbage. Twice a week, we tackle this massive mound of waste. Dozens—Christ, *hundreds*—of industrial garbage bags, black as tar, stacked five or six high.

Up to my fucking chin in Hefty Cinch Saks. I could climb it, I kid you not.

My very own Everest of shit.

We've all got a Mt. Trashmore somewhere on our route. Hell, some of us have to tackle two or three of these projects.

This one's ours. My mountain to dismantle. It's up to me to compact every last black plastic boulder by hand while my partner, Reggie, drives. I grab the bags from the pile, toss them in the hopper, then squeeze them down to a pulp. Listen to them hiss and dribble.

Then it's on to the next pile. Then the next. And the next, 'til the sun comes up.

But Mt. Trashmore feels different. Cursed, somehow. Just when I've strip-mined that summit of rubbish, chiseling the entire pile all the way down to the sidewalk, laying waste to it for yet another night, until there's nothing left to see, not one goddamn garbage bag—*gone*—two days later, the black mountain of offal rises right up again, all on its own, higher than before.

That's some Greek-myth shit for you. Reminds me of that guy. *What's-his-name.* The one with the liver that keeps getting pecked out by vultures? Or who's the guy who pushes the boulder up the mountain? That's me. Those are my kind of myths. I'm the Greek garbageman who's doomed to pick up this city's trash for an eternity. Just when I've grabbed the last garbage bag from the sidewalk—*bam*—they're back again.

But I ain't never found a baby before. Abandoned pups, sure. Dead cats, absofuckinglutely.

Never a newborn.

The dog days haven't sunk in yet, the oven-roast atmosphere hasn't steeped into our skin the way it does come July, slowing you down after ten minutes. There's still a tepid swelter to the air.

These trash bags hold so many secrets. Everything you try to

hide about yourself, it's in there. Your shit. Only your priest and garbageman know who you truly are, am I right?

What you hope to bury about yourself.

Your sins, congealed in bacon fat.

I've been clocking in for nine years now. Practically had the same route the whole time. I'm living in Bay Ridge. Two-bedroom apartment with twice as many kids. Got a seven-month-old now, too, so nobody sleeps. Takes me an hour on the R train just to reach the depot. No sleep for me. Not at night, at least. I close my eyes during the day, losing hours of sunlight. I don't see much of my kids, my wife. Hell, I don't see much of anything anymore.

My kids call me a *nocturnal animal.* A stinky, slumbering beast.

Better not poke the bear, they whisper. I'll crash in one of their beds while they're at school, 'cause my wife's always complaining about me stinking up our sheets. I'll hear my kids crowding around, tiptoeing up to me. Giggling. If I'm still awake and in a good mood, I'll grab whichever kid's closest, shoot my arm out from under the covers real quick and reel them into bed. I'll start growling, tickling the shit out of them, listening to them squeal until I finally let go.

Smash. Crash. Here comes the trashman, ready to bash, mash!

We hit the streets around 2:00 a.m. Me and Reggie got ourselves a good routine going. He chauffeurs, I toss garbage into the hopper. I got an arm for it. Could've been a pitcher for the Mets, but all my curveballs go right into the compression chamber, sending these bags hurtling over a grease-stained home plate. Got to put my golden arm to good use in this city, somehow.

Going pro just wasn't in the cards for me, so yeah . . . I go for the garbage.

Our truck's named Lorraine, no lie, after Reggie's ex. Beats me how he got past management, but he spray-painted her name across the side of the loader in this looping cursive, really

classing up the compactor with this flowery font. *Here comes Lorraine,* Reggie belts out behind the wheel, like he's some soul singer crooning out of tune all through Brooklyn at four in the morning, *through snow and rain . . . She's rumbling down the street, looking for shit to eat . . .*

You got to personalize this job. Make it feel special. Every time I find a stuffed animal in the trash, I'll fish it out. See if it's still good. People will throw out just about anything for no good reason. If it's got all its parts, I'll bring it home to my kids. Let them keep it.

Look what Daddy got you! Every Trash Night is Christmas and I'm motherfucking Santa.

If that animal is missing an arm or a leg, I'll simply tie its leftover limbs to the front grille. There's a whole menagerie of washed-out teddy bears dangling over the bumper. Natty Cabbage Patch dolls with one eye missing. Mildewed Care Bears, their soggy bodies all blanched out by the rain. Gives our truck a little personality. *Panache.* Look at Lorraine, all covered in stuffed animals, a moving zoo, coming right at you, rumbling down the block.

Love your job, right? Take pride in it. That's what I tell my children all the time. *Own that shit, kids.* They're embarrassed their dad's a trashman. They can't tell their classmates their pop's a cop or a doctor, so they shy away from that shit—but nah, I say, embrace it. Take pride in it.

Tell your friends I run this city, I always say. *This town would fall apart if it weren't for your father.* My kids give me this look, like I'm full of crap.

They think I'm lying? Imagine all the pickup crews quitting at the same time. Guess what would happen to the Big Apple if there's a sanitation strike? Remember the big one in '68? How awful that was? Whole city reeked. More than a hundred

thousand tons of trash went nowhere fast, accumulating in the streets. So I'll tell you what happens if we don't show up for work: Your trash piles up, that's what. Sidewalks overflow with refuse. Mountains as far as the eye can see, practically as tall as the skyscrapers along 5th Ave. Oily black peaks mucking up the Manhattan skyline.

And here come the rats, all the rats, taking to the streets, scurrying under your feet . . .

Reggie and me are members of Uniformed Sanitation Workers' Union Local 239. We've been after wage increases for years now. You think our mayor's going to budge? If we're going to pick up your shit in this city, we deserve to be able to afford to live in this fucking city.

You can't push us all out to Staten Island. Don't we deserve to live here, too?

Give it a week. Two weeks of no pickups. You'll beg to have us back.

This city is ours.

Bring us your chicken bones, your lamb chops, your moldy bread and cheese . . . Toss 'em all in the hopper, pull the lever, and listen to that squeeeeeeeeeeze . . . Reggie belts out Motown in the middle of the night. You hear us coming from blocks away with all that Marvin Gaye and Jay & the Techniques. *Apples, peaches, pumpkin pie . . .* The dude's a jukebox for that shit. And if he ever runs out of R&B, he'll make up his own songs. Starts singing about the garbage.

Smash. Crash. Here comes the trashman, ready to bash, mash!

I add to the rhythm section by pulling on the hydraulics. As soon as that ram starts cramming in on those garbage bags, you hear the pressure mounting. This high-pitched squeal lifts into the air, a squelching bellow, like a wet trumpet blaring down the block.

A pulp of percussion. That's my music. The hollow pop of empty milk jugs. Glass bottles shattering, shrill as a pistol going off. The music of the night.

Increase the grease, cram that ham, your trash is gone, thank you, ma'am!

Folks want to believe their trash magically disappears in the middle of the night, thanks to the garbage fairies swooping down and taking it all away—*outa sight, outa mind*—but honestly, it's got more to do with the temperature. It's just hotter during the day. Better to work at night, you know? Cooler. We get more work done without the heat fatigue steeping our bones, slowing us down. We're efficient at night. In the dark. While you sleep.

Here we are. Time to tackle Mt. Trashmore. Scale that motherfucker.

Take it down.

Reggie pulls up alongside the pile and parks. The hiss of hydraulics takes to the air. We ain't going nowhere until this mountain is gone. I'm tossing bags into the compactor. Hitting a pretty good rhythm, too. Once I get in the zone—this headspace where I'm not thinking anymore, simply chiseling away at that stack, one bag at a time—nothing else exists. Nothing else on my mind. Not my kids, my wife. Not even baseball stats. Just destroying this mountain.

My world record for dismantling Mt. Trashmore is three minutes flat. I'm a machine for this shit. You get into this routine. A flow. Just don't let your guard down, you know? That's when you get jabbed with a hypodermic needle. A shard of glass. You get tetanus. Hepatitis. HIV.

Apple cores, cabbage heads, dirty diapers, and moldy bread . . .

Reggie doesn't just drive, he's got to steer the conversation, too. He's got no qualms about shouting over the engine. Really got a throat for it. If there's ever a lull, he simply slips back into

his singing. Pisses the living shit out of people who want to sleep, but you know what? To hell with them. We're out here doing our job. Let the man sing show tunes 'til the sun comes up.

Bash. Smash. Here comes the trash . . .

I finally reach the street. Pavement's glistening in sodium lights. It hasn't rained for days, but the asphalt's soaking up whatever's leaked out from these bags. Gives the concrete a sheen.

Now I'm manning the hydraulics. I hear this familiar squish. A bag bursts open with a hiss, releasing these trapped gases inside like somebody's stomach just popped and—

Out sprouts that foot.

Five tiny toes blossom up from the bag. A pale blue broccoli stalk. I spot a coffee filter. A used diaper. But those toes—they're wiggling at me, wanting to play. *This little piggy went to the market, and this little piggy stayed at home . . .* and this little goddamn piggy got stuffed in a Cinch Sak, tossed in the trash, a breath away from getting crushed in the compactor.

I let go of the throttle and instinctively step back. Hold my breath. Everything halts in the hopper. The blade pins the ruptured plastic bag in place. It's already ripped, sending flecks of lettuce into the basin. There's a juice of milk and grease dribbling out from the split, oozing down the blade. The truck's rumbling, even in park. The vibrations from the engine get everything juddering. There's a hum to it, too. I feel it in my teeth. Deep in my molars.

A foot. A fucking baby's foot.

All that trash quivers in the rear loader, so the thigh jiggles just a bit. Looks like the leg is punting up and down, a pudgy little Rockette performing high kicks through the air.

I'm seeing things, that's all. Any second now, my eyes will adjust and I'll see this leg for whatever the hell it really is. A melon rind sliced into little divots or a husk of pizza crust.

I keep looking at that baby's foot. Staring at it. Waiting.

It's not changing.

Everything okay back there? Reggie calls out, but the words don't sink in. My mind is focused on this foot bunting upward, right into the air, all loose and wobbly, making me think back to every time I bounced my own kids on my knee. I'd grab Sam with both hands, wrapping my fingers around his belly, feeling this familiar squish of baby fat still strapped to his torso, saddling him up on my leg and just letting him hop on top of my knee, like I'm a bucking bronco, listening to him giggle the whole time he's bobbing up and down, up and—

Honk. Honk. Honk.

You get used to pissing people off. Part of the job. I always block the horns out. I don't hear them anymore. The sound doesn't sink in. But our truck's holding up the flow of traffic. This slowly growing line of taxis and delivery trucks forms behind us, its tail starting to snake down the block. They jackhammer their horns, this staccato brass section pouting in rhythm with one another—*honk-honk*—miffed because they're stuck behind a fucking garbage truck. But I'm not moving. I can't.

What am I supposed to do? What the hell am I supposed to do?

Part of me wants to tug. Uproot that foot, you know? Like weeding a garden. Could be a cabbage or a carrot. If I just grab hold of the ankle and pull, I'd find a hunk of fennel.

A toy. That's what it is. Bound to be a baby doll buried below. Just an abandoned toy.

Not flesh. Not blood.

So I wrap my gloved hand gently around its shin, getting a tender grip, fingers sweating in my glove, and just . . . *pull.* It doesn't give, buried deep. I have to yank harder.

So I pull a little harder. *Please don't let it be real,* I think. *Please.*

The garbage slowly starts to relent, letting this pale, fleshy vegetable go, and . . .

I excavate a baby.

A girl.

Our truck becomes a crime scene. I've got to scoop out all the trash, one bag at a time. The cops don't want to touch this shit, so it's up to us to spread everything out along the sidewalk, just to see if they can backtrack which apartment she's from. There's an overdue phone bill clinging to the kid's shoulder, so it's pretty simple to pinpoint the parents. Apartment 5N.

Grace.

Barely a year old. The *Post* picked up her story, splashing some trashy headline on it.

Baby Grace Tossed in the Garbage.

Turns out Grace got her hands on mom's prescription meds, swallowing them like candy. By the time anybody noticed, there was no need to resuscitate. Dad freaks out. Throws Grace in the garbage. Trash Night is only two days away, so they kept their kid in the kitchen can until they tossed her body out along with everything else.

Two nights. Tucked in a trash can.

This fucking city.

If I'd just been looking the other way, Grace would be in some landfill by now and we wouldn't be here, talking about any of this shit. I'm sorry, but it's true. If I hadn't been glancing into the compactor at that exact moment—the very fucking second—I never would've noticed those toes. What if I'd just kept my mouth shut? Kept this kid to myself? Looked the other way?

I want to take it all back. Go back to the way things were before.

I want my old life back. With my family.

So, yeah, maybe it's the baby that fucked everything up. Finding Grace in the trash did it.

Now I see them everywhere. Slithering in the garbage. Every goddamn night.

Trash Night.

● ○

I never hit my kids.

Never.

My wife can say whatever the hell she wants, but it doesn't change the fact that I love my children. You got beef with me? Fine. Get in line. This whole goddamn city's got a problem with me. But I never, *ever*, laid a hand on my kids.

Fucking custody, my ass . . . It's the trash. That's what this is all about.

What's hiding inside.

I just don't trust the touch of things anymore. Would you? How am I supposed to hold my nine-month-old now? Every time I tried, I'd get these queasy feelings in my gut. I'd see Grace swimming through the rear loader, like some mermaid trapped in a landfill. Her blue skin covered in coffee grounds and melon rinds. I hear Reggie singing in my head, a lullaby—*Smash. Bash. Mash that trash!* How the fuck am I supposed to hug my kids with that stuck in my head?

My wife noticed something was off straightaway. We've always slept on separate schedules. She gets the kids ready for school while I pass out. We're living in two separate worlds, her and me. She's always been a day person. Me, I hardly even see the sun anymore. I might as well live in Alaska or wherever there's no light.

She doesn't like me touching her until my third shower. Says

she smells the garbage on me, still steeped into my skin. She wants me to take a Brillo pad to my body.

You just don't notice it anymore, she says. Always says. Fucking broken record.

What's there to notice?

It's like you been rolling around in a landfill.

Fuck off.

You talk like a trash can, too. Even your mouth is full of garbage.

You know what I get for Christmas every year? Cologne. Bottles and bottles of that shit. Ombré Leather. Bleu de Chanel. Axe Body Spray. Now *that* shit smells awful.

Who cares if I can't smell it on myself anymore? The mayor calls me a hero. The *Post* took a photo of Lorraine for their story about Grace. You can see me in the pic. My pitching arm, at least. I tell my kids to squint. *That's me,* I say. *That's your daddy's hand right there. See it?*

Still waiting for the key to the city. Must've got lost in the mail.

Feel like I'm losing my mind now. We got this steel trash can in our kitchen. One of those crappy Ikea cans. It's got one of those plastic foot pedals. You press down and the lid flips open.

Last time I stomped on it, popping the lid, I swear I saw a baby in there, wriggling upside down. I only see their legs. One of them. It's kicking through the air, winnowing deeper into the trash like a fish tail swishing through the trash-ridden sea.

Took me a moment to collect myself. Close my eyes. Breathe in deep. Count down from ten until I'm calm. Collected. Open my eyes. No baby. No Grace in our garbage.

Management wanted me to take time off. Call it a holiday. Mental health leave. My union rep wants me to talk to somebody. A specialist. Get these feelings off my chest.

What the fuck am I supposed to say? *Hey, Doc, I can't hug my own kids without feeling like they're about to pop open. Their skin*

is nothing but thin plastic bursting at the seams. Their insides come spilling out, melon rinds and chicken bones and used tissues . . .

Is that what they all want to hear?

Grace ain't going away.

Can't spell sanitation without insanity, Reggie always says. *'Cause you gotta be crazy to take this fucking job . . .*

Perfect timing for a garbage strike. Turns out Grace was the straw that broke the camel's hump. *We're not getting paid enough to deal with this shit,* our union reps all said. Every goddamn garbageman is on mental health leave now. No pickup until our mayor gives us all a pay bump. Those bags pile up in the streets real quick, don't they? The union timed our strike to hit smack-dab during a heat wave, I swear, holding out until July to make their demands, drop dead center of the dog days, right when the temperature's sweltering so much, it bakes the trash right in their bags. We want folks to know how much they need us sanitation workers.

Tell me: Who runs this city?

Who?

The craziest part, though? I want—*need*—to go back to work. Hit the streets. I don't know what else to do with myself. My hands. If I'm not grabbing bags, I go crazy. Can't think straight in this heat. Our apartment's got this runty window unit. I'm sweating just sitting in the living room. I want to punch the walls. There's this itch in my muscles. Before long, it burns. Feels like my pitching arm is on fire. Only way to put it out is smashing these mountains.

Bash. Smash. Crash.

Don't poke the fucking bear. Rule number one. My kids know that. Should know that by now. Everybody's got to give me some fucking space. Let Dad sleep. I've been stewing in this apartment

for Lord knows how long, not knowing what the hell to do with my hands, just going out of my mind here, screaming in my skull, seeing babies digging into our kitchen trash, while Sam, all nine months of him, he won't stop wailing away, day and night, a tempest in a fucking teapot, so, yeah, a little peace and quiet isn't so much to ask for, is it? My muscles are all wound up by now. Like a spring, you know? A metal spring, coiling up tighter and tighter until—*SMASH. CRASH. HERE COMES THE TRASH.* Someone's getting smacked. Accidents happen.

All I want is to be back out there. In the streets.

I'm desperate to ride. Fucking desperate.

Something about Lorraine weaving down Flatbush Ave. at night. When we're done with our shift and Reggie's driving us back to dispatch, some mornings, just as the sun's rising, I'll hang off the rear loader. Simply grab onto the side railing and stand off the rear bumper. I'll lean my head back, close my eyes, and feel the blistering wind rush over my skin.

I swear, it's like the city itself is exhaling all over me. I feel its breath.

One month. It took our mayor a fucking month to cave. Now it's August and he's begging for us to come back. Pick up this city's shit. I would've let him twist a little longer, get a whiff of this reeking city for one more week, *just one more,* if I wasn't going out of my goddamn mind.

There he is, Reggie says our first night back. *The man of the hour.*

Miss me, asshole?

Like hell. Reggie laughs. *How you holding up, Mr. Hero?*

Peachy.

You didn't go soft on me, did you? Time off give you a beer belly?

You my mother now?

Seriously, though . . . You up for this? He doesn't want to say it. Her name. Grace.

Ready as I'll ever be, Ma. You want to change my diaper, too? Tuck me in?

Suit yourself, boss. Let's do this.

The heat finds us, even at night. The humidity clings to our skin. Gets us sweating even with the sun down. It's everywhere now. There's no escaping it. We want to be done with our shift before the sun thinks about rising, so we can avoid the hike in temperature.

Every minute that slips by, you feel the heat climb another degree. Reggie starts belting—*By seven, you're sweating. By eight, you're baked. By nine, you're blind . . .*

One month on strike and the streets are just lined with trash. As far as the eye can see. Block for block, you got these avalanches of black bags toppling over into the streets.

But goddamn does it ever feel good to ride through the night. Back in the saddle. Feel the air on my face. Through my hair. I breathe in deep, feel the heat settle into my lungs.

I love this fucking city. There ain't no mound of garbage I can't take down. No pile of trash that's going to stop me. I am the destroyer of mountains. The vanquisher of shit.

Fear me, motherfucker.

I'm counting all the flattened rats in the road. Vermin make these heaps their home. The heat slows them down. Makes them stupid. They could give a shit about traffic, coming and going without looking where they're scrambling, until—*splat*—they're tucking their skulls under the tires of taxis, bodies pressed flat against the asphalt. Intestines spill out of their mouths. Nobody picks that shit up, not even us. Leave it for the street sweepers. Rat pancakes frying up on every block. You need a spatula to scrape them off the pavement.

Here we go, Reggie calls out as he pulls Lorraine over. *Showtime, boss!*

We start at the corner of Ashland and DeKalb. Residential. Five-floor walk-up. Piece of cake. A dozen bags, no sweat. This stop will take thirty seconds, at most.

But there it is. This vibration in my hand. I thought it was Lorraine reverberating through my bones, but—no, this is me. I got the shakes. I figured the time off was enough to get over it, move on, but there's a tremble in my wrist. I can't help but hesitate, just for a sec, holding my gloved hand out until it steadies. But it doesn't. The vibrations won't stop.

What if Grace is in there, somewhere? Hiding in the trash?

Waiting for me?

Those seconds add up. When you've got blocks to go, you don't want to slow down the flow. That's all this is. Got to keep this city moving on time. *Ticktock, on the clock . . .*

You asleep back there? Reggie calls from behind the wheel.

Yeah, yeah . . . Nighty night.

Need a hand?

I'm good.

I make a fist. Feel the insulated lining of my gloves tighten around my fingers.

Here we go. Come on. Let's do this.

I lean in and grab a bag. It's soft. Sloshy. Lot of vegetables inside is my best guess.

No time to think about it. Into the hopper.

Next bag's all soggy. There's a squish to it. The plastic must be melting. Everything's a little mushy. I feel the heat lifting off each bag. Rises up in these faint black waves. Greasy shadows. What brand of garbage bags is this apartment using? They're usually made from an industrial heavy-duty plastic. Thicker than your regular Hefty Cinch Sak. The kind that doesn't rip. Sure seems

like they're skimping out on the name brand. This shit is thinner. Squelchier.

I get a tight grip with my gloves. There's that familiar squish. Its insides blend together, a stew of fluids and refuse sloshing around, like it's all a part of some living thing. An egg sac.

You find any furniture back there, Reggie says, *tell me . . . My girl's looking for a chair.*

I don't answer. My attention's on the shadows, swirling in black plastic puddles.

The bags. One of them wriggles.

Garbage bags writhe all the time. You got no idea how often a rat chews through the bottom of a pile. Makes itself at home inside. Got a free pad and a free meal for the night.

But this bag. It . . . pulses. From the inside out. Something about the way it shifts on its own makes me feel like I'm watching something swell within. Something wants out.

Ándale! Ándale! Reggie smacks Lorraine's horn twice. *Let's go go go!*

Next pile is down the street. We haven't hit our rhythm yet. Everything feels off. Maybe it's the heat. Maybe I'm just out of practice. I need to get my head in the game.

Just got to keep it together, I think. *Batten that shit down.*

Fuck it if you can't fry an egg on the sidewalk. Even at night, you feel it. The heat. Absorbs into the concrete. Streets are a fucking sponge for it. Holds on to their hotness, like a fever. The swelter of this city. Soaks up inside every last bag. They start to cook. Each one of them is like a Hot Pocket with shitty filling, getting microwaved by the sun.

Got this film of sweat soaking through my shirt, pooling in my boots. Every time I grab a bag, my gloves slither across my fingers. Got to tighten my grip so it doesn't slip. Last thing I need

is for a bag to rip, spilling its insides across the sidewalk. We get docked for that shit.

I grab a bag and it ruptures the second I pluck it up from the pile. *Fucking hell, motherfuckme.* Splits straight down the middle. Everything inside spills out at my feet.

Out comes a puppy.

I think it's a puppy. Got no fur on it, but still. Got to be a dog. I can see the knobs of its spine lining along its back, all the way to its tail. This dribble of gelatinous crap pools up underneath it. An amber sap of egg yolk and old yogurt covers its pale skin and Christ, all I can think of is amniotic fluid. It's like a newborn foal still covered in its mother. A dusting of coffee grounds leaves everything looking like rust. It's not a dog. Not a possum. Not a raccoon.

It's got fingers. Baby fingers.

This thing stretches its limbs, all covered in used tissues and candy wrappers. The rinds of melons and soggy strawberry slices. It could be a baby, but it can't be human.

It's a kid. Christ, it's a fucking kid. What the fuck is it doing in the garbage?

Everything okay back there? Reggie calls out, rocking me back to the block.

It's gone. Whatever it was. Scurried away on all fours.

All good. I'm trying to keep my voice steady. *We're good to go.*

Already? We just got here . . .

Yeah, on to the next one.

There's a medium-sized mound at 5th Ave. and Bergen. Only comes up to my waist. No biggie. I'll knock them all out in less than a minute.

Just as I'm closing in on the heap, I suddenly see the bottom bag start to wriggle. Could be rats. Cats. Fucking raccoon for all I know. There's a pulse to the plastic.

Reggie's mouthing off about something. I don't know what. My attention drifts.

This new girlfriend, he says—I think he says—to me, *she actually digs the smell. You believe that? She don't want me to shower! Not until after we . . . you know.*

The plastic splits. The trash bag blossoms. Petals of melon pool over the street.

You listening to me, man? She's got a kink for the stink . . .

I spot a dog crawl out. A hairless dog. Has to be. Battered, smothered, and covered.

Hey, yo-yo-yo! Mission control!

Not a dog. A kid. Had to be five or six. Looks just like my boys, only covered in ketchup. No hair. No eyebrows. Nothing but pale blue skin glowing under the streetlamps.

What the fuck, man? Where's your head at, boss?

Then the other bags begin to shift.

Let's go. I smack Lorraine twice, the wet slap of my glove pounding over the truck's engine, loud enough for Reggie to get the message. *Come on, come on, let's move it out!*

We're off to the next pile. The next.

Everything's fucking moving.

Every last pile.

Alive.

I shouldn't be here. I know that now. I should be at home. With my kids. It's too soon. I'm not ready. Not healthy. I'm seeing things. Shadows shifting. The heat's messing with me.

I want to go home. I want to hide under the covers in my kid's bed. I want to be asleep right now, like everyone else in this godforsaken city, not wide-awake at this hour. I want to—

Too late. There it is.

Mt. Trashmore.

I see its peak from halfway down the block, blotting out the surrounding buildings. Mother of God, it's huge . . . I don't recognize the skyline anymore. It's all different. Changed somehow. The silhouette of skyscrapers has reshaped itself, reconfiguring itself.

A new building has popped up overnight. Craggy spires and crooked rooftops.

No, hold up, that's not a building . . .

Trash bags.

Holy shit.

Heaps of garbage block out the apartment complex. At first, I figure the lights are all off—the whole building gone dark, a power outage—but no, fuck no, that's *plastic.* Black plastic. Oily shadows shimmering in the dark. A tower of trash rising up, eclipsing this city.

Do you see that?

See what? Reggie asks.

The trash.

Sure do, boss . . . How 'bout you do something about it? Trash ain't gonna take itself out.

Time to scale Mt. Trashmore.

I take a deep breath, standing before the pile. I got to crick my head back to take it all in. The outright majesticness of this mound. The sheer awe of it all. I've never seen anything like it. The bags reach over my head, towering above, threatening to topple down at any sec. There's just so many. They're all wriggling. Every last bag. A writhing pile. I'm watching them squirm. Something's pushing against the plastic, pressing its body against the inner lining, wrestling to tear its way out. Break free. Its black plastic bubbles, blisters, and splits.

Hatch.

Horns start honking at my back, but I'm not paying them mind. Those cars can turn around if they're in such a hurry. Ride the subway for once. Back the fuck off.

A tiny paw pushes against the plastic until it gives. Turns out it's not a paw, but a hand. A baby's hand. Pudgy fingers and everything. It pushes and pushes against the black egg until the plastic splits, a hiss of trapped gas spilling out. Now I smell warm cold cuts.

Out crawls a newborn . . . something or other. Could be a cat all covered in an afterbirth of orange juice and green pastrami. Got these umbilical cords clinging to its chest. A few blinks and I realize it's just spaghetti. It's crawling deeper into the trash pile.

I got to grab it. Before it gets away. Chase this baby into the trash.

Don't I? Isn't that why I'm here?

Take out the trash?

Horns are really laying into us now. Every son of a bitch blocked behind us just presses their palm flat against their steering wheel, honking in a steady stream.

What's going on, man? Reggie shouts. *You fall in or what?*

Just give me a sec, alright?

Clock's ticking. I don't want to be out here all night . . .

Just a second.

I see them. Spot them crawling across the concrete from the corner of my eye. Our garbage strike must've let them proliferate. Now they're everywhere. Hiding in plain sight.

Eggs. That's all these garbage bags are. Nothing but eggs lining every block in this city.

Yeah, but . . . what's growing inside?

We let it get out of hand. Sanitation shouldn't have let the trash pile up that high. We were just giving them a chance to grow. To spread. Now they're everywhere. In the streets.

Not on my fucking route.

I dive in.

Wade straight into that black morass of plastic. I got to push through. Force my way inside. The balls of this baby's feet are inches away. Just as I reach out to grab it—*Come here, you runty li'l fucker*—that slippery son of a bitch winnows its hips deeper into the pile.

I'm not about to let it get away. I'm tossing trash bags over my shoulder now, letting them land in the street. I don't care if they pop. I got to catch this thing.

The hell, man? Reggie won't let up. He's behind me—right behind my shoulder, I can tell—but his voice sounds so far away. *You fucking crazy? What the fuck are you doing?*

Don't come any closer. Just stay there—

I don't have my feet on the sidewalk anymore. I'm stepping on trash bags. Nothing feels solid. The terrain has gone all soft now. Squishy. Every step collapses under my boots.

The hell's gotten into you? Reggie shouts at my back. Might as well be miles away.

I got to catch them! I'm so deep into Mt. Trashmore, the bags start to collapse. Gravity grabs hold of the garbage and they all start to topple, rolling over me from above.

A cave-in.

Help!

Nothing from Reggie. I can't hear his voice anymore.

Help me! I'm stuck! My arms are pinned at my sides. My right hand, my pitching arm, is sandwiched between bags. I can feel the heat of it, radiating out from the plastic, like tar.

There's no light. No streetlamps. No sodium glow. Nothing but oily black shadows.

They're moving. Writhing. Something slithers against my shoulder. It's got a rubbery touch, like a child's hand wearing a

dish glove five sizes too big for their fingers. Used condoms tumble over the back of my neck, sweaty latex grazing my skin, dribbling down my spine.

The bag at my left presses against me. The black plastic is so tight, I can just barely make out the hollow cavity of a child's open mouth on the other side, desperate to breathe. To exhale.

It's not just one Cinch Sak. Christ, it's all of them. Every last garbage bag pulses. They're all hatching now . . . and I'm stranded in the middle of them.

A nest. That's all it is. Block for block. *Nests.*

I call out for Reggie again, but what's the use? I'm too deep. Too far down. There's no way any sound is making its way out from under here, the bags absorbing every last shout.

An egg begins to crack right in front of my face. Something slender presses against the soggy shell, pushing against the black plastic until the polyurethane peels, then splits.

Out comes a snout. Got the longest jaw. *A doe. A deer. A female deer*. That jawbone is just cantaloupe rinds. Crescent crusts of melon. No fur. Just skin. Pale fish-belly blue. Got some glue on it, all yellow. Egg yolk. I see some flecks of cracked shell caked to its lips.

This kid has got to be ten. The oldest one I've seen so far. He emerges, then crawls. Really wrestles his way out, too, spilling forward inch by inch. First his forelegs, all knobby, then the rest of his body eases out, all slathered in afterbirth of spaghetti sauce and tampons.

His eyes. He's so close, I can see right into his blinking eyes.

They're black. Pools of polyurethane. *Plastic*. His eyes are the color of garbage bags. Sleek rubber glistens, even in the absence of any light, blacker than the surrounding darkness.

He sees me.

Hisses.

He's born from the garbage. He can't stand up. Not yet. Not on his own. He struggles for balance, his haunches slickened in chicken grease. Olive oil. Bacon fat.

We're so close to each other—hugging distance—but this boy snaps his teeth at me. They're all crooked. Craggy. Look more like broken eggshells than teeth. Maybe they are.

I grab his arm but he slithers right out of my grip. I try to hold on, but the kid ends up taking my glove with him. Now my hand's free. Got no protection against this garbage.

Against them.

Fuck this. I start stomping. What the hell else am I going to do? I hear the hollow pop as each bag bursts underneath my boot. I can smell the warm swell of trapped gases as they pass over my face, released into the cramped space. Seedpods popping rotten pollen.

I'm going to kick my way out of here. I don't care what gets in my way.

Smash. Crash. Here comes the trashman, ready to bash, mash!

I spot a broom. Somebody tossed out a useless broom, bristles all bent. So I grab it. With both hands, I bring that broom down against my knee so hard, it snaps. Bingo.

Bring us your chicken bones, your lamb chops, your moldy bread and cheese . . .

I'm jabbing bags. Just stabbing the shit out of this trash.

Toss 'em all in the hopper, pull the lever, and listen to that squeeeeeeeeeeze . . .

I can climb out. Use both stakes as spikes and haul my body back up to the surface.

Increase the grease, cram that ham . . .

Back to the sidewalk. Aboveground.

Your trash is gone, thank you, ma'am!

Then the city just . . . gives. Happens all at once, I can't tell

where the collapse begins. Either above or below, I don't know, but a sinkhole opens up and all that trash just starts to drop.

Fuck it if I'm not falling. Alice tumbling into Wonderland. Feels like forever, just spinning through the darkness. I'm waiting to see the R train skid by any second now.

My face smacks against something soft. A squishy pillow.

Just another trash bag.

I fall end over end, getting a good roll going, plunging even farther down. I try to reach out and grab hold of something, *anything*, that might stop me, but it's not happening.

Not until I reach the very bottom.

Of what . . . I don't know. It's like a landfill beneath the city, bags everywhere. Covering the ground. The walls. Even the ceiling. Hell, they *are* the ceiling. This rubbery lining. Not individual bags anymore. A resin. A shellac of plastic. I'm inside a beehive, only it's black. Honeycombs of garbage bags cluster across the walls, over my head, dripping their juices.

Stalactites of trash.

There's no light down here. My eyes adjust to the dark. A sheen bounces off the plastic. Just the faintest glimmer. They twinkle, black stars, a galaxy of trash, as far as the . . .

Hold up. Those aren't stars.

They're eyes. Blinking back at me. I see them everywhere now. I can just barely make out the blackened silhouettes of their bodies. Little trash hatchlings slithering in closer.

Surrounding me.

If my kids ever ask about me, wanting to know what happened to their dad, tell them . . . tell them I wanted to protect them. Somebody's got to take out this city's trash.

Bash! Smash! Crash! Bash! Smash! Crash! Here comes the trash—

WE TAKE OFF OUR SKIN IN THE DARK

ERIC LaROCCA

There's a preferred way to burn a candle for the first time so that the wax melts properly and does not clot. There's a similar method to be practiced—a similar kind of careful and painstaking ritual of finesse—when I fully remove your dewy coat of skin at nighttime, when I unspool you muscle by muscle and drape your flesh over the back of a chair arranged at our little kitchen table. I'm told that all kinds of gods reveal themselves at nighttime, in the dark.

● ○

Tonight, I cradle you like a newborn lamb, the knife I've twisted into your gut gently slipping out and clattering on the floor beside us. *We don't need that anymore,* I say to you softly with a hope that my tenderness might unravel some of your resistance. It isn't long before I sense a dim pulse throbbing deep inside your skinless body like muffled thunder from storm clouds passing over us on a summer afternoon. You shiver like livid twilight and spill

out onto the tiled floor, a dark tide as black as jelly spreading farther and farther like your shadow. It's a hate-filled current and it seems to want to pull you away from me—away from any harm I can conjure, far away from my trembling hands patterned with the beads of your blood. But I had never meant to hurt you. *Such things are inevitable sometimes,* I whisper. You seem to accept the statement with the reserved dignity you only see in baroque paintings—painstakingly illustrated etchings of statespeople or men of noble birth. To me, you are those stylish, sophisticated things. You are consecrated sinew and hallowed muscle—a cathedral of divine flesh, an idol to be worshipped with such carefulness and devotion. Perhaps once I might have abandoned the thought that I would be worthy of entertaining, of praising such a sacred vessel. After all, I am nothing more than strands of wiry, unkempt hair the color of rust and little, broken bits of yellowing teeth. *I don't deserve your righteousness,* I whisper to you while you continue to tremble, perhaps a little shocked that I went through with the whole ordeal in the first place. If you are in agony, I know it will last for only a moment longer. Godly beings like you are capable of rejecting such agony, such exquisite suffering. *I wonder what you will look like when it finally happens,* I say, pulling you tighter against me and listening to the labored strain of your each and every breath. The way in which you wheeze like a kettle, the quiet manner in which you accept your temporary demise—it's almost too much for me to bear. *You are far too perfect to belong only to me.* I know for certain that I wouldn't have endured the throes of agony with such grace, such poise. That's why you are the holy being and I am merely the conduit for your rebirth. For the first time in a while, you lift your head slightly and regard me with those shimmering eyes—a quiet look of despair crawling at the corners. You've practiced it well enough. You ask me why I've done such a thing. You ask me why

I've removed all your skin and held you like a peasant mother cradling her dying child in some city gutter. *How could you do this to me?* you ask tenderly, almost too upset to speak. It's amusing to think that even in the final moments of your first life—the ending of your human existence—you're so unapologetically dedicated to the horrible ruse. You know that it had to be this way. You already know full well that all gods must endure cruel, merciless torment before they can ascend. I tell you this and you look at me queerly, as if it were a test. But I don't intend to fail this time.

● ○

You are a flawless cosmic basin that was always destined to be refilled with consecrated blood and then reborn. For the past three nights I have told you this. Your suit made of human skin was ill-fitting, and you often looked so tired, as if you were exhausted at the prospect of keeping up this meaningless charade. I chuckle when I think of how easily I could have ignored the telltale signs of your presence as some celestial being in hiding—a holy thing but only in secrecy. It wasn't a strange realization that came to me all at once like some other horrible truths revealed throughout your life—the sudden end of a marriage, the announcement of a loved one's death, unpleasant things like that. Instead, this recognition leaked into my mind slowly—a careful and precise drip that told me bit by bit, night after night, that there was something wrong with you. Nothing terribly wrong to cause alarm or panic, but rather a kind of notice that puts you on edge and prevents you from sleeping properly. When I finally accepted the revelation for what it was—that you were a sacred, hallowed being dressed in a human disguise—I found myself unmoored, unfettered, unable to go about even the most mundane daily tasks. You know this. You asked me what was wrong time after time. *Nothing, dear,* I'd say while we sat at the kitchen table.

After all, I didn't know what I could possibly say to you. I knew for certain that you wouldn't ever reveal your secret to me, but I also knew that to go on living the way we were would be totally pointless. Two people in love can certainly hide secrets from each other, but they cannot exist for long without telling truths to each other. Such things are facts. It is inevitable that secrets eat away at the strength, the integrity of any relationship—an acid that corrodes the spirit, the affection, the love shared between two people. I often wondered if the two of us were actually in love or if rather I was more in love with you. I still wonder if you actually care for me or if you were merely fearful of being on your own. In fact, there's a part of me that wonders if you arranged all of this to happen so that I could be the one to set you free. I tremble when I think of such an honor, such a remarkable kind of dignity. *After all, why me?* You could have had any man crawling at your feet. You always reminded me how you could even attract heterosexual men with your attractiveness, your charm. I believed you. I still do. It fills me with joy to think that you somehow selected me for this task—the gruesome project of slaughtering you so that you can rise again, so that you can perish and then finally come back in your truest, noblest form. I think of how many evenings we sat at the kitchen table, slicing through avocados as we prepared a summer salad, and I remember how you would glance at me when you noticed I was staring at you for a beat too long. *What are you thinking about, darling?* you would ask me with all the curiosity of a small child, your eyes widening with this rehearsed kind of inquisitiveness you must have expected all humans to understand and appreciate. I would smile and merely shrug, hoping you might know what I had planned for you—all the suffering I would make you endure for the sake of your beauty, your grace. I'd shake my head and whisper: *Nothing, dear.*

● ○

At midnight, while the two of us lie together on the bathroom floor—the place where I've murdered you—I think of cleaving you open and searching inside your carcass for the smallest, frailest of your bones. I wish to hold them, to keep them safe and protect them in a way that only another loved one could. I wonder if you'll let me inherit them when you finally pass over, when you finally ascend and take on your true form—a sacred deity, a godly horror. I can't understand why you'd deny me such a silly, meaningless request. After all, what use would you have for such petty trinkets once you've ascended? I hesitate to even call them trinkets. To me, they are divine bits broken off and plucked from distant constellations. You have always been wild, impossible to pin down. Perhaps that's what attracted me to you in the first place. I loved the notion that I never knew exactly where you were headed, what you were doing. I admired that spontaneity, that fervent desire to simply be one's true self. You can imagine my sheer, unadulterated horror when I came to the realization that you weren't actually what you said you were. You weren't a lively and energetic young man from the Berkshires, as you had once told me in a bar in Cambridge. Instead, you were so much more than that. You were this blessed, divine thing—a miraculous being lying dormant inside a slender shell that was eternally on the verge of being cracked open, your remnants being unraveled and exposed for the whole world to see. Or perhaps just for me to notice. Yes, I much prefer that. I much prefer the idea that you are not a gift for the world, but rather a gift for me—a thing to be revered, to be worshipped only by one person. It seems unfair to have to share you with others. Of course, we have discussed time and time again about the possibility of opening our relationship. *Men have such urges,* you'd tell

me. *It would be only natural to do this.* But I loathed the idea of you being passed inconsiderately from man to man. I detested the very notion that you'd pleasure others before returning to the home we had created together—our beautiful sanctuary, the refuge from the madness going on and on outside these walls. It's a pity that I've invited such carnage inside our home, but you must understand that it was only because I knew the situation was dire. It was imperative, after all. You needed me to do this, to accomplish this transgression before you could actually be what you're meant to be. If I had ignored the signs and symptoms, I might have watched you languish. I might have observed you decay slowly, the horrible rot licking away parts of you until you were threadbare and utterly broken. What good is a god that's been dissolved? What could possibly have become of you if I hadn't intervened and done what I did? I look at you while you slump there, your palsied hands trembling slightly and your mouth moving with muted words. I wonder if you'll thank me for all the good that I've done—the help I've provided—when you make the final ascension. Naturally, I never did any of this for the praise. I only did this because I knew you were in need of such a transformation. To be one's true self, to be so completely and utterly free—it's a special gift I'd give you again and again and again.

● ○

I imagine what you will look like when you reveal your form to me. I'm filled with such eagerness, such indescribable longing to see you and recognize the love that we once shared. I turn off all the lights in the room and hold you gently in the dark. There are moments—few and far between—when I hold you and I sense your body shivering slightly. I wonder if you'll pull yourself away and expose who you really are the same way a successful

magician might rematerialize after having disappeared. More dark blood trickles from the wound I've opened in your abdomen, and I can't help but wonder if you'll spill out from the hole I've invited there—a small, sharp thing that flops out onto the floor and then begins to grow in size until you've nearly swallowed the tiny room. But no such enchantment occurs in the dark. Instead, you remain nestled in my arms. Your exposed sinew and tendon feel like they're cooling. *Please let this work*, I say to your skinless body. I haven't yet entertained the thought that I've done this for nothing, that I've butchered you for some worthless suspicion that I invented on a whim one day. I can't bear the thought of that. It's far too horrible to admit. Once I might have entertained that revelation and truly considered it. But I've already done too much. I have believed so fervently in your powers, in your ability to be reborn. I can't quite accept the possibility that it might have been for nothing.

● ○

Hours pass, our nighttime shadows narrowing to thin black spines feathered in the corner of the small room, and you are finally and utterly without movement. You lie there without the beautiful dignity I had noticed earlier. It's now early in the morning. Daylight affords no one a sense of magic, a profound feeling of wonder. Instead, I'm forced to regard the disgusting mess I've made of your body. You no longer resemble the important people venerated in baroque paintings. Instead, you are vile and pathetic—a nasty, obscene thing and totally unsuitable to be worshipped. A horrible recognition to be made in the morning after a night of enchantment. I curse myself for thinking what I had initially thought of you—that you were a celestial creature in disguise, that you required a knife's encouragement to reveal your form. None of those things were true. You had tricked me.

Somehow you had fooled me into believing you were so much more than what you had originally presented. All people are capable of doing that, of course. But the dangerous ones are exceptionally good at it. Perhaps you were one of the dangerous ones all along. If that's the case, maybe it's for the best that I slaughtered you. Perhaps I was justified in taking your life, ending your existence so that others could not be fooled and beguiled by your horrible charm. I think of what's to be done with your lifeless body. There are places I can temporarily hide you, but certainly not for long. After all, your corpse will inevitably begin to rot and then I'll be exposed. When the police uncover what I've done, they won't believe my story—how I believed you were a divine creature that needed to be reborn. I'm distressed when I think of my foolishness—how passionately I believed in you, how I desperately wanted to believe that there were magical beings idling among us, waiting to be caught and revealed. There are no such things. It's stupid to think that there could be deities wandering in our midst, waiting to be killed so that they can be reborn and then finally ascend. I can't believe I held on to such an insipid notion. I feel so thoughtless. I bury my face into my hands and begin to sob. It's a deep, guttural cry that almost shocks me. I wasn't aware that I could be this hurt. I wasn't aware that I could release such an agonizing, distressing noise. In fact, it frightens me. Just then, something soft and warm runs along the length of my shoulder. *Was it someone's hand?* I can't be sure. I look up and I'm met with a pair of eyes that I immediately recognize—they're dark, almost impossibly so, but there's a little bit of emerald light reflecting inside them. *What's wrong, darling?* you ask me, your voice delicate and brittle with a strange kind of warmth. You pull me closer. *Nothing,* I tell you. *Nothing, dear.*

THE DOOR OF SLEEP

STEPHEN GRAHAM JONES

Her favorite song on the radio that summer was Terri Gibbs's "Somebody's Knockin'," so this must be the summer of 1981. It was, to Tonya, a spooky, plaintive song, one that made her eyes smile and her heart swell each time it came on. Though nine years old, she knew enough to relish how Terri Gibbs didn't ever reveal if the guy knocking on the door in the song was a boyfriend or the actual devil.

It was also the summer Tonya's mom's twin brother was living in his camper in their backyard. Tonya and her big sister, Sylvie, worshipped Uncle Lare—his name was sort of short for Larry, but nobody ever called him that. After lights-out, which was thirty minutes later in the summer, Tonya and Sylvie would creep down the hall from their bedroom, become shadows flitting across the living room, tiptoe out the back door by the kitchen table, and finally sit across the fire from Uncle Lare, the backyard not really immense or unexplored, but sneaking out made it feel magical like that. The fire was always in a crumbling,

cutoff barrel between the camper and the back fence. Tonya was fairly certain her and Sylvie's parents knew what was happening just from the smell of smoke on their clothes in the laundry, but Uncle Lare, their mom said, was harmless, was family, was a babysitter who just happened to live in the backyard for the moment. Their dad didn't completely agree—Uncle Lare wasn't welcome at the table, but he did have bathroom privileges—and the fact that one parent trusted Uncle Lare and the other was more suspicious only made their sometimes babysitter more legendary to Tonya and Sylvie.

In the glow of the fire, Uncle Lare sat in his lawn chair and regaled them with his tales from the road: following the Band, seeing once-in-a-lifetime sunsets in the desert, getting in fights in this or that bar, having epic run-ins with biker gangs and police. Tonya and Sylvie were sworn to secrecy, of course. Once, about halfway through June, their dad, saying it like he didn't want to have to be the bearer of this bad news, told the two of them that Uncle Lare was mostly recounting movies, just making himself the star in all of them, but Tonya knew he was just trying to kill the magic.

She chose to believe.

The week before the Fourth, Sylvie sneaked Molly, one of her friends from high school, in through the gate. Because Molly brought a six-pack and was making eyes at Uncle Lare, she was allowed to stay. But she had to, in Uncle Lare's words, "ante a story into the pot."

Molly didn't want to at first because this story, she said, was too scary, but she finally told it. It was how when her grandma's house was being built, one of the construction workers had gotten his arm cut off in an accident, and then died on the way to the hospital. She had lots of details about how many towels they tried to stop the blood with, but Tonya could tell that wasn't where the

scary part really was. Where it was, it turned out, which made her tighten her lips to hide her smile, was in how the ghost of that construction worker found his way back to the house after a few years, and Molly and her cousins would sometimes encounter him in the hallway late at night, where he was forever looking for his lost arm. You could tell it was him behind you in the darkness by if he grabbed hard onto your elbow like maybe he'd found what he was looking for, or found one that was close enough, anyway.

Molly shivered at the end, holding on to her own elbows, and for a moment Tonya wasn't sure she was seeing, Sylvie, dragging her bangs out of her face, was looking through her hair at their uncle. Like sneaking a look at him, but in a different way—seeing him through Molly's eyes, maybe.

Uncle Lare cracked another beer open, toasted Molly's story with it, and then said it reminded him of something he'd heard, about a shadow boy—"shadow boy" was all he knew to call him. Uncle Lare had heard the story when he was a kid, living down the street, so he wasn't sure of the details anymore, but he still had the gist of it: When everyone's asleep in the house at night, there's a shadow boy who steps down from the linen closet, or out from behind the couch, or climbs down through the attic door. What he does is walk around to all the sleeping people and insert two fingers—Uncle Lare held his first and middle up together—into the sleepers' mouths, to feel the wet, corrugated roofs up there.

While he was doing this, he angled his chin up and closed his eyes, trying to give all the sensation he could to his fingertips. Because this shadow boy, he has to find the exact right person.

This made Sylvie and Molly clutch onto each other, ready to shriek.

"And, when he finds the right one . . ." Uncle Lare said, his

eyes closed, and the way he finished that sentence was curling the two fingers he had in the imaginary mouth of a sleeper up sharply.

"*Click*," he said fast and sudden like a dog snapping at fingers, and Molly fell back off the toy truck she was balanced on.

"What?" Tonya said, leaning all the way into this.

"Some people, right up here," Uncle Lare said, opening his mouth to try to show, "they have this square hatch."

Tonya looked over to Sylvie, could tell she was feeling the roof of her mouth with her tongue. Tonya knew because she was already feeling for that hatch just the same.

"And when this shadow boy, when he pushes the hatch up, opening that little door, well," Uncle Lare said, shrugging. Looking down along the side of the camper and taking a long drink of his beer.

"Well what?" Molly asked.

"That's how he gets in," Uncle Lare said like it was so obvious, and Molly closed her eyes, hummed to herself.

Tonya was breathing deep and slow, hearing this.

"Your turn," Molly said to Tonya.

"She's too young," Sylvie said before Tonya could say anything. "She doesn't remember, I mean."

"Remember what?" Tonya asked.

"I shouldn't," Sylvie said, flashing her eyes to Uncle Lare and Molly. "This is . . . It's too real."

"Those are the best kind," Uncle Lare said, and passed her another beer, opening it on the way with one hand, which Tonya was always amazed by.

"You won't tell Mom and Dad?" Sylvie said importantly to Tonya.

Tonya shook her head no, never.

Sylvie breathed in, pursed her lips in argument with herself,

then finally shrugged, said Dale Johnston down the street—her first kiss, Tonya knew—who's lived in the neighborhood forever, probably since their mom and Uncle Lare grew up here, he used to play with this boy Geoffrey Riggs in third grade. Tonya hissed from this. Third was *her* grade.

"Used to?" she heard herself asking.

Sylvie pursed her lips, held her hand over Molly's for strength, and said Geoffrey Riggs had gone, you know, *missing*. Just disappeared—into a car, a storm drain, somebody's side door.

"And he used to live here . . ." Uncle Lare said, something hopeful to his voice.

Sylvie nodded, said, "It's how Neal got the house so cheap."

Neal was what she called Tonya's dad because she had a different one.

"Are you saying he's still there?" Molly asked, looking in the direction of the house.

Tonya wouldn't let herself look, was just staring at Sylvie.

"They never found him," she went on, her voice softer now. "But I don't think he ever found himself, either, if that makes sense? Part of him came home, I mean, what was left after . . . you know." The way she tilted her head over to Tonya meant she couldn't *say* what had happened to Geoffrey Riggs. "But, like that worker with the missing arm, he's still looking for his body, so he can be a little boy again."

For the rest of the night, until Sylvie told her it was time for little girls to go inside while big girls stayed out with Uncle Lare, Tonya was cataloging sounds she'd heard in the house, pencils she'd found in different orientations than she'd left them, and, lying in bed that night, she heard the camper door pulling shut in the backyard, but she didn't think Sylvie and Molly would ever go in there with Uncle Lare.

Why would they?

And, yeah, "1981," I know.

You don't have to believe me on this, but I'm not setting this there to avoid cell phones, or to shuttle these characters around before the whole world was a surveillance machine, when people could still slip through the cracks.

I think I just wanted "Somebody's Knockin'" lilting on the air. I really do like it, and if you read this, look the song up, like it, too—*score*, right? I've spread the gospel of Terri Gibbs a bit wider.

But as for why Tonya is a little girl and I never was, that's easy: I'm making this all up. If he were a boy, even with some other name than mine, then . . . he's going to be some version of me, isn't he?

Just to be sort of honest, here, my mom never had a twin, either. I had no uncle at all. I did have a sister, but she was younger than me. My only campfire stories were from the year I was in Scouts, but there was nothing traumatic on any of those overnight trips, just the usual hijinks.

All the same, I do feel a touch of kinship with Tonya. It's hard to put my finger on, but, when Sylvie cut her off, told her own spooky story instead—I felt for the kid. All you want when you're Tonya's age is to be included, and, suddenly, she isn't. Because she isn't old enough to "remember," even though that memory is made up, is just for fun, for campfire purposes.

I should admit, too, that Geoffrey Riggs is a guy I went to high school with. We never spoke—he was a football star, I was third seat in band, blowing my cornet in hopes it would inspire him to win the game—but I did always watch him, and the way he moved through the cafeteria, through the halls. How every doorway he passed through briefly became a frame for his iconic form. How I longed for him to stand there just one moment longer so I could etch him even deeper into my memory.

He died in a car crash not on prom night, but the night before, and sort of, like happens, stepped into legend, I guess? He's forever seventeen, I mean. A cautionary tale, sure, probably even saved some lives with what gets called his sacrifice, but . . . he's sort of the one who got away, too? The one who found the side door, and got to keep being himself.

Not everybody does.

Anyway, Tonya.

I want to watch her here. See what she does.

It's the end of summer now.

● ○

Tonya was the one who found him, Uncle Lare.

She was humming Terri Gibbs to herself and knocking on the door of the camper, sent to ask if he wanted an egg-and-bologna sandwich or not.

Uncle Lare was dead between the little sink and the couch that folded out into a bed. Not suicide, not drugs, just dead like some people get, surprise.

Tonya sat on the floor by him petting his hair smooth until Sylvie came out looking for them and screamed, and didn't stop screaming for the rest of the day. What her and Tonya's parents didn't know, preparing for the funeral, having the camper hauled away, calling all the relatives, was that Sylvie was still crying in the room because, she claimed to Tonya in a fierce, sobbing whisper, she had been in love with Uncle Lare. He was her "first," which was a thing she had to explain in hushed tones to Tonya.

It made Tonya cross her legs, clench her throat, ball her hand into a fist.

Two weeks later, Tonya woke before dawn to find Sylvie gone from her bed. She ran out into the street in her pajamas, hoping to see her sister receding.

On the kitchen table was the note written fast on a napkin, about how Sylvie was running away to find the real part of herself. It was the same as the note left behind in a detective show they'd watched as a family, but, on the show, the note had been a cover for murder.

Sylvie was back five days later, unmurdered, no big case to solve, but she was a different sister now. Her lip was split. She had different clothes on that didn't fit her. It felt like she was always looking past Tonya, even when they were the only two in the room.

The week after she came home, Sylvie locked the bathroom door, broke the drinking glass stationed by the cold-water faucet, and cut her wrists with it, then stood in the bathtub to keep her death from ruining the rug.

Tonya hid behind the couch in the living room and watched the medics carry her sister's thrashing form away. She was waiting for their eyes to lock for a moment, so she could see if Sylvie was still in there, but it never happened. Her mom, rushing out, trying to cover her head with a scarf like that mattered, stopped to hold Tonya by the shoulders, told her they were trusting her here alone since this was an emergency, did she understand?

Tonya nodded that she did, but she didn't. Not really.

In the bathroom of the now-empty house, she brushed her teeth like a good girl, having to dip her mouth under the faucet to get water, and then she put herself to bed, and if she heard the attic door opening or a footfall below the linen closet, she pretended she didn't.

Two weeks later, Sylvie was back, taking her pills every four hours, and never being alone anymore. Tonya was the main guard on her life.

Her mom explained about how the medication Sylvie was

on made her awake but also sort of asleep. It made her face blank, but the way her hands still trembled around a spoon or a straw, Tonya was pretty sure her sister was still in there somewhere, wrestling for herself.

But, wrestling with what? Or, who?

Tonya looked deep into Sylvie's eyes, trying to see, to know, to understand, and in reply Sylvie, her hand moving in jerky motions, ran her left sleeve up, to show what she'd carved into her skin in the hospital: a tic-tac-toe board with no *X*s or *O*s, but it was also a hash mark, and it was also a pound sign, and the abbreviation for "pound," Uncle Lare had explained to them—they already knew—was "lb.," which were his initials. So, this was the mark he left to prove he'd been somewhere when he didn't want everyone to know. And it was in Sylvie's skin forever now.

When her breathing at night got hitchy and irregular at the end of July, Tonya stepped over to her bed and watched, waiting. Sylvie's mouth was hanging open. Tonya checked the door, the hall, and finally she leaned over to peer up at the roof of her sister's mouth.

"Tonya!" her mom said, startling her.

"I'm just—" she said, not sure how to finish.

And now her dad was looming behind, in the hall.

"She let him in, I know she let him in," he pronounced about Sylvie, his shoulders and his voice all about sadness, and then Tonya's mom and dad were fighting in their bedroom again, like always lately.

She let him in.

Tonya reconsidered her sister.

Had she?

Using the penlight from the amusement park, Tonya leaned over her sister and looked into her mouth again, a scientist doing

her work, and I want to put a single line of black up there in the roof of Sylvie's mouth, just enough to suggest the edge of an opening of some sort, but . . . I don't know.

Aren't campfire stories only real in the backyard?

But what if Sylvie was right, and Tonya was too young to be taking part in this ritual of growing up?

I have a dim suspicion that bringing Molly back might work here—she can be an unwitting element of chaos, an instigator—but she was never even real to me, was just someone to start the whole spooky-stories thing. Well, that, and she brought the beer, which was important if that night was going to open up like it does.

I did know a girl named Molly years and years ago, I suppose, but this isn't her. Not even close.

And, I'm just seeing it: Tonya and Sylvie and Molly all have the letter *y* in their names, don't they? Huh. Can't win them all, I guess. I mean, yeah, I could global replace, that's easy as a keystroke or two, but . . . they've already *got* their names, don't they? Who am I to do some new violence to them, after everything else I'm dragging them through?

It doesn't mean anything, that *y* in all their names.

What does is the noise in the darkness of the garage.

It's Tonya.

We're in present tense now, yes.

She's crawled up onto her dad's workbench, is spidering her fingers across his sacred pegboard until . . . until . . .

She comes back with the long-reach nail punch. It's like a skinny railroad spike, but ten inches to most nail punches' three or four, and it's shaped more like a stop sign until the taper at the business end, its blunt tip mushroomed out because Tonya's dad doesn't use it to give nails in the baseboards one last tap, but to drive big things deeper.

It's cold, heavy, and perfect, and the reason I know about it is my wife and I just remodeled my study into a nursery because this hobby of mine is just that: a hobby. So: all new trim, and baseboards, and a casement for the door not exactly in keeping with the style of the rest of the house, like this room is different, special, maybe one where the rules don't hold the same—it's exactly the kind of magical a kid needs for their early years. I'm thrilled about all of this, too, please don't misunderstand. I can work at the kitchen table as easy as I can work at my own desk. Children are far more important. Family over hobbies and dreams, always.

But I'm just stalling because I know what's about to happen.

With her sister zonked on meds, Tonya is able to lean over her chest, line the punch up on the roof of her sister's mouth, and draw the mallet back. A hammer would be better, for that metal-on-metal *thunk*, but Tonya doesn't know tools, so just grabbed the mallet that, on the pegboard, looked biggest.

Sylvie *did* let him in, she knows. Not Uncle Lare, but Geoffrey Riggs.

All Tonya has to do now is let him back out. She imagines him in the cab of the tractor that's Sylvie's life. He's up there pulling handles and steering over and back, and Sylvie's banging her open hand on the cab of that tractor and crying because he's in her seat.

This is what sisters are for, though. They save each other.

"Hold on," Tonya says, and swings the mallet as hard as she can.

The nail punch opens a perfect little hatch in the roof of Sylvie's mouth, and it doesn't stop there, keeps going, doesn't have quite enough oomph to break through the top of the skull. Sylvie's left eye deviates radically, like tracking her life, leaking down onto the pillow.

Tonya steps back to the middle of the room and shines her dad's flashlight at her sister's face, waiting for the shadow she

knows is there to seep out like smoke, shape itself into a ghost boy suddenly without a boy. When that doesn't happen, she puts her sister's left hand around the nail punch, the mallet in her other hand, and then lies awake in her bed all night, waiting for her mother to come wake them for breakfast, singing the same song she always does.

This time, it stops halfway through a line, never gets to the rhyme.

• ◦

If I'd done this right, I guess I would have had Tonya practicing, looking for "The Door of Sleep"—which is what this wants to be called, I think—in cats and dogs in the neighborhood. It's a bit Dahmer, but it's really shorthand, isn't it? Like a smuggled-across communication, a signal, a nod of acknowledgment.

I don't want to go back, though.

I already wonder if I ever even finish this. You can't tell, but it's been three months since Tonya killed her sister. Of real time, *my* time, not story time.

I'm a dad now, rah-rah. What that means is all my extra minutes are used up before I ever get to them. I'm a washcloth being wrung over a utility sink, and I'm almost dry, but still that twisting squeeze keeps ratcheting around, probably until what hits the drain is one big dollop of blood.

But I'm being dramatic. Deny someone their sleep for long enough, they get grim, don't they?

And, yes, I seriously considered staging the crisp silhouette of Uncle Lare in a doorway at the end of the hall. Or, even better, having Tonya walk outside way after lights-out to sit at the fire with him one more time—maybe even right after she does what she did to Sylvie. That is, what Sylvie "did to herself," as far as

her parents and the medics and the law know. Which—I agree: They can really buy that, that she'd off herself in such an extreme manner?

Probably not. Unless, say . . . the other option is the little sister did it?

Yeah, I think it passes muster . . . *barely*. And the impinging factor, the pressure I have writing a story like this, that I have to balance against believability, is that I'm supposed to come up with novel death scenes, shocking kills, haunting imagery.

Hopefully a nail punch to the roof of the mouth qualifies?

That's not exactly what I'm interested in, though.

The same way Tonya was leaning over her sister, to look up into her mouth? I feel like that's what I'm doing now, with Tonya.

She's lying there, her covers pulled up prim and proper, and when her mother's song stops halfway through that one line, a line I'm being vague about because I can't hear it very well, she rolls over, sits up fast, and then the rest of that day and week and month and year happens, and it's next summer already.

Next summer in that same present tense, yes. I think I'm kind of gearing down into that from the past this opens up with because it starts out with almost a campfire tale delivery itself, "summary mode," flashlight under the face and the rest of those trappings, and that delivery's usually past tense, isn't? "*X* happened here *Y* years ago," until, *surprise*, the past is actually present. It's a good thrill, one you don't have to take too seriously—one you sign up for when you sit down across from your own Uncle Lare.

And, I say Tonya's who I'm interested in here, but I wonder if she's just my best bet for seeing the ghost in this house?

I think there is one, yes.

For Molly, it was a construction worker. For Uncle Lare, it was a shadow boy. For Sylvie, it was Geoffrey Riggs—and, again,

never mind that I knew the real Geoffrey Riggs. I'll go back and change his name when I'm done, if I'm *ever* done, what with diaper changes and baby monitors and wellness checks and dinners eaten pacing back and forth, my lower back singing with each step.

But, those campfire stories.

My instinct anytime I'm presented with three things at once, or one after the other, is that this is a shell game, where I'm supposed to pick the right one. So, in this case, with these three stories, I'm supposed to pick the *real* one, the other two just being distraction.

The construction worker is easy to dismiss, of course. It's a tale told over and over, in so many variations. I think why it's usually a missing arm and not a leg is that it means this "ghost" can shuffle up behind you for a fun jump scare.

But I can't decide between the shadow boy and Geoffrey Riggs.

I'm standing in the street in my head, am looking down at this folding table, at these three red cups hiding the ball, and . . . I don't know.

I blame Sylvie. She elided Uncle Lare's shadow boy with her secondhand story of Geoffrey Riggs. I am pretty sure she just made it up from whole cloth, on the spot, but . . . there's something there, too. Or, by using a real name, did I *put* something there?

Oh, but I get it now: The reason I can't decide which of these to invest in is simply because Sylvie's is just the shadow boy with more focus. With details. With that *name*. It does introduce the element of a kid who got snatched, suffered some unspeakable end, meaning what's left of him now has a grudge or a hunger, but . . . yeah, yeah. There's only *two* cups, not three, and I've already eliminated one, so: Shadow boy it is. Geoffrey Riggs.

I'm glad I didn't go back, have Sylvie tell a different story. I think this is the lucky path through to the end, maybe.

I mean, lucky for me.

Not for the people in this story.

Like I was saying, it's next summer already.

And Tonya's back in the garage.

• ◦

With Sylvie out of the picture, this has been a charmed year for Tonya. She can do no wrong. She's fragile: "She slept with her dead sister for that whole night and didn't even *know*!"

Instead of donating Sylvie's closet and dresser of clothes, Tonya's parents are saving them all for when she grows into them. Which says something about how immune adults can be to the vicissitudes of fashion, but it comes from a place of love, anyway.

They blame themselves for Sylvie, of course.

They should have listened better, watched closer. One night, Tonya's dad gets arrested for vandalism, even—his first brush with the law. He gets caught at the cemetery with a bottle of lighter fluid he's using to burn Uncle Lare's headstone, which is really just burning accelerant on stone. For most of the fall he sleeps in the guest room beside Tonya, and her mom, not wanting to occupy the bedroom since that makes her husband the good guy for "giving" it to her, stays up most nights in the living room, watching talk show reruns and infomercials.

It's a good year for Tonya, but a bad one for the family, and the house itself.

The square of yellow grass in the backyard where the camper squatted stays yellow, and the fire barrel still swirls black ash up when the wind blows, and nobody cares about any of it.

Finally, narrating it as she does it, explaining how the eighth or sixteenth or whatever of Blackfoot blood in her veins means

she's entitled to do this, Tonya's mom stands at the oval mirror in the hallway and uses scissors to chop her hair out in great grieving hanks, until Tonya's dad hugs her to him and they fall to their knees in the hall and hold each other, finally start sleeping in the same bedroom again.

Except.

Walking back from the bathroom on a school night in late May, Tonya looks up and sees her Uncle Lare coming for her in his tatty robe and slippers, his hair uncombed like always, his face hidden in shadow, but definitely that same cast she remembers from across the fire.

She falls back, runs silently through the living room, and is two houses down before her mom catches her, tackles her into the wet grass of the lawn and holds her there, telling her to wake up, wake up!

She was never asleep, though.

Just, she forgot her mom and Uncle Lare have always had basically the same face. Just, now, they also have pretty much the same hair.

Tonya's dad never wakes for this.

After this, after the last day of fourth grade, Tonya carries herself the same through the house, she sits in the same place at the table, but she's watching her mom in a new way, like trying to catch her when she doesn't know she's being watched, like she's going to give an evil leer while spreading jelly, or show her true face in an accidental reflection.

Twice, Tonya sees her mom scratching the top of her mouth with her tongue. It makes the loose skin under her jawline pooch down, from the muscles bunching up.

This is how Tonya knows.

Geoffrey Riggs is back.

All Tonya did when she used the nail punch on Sylvie was let

him back out. Tonya's dad must not be a good candidate, but her mom, having just lost her mirror image, or maybe because she found Sylvie first, must be compromised, cracked in a way that lets darkness in.

Tonya starts listening to the Terri Gibbs song again.

Somebody *is* knocking, she's pretty sure.

It might be her herself, even. And she's not really a sister anymore, so . . . what is she now?

She shakes that possibility from her head, and, for the next two weeks, she watches, she waits. When her parents are at work, her dad full-time, her mom part-, most of her shifts starting at three in the morning, Tonya turns the light on in the garage and uses her dad's workbench.

She knows now that the nail punch wasn't quite right. It was like using a battering ram on the door of sleep—there, I got the title in, now no editor can change it, right? It's got an anchor in the text.

There has to be something better on the pegboard, Tonya thinks, knows. Or . . . in the drawers of the tool chest? Her mom got the chest for Tonya's dad three Christmases ago, and he spent the rest of the week in a frenzy of organization.

What Tonya finally finds is an inch-and-a-quarter hole saw. It's basically a stout little saw blade looped into a circle, to go on a drill, for punching doorknob holes and the like—I'm actually not sure. I have a set of these, I don't know why, but I've never used them, am not that kind of handy. When I got *my* tool chest, though, and fell into the manic organizing hole I think's natural after a gift like that, I did snag my fingers on the grabby little teeth of these saws over and over, until I was wearing Band-Aids like gloves. Hole saws are wicked.

Problem is, though: They're *round*, where doors are supposed to be square.

Tonya solves this with her dad's vise. It's mounted at the opposite corner of the workbench from the grinder, which she's under strict orders to never touch, her having long "beautiful" hair.

What Tonya does is tighten the vise down on the hole saw until it's got two square sides. Then she rotates it over, flattens the remaining roundness down. It's not perfect—she finally has to wedge a scrap board under the hole saw in the vise to keep the bottom from bulging back to round, and then has to use a metal hammer to flatten the top, but the end result is a little door-shaped punch, hollow in the middle, with sharp teeth all around. It's even got the stud part coming out the back that's meant to go in the drill—perfect for the new mallet, which is still her choice instrument, I think because that soft head is quieter than a metal one.

The elegance of this hole saw makes her want to apologize to Sylvie for having been so crude with the nail punch.

This time, trying to do it right, she steals a mason jar from the kitchen and practices with the two-piece canning lid. If all she does is let Geoffrey Riggs free to feel his way into some other sleeper, then what use is all this effort?

She waits until her mom's back from book club, is zoned out on infomercials with one more glass of wine. Back in the master bedroom, Tonya's dad is watching his crime show on mute, reading the subtitles like he does late at night, so he doesn't keep the rest of the house awake.

Tonya paces her bedroom, going through all the steps in her head to get them just perfect, and, on the way to the living room, she pads barefoot into the kitchen, stands at the sink watching the backyard.

After long minutes, just like she knew would happen, the fire barrel exhales a breathful of sparks that trail up into the night.

Uncle Lare, giving her the nod from the other side.

She's doing the right thing, here.

What she doesn't realize—she's only ten now—is that she leaves the mason jar there by the sink, on the side with the sign that reads WASH ME.

In her left hand she has the square hole saw, holding it by the long stud, and in the right, heavy by her thigh, the blue-handled mallet still with its price tag.

For a hundred count—counting with her heartbeat, trying to make it slow—Tonya stands in the doorway between the kitchen and the living room, but her mom really is sleeping, she's pretty sure. The blue glow of the infomercials is like a flashlight shining up her body, deepening the scary shadows.

Because her mom's recliner will tip over if Tonya straddles her, she has to lean far over again. When the metal of the hole saw makes that bad sound against her mom's lower teeth, her mom starts to jerk awake.

This is when Tonya drives the mallet up, as hard as she can.

The teeth of the hole saw, each about a quarter-inch long, and, like I said, grabby as hell, a ragged kind of sharpness that must be good at hundreds of rounds per minute, they jam up into the top of Tonya's mom's mouth. But, with the hole saw not lined up quite perfectly, it's open mouth is also over Tonya's mom's teeth, meaning some of them jerk to the side or chip away, and the saw doesn't go as deep as it should, is wedged deep into the top gum, or gums, between the incisor and whatever's right beside the incisor.

The recliner tips back and Tonya goes with it, and, without this, her small self has no chance. With the momentum of this fall, though, with how her mom's hands reach out to the side like anybody's would, Tonya manages to get one last mallet swing in.

It's enough.

A burble of blood spurts from Tonya's mom's right nostril, her hands find Tonya's sides, trying to push her away, and then she's panicked, she's choking—

"Tonya!" Tonya's dad bellows from the hallway, and when Tonya looks up to him, she can almost see her name at his thighs like a bright subtitle, he's so loud with it.

Tonya rolls off, the stud part of the hole saw still standing up from her mom's mouth, and Tonya's dad rushes to his wife, his hands not sure where or if to touch, his eyes and breath not wanting to believe, and when he looks up to Tonya for the explanation he's maybe two seconds from not needing, as this is obviously what it is, Tonya's mallet comes sideways into the eggshell bone behind his right ear, and the head of the mallet is soft compared to a hammer, but its corners are hard. Hard enough.

Tonya's dad slumps over his wife, his left foot twitching fast, which is when Tonya realizes she left the jar in the kitchen.

But it doesn't matter.

In the glow from the television, she would be able to see any shadow boys standing up from this wreckage, and it's just her here.

What does this mean?

I think that's where I've been trying to get to this whole time, through all this blood and grief, all this destruction and misguided love.

Tonya's just staring down at what she's done.

Finally putting enough pieces together in her head to suspect there might be a different way to understand what's happened—what she's *done*, okay—she makes her way into the hall, pulls the box of photos out to stand on so she can look into the oval mirror.

She tilts her head up, trying to see into her own mouth, which is—

I don't want to do this, God.

Okay.

She's tilted her head back, is trying to look down past her face at her reflection, and what she feels more than really sees, it's three smoky fingers reaching up from inside her mouth. It was her all along, wasn't it? It was her Geoffrey Riggs sneaked into. His fingers wrap up around her top lip, around her nose, and it's the kind of handhold something climbing uses, needs, and it means—I guess it means that, inside her head, past this "door" or whatever, gravity and up/down is different.

Different for whatever's crawling out, birthing itself.

This is what I'm interested in: Geoffrey Riggs, standing from the twisted wreckage of his death-wrecked car; Geoffrey Riggs, coming alive under my pen, letter by letter, step by step, radiator steam shrouding his legs, his eyes fixed right on me.

But I don't think I want to stay there in that hallway with Tonya anymore.

It's best I just go down to the nursery that used to be my study, when I was going to be a writer, share my nightmares with the world.

Coincidentally—*ha*—we also have this antique oval mirror hanging over an umbrella stand in our hallway.

Though there's a pencil on the flat top of the umbrella stand by the notepad that I'm forever straightening, I won't stop to do it this time because I might look up into my reflection. My back is too straight for that right now, my nerves too jangly, my breathing too shallow and fast. But this could be from thirty hours of no sleep, I know. Believe me, I know.

Gregory's crying again, down there. He has been for the last twenty minutes. The eternal chorus I'm damned with, evidently.

But: "dramatic," pity me, I know.

Still.

The reason I'm not going to stop, flick the hallway light on, check my mouth in that mirror?

It's because Gregory, not Geoffrey, Gregory Gregory *Gregory*, he's pedaling his little socked feet in his crib, I know, he's waiting to see a face he recognizes and depends upon come into focus in his sky.

It'll be me. I'm the only one up this late.

And, I don't want to, I don't want to have to, but I know when I reach down for him, I can slip two fingers into his crying mouth. I can stretch my chin up, close my eyes, and I can feel the roof of his baby mouth for the presence I'm starting to think might be there, just a sharp push away. Just a single, wet *click*.

Babies have more than one fontanel, I think. We're told to be careful of that soft spot at the crown of their heads, since it can collapse at the slightest touch, crash splinters down into their just-forming brains. But there's another.

These babies were asleep a long time in the womb, weren't they?

I think this might mean that the little door in the top of their little mouths, somebody might be able to knock at it in *just* the right way—not to open it, leave it yawning, spilling, nobody wants that, but to nudge it shut, since it's been left open the slightest bit, is corrupting the waking world.

That's all I'm going to do here. If I push just hard enough, my fingers already curled, my arm doing most of that upward twitch, I think I can latch it back shut, and maybe get some sleep at last, never mind if there's a shadow girl standing in the doorway behind me. There's no rule saying I have to look there, at her.

Hold on, Gregory, Geoffrey.

Daddy's coming.

AT NIGHT, MY DAD

DAN CHAON

At night, my dad sits by my bed while I twitch, while my toes gnarl and my fingers scrabble and I cough up some phlegmy glossolalia.

● ○

It's always night when I wake up, ten o'clock, midnight, one in the morning, but nevertheless he's always there, holding me down while I seize and shudder and sweat, offering a sip of water and a pill, "to make you feel better," he says, and wipes the yellow goop from the corners of my eyes.

Here is my old childhood bedroom—the framed map of the Land of Make Believe, bookshelf stuffed with my collections of C. S. Lewis and Tolkien and Madeleine L'Engle, a calculus text-book from senior year of high school, which I'd defaced with a black marker—drawings of demons and ooze monsters and what I imagined satanic runes might look like. I used to enjoy reading up on exotic mental illnesses, wishing I had one.

• ◦

And now here I am. Meds for anxiety. Meds for psychosis. Meds for schizoaffective disorder and depression, meds to protect me from opiate withdrawal, meds that smooth out the other medications.

"Why is it always dark out?" I ask my dad when he brings me some soup.

And he's like, "Well." He stirs the spoon in the broth and scoops up some vegetables. "I mean," he says. "It's Minnesota. And it's winter. So . . ."

But the thing is, I can't seem to wake up during the daytime.

Last time I remember seeing the sun I was in rehab, and I was trying to drape a blanket over the window, and even though it was heavy gray wool the golden light crept in as a partial rectangle, and I knew if I put my hands near it I would get burned. I poked a finger into a sun mote and it felt like a puff of flame igniting down from my fingernail to the knuckle.

• ◦

This was six months ago? A year?

"What day is it?" I ask my dad as he picks up one of my dirty socks and a crumpled empty pack of cigarettes.

"It's Saturday," he says. He lets out the soft grunt he's started making when he straightens up. "The twenty-ninth." Then he spots an empty cereal bowl under the edge of my bed and frowns grimly, considers. He decides he has to collect it.

"Is it March?" I say. "It can't be April yet."

Grunt. He nabs the cereal bowl with Pokémon on it, the bowl of my youth, and sniffs it with melancholy displeasure. "It's February," he says in the gently corrective voice you might

use on an adult child who has been diagnosed with paranoid delusions.

"Wait," I say. "It was February last month."

• ○

Before this—six months ago? A year ago?—I was going to college at Loyola in Chicago and doing well enough, considering majoring in visual communication, and then one day in the fall this girl Sophie took my order at a donut shop on Sheridan Road, and she watched from the counter as I tore open six sugar packets and poured them into my coffee, and she came over and touched the back of my neck. "I know your type," she said. She had the smile of a person who knows how to wound you with insults and will still convince you she's just joking. *Oh,* I thought. *Interesting.*

My dad has the idea that Sophie somehow "led me astray" or whatever—if it wasn't for her, I wouldn't have gotten hooked on heroin, I wouldn't have had my "nervous breakdown," as he quaintly calls it—as if I were a sensitive artist who worked for a New York advertising agency in the 1960s. In an alternate universe, he imagines that if I didn't meet Sophie, I'd have graduated and gotten a job designing websites for some kind of semibenign corporation and I'd get married and give him a sweet little fat grandbaby. But in his fantasy, Sophie stole me from him, and I guess if it makes him feel better to reduce me to a blameless dupe, if the story helps him sleep, what kind of son would I be to deny him comfort?

The fact is, I was already messing with heroin before I met her. Fact is, he knew something was wrong with me when he sent me off to college, but he convinced himself everything would work out. He might as well have dropped a coin down a well and waited for his wish to come true.

• ○

Prospect Park is a neighborhood in Minneapolis, the kind of place where an assistant professor of sociology can buy a house and raise a family on a tree-lined street of older two-story homes. From my attic window I stare down at the snow falling and the plow truck with its blinking yellow lights drags past, its blades grinding the asphalt. February. I can see the old water tower, with its roof like a witch's hat. My hands spasm and I wipe away the constant slobber trickling out the side of my mouth. From outside not far beyond our yard I can hear whispers.

"You're still awake?" says my dad, and I turn and he's in the doorway with a glass of water and a bottle of pills. "If you're up all night, it's no wonder you have such a hard time getting out of bed in the morning."

According to my dad, he wakes me with difficulty at 10:00 a.m. and he drives me to therapy appointments and so forth, but I don't recall any of it. I'm not sure if I believe him. He says I have a doctor named Brooke, and she and I have hour-long conversations, and I take injections of Suboxone, and he says we went to a fast-food restaurant and got their spicy chicken sandwich, which I don't have any recollection of whatsoever. Is he lying?

But—*why* would he try to trick me?

His eyes shift. He glances at the screen my Xbox is connected to.

"How's *Elden Ring* going for you?" he says.

• ○

Sophie liked for me to put the needle in. I'd sit on the floor of my dorm room, crisscross applesauce, and she'd sit in my lap and lean her head back so her soft neck was exposed and you could see the pulsing blue veins and I'd cuddle her and give her

hickeys and lolling tongue kisses and she'd whisper, "Shoot me up, Scotty, shoot me up," and afterward she'd lotion her hands and idly jerk me off while we watched original episodes of *Star Trek* and chortled at the corniness of it and dozed—

● ○

I wake up and I'm withdrawing again. The ache is so bad in the sweet spots on my forearm, the place on the other side of the elbow where the veins will just pop for you, that's the worst, the phantom needle marks aren't there anymore but still they open and close like hungry mouths, burning, burning, and my legs cramp and uncramp from thigh to ankle. My feet jitter.

And now here's my dad with a glass of water and a heating pad. He puts a wet cloth on my hot forehead. "Shh," he says. "You're going to get better, you just have to weather it out."

● ○

Weather it out. That's what he used to say after my mom died—I was a junior in high school then, and I couldn't stand to be around him. The grasping, grief-addled shadow in my doorway, watching me sleep, the grinning breakfast goblin, gurgling with hopeful prattle as I shoveled cereal into my mouth and scrolled on my phone. "Do you want me to make my special tacos for dinner," he'd say. "Do you want to watch a movie. Let me show you a funny picture I took of the cat."

Hovering, scooping up my bowl before I'd barely finished eating and hurrying it to the dishwasher to be cleansed.

"He was such a nightmare," I told Sophie. "Like, cringy and fawning and exuding this sort of grayish spiritual glop. Like a vampire's familiar, you know what I mean?"

She threw back her head and laughed. "Daddy Renfield! Aw! How sweet!"

"It's creepy," I said. "If I asked him to bring me blood, actual human blood, he would probably do it, eventually. He could be talked into it."

"Oh my God, do it!" Sophie said. "Call him up. Ask him. Tell him you've been having such terrible cravings."

●○

When Sophie died—when I killed her by accident—it happened so much more quietly than you'd think. When you see people overdosing on TV, they go into convulsions and maybe oatmealy vomit pours out of their mouth, or bubbling spittle, etc. But Sophie just went to sleep and never awakened.

She was nestled in my lap with her head resting on my shoulder, eyes closed, a secretive smile on her face. It looked like she was having the best nap of all time, but her skin was cold, and rigor mortis had already begun to set in. When I realized what had happened, I had to push her stiffened body off of me.

●○

I wake up thrashing with the feeling of her corpse in my arms and Jesus fuck I'm withdrawing again worse than ever, I stiffen and my hands and feet flop like desperate fish and here is my dad with a goblet of blood—or possibly a mug of bouillon—telling me how much he loves me and everything is going to be okay. "I promise you're going to get better, I promise, I swear."

●○

He thinks my mom's death or Sophie or some combination triggered this. Or is it his fault? he wonders. Something he transmitted in his genes, some failure of parenting, some small cruelty he committed when I was but a baby, which fluttered,

butterfly-effectly, to transform me into the tormented creature you see before you?

● ○

Or was I always meant to be like this? I wake up and it's dark again and I shiver. I can hear the gravelly purr of the snowplow, dragging whispering voices behind it. I have seen pictures of us in photo albums, the three of us—mom and dad and baby, mom and dad and toddler, mom and dad and kindergartner—but it doesn't feel like any of this really happened. It's like they planted these images of childhood, of happiness, just to make me feel more lonely and lost.

● ○

The shakes are starting again.

My dad sometimes points out that I haven't used heroin in a long time. "You take a blood test before you get your Suboxone injection, so we would know if you had opioids in your system. Right?"

Did he think I was making it up? Playacting?

"No, no," he said in his cringy Renfield voice. "I'm sure what you're experiencing feels very real . . . to you."

● ○

Do you think I'm being punished? Have I been cursed? Is it like the old movie my dad likes, where that actor from *Ghostbusters* has to relive the same day over and over? He tries to kill himself but he can't die, he just wakes up and the day starts over again.

I was never prosecuted for murder or whatever, even though I was the one who pushed the fatal dose into Sophie's vein, it was my thumb on the plunger of the syringe.

And do you know that my mom never speaks to me anymore? I mean, she's dead, of course, but I can't remember the sound of her voice, or even anything she might have said to me. All I recall about her is the day when we had to go to the funeral home and identify her body before she was cremated. Apparently, even if a person dies in a hospital, you have to do this, and you stand there at a window while they uncover the face of a corpse on a slab. Here is the last image of your mom you will ever see, and then it is the only image.

"I should have never put you through that," my father told me later. "I regret it a lot! You were only sixteen, and I didn't expect her to look . . . Well. As bad as she did. But at the time I thought it was important for you to be there. For you to know it was real."

● ○

I hear his tread on the stair. The cramps are beginning to clench in my lower gut, and I'm guessing it's probably February 29 again, and there is probably a dirty spoon on the floor near my nightstand that has been collecting cat hair and he will grunt and bend to pick it up, and the snowplow will murmur past, and there will be a cup of some liquid that he will offer like a very chalice of light.

"I feel like you are getting better," he will say. "Here. Drink this."

THE NIGHT HOUSE

GEMMA FILES

They say there's nothing in the dark that isn't there in the light, but that's not always true. Yes, half of the world is always in darkness; yes, half the world is night. More than half. But the world is round and keeps on spinning, no matter what some morons on the Web might claim. So which half, and when? It should be obvious.

Should be.

Here's what you need to know—one thing, anyway—

The darkness is inside already: inside buildings, inside objects. Inside everything, even you. We're born into it. We carry it, and we make it. And it's the same sort of darkness, everywhere. The dark we're instinctively afraid of because it breeds monsters.

Because it breeds *us*.

We fear the night because when night falls, that's when the darkness inside things and people emerges, given immediate license. That's when anyone you meet on the road could be capable of . . . well, at least as much evil as none of us want to think

we're capable of, maybe more. Every dream is a wish, the old phrase goes, and night is when those wishes are released, when they brush up so close against reality that they start to come true. When every shadow darkens what it touches in turn, blending together until light is lost completely.

Unless what it meets is an even deeper darkness, one so deep it swallows our own darkness whole.

● ○

Of course, some of us learn hard truths about the daytime, as well.

Even now, so many years later, I don't much like being outside while the sun's up. It still strikes me as unsafe, or maybe just unfamiliar—too many strangers, too much noise. People tend to go with what they know, the wisdom of earliest childhood, whatever scripture those around you first made sure to scrimshaw deepest on the inside of your skull. Not saying it's impossible to overwrite these things, but it *is* hard, sometimes harder than seems worth the effort, depending on circumstances. Which probably explains why I only go to recovery groups that meet at night.

I've cycled through over a baker's dozen of these groups thus far, enrolling late and quitting quickly, sometimes for what seem (in hindsight) purely cosmetic reasons. Because it's not *surprising*, just more than a bit bemusing, how their leaders tend to present themselves similarly, whatever their physical appearance or background: Earnest, kind, patient, friendly. Apparently impossible to anger or perturb. Mommy-lite, or auntie/counselor, or Cool Teacher Storytime Leader at absolute best, gently but inexorably urging everyone else's participation—and that's when I start getting restless, feel my hackles rise and feet begin to itch. It's like being asked to disembowel yourself in public once

a week to convince a bunch of fellow Crohn's disease sufferers they don't have the ugliest intestines around, 'cause take a look at *these* sausages!

And everything done under the vaguely approving stare of some empty-smiling, flat-eyed leader-shill with a trauma story that sounds like patter because they've told it so many times to so many different survivors who they know damn well are still caught up in their own barely escaped nightmares; nobody's listening, on either side, and that's just fine for the immediate purpose, I guess. A bunch of robots running off the same sparky program, throwing too-familiar details at one another, but with hard plastic chairs, buzzing lights, and bad coffee. I take it as long as I can, before bouncing.

Ash (short for Ashley, which she hates and never uses) is different. Blatantly so. She brought alcohol to the first meeting, for one thing—cheap, strong, blended whiskey in an aluminum flask, which she smacked down next to the coffee urn before taking her own folding chair. "That's not for me," she told us as we stared. "I've stopped. But if *you* find it helpful to get through some of the stuff you want to say, least for an evening, then go for it. This isn't AA, *or* NA. Same token, though. Anybody who tries that and fucks up? Be warned, I *will* dump your ass on the sidewalk and not look back. We focus on one healing process at a time here. Anything else is your own lookout."

I liked her from that moment on. I still like her now. I like all these people.

I do keep on making that mistake.

● ○

The day we found the Night House was overcast but verging into twilight, horizon low, and the dark was opening wide. Driving on fumes, in formation: Him in the first car, me in the last, sitting

next to my little sister Scarlett as one of our mothers drove. The van in between, three of our other mothers shepherding my youngest siblings. I was the oldest now, since Blue and Indi ran off—or since *He* ran them off, maybe. There's more than enough similar situations where the boys don't tend to be allowed to stick around long, after puberty, not that I would've known that, back then.

I'll never get to know what adult names He would have chosen for them, I remember thinking. *And they'll never get to know mine, when He chooses it for me.*

My childhood was different from yours, almost certainly. Hopefully so.

We didn't know where we were going, just that we'd had to leave, like always. No more money, too much scrutiny. People calling the police every time they saw us kids out walking together, foraging the vacant lots, gathering stovewood. Plus, the crawls weren't going that well anymore, not with Blue and Indi gone—"crawl" cut down from creepy-crawl, something He'd stolen from Charles Manson, which basically meant scouting around at night for places you could break into easily, then grabbing whatever food, batteries, clothing, appliances, or other potential salable goods came to hand. I knew He wanted me to take charge of the little kids on that front, teach them by example. And if I didn't step up and do it myself before He made me, I'd suffer for it.

I still remember my own training, every day, when it came to what to do if you got caught on a crawl: Grab something, break it, make a sharp edge—don't cut, punch; stick it in, twist it, pull it back out. Then hurt whoever you have to with it, wreck their bodies as effectively as possible. Create a hole, deep and messy, where two veins meet; let out some air, some blood. Let out the ghost.

My mothers taught me this mantra through sheer repetition, trial and error, and painful physical punishment, the same way He taught them. He wanted us to be strong, just not strong enough to leave. He wanted us to know how to defend ourselves because we were His property—Him, my biological father, and Blue's, and Indi's. Father to all of us, in both that and every other sense, too, except for a few of those to whom He was also husband.

I was taught since toddlerhood to examine things without seeming to look at them, cast my attention out 360 degrees whenever forced to interact with heathens, clock and codify those around me constantly. Taught to steal and lie and hurt without guilt because everyone unlucky enough to be born outside our enchanted circle was already doomed and damned, already dead, and just didn't know it. Already halfway into the fire, burning forever. So what did it matter, what I did or didn't do to them? What did anything, anyone, matter?

Only we mattered, and only because of Him. Which meant only He mattered—but without us to pray to Him and steal for Him, to impregnate and to banish, to fuck and to punish, how would He even have known He existed?

Which, in hindsight, made Him just like any *other* god, I guess.

Mother Joan, Mother Jane. Mother Jean and Mother Jenny. Mother Janet, Mother Jasika, Mother Jael. My mothers.

I came out of one of them, but which one? That was the question. One none of them would ever even dare to *try* to answer, not within His potential hearing... and He was listening, always.

Our destroyed selves, living sacrifices to Him. Hollowed and broken and empty.

But no, there was something else inside me, even then, always was.

The possibility of it haunted me back then, like what turned out to haunt the Night House still haunts it today.

● ○

I know what you're thinking: *Dude, that's some weird shit. What were you, raised in a cult?*

(Long pause, eye contact held with a level gaze, not stating the obvious.)

Oh man, I'm so sorry; I didn't know.

It's fine. How could you?

I mean, you just seem so . . .

Normal?

Yeah, kind of. So—when did you leave?

Well . . .

. . . It's complicated.

● ○

Anyhow, the Night House.

We didn't buy it; it was just waiting for us, abandoned. No one left to buy it *from*, probably, not that any of us checked. It was synchronicity, the universe unfolding itself, giving us gifts. A handy answered prayer—but no, not that: *He* didn't need to pray. Us, either, we'd been taught—except to Him.

Just another mystery of the sort that never has a solution, i.e., a religious one. How God—*one* God—can be three and one at the same time, for example; how wine can be suddenly made blood, or bread, flesh. How three different faiths can share most of the same scriptures and acknowledge most of the same prophets, but still go on killing each other over the assumption that their personal version of the One True Creator is better than anybody else's. Or how said creator—*any* creator—can love us enough to assemble us from nothingness, supposedly, only to leave us alone

to blunder around down here in the endless night forever, moving from darkness to darkness to darkness.

Do I sound bitter? Looking back, I know now that I must have lost my faith long before I left my church, which was also (by necessity, as well as design) my home. And this house . . .

. . . As you might guess, it's where that loss finally became apparent.

The house sat inside a thicket, branches and trunks grown so close-knit it seemed from the outside like a single, massive tree, 'til you looked up and saw a sheaf of rucked-together roof shingles poking out the top. That's how we spotted it. Fold yourself through the gaps, though, feel your way without seeing, and eventually your hands would touch wood, touch glass, touch brick. The trees kept it weirdly intact, like they held it together. A tight embrace.

Inside, the house was tall and narrow. A cellar with storm doors, then three stories stacked on top, floor space decreasing by increments. The attic was the smallest, almost closet-sized, yet with a tiny door leading off it into an even tinier side storage area. That's where He made us set up the temple.

Always a space like that in every place we occupied—hot, and dark, and close. A place to kneel and think about whatever it was He said you'd done wrong until you couldn't remember whether or not you'd done it. A place to lose what little sense of yourself you had. Once it was a box, hammered together from rough, unfinished boards full of splinters and painted black on the inside; once it was a trunk big enough to crawl inside, bound tight with straps and tipped up on its end against one wall, kept locked until you stopped crying, puking, answering back.

And here it was *this* place, with the door's lintel only slightly higher than its low, low ceiling, a coffin-sized space whose floor was tiled in sandpaper and pocked irregularly with square-head

nails. No windows, no light, door handle on the inside knocked off so you won't tempt yourself with reaching for an exit. And after you've been in there long enough, it's like a lid in your mind slides open because kneeling on sandpaper is better than trying to stand or crouch, even with the nails wearing holes in your knees; the pain becomes a hum, a frequency tuning you to a different station. Which is when you open your eyes at last, only to find the whole inside of the room watching you back.

That's where I saw it, for the first time—felt it, maybe. There in the dark, the *true* dark . . . not the kind that seemed to seep in everywhere else like a dimming bulb, so you had to squint to see, even in the middle of the day . . . with nothing else around to distract me.

A touch, more inside me than on me, fluttering through, vague and cold and indistinct. Plus the barest shade of a voice, asking:

Who are you?

Why are you here?

Who said you could be here?

This is my *house.*

It didn't scare me, though—not any more than normal, at any rate. Not any more than anything else did. Because I'd never developed any of the self-protective instincts a person who wasn't born into what I was does. Because, you see, I was *used* to being scared.

So here was the problem, and it took me quite a while to solve it . . . though in hindsight, I'm sort of proud of myself that I did. When every place you come to already seems full of fear—because your normal, everyday life is full of fear—how can you possibly trust yourself to figure out that a house is haunted?

How indeed.

● ○

"The Trilectors used to tell us water fasting would help us meet our True Selves," Derek puts in, eagerly, when I pause a minute to figure out what to say next. He's got big gaunt hands, a scraggly beard, and teeth too white and even to be real, but he always relaxes when he sits down in the circle. "'Course, when your blood sugar's crashing and they sneak a hit of LSD into your pitcher, it's no goddam surprise you're gonna meet *something* feels like some kinda divine messenger."

Ash nods. "Which is just another example of Lesson #2, and I know you know it, but I love hearing you say it, so what is it again?" With a fierce grin as we cheerfully repeat it along with her: "*Cultists—fucking—lie!*" She laughs; we do, too. There's more laughter in these meetings than I've heard in years. Something aches inside me.

"Do you think that was it, Anke?" Jiayi asks me in her soft, heavy accent. Like Derek, she looks older than she is, doughily pudgy with limp black hair, but she's always been incredibly kind. Her group—apparently a Falun Gong chapter that went rogue, which takes some doing—expelled her after her third miscarriage in a row. "If you were not, not *scared* enough in the box, then perhaps He, or those women, gave you something. To make you *more* scared."

I sip my coffee.

"Always a possibility," I say.

• ◦

I started to dream, after that—dream in that same voice. Its voice. *Her* voice.

(Yes, definitely Her, with a big *H*.)

(Just like Him.)

Dreams like a river, current-driven and washed half mad, an internal monologue. Here's how they sounded:

This has always been your house. Maybe you were born here; maybe you died here. Maybe you live here still. Sometimes you wonder, given the unfamiliar items you encounter as you do your chores, but . . . no, no, you're sure, you think, whenever the question occurs to you. You're almost *sure.*

Drifting from room to room on a cyclic track of task-memory, occupying every era the house passes through at once—upstairs and downstairs, at the same time. And always with that blending of time, minute shoehorned into minute 'til the chain of them bends and snaps, hours gone with a stutter or jerk, the slow spin of sun, stars, evening and dawn fusing somehow into some deeper, darker night that never goes away.

Things reset, again and again. Things jell, things freeze. The air gone suddenly solid around you, everything muffled, blood-slosh and beat dimmed by whatever keeps you rigid, motionless. Like a dead thing in aspic, waiting to be eaten. A dead—

(thing)

—moment, echoing, with no one to listen to it.

Sometimes you look up, abruptly aware of a noise whose source you can't identify; it sounds like a gasp, a drawn breath, a moan. Like half a word in a voice you almost think you recognize, before you forget once more why it matters that you should try to.

This faintest trauma-trace, left behind, and shrinking. A hair-fine sliver dug deep in time's own meat and sore with it, aching, infected: a glass shard stuck in the world's own skin, just itching for someone to dig 'til they tweeze it forth and throw it down in a bright red splash, grinding it smaller yet beneath their heel.

And sometimes you still hurt, or think you do, and sometimes you don't hurt at all anymore, or not so much that you notice.

Always here, caught and fading. Dried to a smear. Soon you'll be gone altogether. And you can't tell if that's what you wanted to

happen or not anymore, if that's what you've spent most of your time longing for, these many, many years.

Or if that's what you're most afraid of.

Just dozing upstairs and downstairs at the same time, lying on a bed that's no longer there (so you seem to float), inside a room that's no longer there (so you're half in, half out of the two rooms that are). Aware of noises you can't identify, whose source you can't trace, and when you run across people they don't seem human to you—trapped inside time, apportioned and scattered: a leg here, a hand there, a head grinning and blinking at you from inside a cabinet. Fingers grasping the frame of a door, with nothing else attached.

And sometimes you hurt, and sometimes you don't. Sometimes your wounds unseam. You leave blood trailing behind you like red string, looping from object to object. Sometimes the breath of your passage pulls the string taut, tight, and the objects linked by it fall, some of them breaking—a crash, a clatter, a spasm of undirected rage and hatred. The only sort of scream that's left to you.

Try to leave and you just reset, forget that you haven't always been here, in this one moment, this endless inner dark, this red, repetitive moment of decision. So you don't do that anymore.

That's one thing different, anyhow.

Cold, so cold. Always cold. It doesn't matter what you're doing. It doesn't matter where you find yourself; you're always here. Where else would you ever be?

An empty house, for no one. A full house, far too *full. Both. Neither. And all for you.*

● ○

The room is silent for a long time.

"Jesus jumping Christ on a crutch," says Will at last, with something not quite a laugh. He bailed on his doomsday-prep

militia when they made the mistake of letting him travel out of state on an arms-purchase trip, and he fell hard for a girl who convinced him to go straight to the local FBI field office, hormones driving the smart choice, for once. They're living together now under different names. "If they did give you something, dude, I wanna try some of that."

"Got the point, though, didn't you?" says Ash. She looks pale, too, but she's got her mission between her teeth like a bit. She ticks points off on her fingers as she notes them. "Destabilizing memories. Paralysis. Untrustworthy perceptions. Trauma that is very fucking deliberately not *allowed* to heal." I've always loved that Ash never feels any need to hide her anger. "That dream's the perfect representation of what Anke went through. What everybody here's gone through, in one way or another." She looks at me. "And that's Lesson #1, right, Anke?"

I need a moment. "If you can't stop thinking it, then it just might be the truth," I say. It's harder than I expect, and they hear it in my voice. They wait while I try to collect myself. The kindness only makes it hurt more.

The worst lies are always the ones you don't need anything but the truth to say.

● ○

Tide-caught, Her dim thoughts seeping up toward us from far, far down. She'd been here a long time, I slowly came to understand—alone, but never lonely. Everything only to Her liking, at last; a place for everything, and everything in its place.

Until we came, at least.

I remember Him looking around with satisfaction after our work was done: clearing and cleaning, sanding and painting, disinfection. The vermin made short work of. "This house is *ours* now," He proclaimed proudly.

Someone disagrees, I thought, but didn't say; always the best idea to keep your mouth shut, around Him—your dumb mouth, your smart mouth. The safest option in an utterly unsafe world.

And kept my head down for the next month at least, knowing I was stranded without options or choice, caught between the two of them.

● ○

This is my *house.* Mine, *not yours. Never yours.*

(I know, ma'am. I'm sorry.)

Who are *these women, little girl? That man?*

(He's Him. Who He is. We belong to Him.)

No, you don't.

No one belongs to anyone.

Does he make you stay?

(Yes.)

If he wasn't here, would you go?

(. . . Yes.)

I would, anyhow. I knew that much.

. . . *Well, then,* the voice inside my head said with satisfaction.

I could have warned Him about what She was planning, I guess, after that. Warned *them.*

But I didn't.

● ○

"I'm gonna hit pause on you for a second, Anke," Ash says. She looks around at us. "I forget if this is Lesson #4 or #5, but I'm guessing you know which one I mean?"

It's Jiayi who answers, surprisingly; she's staring at the floor but her voice is steady. "Nobody judges what someone else has to do," she says. Around the circle, people nod.

Ash leans forward, elbows on knees, hands clasped. "I'm not

a lawyer or a shrink or a priest, guys. Nobody here is. The only protection we have is each other. No leaks. So if anybody doesn't want to risk hearing something they can't stay quiet about, you better go upstairs. Last chance."

After a moment, Will rises. He shrugs guiltily at me as he leaves, but I don't blame him; he's still got federal agents looking over his shoulder. He's the only one. Ash watches him close the door and then looks back at me. So do Derek, Jiayi, and the rest.

"Say what you need to say, Anke," she tells me. "And stop when you have to."

• ○

In one way, He *was* like a prophet; He had the ability to change His teachings on a whim, making whatever swerve He came up with sound like just the next logical, inevitable step in a well-thought-out plan only He knew best. Henceforth, He proclaimed, we'd only go out at night, resting inside during the day. None had any right to see our comings and goings. The days of the recent plague had been a foreshadowing, He said: While the heathens rejoined their ridiculous, meaningless bustlings, we were no longer of their world. We would go out only to take our due, and wait within until . . .

. . . Well, that part He was never too clear on.

Daylight became the reddish glow behind drawn curtains. We boarded up the windows to hide our lanterns, fires, and candles. We mastered the paths in and out between the trees with sure, blind feet, learning the sounds of the night, of the nearby city. We stole food from grocery store skips, blankets from donation boxes. Our eyes grew painfully sensitive to light. And He became more serene, more peaceful than we'd seen in months. But then, why shouldn't He? He had what He'd wanted all along: a tiny little pocket universe, hidden from the sun and the world,

full of nothing but His servants. The nights passed by like slow, unchanging dreams.

Then He fell down the stairs.

He raved and cursed and screamed at Mother Jael, though she hadn't even been in the house when it happened: *Treacherous whore! Bitch! Filthy slut!* And He ordered the rest of us to take turns whipping her, since He couldn't stand. I tried to be as gentle as I could, but some of the others must still have believed Him; by the time He was satisfied, she was a bleeding, sobbing heap. *Any of you pulls this kind of shit again,* He snarled as she wept, *and you'll be fucking praying to get off* this *easy.*

Three nights later, as He rested His splinted leg in bed waiting sullenly for his meal, the heavy oaken bookshelf toppled over on Him. It was empty, so He took nothing worse than bruises, but when some of the children ran to answer his yells (me among them), we did something far more hurtful, without ever thinking to. We laughed. Laughed . . . at *Him*.

All the children got beaten, this time. But I could see He'd made His first real mistake. We might not know who our mothers were, but *they* knew. No matter how they feared or adored Him, they couldn't easily turn His rage on their own daughters, not the way they could on each other. Some of them must have understood the truth in our tears and pleadings, as well: None of us had done this. Nobody knew how it had happened. They threw quick looks at each other, looks they were careful not to let Him see.

I knew, of course. I slipped into the temple during the day, rolling myself up into a small, silent ball. Not thinking so much as just letting what I knew sit quiet in my head, waiting—waiting to be picked up, turned over, and examined, almost aimlessly. The air was sweltering and stuffy.

(You have to stop.)

No answer.

(He won't go. He'll just stay, and keep on hurting us.)

The house seemed to boil for a minute, like She was simmering along with it.

(You know He beats us, right? You saw. What he did to me . . .)

Everything he did to me was what I meant. To us. Taking advantage in every possible way because our mothers let Him. Because they'd given Him us, along with themselves.

Because why the fuck does anyone start a cult? To do whatever they want, and feel justified in doing it. Feel wanted. Feel *loved*, even by the ones who also hate them most.

I knew She knew what I meant, deep inside me. She'd forgotten a lot of Her life, I think; maybe She'd *made* herself forget, folded trauma over her like a blanket and dived deep, trying to drown. How She'd suffered, and who'd made her suffer; who She'd killed, or been killed by, or both. That She'd woken up here afterward, alone but never lonely, queen of all She surveyed. That this house, this empty house (*and all for Her*) had become not just everything She had of heaven, but everything She needed . . . She who needed nothing, anymore, aside from what she'd decided was forever Hers. She who was barely more than a smudge of motiveless rage, a memory of nameless hunger. A possessive, selfish queen on a throne made from splayed and moldy bones.

But I knew how to deal with something like Her, or thought I did.

What makes you think I care what He does to you? She answered at last, so quiet I could barely pick the words from the sigh, the thrum, a single phantom finger dug into my chest fading further away with every sketch of a syllable, until it was gone. Before then the sigh went out, too, like a light. Nothing but black on black in that hot, hot little room.

Okay, I thought. *Fine.*

So it was up to *me* to do something, like usual, no matter what it cost. Just so long as the only one who hurt the worst was me.

(Fuck you, then, dead woman. *My* family's still alive. And they need help.)

As if on cue I heard Mother Jasika from downstairs, calling loud but not *too* loud, voice half-cracked with fear: "Lilac, where are you? He's asking for you, gal. Lilac? Don't make Him mad!"

Mad, right, or madder than He already was. I understood.

"Coming, Mom," I told her, getting up. And closed the door behind me.

● ○

Nothing for almost a week, aside from pain—me putting myself between Him and my siblings, Him and my mothers. Bruises and blood and cracked teeth, damage inside and out. Sometimes I caught Him looking at me sideways, like He might've thought I was enjoying this on some level, too much so to be worth the effort . . . But guys like Him, they're kind of lazy where it counts, aren't they? Offer them the easy way out, they'll almost always take it.

Still, we could feel something building. The house was watching, at first dispassionately, but consistently. Increasingly disapproving.

Please, I thought. *Please, please, please . . .*

And then it was night again. Some of our mothers were getting ready to go out and crawl, the rest trying to keep themselves and everybody else out of His way as He sat at the head of the table, brooding and drinking, drinking and brooding. Once upon a time he'd said alcohol made you stupid, that's why you could find it in corner stores. That was before He found those crates full of dusty wine bottles suddenly spilled out from that bolt-hole

underneath the stairs—tripped over 'em, almost, just when He'd graduated to stumping around with a pair of canes, making His leg jolt and His wrist creak as he grabbed for a doorframe to stop Himself falling. Which meant He just *had* to make us drag them into the kitchen and stick them next to His chair, handy for grabbing.

Then a heavy china plate I'd just finished drying leapt off the counter the instant I put it down, whipping through my fingers to break right across His head as He was turning to look at me; He slapped both hands up against the wreckage, blood leaking through His fingers, porcelain shards clattered across the floor. I stared. Beside me, Scarlett screamed, as much at me as at Him. She'd seen the plate move by itself. She *knew.*

Which of you bitches?! He yelled, the way we knew He would. "Me," I answered automatically. Hearing something hiss inside my head at the same time, like rotten linen tearing: Shut up*, girl. Stay quiet. Let me—*

(I can't. You know why.)

No reply. Just Him stamping His way up to loom full-size over me, even drunk and with the cane to help him, grabbing me by the hair. Hissing: *Always fucking* you*, Lilac.*

That's right, I thought, neck too twisted to talk. *Dad.*

Heard our mothers screaming—for each other, at the kids, in general. *Not* at Him; never that. Not that I expected them to. Because I was just *done,* suddenly, more than ready to die if it made my point, and She—I think She could tell? Just still wasn't completely certain whether or not it was worth going back on Her own words, even now . . .

That's when Scarlett surprised us all by jumping at him, blurting out: "Don't! She didn't—it was the *ghost*—"

It's never good to sound crazy, even among other crazy people. Even He seemed nonplussed. Maybe some last little part of

Him that was still sane had muttered dubiously how *no way* a small, scrawny girl like me could throw a plate that heavy that hard and fast . . . but the eyes of the rest were on us now, from where they stood in the kitchen door, and He didn't dare look weak, or indecisive.

"There's no 'ghost,'" He told Scarlett, spitting the word back out, like it tasted bad. Then backhanded her, hard enough I thought her jaw might come loose. After which He told Mother Joan and Mother Jane to haul me back up to the temple and lock me in—and it seemed to me they could feel something different than just the usual, as well, when they did. Mother Joan peered around, shivered a bit, as if she were trying to shake it off. "You smell that?" she asked Mother Jane.

"Smell what?" Mother Jane replied, squatting down. Murmuring, to me, while Mother Joan kept on scanning the walls: "Look, Lilac, you gotta stop winding Him up, okay? And don't tell lies that scare the other kids, either."

"I didn't tell Scarlett anything, Mom."

"Well, she didn't hear about it from *us* . . ."

Oh, and *that* was a surprise.

One hour alone in the heat, another, yet one more. Then I heard Her at last, inside me.

. . . They know about me too?

(Seems like.)

"But why would you care," I mumbled out loud, through thirst-swollen lips. And fell into darkness.

● ○

This time it was five days. I didn't cry. Barely opened my eyes. I think He must have waited outside sometimes, listening to hear if I was, because when He opened the door and hauled me out

in my stinking, soiled dress, He looked just as pissed off as usual. *Don't test Me, girl,* He said. *You set yourself against God, doing that. Go. Get yourself washed. You reek.*

Which I did. I was happy to.

It'd put the rest of it off for longer, if never forever.

But that night, after, He coughed out the wine Mother Jenny poured him at supper in revulsion. *Blood!* He shouted. *It's blood! Who dares? Who—?*

Even He stared when I calmly raised my hand. I could see Him trembling to ask, *How?* but prophets can't ask that. So He made my mothers run the gauntlet, punch and slap me around a circle of their fists not once, not twice, but three times. Two days later, He barely dodged a pot of boiling water as it tipped off the stove by itself, while I chopped onions at the table eight feet away, not even looking up. And four nights after that, the house awoke to His screams echoing in the sole working bathroom; He was crouching in the corner, staring at the smashed mirror, naked and shaking. This time, I only smirked.

"Easy trick, if you know how," I said, now everyone was watching. "Go on, *God*; tell 'em what You saw."

I didn't know what He'd seen, of course. I still don't. But I should have seen the reaction coming, looking at His maddened eyes. He rose slowly to His feet, leg mainly healed, but still a little shaky.

It's all *of you,* He said, almost wonderingly, looking around. *Isn't it? Oh, you fucking whores. How you'll pay for this, trying to deceive* Me. *But you the most, little Lilac.*

Not bothering to dress, He summoned everyone to the living room, shoved the furniture aside to clear space, then grabbed me and threw me to the floor, face down. A heavy foot planted itself between my shoulder blades and drove the breath out of

me. *Lilac,* He said. *You're going to watch, this time. So you can see what your snot-nosed insolence gets your sisters. So you'll remember.* Tossing His whip to Mother Jasika: *All of you, now, in the circle. Oh yes, little Scarlett, little Rose, little whatever the fuck the rest of you got named. Babies, too. Face right. Three strokes on the back of the one in front of you. Then pass it forward. I see anyone shirking or holding back, I'll break Lilac's fingers, one by one. Then we'll start with her knees. Then we'll start . . . removing things. Until someone tells the truth.*

Now. Begin.

The mothers did their best, only whimpering. But the first time poor Scarlett took a whip stroke across her spine she shrieked, and Mother Jael—who held the whip—burst out in wailing sobs but didn't dare stop, even though by then *I* was screeching, telling Him it was me, only me, it had only ever been me, but it was like throwing water at glass, hoping for it to melt. Mother Jael hit Scarlett again, and again. The third time, Scarlett fell, writhing on the floor like a broken-backed snake.

Mother Jael was kneeling down to pass the whip to her when the brutal weight on my back suddenly vanished; I sucked in a huge gasp of air. He'd leapt forward, dropping to his knees beside Scarlett. *What?* He demanded. *What did you say? What did you say? Was it you? Has it been* you, always? He bent down, listening close, turning Scarlett's head toward him.

She coughed, sprayed His face with blood and snot.

He jerked back, eyes widening. *Fucking* bitch! He screamed. *Time for a fucking sacrifice!* He pinned Scarlett down, one hand around her throat, pointing at me. *Bring a knife!* He roared. *Now!*

I met his eyes, but didn't move. His face went slack, but not in a good way. *Your turn next, then,* He rasped. Then He was upright, Scarlett hanging by the throat from one fist, the other

clamped between her legs—lifting her like he was going to break her across his knee. Blood dripped from her torn back. Fuck, I'd forgotten how *strong* He was, even like this.

Everyone recoiling. Kids howling in terror. Our mothers—Jael and Jenny, Jasika and Janet, Jean and Joan and Jane—frozen helpless, like they couldn't even hear me screaming at them to do something, anything . . . until the voice, louder than I'd ever heard it, was inside us all at once.

PUT HER DOWN.

The walls vibrated. It sent shocks through my bones. The windows shattered, explosively. He tottered, dropped to his bad knee and yelped, fell back onto His ass; Scarlett tumbled away, limply, into Mother Jasika's clutching arms. I saw blood running from His ears.

What? He asked, blinking, like a child. *What?*

DON'T TALK.

We crumpled to the floor, hunched over, arms shielding heads and ears. He howled, His face screwed up. Blood *pouring* from His nostrils and eye sockets. But He'd thought of Himself as God for too long now to stop, even in the face of an apocalypse.

You, He choked out wetly, *whoever you are, you will, not,* dare—

YES. I WILL.

I DO.

And this time I *did* see a jaw break—His. Saw it skew violently, like an invisible sledgehammer'd been swung up into it from below. Saw half His tongue fly forward on a jet of blood, smack the floor, bounce stickily. Saw Him slammed backward, hands over His ruined face, bucking and shrieking in wordless agony as he puked out great gouts of blood. Steaming crimson

sprayed over the floor, hit Scarlett and me, so hot it almost scalded. And I saw Him, writhing and twisting, puking and screaming like a sick fucking dog. Like some poor innocent dog we'd poisoned in order to crawl some heathen's house, looking for shit to bring back home to *Him*.

Without warning, something lifted Him up off the bloody floor and high in the air, hovering above. We gaped up: Apotheosis, at last? Ascension? But no, whatever had Him only paused a second before *crunching* Him back and forth, same way you'd wring out a washcloth. Bones cracked like celery. Ribs collapsed inward. The pelvis broke in half, like chalk. Collarbones splintered, snapped like chopsticks. His skin bloomed bruises, ripping and mashing itself, bleeding smoking jets, crumpled like paper. I saw Him shrink, roll up into a mess of shredded flesh and shattered bone but keep on flapping back and forth at the waist like something was riding Him midair, twisting his broken spine with a steady, pleasurable rhythm . . . *penetrating* Him. Raping *Him* to death.

I was good with it. Still am.

And somehow, all the while, He was still screaming. Even though His lungs, and throat, and larynx were nothing but ruined masses of meat. Like She was keeping Him alive throughout, so He could feel for Himself what He'd done. What She'd *seen* Him do to us, over and over.

And the blood kept pouring down, impossible, unceasing, like warm rain. Gentle. Tender.

I saw my mothers raise their arms to it. Open their mouths to take it in, like milk: His final gift to us, through Her, as He unravelled everywhere, dissolving into oblivion. Saw them hold the kids up one by one, into that gross baptism. None of them struggled; it was like they were drunk, shocked silent. I rolled

over, tried to crawl away, but two of my mothers caught me and cradled me between them so I'd get my fair share of the gore. It was the softest, warmest lap I'd ever cuddled in, the gentlest, most welcoming embrace I'd ever known. Well worth the butcher-shop shit still happening up above, while She kept on grinding Him apart, by inches.

You were right, Lilac, they whispered, holding me close. *You tried to tell us, and you were right. Thank you. Thank you* so *much.*

This is the way it always should have been.

And that was when I knew . . . It had all, *all* of it, been for fucking nothing.

They had a new god now.

• ○

It takes me a long time to come back to myself. To look up, slowly, at the faces in the circle, staring at me with disbelief, confusion, bemusement. Anger, even, or disgust, like: *Oh, come* on*!* And fear, of course. Always fear. Even Ash, fiercely supportive Ash, looks for the first time like she has no idea what to do. Like she's wondering who to call.

But when her face changes at last, it isn't to what I expect. The mask was always the same with the others: friendly, nonthreatening, the careful reassurance you show a growling dog while groping for a rock. Ash just draws a deep breath, and looks me straight in the eye.

"Lesson #3," she says. "Your experience is valid. However you experience it."

It isn't what I truly hoped for, but it's so much closer than anything else I've ever been given, from an outsider. I feel my eyes burn, my throat thicken. I have to swallow, again and again.

"But—" Derek begins, looking bewildered.

Ash cuts him off, hand up. "*However* you experience it," she repeats.

Nobody dares to argue.

● ○

I got out, obviously. Got a job, saved up, went to school, got my GED. I haunted libraries, almost literally; I was the too-young-looking volunteer reorganizing in the back, sorting and culling, making lists of things to google once the place shut down. That's how I found out His real name, even if I still can't bring myself to use it—and found out the rest, as well. The house's history.

That's how I found Her, long after She'd first revealed Herself to me.

And yes, She *did* have children, once, as I'd suspected. Until her own personal version of a Him took them from Her.

They died together in that house, her He and She. But He died first.

I was in my first year of college when Scarlett tracked me down—night school, various courses in criminology, abnormal psychology. Almost three years since I'd seen her, and she looked like a mother herself now, full-blown: crawl clothes, black on black, good for hiding in shadows; thought I could see a little paring knife taped to the inside of her left wrist, handle ready to drop into her palm if she ripped fast enough, and another strapped inside her boot. Not to mention she was visibly pregnant already, at maybe fourteen.

"Lilac—"

"I'm Anke now," I told her, barely slowing, once I'd squinted just enough to recognize the child-face beneath her adult one. "Chose it myself . . . You could, too, if you wanted. Or are you still fine with being named after a colour *He* picked out of a hat?"

She shrugged. "I always liked being Scarlett. And besides—doesn't matter where it came from *now*, does it?"

"Glad for you, then. But I'm not Lilac, and Anke's late for class."

"We fixed it, Anke."

"Fixed it? It's a fucking cult still, Scar. How the fuck can you fix that?"

"Well, He had the right shape of things, but *He* was what was wrong with it. His view was skewed. He couldn't see what He was seeing. So we . . . readjusted things."

"You mean She did."

"Yes. Yes, oh *yes*. That's *exactly* what I mean."

(*Thank you for putting it into words, sister.*)

We stood looking at each other for a minute.

"He talked a good game," she said, "but He never showed us anything, did He? Not anything real."

Nothing like Her, yeah.

"Please, Li— Anke. Come home. Just for a day, okay? Come home, and see."

● ○

"And you did," Ash says. I nod.

"And I did," I repeat.

● ○

Just once, I thought. Knowing how wrong I already was, even to dream that'd be the end of it.

The whole house felt different, the minute I walked in the front door, excited and welcoming, filled with a great sense of peace. It knew itself loved, and it loved them back—my mothers, my siblings. *She* knew. And the whole thing is, it was because they *liked* Her being what She is. She'd given them what they could never have dared to admit they'd wanted most all along, at

least not out loud. Not like I hadn't wanted that, too, of course, back then—for them. For all of us.

I could feel Her watching, waiting. That light in my mothers' eyes, mimicking Her unseen own—calm and murmuring, humming with satisfaction at a house set once more to rights. Finally happy. Finally *free*.

(For certain values of the word.)

So . . .

I could leave again, sure. Definitely. I'm an adult now; Blue and Indi were kids, and *they* left. Of course, they did have each other to rely on when they went, if nothing else . . .

I couldn't've ever left *them*, though, and that's the truth. Because they were part of my family, the only family I've ever had—and She knows that about me, just like He did. She's cunning that way.

So I stayed, that day, and every day after. I went home, to them. To Her.

I still do.

●○

This desperate wanting to believe. To *be* believed. I know it so well. I was born into it. So I yearn to believe in people, but people are ghosts waiting to happen, and all ghosts are liars.

Me too.

●○

The group ends then, and everyone else wanders away, trying not to look back at me while I help Ash break down—put the coffee maker away, put the chairs up, lock the storage room. Pause for a moment after stepping outside, to let her catch up. To let her say what I know she's going to say.

"'The only person you have left is me.' That's what She'd

probably say to you, if She was real, just like He would've. But that's not true, is it, Anke?"

"No. It never was."

"Yeah, exactly! Fuckin' right. Oh, I knew it; I *knew* you didn't think some ghost saved you from your cult."

I shake my head, smiling: Damn, I like her so much. I really do.

"'Course not," I agree. "I mean . . . ghosts don't exist, right? Just like God. We *both* know that. Right?"

"Bet your ass," Ash says. "See you next week?"

"You know it."

And I smile again—we smile at each other—before turning away, her for her car, me for the shortcut through the trees into the next strip mall's parking lot. Gotta cross a good eight of those to get where I'm going, plus a dirt road and a gravel path up into the woods that runs for half a mile before I see Her house's beams sticking out the top of that one huge tree made from trees. Before I'm home at last.

I'm gonna miss her most, I think, then file that thought away down deep in my own interior darkness where I can forget it, as soon as humanly possible. Because I'm sure as hell never coming back to *this* nighttime survivor group again.

● ○

It's strange, like I said, how you just can't seem to stop yourself making some mistakes, even after you've grasped that's what you're doing. Maybe because when you're used to always doing things for the wrong reasons, it's hard to see why you shouldn't indulge yourself in doing something for the right one. Just the once.

I'd like to tell the truth, just the once, and have it be believed.

Instead, as the sun is coming up, I simply slip back inside this house, where it's always night, even when it isn't. I come home.

And the first thing I hear is Her inside me, welcoming, happy. She *does* care, now. Now that I've given her what she never knew she wanted: a family. *My* family.

We have to share. She has to understand that. I'll make her, even if it kills me.

Because—

—Then there'll be two of us in here, won't there?

THE NIGHT-MIRRORS

PAT CADIGAN

The Grandmas were so busy talking over one another about what was on TV, they didn't notice Flo peeking through the drapes at the night-mirror behind the sofa.

Of all the discoveries she'd made (not that many, but she was only five), Flo's absolute favorite was how nighttime turned windows into mirrors. Everyone else seemed to think this was as ordinary as breakfast. But then, most people took regular mirrors for granted, too, as if they weren't sort-of windows.

"Florence!" Grandma 1 said suddenly, and Flo sagged against the couch cushion. She'd stopped thinking about the Grandmas not noticing her. Every time she did that, at least one of them would wonder what she was up to. "What have we told you about fidgeting with the drapes?"

"Don't do it." Sighing, Flo crossed her arms and hid her hands in her armpits. "The oils on my fingers stain the cloth."

"They certainly do," Grandma 1 scolded. "Look at the drape. Just *look*."

Flo saw only the slight gap she'd been peering through, and the tiny section of the reflected living room.

"We just had those drapes cleaned last month," Grandma 1 was saying. "And you've already got finger marks on them. It's not easy to take those drapes down and put them up again. And the part in between, where they go to the cleaners? That's not free."

Grandma 2 had grabbed the clicker to turn down the volume on the TV. Now she cleared her throat. "Alright, Sophie, you made your point. Unless you want to send her out to look for a job in the morning."

"Maybe that would make her stop playing with the drapes," Grandma 1 said. She and Grandma 2 turned to look at Grandma 3.

"What?" Grandma 3 said, bristling. "I'm not in this. If I were, I'd tell you to give it a rest. They're drapes, not the sacred swaddling of the baby Jesus."

Grandma 1's forehead wrinkled the way it always did when she was worried. Flo's mother had been her daughter and Grandma 1 felt it was her special responsibility to make sure Flo was raised right. Grandma 2 was Grandma 1's sister, while Grandma 3 was Grandma 2's wife. This wasn't like most families Flo knew of; her parents had died in a car accident. Flo barely remembered them—nothing about her father and only bits about her mother. Having three grandmas instead of a mom and dad felt as normal to her as mirrors did to everyone else.

"Were you looking at something out there?" Grandma 1 asked. There was a suspicious edge in her voice as she came over to kneel on the sofa and look for herself.

There wasn't much to see—the side street that ran past the house was just an alley. It didn't get much traffic other than vans delivering to the back entrances of stores and restaurants across the way; the kids from nearby apartment buildings played there when school was out. Sometimes Flo played with them, while

one of the Grandmas sat on the porch with a newspaper or a magazine or a book, keeping an eye on everyone and picking up some neighborhood gossip.

"God, it's only five thirty in the afternoon and it's already like the dead of night," Grandma 1 said.

"The clocks just went back, remember?" Grandma 2 sounded like she wanted to laugh.

"Happens right around this time every year," Grandma 3 added, with the same almost-laugh in her voice.

"I know that," Grandma 1 said. Her gaze fell on Flo. "Don't be opening the curtains. We're not putting on a show for the neighbors."

"Hey, quiet, you guys," Grandma 3 said, taking the clicker from Grandma 2 and turning the TV sound up. "This is the segment I've been waiting for." She let out a long sigh as the screen showed a dark-haired man playing the piano; the music was what Flo thought of as brave-lonely—Grandma 3's favorite kind. "There'll never be another Freddie Mercury."

"I've seen this clip three times this month," said Grandma 1.

"Shush," Grandma 3 said. "I don't care."

Flo waited until the six o'clock news came on before snaking her arm along the back of the sofa again to the break in the drapes. The news usually held the Grandmas' attention enough that they practically forgot she was there, at least until the regional news from Boston came on and it was time for supper.

● ○

The night-mirror in the living room was the biggest one in the house and piqued Flo's interest the most, partly because Grandma 1 was so fussy about keeping the drapes closed after dark. But Flo had her own personal night-mirror in her bedroom.

Grandma 1 always closed its curtains, too—it was the first thing she did, before Flo even changed into her pajamas.

After Grandma 1 finished the usual bedtime reading, Flo waited 'til she was sure she wasn't coming back. Then she would get up and open the curtains again to look at the reflection of her room in the soft glow of the night-light on the stand beside her bed.

Her window looked out on the Grandmas' flower garden and the busier street it backed onto. When she sat on her bed, however, the night-mirror reflection covered up most of the outside. She had to get up close to the glass and cup her hands on either side of her head if she wanted to see the garden.

Now she took the flashlight out of the nightstand and turned it on, resting it on her pillow with the beam aimed at the far corner before she got up and went over to kneel at the window.

Her head made a dark half circle (with curly hair) that cut into the beam and let the outside show through. While she was looking, a large dog on a leash led a man from her right ear across to her left and disappeared into the reflection of her night-light. That would be Mr. Ramirez, who lived down the street by the bridge. He was a good guy. So was his dog, Elmo.

Leaning one arm on the windowsill, Flo stared at the reflection of the night-light. It was a big one that looked like a fancy circus tent. The top was yellow with a pattern of shooting stars; below that, it was multicolored stripes. And inside, Grandma 1 said, was anything she could imagine.

Flo had tried imagining tiny trapeze artists, miniature trained elephants playing catch with beach balls, clowns running around frantically, but none of it felt right to her. Grandma 1 had given her the night-light so she wouldn't be afraid. But she wasn't scared of the dark, never had been. What she really liked about the big

circus tent was how the warm golden light made her window into a perfect night-mirror.

A car slid into her head's half circle and stopped. Flo blinked, startled; she'd never seen that happen before, although the car seemed kind of familiar. Her knowledge of cars was limited to which one belonged to the Grandmas and which ones belonged to the nearest neighbors, and she differentiated them either by color or by dents, scratches, or bumper stickers, but never by manufacturer, even though she had a collection of toy cars. They were neatly contained in a carrying case that had a tendency to appear anywhere in the house, even if Flo had put it under her bed the last time she'd finished playing drive-in or car school or rug race.

It could be worse, Flo had overheard Grandma 3 say once over breakfast coffee. *One word, ladies: "Legos." Can you say "Ow"? You will.*

Flo was vaguely aware of Legos but had no strong feelings about them one way or the other. At the moment, she was thinking about the case full of cars and trying to remember if she had a car like the one that had just parked across the street. Except it shouldn't have been able to because there had already been a car there; it belonged to Mr. DiAngelo, who lived in the house it was parked in front of. Everybody knew that was his space and nobody else ever parked there.

The trespasser car was turquoise, which was one of Flo's favorite colors. As she stared at it, wishing a color she liked so much wasn't involved, the driver's-side door opened and a woman dressed in a silky-looking blouse and pants got out. Her window was rolled all the way down; she left it that way as she closed the door and leaned against the car. Flo thought she looked like she was posing for a magazine ad, either for cars or silky clothes, and she seemed to be staring directly up at Flo's window with a dreamy smile on her face. It was like she knew someone was watching her. Like she knew it was Flo.

A man got out of the passenger side and walked around the back of the car to the woman. Smiling the same dreamy smile, he slipped his arm around her shoulders and she cuddled up to him. They both stared up at Flo's window.

Slowly, Flo went from kneeling to a crouch and backed away across the room, until she bumped into the bed. Now she couldn't see the couple and their trespasser car, which meant they couldn't see her, either, but it didn't matter. She knew they were there and they knew that window was hers. Those dreamy smiles were for her.

Go away, she mouthed.

But they didn't; she could feel it.

● ○

After lunch the next day, Flo found the carrying case with her toy cars behind the sofa. As usual, she didn't remember leaving it there. When things turned up in random places, Grandma 3 would say they had fallen into a wormhole in one spot and fallen out somewhere else. She knew Grandma 3 was just kidding, so she didn't have to worry about giant worms crawling into her room or coming up through the toilet, but it gave her the icks anyway.

That man and woman, though, they didn't give her the icks—they gave her the creeps. Worse, they looked kind of familiar, like they were people she knew. She tried to remember if she'd ever seen them around the neighborhood. Maybe they'd come to get one of the girls playing hopscotch? But even as she thought it she knew that wasn't it.

Flo started lining the cars up bumper to bumper on the windowsill, pausing to look out at the empty alley wistfully. All the kids were in school now. The Grandmas were talking about putting her in first grade next year and she wasn't sure how she felt

about that because the Grandmas couldn't seem to decide which first grade was best.

Public schools here are rough, Grandma 3 had said in one of the discussions Flo had overheard. *You two don't know because you didn't grow up here, but I did. When the other kids find out what a brainiac she is, she'll need bodyguards. And God help her if they even* think *she's queer.*

The memory fell away as Flo examined the line of cars. There were three turquoise cars, but none of them had a metallic finish. She put those three in the center of the line anyway and took another long, careful look, searching for a car that was the same shape as the trespasser. That took longer, but she finally chose one of two white cars, the one with rainbow stripes along each side. It wasn't quite right—the angles weren't as sharp—but it was close enough. Tucking the car into her pants pocket, she went in search of a Grandma.

● ○

"Metallic turquoise paint?" In the basement, Grandma 3 closed the washer lid, twisted the settings knob, and pushed on it. Flo heard water rushing into the machine. "Whatever for?"

Flo showed her the car and explained about the trespasser car parked in front of Mr. DiAngelo's house. "It looks kind of like this, but turquoise, shiny. Almost like glitter."

"Let's have a look." Grandma 3 went to the basement door, which opened onto a patio under the back porch. Just beyond it was the garden and the street, which was mostly empty, giving them a clear view of Mr. DiAngelo's house.

"Nobody's parked there now," Grandma 3 said, closing the door again. "Not even Mr. DiAngelo, who won't be home from work for a while yet. Tell me, kiddo, when did you see that car last

night—was it before or after Grandma Sophie finished reading to you?"

Flo couldn't help squirming. "Uh . . ." She slipped the car back into her pocket. "I don't remember exactly."

"I bet you don't," Grandma 3 said with a knowing chuckle. "So here's my theory—*somebody* got up after she was tucked in, even though she knows she's not supposed to. She opened her curtains, which she also knows she's not supposed to do. *However,* she was *so* sleepy, she doesn't remember getting back into bed, dozing off, and dreaming someone parked in Mr. DiAngelo's space. Just a theory, but I think it's a good one. What do you think?"

"Well . . ." Flo squirmed some more.

"Of course, if someone promises not to break the rules anymore, I'll keep my theory to myself," Grandma 3 went on. "While I'm looking for some metallic turquoise paint, of course. There might be some in one of Grandma Carol's paint-by-numbers kits."

"Oh. Okay." Flo suddenly felt like she had too many hands and stuffed them in her pockets.

"Anything else?" Grandma 3 asked cheerfully. Flo shook her head. "Dismissed."

Flo ran for the stairs.

● ○

Back behind the sofa, Flo turned the cars on the sill so they were facing outward, pretending the window was a giant drive-in screen. The Grandmas had taken her to the local drive-in a couple of times over the summer, when it had reopened to show what the Grandmas called B movies. The sign claimed it was the last one between here and Worcester. Also, Nashua, New

Hampshire, Grandma 3 said. Flo wished they'd gone to that one and then had clams at their favorite restaurant at Lake Winnipesaukee afterward.

It took some pretty strong imagining, as it was still daytime, but Flo was up to the task. All she had to do was picture *King Kong vs. Godzilla* playing on the glass. That was one of her most favorite monster movies (she had seen three). Right in the middle, there was a shot looking down on a battleship from above and it was obvious the boat was a toy. The Grandmas had groaned but Flo had liked it. The movie was pretend anyway and it was like the people who'd made it were showing they were doing their best pretending with what they had, the same as she did.

The second feature at her window drive-in was a movie about the Mummy and Frankenstein's wife. Flo had never seen a movie about either of them let alone both together. She'd only seen a bunch of photos in Grandma 1's book about horror movies.

The book had been in the magazine holder next to Grandma 1's chair and she'd known immediately it was something she wasn't supposed to be looking at. Enthralled, Flo managed to pore over it several times. She had learned to read from following along in the nighttime books the Grandmas read to her, well enough that she'd learned about the Mummy, Frankenstein and his bride, Dracula (who was also married), the Wolfman (who wasn't), and an ugly guy who liked opera.

Every time she'd curled up behind Grandma 1's chair with the book, she'd wondered if this would be the time when she got caught; eventually, it was. Grandma 1 had taken the book away, but to Flo's surprise, she hadn't scolded her. She'd said that Flo was too young to look at *this kind of material,* but she herself was at fault for not putting the book away properly. If Flo had any questions about horror movies, Grandma 1 said, she would be happy to answer them. Flo hadn't been able to think of any,

partly because she was distracted by Grandmas 2 and 3 laughing in the kitchen.

In the window drive-in, the Mummy and Mrs. Frankenstein came out of the screen, causing the cars to throw themselves off the sill onto the carpet, where they bought refreshments before Flo put them back for the next movie, *Godzilla Beach Party.*

Not long after Godzilla crashed the party and scared the surf bullies away, Grandmas 1 and 2 came home from shopping. Grandma 1 insisted she come out from behind the sofa for a snack. Flo wasn't hungry and got away with eating half a banana before going back to the drive-in to add King Kong to the party.

Somehow, the drive-in morphed into a drive-in school, which Flo thought had to be real somewhere because it was such a great idea. She'd never heard of any drive-in schools but she was going to ask the Grandmas about it. If there were no drive-in public schools, maybe there was a private one in Worcester, or Nashua, New Hampshire.

When it started getting chilly, she moved to the sofa and played drive-in school from there. Daylight began to fade and the window started to turn into a drive-in night-mirror, which was exciting. Flo had never seen her cars in a night-mirror and she hoped the Grandmas would be so wrapped up in what they were doing, they'd forget about closing the drapes.

No such luck.

● ○

Flo woke to find she'd dozed off with her head in Grandma 3's lap. There was some program on TV where grown-ups were talking like they were trying not to panic. The Grandmas never panicked. They always sounded like they knew everything was going to be okay, like when the boiler broke and the basement filled up with water, or the time a windstorm tore most of the tiles off the roof.

Or another time Flo remembered only in dim patches, when someone was on their way to the house and the Grandmas had to stop them because they were bad. Flo seldom thought about that time, but the way the Grandmas were talking to each other now reminded her of it.

Grandma 1 kept talking about things called sigils—or sijils, maybe? These were circles with funny little drawings inside them. The Mummy had something like that, except the drawings weren't in circles. There was a special name for them, a long word she couldn't read, but it started with *H*, so they weren't sigils. Or higils.

Grandma 2 was saying the whole thing might be over because nothing had happened last year, so maybe Grandma 1 was simply being jumpy.

"Different years have different energies," Grandma 1 said. "One year, there's a lot of activity, then virtually nothing the next. But it's only an intermission."

"And you think this year's active?" Grandma 2 had an arguing kind of edge in her voice.

"I *know* it is." Grandma 1's edge was larger and sharper. "I can feel it. I felt it back in March."

"Maybe if we'd poured her ashes out off Cape Cod or Gloucester—" Grandma 2 started.

"And then we'd have nothing to worry about? Seriously?" Grandma 1 gave a single laugh that was almost a bark.

"It might have diffused her, reduced her potency."

"You're forgetting how clever Chloe was," Grandma 1 said. "She'd find a way to get to us and damn the torpedoes. I don't want collateral damage on my conscience. We agreed to keep the cremains here, under our control."

"Yes, but we've got boxes of their personal effects, hers and his both," Grandma 2 argued. "Plenty of hair, skin cells, DNA.

Not to mention three out of four people in this house are *her* blood relatives."

"I will *not* allow Florence to be mixed up in this," Grandma 1 said in a firm, final way.

"That's good," Grandma 3 said, talking over Grandma 2 as she started to reply. "Because I've got a possum in my lap. Don't I, Miss Flo?"

Grandma 3's calling her Miss Flo usually made her smile; now she was just annoyed that she'd given herself away. But to keep up appearances, she stretched one arm and gave an exaggerated yawn. "Is it morning already?" she asked in a fake sleepy voice.

"The kid sleeps through *thunderstorms,*" Grandma 2 said. "But mention *them,* and her ears prick up like a spaniel's."

"A bat's," Grandma 3 corrected her.

"Come on now," Grandma 1 sighed, pulling Flo to a sitting position. "You're way too big for me to carry upstairs."

● ○

Flo opened her eyes. *Now* was it morning? Her quilt was barely disturbed so she hadn't been in bed for very long. There was no sunshine, just the dim, golden glow from her night-light. She sat up, wondering if someone had called her name.

No, she was alone in the room. But the curtains were open.

Grandma 1 must have been in such a rush to put her to bed, she hadn't noticed. That was different—normally, Grandma 1 could spot a pin on the carpet in a blackout.

Flo swung her legs over the side of the bed and stepped into her bunny slippers. If Grandma 1 had missed the curtains, who knew what else had gotten by her? She hurried over to kneel at the window, keeping her eyes on the reflection of her night-light.

Then she caught sight of the reflection of the wall calendar hanging above her bed.

The real calendar had photos of exotic flowers and plants that didn't grow in New England—orchids, birds-of-paradise, fuchsias, other things she could never remember the names of. The night-mirror calendar showed even stranger blooms that weren't like any flowers she'd ever seen, bizarre blossoms that looked more like insects or lizards than plants. They were almost scary, like some of the photos in Grandma 1's horror-movie book. But pictures couldn't hurt you, no matter how creepy they were. Nothing could get out of a picture and do something bad. Things stayed in photos and reflections stayed in mirrors.

Night-mirrors, too?

Flo's gaze moved to the peaked roof of Mr. DiAngelo's house and traveled downward. The trespasser car was back.

When had it slid into Mr. DiAngelo's parking space—while she'd been asleep downstairs? Or after Grandma 1 had put her to bed and forgotten to close the curtains?

Or had it been there since last night?

The driver's-side door opened and the woman got out. Flo thought she could see her a little better tonight, almost like she was closer somehow. She and her silky clothes.

And there was the man, coming around the back of the car to stand next to her with his arm around her shoulders. They smiled up at her with those perfect, dreamy smiles. Because they were her real parents and they were coming to take her. She would be perfect with them forever.

"*No,* you're *not* my parents, not anymore," Flo whispered. "The Grandmas are my parents, my *true* parents, my *real* parents. Because *we're alive.*"

She backed away from the window in a crouch like she had before, careful to keep them and their trespasser car within the

frame of the night-mirror. Whatever was in the night-mirror couldn't get out any more than something could escape from a photograph.

Except they weren't reflections, she remembered uneasily as the bed bumped against her legs. They were trespassers.

● ○

The photo album was so heavy and awkward that Flo had to ask Grandma 3 to get it out of the cabinet for her. She would rather have gotten it herself so she wouldn't have to explain why she wanted to look at it. But Grandma 3 only said she had a million things to do while the other two Grandmas were out.

"Just leave it on the sofa when you're done. I'll put it away later," she said before she went down to the basement, leaving the door open. Grandma 3 rarely asked her why she wanted to do something, unlike Grandma 1. Flo thought it might have something to do with Grandma 1's special-responsibility thing.

Lying on her stomach, Flo paged through the album propped up on a sofa pillow until she came to the section with the photos of the baby, the woman, and the man—her and her parents, according to the Grandmas.

Grandma 1's favorite was one that showed Flo and her mother cheek to cheek. *You were about six months old there,* Grandma 1 had told her. *Your eyes were just starting to change from blue to gray. For a while, they looked like they were glowing.*

To Flo, the baby looked like any other baby, with unremarkable blue eyes. The woman had dark, pixie-cut hair; her eyes were the color of dirty cement, not light gray like Flo's. She was smiling, not dreamily but like she knew something that nobody else did, and it wasn't a very nice thing.

The Grandmas said it was wrong to think someone could do something bad just by the way they looked. You weren't

supposed to judge a book by the cover. But Flo wondered if there was a camera that showed the real person underneath their disguise. Or what if some people had special eyesight that let them see when certain people had more bad than good in them?

She had a feeling that if she asked the Grandmas about such a thing, they'd say it was impossible. Because they thought the subject was too grown-up for her? Or because they didn't know?

The dark-haired man had hazel eyes and he wasn't in as many of the photos. Flo thought he looked like a Ken doll—had her mother stolen him from Barbie? It was a pretty mean thought but she couldn't find it in herself to be sorry about it.

If those two ever came to the door and announced they weren't dead, it had all been a big mistake and now they were going to take her with them, she would refuse to go. And if they insisted, she would chain herself to her bedroom door and swallow the padlock key.

She could practically hear the Grandmas reassuring her: You never have to worry about anyone trying to take you away. Nobody like that will ever ring the doorbell. It's impossible.

Her gaze fell on the photo of the baby and the woman's dirty-cement eyes and she scooted to the other end of the sofa.

"What *are* you doing?"

Flo jumped, startled. Grandma 3 was standing in the open door to the basement. "Nothing," she said. "I had an idea."

Grandma 3 chuckled. "You and a million other creative minds in New England. What's yours?"

"I want long hair," Flo said. It was the first thing that popped into her head.

Grandma 3 laughed a little more. "That would be very pretty. It's more work but it's not like you'd have to walk it or milk it. Never mind," she added in response to Flo's baffled look. "I came

up because *I* had an idea—that *you* might feel like a snack about now. Am I right?"

Flo nodded and followed her to the kitchen.

● ○

That evening, Grandma 1 fell asleep in her chair early and Grandma 3 was Skyping with her niece, so Grandma 2 read the nighttime book. Flo was tempted to tell her about the trespasser car and the man and woman but she wasn't sure how Grandma 2 would take it. Grandma 2 was usually more relaxed than Grandma 1, but this wasn't a usual kind of thing.

"Anything on your mind tonight?" Grandma 2 asked when she closed the book.

Flo turned from the window with its closed curtains to blink up at her in surprise. "Huh?"

"You've been checking that window like you're expecting—well, I don't know who to come crashing through it. Peter Pan or a tiger."

Impulsively, Flo sat up and hugged her tightly.

"Oh, my," Grandma 2 said, laughing a little as she hugged her back. "What did I do to deserve this?"

"Just because you're you," Flo said. It wasn't really a lie.

"Thank you for that," Grandma 2 said as Flo lay down again. "But I know something's bothering you. Anything you want to talk about?" She was smiling but her eyes were serious.

"Do you think everyone in the world has a twin?" Flo asked her.

Grandma 2 raised her eyebrows, surprised. "Sure. There are so many people in the world, we're bound to have someone who looks just like us. Maybe even more than one."

"Like triplets? Or, um, what's four—quartets?"

"Close enough for jazz," Grandma 2 said, tweaking her nose.

Flo took a breath and plunged ahead. "Do you think there could be someone who looks like a dead person?"

Grandma 2's smile faded. "How do you mean?"

"Do you think"—Flo took another breath—"there could be people who look like my mom and dad?"

"I'm sure there are." Grandma 2's forehead wrinkled with concern. "Why? Did you see some people you thought looked like your parents?"

"Oh, no," Flo said, trying to sound casual. "I was just wondering. Have you ever seen anyone you thought could be your twin?"

"No, but I haven't been looking." Grandma 2 was smiling again but Flo could see the worry underneath. "How about you?"

Flo shook her head. "If so many of us have twins, how come we've never met ours?"

Grandma 2 laughed. "Probably for the same reason we've never met aliens from other planets."

"Why's that?" Flo asked, curious.

"Because we're too busy, the aliens and us and our twins. We've all got work or school, not to mention curious little kids who ought to be asleep by now." Grandma 2 kissed the tip of her index finger and pressed it to the spot just under Flo's nose. "There—I've shut off the question box. 'Til morning, it's emergency calls only."

Flo giggled. It was silly but she went along with it anyway and mouthed, *Good night.*

Grandma 2 looked at her finger with a pleased expression. "I'm glad to know this thing still has some juice in it." She leaned over and kissed Flo's forehead before she left, turning off the overhead light and leaving the door partly open.

Flo counted to sixty three times, in case Grandma 1 had woken up and decided to come up and kiss her good night to make up for missing reading time. All the Grandmas read to her,

but lately Grandma 1 had taken over the job. Maybe she thought it was part of her special responsibility or something.

She could hear the murmur of voices from downstairs; they sounded serious. Flo glanced at the night-mirror still hidden behind the curtains, then got up to tiptoe to the doorway. Lying down on her side, she wiggled past the edge of the door without touching it to the top of the stairs. From there, she could hear everything unless they went into the kitchen for tea.

". . . not sure if it's a matter of mirrors or doppelgängers," Grandma 2 was saying. "I asked her right out if she'd seen anyone who looked like *them* and she said no."

"She's a kid," Grandma 3 said. "Twins, reflections—it's almost the same thing. And then there are photos—she spent time looking at old pictures of the three of them together. That surprised me."

"I'm sure she thinks about them more often than she lets on," Grandma 1 said.

"Totally normal," said Grandma 2. "Even if Chloe and Richard hadn't been—well, you know, what they are—she'd think about them, wonder about them, about her family as it was. Any kid would. But we're well past All Souls' Day. I doubt that they're, ah, even in the vicinity of proximate, let alone imminent."

"It still won't do any harm to make sure the curtains and drapes are drawn after dark. When it *starts* to get dark."

"Oh, Jesus," Grandma 3 said suddenly. "It completely slipped my mind. Flo claimed she saw a trespasser car—unquote—parked in front of Manny DiAngelo's house. A metallic turquoise trespasser car. Sounded like that old Chevy Impala they had when they—you know. Anyhow, it slipped my mind because she asked for the photo album, I was thinking about that."

"Should we send you for cognitive testing?" Grandma 1's voice had that edge in it again.

"No need to be nasty," Grandma 2 admonished her.

"Don't scold Sophie," Grandma 3 said to Grandma 2. "I should have remembered. I was right there with you when it happened."

Flo's heart started to beat a little faster. Grandma 3 meant the car accident. The Grandmas hardly ever talked about it. Grandma 1 had promised Flo she would tell her the whole story when she was older. Unfortunately for Flo, Grandma 1 hadn't specified how much older. This was one of those tricky things grown-ups pulled on kids (and sometimes one another) when they wanted to get out of doing something without actually saying no.

Talk about it, Flo thought at them with all her might. *Remember and talk, talk, talk.*

Most of the time when the Grandmas did this, it was something she already knew about, like the time when Grandmas 2 and 3 got married or when Grandma 3's nephew had to drive them home in a blizzard from some place near Nashua, New Hampshire. But once in a while they got wrapped up in past events and then Flo might hear something she'd never heard before.

She knew eavesdropping was wrong, but it wasn't *too* wrong, not as wrong as, say, talking back with bad language, or going through the Grandmas' private belongings without permission. They were sitting in the living room talking to each other in their normal voices, not huddled in the kitchen, whispering. This was more like Grandma 1 not putting her horror-movie book away and Flo finding it and looking through it; no big crime.

At the same time, Flo knew it wasn't the same thing and the knowledge made a guilt lump in her middle that bothered her as much as not knowing about her parents' car accident. But she stayed where she was. *Knowing* something *is better than* not *knowing* anything *at all*; she had overheard Grandma 1 say that once.

"... hardwired, in a way," Grandma 2 was saying and Flo realized she had nearly dozed off.

"What worries me is how smart she is," Grandma 1 said. "That big brain of hers makes her vulnerable."

"What if we tried to channel Chloe's maternal instincts?" Grandma 2 suggested.

"Maternal instincts enable *survival*," Grandma 1 said. "The dead don't want to keep anyone alive—the dead want company."

"I'd have thought the bond would have diminished by now," said Grandma 3. "How long has it been?"

"Flo was only two when it happened," Grandma 1 replied. "From Chloe's point of view, not very long since Flo was part of her body." Pause. "And Chloe always was pretty selfish and self-centered."

"Oh, Sophie," Grandma 2 said, her voice so sad that Flo winced.

"No, it's true and we all know it," Grandma 1 said firmly.

"But you never gave up on her—" Grandma 2 started.

Grandma 1 cut her off. "She was what she was, and still is—the dead don't change for the better."

Flo rolled onto her back with a yawn. This was nothing she hadn't already heard. She should get back into bed before she fell asleep. If the Grandmas found her here, they'd know she'd been listening in on their private conversation and they wouldn't be too happy about it. Except it took so much *effort* to get up.

"The last time we turned her and Richard away, Chloe said she'd never stop coming for Flo," Grandma 1 continued. "She's going to keep trying until either she gets her or we find a way to stop her for good." Pause. "Please, let's talk about something else. What's on TV?"

Flo's drowsiness was suddenly gone. Her mother was coming to take her away from the Grandmas? Her *dead* mother?

No, the Grandmas would never allow it. Grandma 1 had just

said they'd find a way to stop her. They would, wouldn't they? They had to.

Flo crawled backward into her room and sat on the edge of her bed, eyeing the closed curtains on her window. She had a strong urge to go and see if the trespasser car was back. At the same time, however, she didn't have to look to know it was there. When the woman saw the curtains were open, she'd get out of the car and so would the man. The both of them would smile dreamily up at her because they'd be that much closer. The more Flo looked at them, the closer they'd get with their dreamy smiles, until they trespassed all the way through the night-mirror and right into the air she breathed.

Did they think smiling at her would make her want to go with them? And where would they go? To a cemetery? Or to wherever the dead stayed when they weren't trespassing on the world of the living? Didn't you have to be dead to get into that place?

Would they kill her?

Only the worst kind of people would do something like that, Flo thought. Not just very bad, like thieves or liars—*evil.*

Flo's throat tightened. The feeling was very faint, but soon her eyes would start filling up with tears and then she wouldn't be able to keep them from spilling over.

It wasn't fair. She had the Grandmas and she tried so hard to be good. Why did her dead parents have to be evil?

In spite of everything, she almost got up and went to the window. Instead, she lay down, putting her back to the window. As she did, tears spilled out of her eyes, wetting the pillowcase. Her mean, dead, evil parents were ruining the night-mirrors; she had to find some way to get rid of them.

Only, how did you get rid of people who were supposed to be gone already?

• ○

"I'm sorry, honey, I clean forgot to look for turquoise paint." Grandma 3 looked a little embarrassed. Flo wondered if she were embarrassed about lying or lying about being embarrassed.

"*Metallic* turquoise," Flo corrected her.

Grandma 3 laughed a little. "Right. I guess I forgot about that, too. Now that I'm thinking about it, there probably isn't any in Grandma Carol's paint-by-numbers kits because those are mostly outdoor scenes—"

"Landscapes," Flo put in helpfully.

Grandma 3 laughed some more. "Yes, landscapes. I'll check anyway. You never know."

"If you don't find any, can we order some online?"

"We'll see," Grandma 3 said, which generally meant no. "Anything else I can do for you? If not, I'll be working down in the basement again today."

"Doing what?" Flo asked before she could think better of it.

Grandma 3 blinked at her, surprised at the question, though no more than Flo herself. "Important Grandma stuff. That okay with you?"

"Can I help?"

"No, but thanks for the offer, kid," Grandma 3 said. "I'm still going through old boxes and things. It kicks up a lot of dust and would probably make you sneeze and wheeze and honk like a Canada goose, which wouldn't be much fun for you. But I'm leaving the door open, of course, so you can yell if you need me."

"And vicey-versy," Flo said, making Grandma 3 laugh even more.

"And if I find any turquoise paint—excuse me, *metallic* turquoise paint," Grandma 3 said as Flo opened her mouth to correct her, "you'll be the first to know."

She went down the stairs to the basement and Flo went behind the sofa, where her toy cars were waiting. Today she didn't bother with bumper-to-bumper traffic on the windowsill but set them out for the drive-in. What was playing today?

King Kong and Godzilla vs. Dracula and the Wolfman sounded pretty good; she just had to decide if King Kong and Godzilla were people-sized or if Dracula and the Wolfman were giants. Making everybody gigantic was much more exciting, she thought. Small King Kong and Godzilla might frighten babies but a giant vampire and werewolf would scare the H-E-double-hockey-sticks out of just about anybody.

All the cars were duly terrified and threw themselves off the sill even though none of the monsters came out of the screen. After they bought their refreshments, she put about half of them back, then paused to think about what the next movie would be. Mrs. Frankenstein hadn't scared anybody lately. But Flo had a hard time choosing a partner for her. Mr. Frankenstein was too easy. And, frankly, too ugly.

• ◦

She opened her eyes to find Grandma 3 shaking her foot and scolding her about sleeping so close to the window. "You could wake up with a stiff neck," Grandma 3 said, helping her up. "Then you'd be walking around like Frankenstein."

Flo giggled politely, too groggy to show her full appreciation. She stumbled out from behind the sofa and then caught sight of the reflection in the window.

"Don't!" she said as Grandma 3 started to close the drapes. "I want to see!"

"See what?" Grandma 3 looked from her to the window and back again, mystified.

"The living room in the night-mirror," Flo replied, wide-eyed as she climbed onto the sofa.

"The what?" Grandma 3 stood behind her. In the night-mirror, she was dressed in something like a costume or a kind of uniform. It was deep black and imprinted with those silver circles. *Sigils.*

Flo turned to look at Grandma 3 in amazement. But in the living room they were really in, Grandma 3 was wearing the same ordinary shirt and jeans she'd been wearing all day, and there were no sigils on them. Or rather, none Flo could see. Still, they were there, and now that Flo knew about them, she could sort of feel them, too.

Did Grandma 3 know? Flo looked up at her face, then turned back to her reflection in the night-mirror. Night-Mirror Grandma 3 definitely knew, but Flo thought the one in the regular living room didn't.

"Where are Grandmas 1 and 2?" Flo asked, keeping her eyes on Grandma 3's reflection.

"Grandma Sophie and Carol are still out. I thought Sophie told you not to call us numbers, it's disrespectful—"

Flo barely heard her. A car was rolling into view in the alley. It wasn't that easy to see under the night-mirror reflection but Flo could tell it was metallic turquoise, although it wasn't very shiny. It was an old car, little more than a box on wheels with seat belts, as Grandma 1 had said once, a very long time ago, the car Flo's parents had died in but she had not. The trespasser car. Not in front of Mr. DiAngelo's house tonight, so not small enough to fit inside the frame of the night-mirror in her room, but life-size. As big as King Kong and Godzilla, if not bigger.

Flo put her hands behind her back and traced an *X* on her left palm with her right index finger, then put a circle around it. It

wasn't that difficult but she had to concentrate on feeling exactly where the *X* lines ended so the circle didn't cut them off.

If the border cuts into what it contains, the power bleeds out.

When had she heard that, who had said it? One of the Grandmas? Or—

She heard the car door open and close, so she wasn't surprised when the woman appeared in the center of the window, not small and distant but regular people-sized. The night-mirror reflections seemed to fade under the force of her smile, which wasn't so much dreamy now as it was knowing, like in the photo. The trespasser smile said the woman knew her because Flo was the flesh of her flesh and the soul of her soul and she was here to claim her own.

The woman pressed her right hand to the glass. On the sofa, Flo drew back a little, though the urge to press her own hand to the same place on her side of the night-mirror was strong and getting stronger.

Flo knew what would happen if she did. The glass would vanish and their palms would meet, mother and child. Then her mother would lift her through the empty frame and take her away from the house, from the Grandmas, from her life.

And there was the man coming around the front of the car this time to stand with her mother and put one hand on the back of hers. Flo felt the pull toward them increase.

"Florence," Grandma 3 said in a tight, tense voice, and now Flo felt a pull in the opposite direction, although not strong enough to override the one from her parents. Her mother sensed it, as well, and turned her angry face toward Grandma 3 in a hard, jerky movement. Flo could all but hear the slap her mother wanted it to be.

Flo looked at Night-Mirror Grandma 3. Her face was set in a determined expression Flo recognized; she'd seen it on the other Grandmas as well as her own. It took all her willpower not to turn and look at the regular Grandma 3 in the living room. If she

did, the window would pop like a soap bubble; then her mother would pluck her out of the world of the living, stick her in the front seat of the trespasser car between her and the man so they could ride the endless highways of the land of the dead. Because that was how it was supposed to have been that night. She had been in the car with her parents.

The Grandmas hadn't told her but she knew; maybe she'd always known. Grandma 1 planned to tell her when she was old enough to understand certain things about the daytime world and the one reflected in the night-mirrors. Flo had picked up bits and pieces from conversations they hadn't meant her to overhear. It didn't make sense to her, but very little about grown-ups ever made sense anyway.

Why the Grandmas didn't want her to know she'd been in the car accident baffled her. It wasn't like it was a big secret—the police would know, and so would the ambulance people and the hospital they'd brought her to. So why keep it secret from her?

Her mother's expression was deeply sympathetic. And yet Flo could see the lie as plain and clear as day in her mother's cement-colored eyes. Whatever the Grandmas weren't telling her, her mother wasn't telling her the same thing. Same lie, different reasons. Knowing that kept Flo from putting her hand up to her mother's, her parents', on the glass so they could be together. So they could be a family again.

Flo frowned. They were already a family. That was beside the point.

The problem was, she was still alive. The sacrifice was incomplete.

Sacrifice? For what? To what?

Her mother's muddy-gray gaze told her that wasn't important. Only the sacrifice was important. They had been given one last chance to finish the ritual, complete the offering. Then they

would be more than mere servants of the Dark—they would be *of* the Dark themselves. But only if she joined them.

Flo wanted that, didn't she? Her mother's eyes seemed to penetrate her mind like the sharpest knife. Of course she did. Every little girl wanted her mommy and daddy, *needed* them.

Flo looked at Grandma 3's reflection. She was frozen in place, unable to move her arms. Grandma 3 couldn't touch her or hug her or pick her up and take her away.

But neither could her parents. It was up to her.

Flo brought her left hand up, and for a moment she could only stare in surprise. The lines she had traced on her palm glowed a vivid red; the skin had been scraped off and she could see blood oozing through the flesh underneath.

She turned her hand toward her parents. Her mother looked delighted for all of a second. Then Flo slammed her palm squarely over the woman's face.

Flo heard a scream, maybe with her ears or maybe just in her mind. Trickles of blood were running down the glass and somewhere in the distance, a door banged open, smashing against the wall so hard, the living room night-mirror rattled. But it didn't break.

● ○

When her vision cleared, she was sitting on Grandma 3's lap; Grandma 1 was putting a pad of gauze on her left hand, which felt like it was on fire, and Grandma 2 was holding her other hand.

". . . knew what to do?" Grandma 1 was saying. "Florence? Can you hear me?"

"Give her another minute or two," Grandma 3 said.

Flo tried to pull her left hand away but Grandma 1 was pressing the gauze firmly against her palm. "That *hurts.*"

"We know, kiddo," Grandma 3 told her. "Sorry to say it's gonna hurt for a while."

"Flo, can you tell me how you knew what to do?" Grandma 1 said.

"What did I do?" Flo asked, wiping her tears with a tissue Grandma 2 had just given her. There was no answer; the Grandmas were all looking at one another. "What?" she said.

Grandma 1 peeled the gauze off her bloody palm, making her wince. "Both your parents had gone through the windshield. They found you on the floor in the front seat. Broken glass all over the place but not a mark on you, not even a bruise. We knew then you'd inherited the family gifts."

Flo yawned; all of a sudden, she was exhausted. "Was there a sigil?"

"What do you know about sigils?" Grandma 2 asked her, surprised.

Flo shrugged, yawning again.

"Looks like you're going to have to have *the Talk* early," said Grandma 3, chuckling a little in a grim way that gave Flo a chill.

Grandma 1 put another pad of gauze on her palm and then wrapped her whole hand in the stuff, including her fingers. "I was hoping she'd get a few more happy years of childhood," she said sadly.

"She's got her whole life ahead of her," Grandma 3 said. "Plenty of time to have a happy childhood."

Leaning back against Grandma 3, Flo saw the sigil she'd left on the living room night-mirror. It was smeared now, and so were the forms trapped within it. They wouldn't be trespassing in any more night-mirrors anytime soon. Good thing; as smeared as they were, she could tell how angry they were with her.

She could understand that, Flo thought. It was going to be pretty boring for them, stuck in the smear. If they ever stopped screaming, maybe she'd let them watch the drive-in movies.

FEAR OF THE DARK

BENJAMIN PERCY

A power strip is plugged into every outlet in the bedroom. Each receptacle is full. Cords tentacle across the floor, connecting to lamps, forty-eight of them altogether. They are of varying heights and styles: some cheap plastic, others brass or wrought iron, one leather-sleeved, another wooden-necked. All are unshaded, their bulbs bare. The room is hot with their heat. The buzz of electricity shivers the air.

There is no furniture except for the mattress that centers the room. On it lies Penelope. She is seventeen with a long, curly mop of black hair. She wears a T-shirt, pajama pants, and a black cloth eye mask. Her pale skin is crosshatched with scratches and cuts. Her mouth is open and she breathes deeply, lost in a dream. Her face twitches at some disturbance.

• ∘

Malcolm can't see the Chugach Mountains, but he knows he's driving toward them, the road rising among their foothills. It is

midafternoon, but the sun is a distant memory. This is December in Anchorage, Alaska. The darkness grows longer by several minutes every day, and every one of those minutes feels like a pound of weight he has to carry around. He is never not drinking coffee, unless he is drinking whiskey to knock him into a narcotic sleep.

Snow falls. It is a fine powdery mix that swirls and billows as the Grand Cherokee charges through it. Malcolm leans forward to see better, the road ahead a vertiginous white. The windshield fogs over, making visibility worse. He cranks up the defrost.

He passes the occasional house, islanded in the dark. There are no streetlights nor guardrails, and it is difficult at times to figure out where the asphalt ends and the shoulder begins. He feels the right tire drag into gravel and he yanks hard at the steering wheel, correcting his course.

He has a stubby nose and his glasses are always sliding down it. His big body needs less fast food and more exercise. He fishes when he can and his fingers are scarred from slipped hooks and yanked lines. His wardrobe consists almost entirely of flannel and denim. He operates a private clinic, but spends a lot of his time making house calls. People around here don't want to deal with fluorescent-lit waiting rooms and X-ray machines and paperwork. He's set and plastered broken arms at kitchen tables. He's delivered babies on garage floors. Some of his patients are insured. Others pay him with venison or elk or salmon or whatever service they can offer. He hasn't been charged for an oil change in three years. His boots have been resoled twice. An antler chandelier hangs in the entryway to his office. He wears a pair of hand-stitched sealskin gloves when the temperature drops below zero.

That's the way things work in Alaska. You patch together your own rules. Sometimes it feels like everyone here is from somewhere else. Starting over after a failed marriage. Searching

for a new job after getting fired. Escaping a prison sentence. Or, like him, running away from grief. He ran as far as he could. He ran to the edge of the map.

He's not going to get better. But if he can help others heal, he can justify why he's still alive. Otherwise he'd rather fill his mouth with buckshot or cut a hole in the ice and drop into the black water.

The GPS indicates he's approaching the address. Mrs. Spivey, when she called, said that he would know the place by the Christmas wreath hanging off the mailbox. He turns down the driveway and almost loses control of the vehicle. Because a dozen motion-detector lights click on and flood the yard. Their brightness feels like an assault.

He pulls down the visor. That's not enough, so he holds up a hand, too, shielding his eyes. He creeps forward and finds a spot near the garage. He can barely see the house—the two-story structure looking like a crouched shadow behind all that light. He grabs his bag and keeps his head down and tromps through the six inches of snow. It's so light that it kicks and plumes out of his way.

The front door is already open by the time he gets to the porch. A woman stands in it, with light pouring around her.

● ○

Mrs. Spivey turns out to be Miss Spivey. Laura. That's what she asks him to call her, as she waves him into the house. He has trouble seeing her at first, since his glasses instantly fog up. He takes them off and blinks at her, trying to find his focus. She wears a T-shirt and running shorts. Her eyes appear bruised from lack of sleep. Her hair hasn't been brushed, a tangle of curls. She's chewed her fingernails down to blood. On her hip, a baby is

balanced. The boy wears nothing but a diaper. His arms and legs are rolled with fat. In his mouth is a green pacifier.

Malcolm begins to sweat. Maybe the thermostat is set high. Maybe the fire in the living room hearth is to blame. Or maybe it has something to do with the lights. They are everywhere, all of them blazing high-wattage bulbs. Not just the ceiling fixtures and wall sconces. But lamps. In the foyer alone there are four. He returns his glasses to his nose. He can see only so much of the house from here, but he tracks the extension cords threading the floor, the living room a garden of bare bulbs.

A teapot begins to whistle, and Laura excuses herself to the kitchen, padding away from him on bare feet. He hears the scrape of the kettle pulled off the burner. A second later she appears again, trying to smile and failing.

He asks if he should take off his boots, and she says no, and then she says, "You can put them over there." She asks if he would like a cup of tea, and when he says that sounds nice, she makes no move to fetch a mug. She seems so distracted that she's barely present.

The baby sucks the pacifier at a steady rhythm, making a damp clicking sound. "This is Tommy," she says. The boy clings to his mother and stares at Malcolm worriedly. "He doesn't like to be put down."

"Is Tommy the patient?" Malcolm says.

"No," she says, and her face tilts toward the stairs. "It's not Tommy that's having trouble."

Earlier, on the phone, she was hesitant, not telling Malcolm what was wrong, only saying her child was terribly sick and begging him to hurry. Now he is here, stepping out of his snow-slick boots, and he still doesn't understand what he's dealing with, maybe a mental health crisis. His lungs feel choked with the heat.

He unzips his parka and shrugs out of it. She makes no offer to hang it up, so he flops it over the newel post at the base of the stairs. "Can I ask what the trouble is?" he says.

"What?"

"Why did you call me? Why am I here?"

Her gaze meets his and then flits away. "It's easier to show you, I think. That's the only way you'll understand." Then her voice rises to a shout. "Penelope!" She waits a few seconds, and when she gets no response, she says, almost apologetically, "She's sleeping. She spends a lot of time sleeping these days."

● ○

Malcolm has been in every kind of home in Anchorage. Luxury log cabins owned by oil and mining execs. Hunting shacks with plastic stapled over broken windows. Yurts. Trailers. Bunkers. A home built from welded-together shipping containers. You can usually count on a mounted elk rack or a bearskin nailed to the wall. Maybe some lacquered fish. Rifles and snowshoes and fishing gear laid out openly. Pine panels. Cinder blocks. A mismatched cabinet door. A Pendleton blanket. A giant flat-screen TV set on top of a plastic crate. Exposed studs from an abandoned home-repair project. Things not really matching is kind of the standard, since everything here comes from far away. People cobble together what they can.

This home seems—by Alaskan standards—to be startlingly normal. Like something found in a lower-forty-eight suburb. The walls are a freshly painted gray. The couch matches the chairs. There is a woolen rug pinned down by the lacquered stump of a coffee table.

Except for the lamps. There are so many of them that it's difficult to walk without tripping over a cord or knocking an elbow

into a stand. None of them have shades. Their light stains his eyes, so that wherever he looks, there are ghostly afterimages.

Malcolm settles onto the couch. Across from him are two chairs. In one sits Laura. She clutches Tommy in her arms, bouncing him slightly, trying to get him to nap. His eyes droop and his pacifier clicks with less and less frequency.

In the other chair sits Penelope, the teenage daughter. Her legs are folded underneath her. Her arms are reddened with scratches and purpled with bruises. Malcolm tracks the gummy gash running from her wrist halfway to her elbow; she had attempted suicide and she had made the correct cut. Her hair is long and thick enough to hide most of her neck, but he spots at least one red gash along her throat. Her forehead is beaded with sweat and her shirt is soaked through at the armpits. She doesn't look at him, her eyes on the fireplace. A pitch pocket snaps and sparks fly. There is an iron wood rack beside the hearth with a dozen pieces of wood stacked in it.

"It's hot in here," Malcom says. "Isn't it?"

She doesn't register that she's heard him.

"I did a little bit of theater in high school. This brings back a memory. Of when I played Falstaff. It was so hot onstage—with the lights burning down on me—that the makeup melted right off my face. Have you ever done any theater?"

She shakes her head no.

"What do you like to do? For fun? Any sports?"

Her voice is husky and strained, as if raw from screaming. "I used to be play tennis. But that was . . . before."

"Before what?"

"Before we moved here. And before . . ." She gives up on the sentence. When she speaks again, it's to her mother. "He's not going to be able to help."

"Now hold on," he says. "Let's give this a chance. Earlier, your mother said she wanted to show me what was wrong. Can we do that? Can you show me?" He makes his voice as gentle as possible. "Penelope?"

"No," she says.

"Hey," Laura says. "It's okay. I'm right here."

"I really don't want to."

"You have to. This can't go on. We need to do something."

Penelope makes no move to get up.

"I'll help," Laura says. The baby is now asleep, and she rises carefully and picks her way through the cords until she stands over Malcolm. "Here," she says, and offers the baby. "Tommy'll keep sleeping as long as someone holds him. If I put him down, he'll scream bloody murder. Do you have him?"

"I've got him," he says and accepts the warm, sticky body.

"Do you know how to hold a baby?"

He renegotiates Tommy so that the boy's head rests in his elbow. The pacifier gently pulses. "I know how to hold a baby. I had . . ." Here he stops. "I know how to hold a baby."

Laura stares at him searchingly for a moment, and then seems satisfied. She goes to her daughter and snaps her fingers and says, "Up. Now."

With some reluctance, Penelope unfolds herself from the chair.

The two of them go to the corner of the living room. "How about here?" Laura says, and pulls back a few lamps, clearing an area for her daughter to stand.

Penelope steps into the space her mother indicates. Then glances back at where the walls make their corner. "This feels kind of close."

"So take another step toward me." Laura pulls the lamps back farther to give her daughter more space. "How does that feel?"

Penelope says, "That feels better." She absently picks at a scab on her forearm. It begins to bleed, a red trail oozing along her wrist, the back of her hand, her thumb, where the blood beads—and then drops to the carpet.

Her mother doesn't notice. Her attention is focused on a power strip, picking it up and toying with the cords, making sure she's accounted for all the lamps connected to it. Satisfied, she says, "Ready?" and hovers her thumb over the red button.

Penelope takes a deep steadying breath. "Ready."

There is a click. Five lamps go dark.

In that corner—the corner where Penelope is standing—a cluster of shadows forms. They are hers. They are her, various versions of her, black and gray, tall and short, and everything in between, thrown against the walls by the lamplight.

Some frequency in the air seems to shift. There is a sound—like an old door moaning open—followed by a quick whispering.

Penelope closes her eyes. Her fists clench at her side. Her whole body tightens. She breathes so heavily that her nostrils flare and her throat surges.

And then Malcolm notices the dark. The dark of the shadows. Something seems to move in them. As if there were shadows inside of shadows. More whispering follows. Then a scraping, like that of claws against wood.

Penelope flinches. A whimper escapes her mouth.

Malcolm doesn't trust his eyes at first. So he stands up to shift his view. Yes. A blackness—an *under*shadow—steadily stains the corner of the room, like a sudden moldering of drywall from water rot.

"Is that enough?" Penelope says in a strangled voice.

A boom sounds—a heavy impact that shakes the house—and a jagged crack opens in the wall.

Penelope cries out, "I said! Is that enough?"

Her mother clicks the button. "That's enough." The lights buzz back on. The sounds instantly recede.

Penelope hurries away from the corner of the room, returning to her seat, where she tucks her body into a shivering ball. Laura goes to sit on the arm of the chair, rubbing her daughter's back, saying, "You did so good. You were so brave."

Malcolm wants a better look. If before he stepped carefully among the lamps because he didn't want to knock them over, he now takes care because he wants to preserve the light.

The shadows in the corner are gone. But something lingers. A stain. It's a smeary abstraction, like a pencil drawing rubbed over by a wet thumb, or a mold that grew in the place where something dead slowly decayed. It is recognizable as a figure, but with a warped, tortured anatomy and the vague impression of hollow eyes and a gaping mouth.

He leans in to study it further and then gags at the carrion smell.

He is surprised to feel the baby squirming in his arms. He forgot it was there. He was squeezing the boy to his chest. He loosens his grip. Then he swings his hips and rocks his legs and says shh-shh-shh, falling into the familiar comforting rhythm, a vestige of fatherhood still in him. The baby coos and settles back into sleep.

Only then does he face Laura and Penelope again. They watch him carefully, hopefully.

"Can you help us?" Laura says.

He doesn't know how to respond. There is a part of him that wants to march right out the door, climb into his Jeep, slam on the gas, and get as far away from here as fast as possible. That's exactly what Penelope expects him to do. He can hear it in her

voice and see it in her defeated posture when she says, "Nobody can help us."

He has run before. Running is what brought him to Alaska. After his wife and son were T-boned by a drunk driver who ran a red light, he no longer fit in his house, his neighborhood, his job. Everything was a reminder of what used to be. His wife's brush, tangled with hair, sat on the bathroom counter. His son's half-drunk glass of milk remained in the kitchen until it evaporated into a ghostly rime. In the grocery store, people gave him pinched smiles and touched his shoulder when they said, "We heard about what happened." He hasn't escaped the pain, moving here, but sometimes a few hours or even a day passes without him remembering them. That's the mercy he needs.

"Can you help us?" Laura says again.

"You offered me tea before . . ."

"I did, didn't I? I'm sorry. I can't seem to focus. I haven't slept in . . ." Her eyes blink fast—one, two, three—as if accounting for days.

"I understand."

"Would you like some?" she says. "Tea?"

"I was actually wondering if you had anything stronger."

"Whiskey?"

"Whiskey's good."

"Of course," she says and leaves him. His eyes return to the corner, to the stain. He notices then the color variations throughout the room. The walls are freshly painted gray, but the gray is not uniform. Several sections of the room are patched, and he can guess what kind of shapes hide beneath them.

He startles at the sound of ice cubes tossed in a glass. He finds his breath again when he hears the soothing pop of a cork and the glug of the pour. He needs to calm himself. That's what

this family is looking for. A calm voice to counter the screams they must be choking down. Laura returns from the kitchen with a short glass of bourbon. He trades her the baby for it.

He holds the glass in both hands. The cold feels good. He fills his mouth, swallows, and lets the burn spread through his body before he speaks again. "You asked me for help. I'm going to approach this the only way I know how. I'll ask you the same questions I would any patient. So let's start with . . . when and how did the symptoms begin?"

● ○

They came here for a new beginning. Alaska was as far away as you could get without leaving the country. That's what they wanted. Distance. Her mother had the money from the divorce settlement and the money from the lawsuits. They bought a five-bedroom home on ten acres in the foothills outside Anchorage. The air smelled like ocean salt and pine resin and campfires.

Penelope entered West Anchorage High with music roaring in her ears. Her back was hunched beneath a pack and a thrift-store army jacket, as if she wished she could curl up and disappear herself. Most of the students were happy to ignore her. She moved through her first week invisibly, always in the rear row of every class, never raising her hand. But on a few occasions, she noticed someone watching her. The girl's hair was dyed black and purple on one side, shaved on the other. Her eyeshadow was blue and she had three black lines running from her lower lip to her chin. She wore a jean jacket busy with patches and pins for everything from the Misfits to the X-Men.

At lunch, Penelope avoided the cafeteria, preferring to eat outside, even in the cold gray of September. She was seated on the blacktop, her back against a brick wall, with a wrinkled brown bag beside her. She snapped into an apple and a shadow fell over her.

It was the girl with the black-and-purple hair. Mandy was her name. She was joined by a boy named Isaac. His hair was styled in a mullet. He wore a black shirt, black jeans, and oversize boots. He was skinny and long limbed, with a neck as thin as a wrist.

"What?" Penelope said, pulling out her earbuds.

"You're that girl from the news," Mandy said. "The one from Oregon."

This was the worst possible thing that could have been said. Penelope stiffened and looked around, making sure no one else had heard.

A basketball bounced. A group of boys joked and laughed. Somebody snuck a vape.

No one was looking their way.

"Don't worry," Mandy said. "The normals don't know. They don't pay attention to that kind of thing. But we do."

At this Mandy pulled back the sleeve of her jean jacket, revealing the razor tracks on her wrist. Isaac did the same. "We're part of the same club."

Penelope relaxed some, but still didn't know how to respond.

Mandy said, "You must have moved here to get away from all of that, right?"

"My mom thought it would be best."

"It's always going to follow you, though. No matter where you go." This wasn't said with cruelty, but understanding.

Penelope brought the apple to her mouth, but didn't bite. Her appetite had abandoned her.

"Meet us after school," Isaac said, his voice unnaturally high.

"For what?"

The two teenagers just smiled before departing.

They walked through Anchorage in a misting rain. The sky matched the gray of the sidewalk they followed. Seagulls shrieked and wheeled above them. Clouds shrouded the mountains. "Do you like it here?" Mandy said.

"I don't know," Penelope said. "Do you?"

"I don't know, either," Mandy said. "Except for the winter. I know I don't like that."

"Because it gets so cold?"

"Because it gets so dark," Mandy said, and Isaac said, "The dark makes people crazy."

The dark was already coming. It was only three in the afternoon, but in the gloom, the streetlights were buzzing to life.

They took her to Mandy's apartment. She lived above a laundromat, and even though the kitchen was a mess of dirty dishes, everything smelled like detergent and dryer sheets. Her mother was bartending and wouldn't be home until midnight. Isaac collapsed on a beanbag and Mandy and Penelope sat on a couch that was covered with a fitted sheet. The flat-screen TV remained dark. No one messaged on their phone or played music. No one even turned on a lamp. They just listened to the rain in the graying light. There wasn't much in the way of decor. A framed photo of a whale. Some Athabascan beadwork. A shelving unit full of novels and DVDs and video games.

Penelope kept expecting them to ask about what had happened. She drank too much at a house party. A few boys carried her unconscious body to a room. They stripped off her clothes and took turns with her while recording on their phones. She woke up bruised and unclean, a feeling that persisted to this day. What happened that night was ugly enough, but it was made worse by the videos that circulated—first among her schoolmates, then online in pornography forums. There was a police investigation. Lawsuits followed, as did countersuits, when the

boys were expelled from school. There had been media coverage due to her case matching others and a federal court ruling against sites that were willfully blind to distributing videos of minors. Somewhere in the middle of all of this, dying had seemed easier to Penelope than living.

This was the only thing that Mandy and Isaac cared about. The moment she cut her wrists and bled out in the bathtub. "How close did you get?"

"They barely got me back. I think they said I lost forty percent of my blood."

"Do you remember anything?" Mandy said. "About what happened?"

"When I died?"

They stared at her, unblinking.

"I just remember how everything hurt when I came back. My eyes hurt from the light in the hospital. My stomach hurt when they made me drink all those electrolytes. Even my skin hurt. Like, the feel of the cotton sheet rubbing against me made me want to throw up."

"Life hurts," Mandy said and nodded.

"But . . . I guess I also felt kind of amazing? I know that sounds weird."

"No," Mandy said. "That doesn't sound weird. Does it, Isaac?"

"No," Isaac said in his curiously high voice. "It doesn't sound weird at all."

"Because nothing," Mandy said, "nothing makes you feel more alive than dying."

● ○

They made Penelope watch. Because they wanted her to feel comfortable. They had tried a few different methods—drowning in a bathtub, choking in a plastic bag—before settling on this one

as the most controllable. They had a shoebox full of Vicodin and Percocet and a shoebox full of naloxone.

"It takes a while," Mandy said. "To find your sweet spot."

"Is this safe?" Penelope said.

"It wouldn't be fun if it was safe," Mandy said.

Isaac was easy to knock out because of his weight. Mandy counted out five pills on the coffee table. With the bottom of a glass she crushed them to powder. She used her student ID card to cut the white mess into lines. Isaac snorted them one after another with a rolled-up dollar bill. He sneezed. A chalky sludge dribbled down his upper lip. He licked it up. Then he plugged one nostril, sniffed hard, plugged the other, sniffed again. He settled back onto the beanbag chair, burrowing in so that his neck was supported. His eyes were already half shuttered as he studied the ceiling. "Damn," he said. "Fuck."

"How you feeling, Isaac?" Mandy said.

He opened his mouth to reply, but the words never came. He was already gone.

Mandy dug a Narcan out of the shoebox. "They give away Narcan at the clinic downtown. No questions asked." She ripped open the foil packaging and tossed it aside.

She slid off the couch and invited Penelope to join her on the floor. They listened to Isaac's breathing, over the course of several minutes, as it slowed and shallowed. His crotch dampened with urine. Mandy put two fingers to his neck, finding the jugular.

"How do you know—" Penelope started to say, but Mandy cut her off with a *shh*. She was concentrating, pressing her fingers so hard the skin of his neck whitened against them. She nodded, satisfied with something. Then she shoved the nozzle up Isaac's nose and depressed the plunger halfway. She repeated this on the other side.

He didn't open his eyes. He didn't gasp and sit upright. Nothing happened. Penelope felt a panic rising in her and Mandy said, "Chill. Sometimes it takes a bit."

When he did wake up, it didn't happen all at once. A finger fluttered. His eyelid twitched. A whimpering came from deep in his throat. She was reminded of her baby brother rising slowly from a nap.

"Here," Mandy said. "Help me turn him." Together they tugged and pushed at Isaac so that his body flopped sideways. "Just in case he pukes."

After a few minutes, he was drooling through a big smile. His voice was slurred when he said, "I am so goddamn happy to see you guys."

● ○

They met every Friday so that they had the weekend to recover. The suicide club, they called themselves. They rotated who died, week to week, with Penelope the third in line.

She almost didn't do it. "I'm not worried about myself," she said. "I'm worried about my mom. My dad left. Then all this shit happened to me. Plus she's got the baby. She's been trying so hard to make things work for us."

"You'll be fine," Mandy said.

"You'll be better than fine," Isaac said. "It's, like, medicine. You'll appreciate life more every time you almost lose it."

They were right—at first. She plunged into darkness and rose out of it sobbing and laughing. She hugged and kissed whoever was closest to her. Her nerves felt freshly scrubbed. Colors burned brighter. She drank down every breath like a cold gulp of water.

Usually she remembered nothing. But every now and then there was a wispy memory, like the rotten cobwebs of a dream.

Something was on top of her or below her. There were teeth and tongues and hands. She couldn't wrestle free. They had her. They claimed her. They—

The panic faded when her eyes snapped open and her friends came into bleary focus. They were smiling at her and welcoming her back. They were happy she was alive. And so was she.

"Didn't I tell you?" Isaac said. "We always come back."

But the next time they met, a week later, something came back with them.

• ○

Mandy couldn't scream. She couldn't move. But her skin darkened with bruises that made her pain evident. First her face, a swelling purple near her eye. Then her neck, where what looked like a long-fingered hand left its grip. A ribbon of blood fell from her nose when it snapped sideways, broken by an invisible force. More blood curled from her ear. A section of her hair tore away, revealing the candy-red slickness beneath her scalp.

She was lying on the couch in her apartment. Penelope and Isaac were hovering over her. Penelope screamed at Isaac to hurry, even though he was already pumping her full of Narcan. "I'm doing it," he said. "I'm fucking doing it already."

Penelope was shaking Mandy, telling her to wake up, and her hands came away bloody. Mandy's jean jacket—and the shirt beneath—were sopping wet. When Penelope pulled open the fabric to locate the injury, she found the skin of Mandy's belly torn away, revealing a mound of innards.

"Holy fuck," Isaac said, and scrambled back. "What the fuck is that? What the fuck is happening?"

The Narcan was beginning to kick in. Mandy was coming back into her body, but it was a ruined body, circuited with pain. Her lungs hitched. She released an uneven scream that

began to burble with blood. Her eyes snapped open, one of them a red marble.

The room was dark—the only light coming from the gray square of the window—and something joined them. Arms—six, no seven—rose out of the couch cushions and wrapped around Mandy. Their skin glistened like cellar-floor mushrooms. The nails were yellow and horned and chipped. A long finger curled into Mandy's open mouth, slipping down into her throat. Another burrowed into her eye up to the knuckle. Another peeled off her ear.

Isaac released an animal screech. A hand had slipped out from beneath the couch and seized his ankle. His weight was dragged out beneath him. He fell to the floor with such force he lost his breath. He pantomimed a scream as something ripped him out of sight.

Penelope said, "No, no, no, no," and retreated until her back hit a wall. Beside her was the light switch. She flipped it on. Because she needed to see better what had come for them, and because the dark felt sickening and oppressive.

The overhead fixture glowed a sudden yellow and chased the shadows to the corners. Beneath this sickly light lay Mandy's body. Everything was quiet except for the dripping.

● ○

Penelope has been questioned repeatedly by the police. They believe her story to be a drug-fueled hallucination. She hasn't been charged with anything, not yet, the case still underway. Isaac is considered their primary suspect, and she has been recommended for drug and psychiatric counseling.

Malcolm doesn't get this information from Penelope all at once. For more than an hour, he asks questions, sometimes searching for more detail, sometimes circling back to an earlier

moment for clarification. He tries to be as methodical as possible, as if this is something he can diagnose and treat. He doesn't express any disbelief. He knows what he saw. And somehow the affliction feels familiar.

Penelope had visited death, and death had clung to her. It didn't want to let her go. It would claim her yet. The same could be said of his wife and child. Their deaths stained him. Their foul, rotten bodies crouch inside him, peeking out at the world through the hollows of his skull and the slats of his ribs. They claw and chew at him. When he's not drinking coffee to stay awake, he's drinking whiskey to knock himself out. Whether his eyes are open or closed, it's night that he sees. He might have come here to escape, but he instead found a place that matched his mood—a permanent winter, a brewing darkness.

Something similar has manifested in this house, this family.

He sets down his empty glass. He takes off his glasses and rubs his eyes. His vision is smeary and full of phantoms.

"What do we do next?" Laura says.

"We do everything we can to keep your kid alive," he says.

A hard wind comes rolling off the mountains. The chimney whistles and the fire roars. The timbers of the house groan. "That's a big wind," Malcolm says, guessing it to be a fifty-mile-per-hour gust. He rises from the couch and walks to the entryway, where he peers out a window into the front yard. The snow whips into a white frenzy. The shaking of the trees is enough to set off the motion-detector lights. The swirling flakes make a dizzying conflict of shadows.

For a second, he thinks he sees someone out there. His wife. His wife and son. But then the wind changes direction and their shapes dispel.

The wind rises again, its roar joined by a crackling symphony of broken branches.

"Do you have a generator?" he says to Laura, and just then the power goes out.

● ○

There is no light except the fireplace. The rest of the living room is draped in tremoring shadows. The walls and floor and ceiling shake with a doom, doom, *doom*. A chair skids across the floor. Several lamps fall over and their bulbs explode.

The baby begins to wail. His pacifier falls and bounces into the darkness below the chair. Its rubber is glow-in-the-dark, a faint green color. For a second Malcolm stares at it—and then it pulses, as if another mouth has found it, and disappears.

"Go to the fire," he says. "Now."

Something curls around his ankle and he rips it away. Something claws the side of his head and tears off his glasses. He hurries forward in a stumbling rush. Penelope looks back, her eyes wide, and whatever she sees stills her. Malcolm reaches out an arm and scoops her up and carries her to the fireplace, where Laura waits with the baby. "Get down," he says. "Get in front of me." The four of them crouch there, and he shields them with his big body, his back to the room. "Don't look," he says. "And try not to listen."

The cracking of wood and drywall sounds like someone stepping out onto thin ice. More light bulbs shatter. Something damp squelches, like a mouth full of tongues. A hissing and a whispering fill the air. The wailing of the baby disguises some of this, but not enough.

Laura is talking to herself in a hurried, quiet voice, as if in prayer: "I wouldn't have moved us here. I shouldn't have moved us here. It's so dark here. It's always dark. We can't survive in the dark. I shouldn't have brought us here, we shouldn't have come."

Penelope, too, babbles wildly: "I'm sorry. This is my fault. I'm so sorry. I'm sorry."

He tells them to stop. He says it's nobody's fault. He says they're here—the four of them—and there's no way to change that. What they can focus on is survival. She asked him here to help, so he's going to help as best he can. "We've still got the fire," he says and feeds it another log. "Just focus on the fire."

Malcolm stares at the flames until his eyes feel seared. He curls his back until his spine screams and he grips their bodies until his shoulders ache. He knows not to look behind him. He knows the room is full of gray shapes that pace the flickering perimeter of light and wait for the fire to die or the sun to rise. What else can they do except hold on to one another as long as they can and hope that the night doesn't claim them.

THE PICNICKER

JOSH MALERMAN

The young man, Arnold Fabian, was reading *Beloved* for senior-year English, his bedroom barely lit by the beside lamp shaped like a basketball, when he jumped at the sound of a knocking at the second-floor window.

He closed the book, his heart thudding, and stepped to the glass.

But he knew who it was going to be. Who else? Both had felt the time coming for weeks now. Months. Both had sensed the future—college, distance, separate lives ahead.

He looked down into the yard and saw Natalie Wilson looking back up at him, pebbles in the palm of her hand. She was visible mostly by the Fabians' motion-detector spotlights, but her face was illuminated by moonlight alone. And in her eyes, Arnold saw the same flat resignation he felt in his own.

Alright, then. The end had come.

It was time for them to break up.

He nodded once to let her know he was coming down, then

set the book on his unmade bed. It wasn't quite midnight yet, an eternity to go in a teenage night.

He took the steps quietly, though Arnold wondered if his folks would've respected the moment. It felt plastered upon him: as though he, and all people, were made for these particular rites of passage.

Ned Fabian had already spoken to his son about "more fish in the sea."

Outside, Natalie was draped in the moment, too. Arnold closed the door behind him, and saw her form, wearing a hooded sweatshirt despite the summer heat, her auburn hair hanging as limp as her shoulders.

"Hey," she said. "Wanna walk to the meadow?"

Arnold nodded. The meadow was as good a place as any. It was where they'd spent their early days. It was where they'd fallen in love.

But, as they had learned together, love was a tricky thing.

"Sounds good."

Arnold wore his jean jacket. A new addition to his wardrobe, one that made him feel older somehow, closer to the man he was becoming.

Neither looked back to the Fabian house as they crossed the backyard, then out of range of the motion detectors. Then it was through the Nethers' uncut grass and the obstacle course of the Clutes' summer sprinklers, always running at night.

"This would've been funny to us before," Natalie said.

Arnold knew what she meant. Dodging a sprinkler, potentially getting wet . . . Hadn't they done that very thing a year ago? And hadn't it made them laugh?

But tonight they traveled with heavy hearts.

At the dirt road of Loori Way, Arnold put his hands in his pockets, Natalie took the flashlight from the pouch of her hoodie.

"I was reading more of that Toni Morrison book," Arnold said. "I think it's a little above me."

"Same," Natalie said. "Mom told me it's the kind of book we'll grow into."

"Well, I wish Mr. Carmichael would give us books we can understand."

"Maybe we're not supposed to yet."

Arnold wanted to tell her he loved her then. Because he did. And because the farther they walked, the more it felt like they were stepping down into a body of water, a lake of emotions so deep and dark as to overwhelm them.

Would they drown out here? Could one drown from a broken heart?

The trees here made a tunnel of the dirt road, and Natalie allowed the flashlight's beam to show them bent branches, black hollows, the organic tangle of all woods, before settling again on the bumpy road they walked.

"You doing okay?" Natalie asked. And her voice was compassion. For him, for her. For the moment in time.

"No," Arnold said. "Not really, Nat."

But they did not turn to face one another. They did not change their minds.

"Are you getting excited for Chaps?" he asked.

Chaps University. Only ninety minutes from Chowder, but it felt as far away as France. A place Natalie would vanish into, likely never to be seen again. New friends. New experiences. Possibly new love.

"I don't know if 'excited' is the right word," she said. And it didn't feel like the word had any place out here with them tonight.

He expected her to ask him if he'd finally decided what he was going to do. Would it be college or not? Would he stay in

the state or not? But she didn't. And Arnold understood how meaningless the answers to these questions would become, after they'd done what they were setting out to do tonight.

"Listen, Nat," he began. But she cut him off.

"The entrance is right there."

She shined the light on the small break in the trees, the natural gate they'd already passed through together a dozen times. He knew where the entrance was. But it seemed to come too fast tonight.

Natalie went first, the beam of light the path of life they were following as the dirt gave way to fallen branches and the branches then to the soft summer grass of the meadow.

"This sucks," she said. But that didn't feel right, either. Just as wrong as "excited." The weeds and short flowers were bathed in moonlight. Everything swayed in the warm wind.

Wasn't this once a beautiful place? And wouldn't it always be?

Natalie wanted to tell Arnold she loved him then. Because she did. But the confusion, the inevitable distance, the unmistakable proximity to the end . . .

She at Chaps University. Arnold . . . anywhere. And that anywhere felt bigger than it ever had before.

Their shoes momentarily flattened the soft grass until they reached the taller flowers and weeds, and both recalled lying out here, hidden, it felt, from their families, their homes, the cities, the world.

They'd had their first kiss in this meadow.

"I'm struggling with school stuff, too," Natalie said.

"With what?"

"Spanish. I'm trying. I really am. I just don't know if my mouth works that way."

Three months ago, Arnold would've laughed at this. She

would've, too. But tonight her struggle with Spanish felt like her struggle with him.

A stronger gust of wind blew the tall grass to the left and Arnold almost removed his hands from his denim pockets to hold her, to steady them both. The beam of Natalie's light tilted a little his way, too. But neither completed the gestures.

They walked. And they thought. And they felt. And they wondered when they should speak their minds and their hearts. When they should do what they came out here to do.

"I don't think there's any right or wrong here," Natalie finally said.

Arnold knew what she meant.

"There doesn't have to be a good guy and a bad girl," she said.

"But there could be regret," Arnold said.

He wanted her to agree. He thought she might. He thought maybe there was a chance, suddenly, a piece of hope, a—

But Natalie stopped walking mid-step, instead.

It happened so suddenly that Arnold stiffened, expecting to see an animal ahead.

"Shh," Natalie said sharply. "Do you see that?"

She trained the light ten feet beyond where they stood.

"I don't see—" Arnold began.

"Shh. Look, a basket."

He did see it then. A basket, yes. The very top of a picnic basket. One of its twin lids open.

"Weird," Arnold said. "Someone must've forgotten it."

The two walked slowly, in tandem, the light fixed to that basket. Then a checkered blanket, too, a bottle of wine, a small guitar.

And shoes, too. Shoes that led to ankles and legs.

"Holy *shit*," Arnold said.

A dead man. On his back on a picnic blanket.

Natalie moaned in a fearful way. A sound Arnold had never heard her make before.

Now they did reach for one another. They stood beside it, above it, the spread blanket, framed by the swaying grass. And the man, on his back, khaki pants and a yellow buttoned-up short-sleeved shirt. And in the light of the beam, they saw he was not only dead but had been for a very long time.

"My God," Arnold said. "Nat, what happened here?"

The two looked to the dead man's wrists, his fingers like bent wire, as if gripping something unseen.

Natalie raised the light to the man's face and the pair took a step back in unison.

His thin brown hair sat straw-like upon a leathery forehead, deep pockets cupping his closed eyes.

"Check out the basket," Natalie said.

But Arnold already was. One lid lay folded back, open, and by Natalie's beam they saw a fresh wheel of cheese, apples, two wineglasses, and a sleeve of crackers.

The warm wind tousled the grass, the dead man's hair, and a piece of paper, too, seen now in Natalie's light.

Words written by hand. The single page held beneath an impossibly bony elbow.

"We need to tell someone about this," Arnold said.

"He looks like he was supposed to meet someone," Natalie said.

Arnold hadn't seen it that way at first, he'd only seen the horror of it, without possible context. But Natalie was right. The open space on the blanket, the two glasses in the basket. And just like the books he'd been assigned in school, and just like the Spanish she struggled with, whatever the man might have been waiting for felt beyond them.

"What are we supposed to do?" Arnold asked.

Natalie stepped toward the sheet of paper.

"Don't touch him," Arnold said.

She didn't. She pulled the paper out from under the elbow.

"It's a song," Natalie said.

"How do you know?"

She shined the light on the small guitar.

"That's a mandolin," she said.

"How do you know?"

"My aunt Sherry plays one."

Natalie shined the light on the dead man's face.

"Jesus," Arnold said. "Do you think he was poisoned?"

They both looked to the unopened bottle of wine. The contents of the open basket. The cheese and crackers were still sealed. The apples uneaten.

The wind rustled the paper and Arnold reached for it so that both he and Natalie were holding a side. Natalie was right; it was a lyric sheet.

She read:

I'll wait for you, my dear,
As long as I must wait.
I'll sit in place and hold my breath,
Until I face my fate.
You said you'd meet me by the flowers,
That grew up to our knees.
And even if they were planted now,
I'd wait for them to reach our knees.
I'll wait, my dear, for you to come,
As you told me you would come.
You are my present, my future, past,
You are my first, my last . . .

You exist for me past hope and fear.
I'll wait for you, my dear.
You exist for me past hope and fear . . .
I'll wait for you, my dear.

A gust too strong took the paper from their hands and the two watched it sail slowly back down to the checkered blanket.

"A love song," Natalie said.

"It's impossible," Arnold said. "He couldn't have died by . . . waiting . . ."

"Are we doing the right thing?" Natalie asked.

And Arnold knew what she meant.

He heard tears in her voice. He felt them in his own.

Natalie shined the light on the dead man's face.

"There doesn't have to be a good girl and a bad guy," Arnold said.

"But there might be regret," Natalie said.

They stepped closer to the dead lover.

"Look," Arnold said.

He went to his knees on the blanket and took a small white box from a pocket of the man's khaki pants.

"Oh, no," Natalie said.

Because they both knew what it was.

Arnold rose and opened it anyway. They saw a gold ring within.

"I'll wait for you . . ."

The lyrics already as familiar to the teens as the wind. As the meadow. As their own first kiss.

"He died here . . . Yes, waiting," Natalie said.

"Waiting," Arnold echoed.

"Is it above us?" Natalie asked then. "The future?" And Arnold knew what she meant. "Will we regret letting go of what we have?"

For the first time since Arnold looked out his bedroom window, they faced one another. And they felt the power of doing so.

"Chaps University for you," he said. "And me . . . here . . ."

Natalie knelt beside the basket.

"Don't eat any of it," Arnold said.

But she wasn't going to.

She opened the second lid. Inside, a bottle opener.

She shined the light on the dead man's face again.

The pain, so clear. The open mouth, as if wanting to sing the lyrics, the curled fingers, as if wanting to accompany them. A corpse of a man who had done as he presumably sang: He had waited. For his love, he had waited. For the woman he was to marry, he had waited. For the future . . .

Flies crawled lightly on the man's forehead. One flew and landed upon a fingertip. Another on his lower lip.

"I love you, Arnold," Natalie suddenly said.

"I love you, too."

They both looked to the dead man's face.

"Will we regret it?" Arnold asked.

"I think it's above us," Natalie said. "I don't think we're ready to understand something like that yet."

They looked at one another with the same resolve they had when she was in the yard, he at the window.

Arnold saw her eyes were wet in the flashlight. He knew his were the same.

"We've made up our minds," Arnold said.

"Yes," Natalie said.

And their faces contorted into expressions each would remember for the rest of their lives, when they thought of their youth, with any mention of the years when things were above them, when things were too big to comprehend.

Facing one another, they allowed the tears to flow. And when

they turned to face the dead man on the blanket, they saw his eyes were now open.

"*Natalie!*" Arnold cried.

But Natalie had seen it, too.

And the sound . . . of twigs snapping . . . as the man turned his head toward them, as he made to sit up.

And from his dry, fly-encrusted lips . . . the lyrics . . .

"I'll wait for you . . ."

"We have to run," Arnold said, backing up.

"We have to leave this place now," Natalie said.

But neither ran. Not yet.

"I'll sit in place and hold my breath . . ."

Like rope stretched to its limit, the sound of the tendons of his arm extending, reaching for the mandolin by the picnic basket upon the checkered blanket.

"Until I face my fate . . ."

"Arnold . . . He's . . ."

"He's still waiting, Natalie . . . He's still waiting . . ."

The man snapped to a sitting position then, and the sound was like the death of a tree, wood cracked in half, echoing out upon the warm wind in the meadow of first kisses.

"I'll wait for you . . ."

But by then, Natalie and Arnold were already running, their legs whipped by the flowers and weeds, even as the first atonal plucks of the mandolin sounded behind them, a song neither would ever forget.

"You are my present, my future, past . . ."

The teens reached for one another, but their hands did not connect. Just as the throaty lyrics of love came without a key, the dead man's voice as troubled as the teens who fled it.

". . . past hope and fear . . . I'll wait for you . . . my dear . . ."

They did not stop when the grass got shorter. They did not

stop at the break between the trees. And they did not stop once their shoes connected with the dirt road that would take them back to their homes.

". . . past hope and fear . . . I'll wait for you . . . my dear . . ."

To the rhythm of snapping tendons in petrified fingers plucking the mandolin.

Arnold and Natalie did not look back.

Back to something they did not have themselves.

And they did not wait.

Wait for something they had already decided to end.

The song would haunt them. This was not beyond their comprehension. They would hear those dry strings, the knurled melody, the voice of a dead man's song, wherever their lives took them from here.

Yet, their minds made up, they fled a love they did not have.

SECRET NIGHT

NATHAN BALLINGRUD

State trooper Terry Vicks sped along the road between the mountains, the Dodge Charger alone on the highway, hugging the tight cliffside curves with graceful confidence. The sky was awash with stars and the Appalachians were a monolithic darkness on either side of him, the twisting road a narrow thread of human will extending through thousands of acres of wilderness on the border separating North Carolina from Tennessee. The worn old mountains seemed to him like sleeping giants, festering with occult histories. On nights like this he felt like a Jesuit priest, bearing the true light to lightless places.

He rounded a bend and the road erupted in a million stars from a constellation of broken glass sprayed across the asphalt. He braked hard, bringing the car to a growling idle about ten feet from the scene of a bad accident.

Vicks pulled slowly to the curb, illuminating the scene. A Subaru Outback lay on its left side. Its right side was crumpled inward; both the front and rear passenger doors had sustained a

massive hit. Oil, gasoline, and coolant pooled beneath the car. It looked like blood in the flat hard light of his cruiser's high beams.

Another car was parked about twenty feet farther up the road, on the far side of the wreck. He couldn't see the make or model yet.

He picked up the handset. "Dispatch, this is Officer Vicks on US 63 calling in a 10-50. A little past mile marker 33. Two vehicles. I'm going to need a tow and an ambulance, possibly two."

"Copy, Vicks. How bad is it?"

"Don't know yet. Pretty bad. Over and out."

He set the receiver back in its cradle and surveyed the scene another moment. He needed to move—someone might be dying. Almost certainly was. But something made him uneasy. An old, forgotten fear. He was reluctant to get out of the car.

"For Christ's sake," he said, ashamed of himself. He flicked on the blue lights and opened the door.

He liked to use the lights. He liked the way they muscled back the night, liked the brute intrusion of order and clarity into the darkness. They made him feel strong, and they lent him confidence now.

Vicks was twenty-four years old.

He approached the overturned Outback. "I'm Trooper Terry Vicks! Can anybody hear me?"

Nothing but the sound of the woods: crickets, rustling in the underbrush, wind in the branches.

He moved to the front of the vehicle. Its cooling engine still ticked. One headlight sent a weak beam into the forest. The windshield was a cracked white mass, leaning in like a hammock. From this vantage he could see the other car clearly now. It was a Chevy of a make he didn't recognize, a station wagon for God's sake, clearly from a time before Vicks was even born. Its engine was off and at least from this angle it seemed to have taken no damage.

"Hey! Is anybody in there? Can you hear me? An ambulance is on the way!"

He trotted over to the Chevy and shone his flashlight through the windows. They were filthy, covered in dirt and mud, though he could see that the car was empty. The interior looked clean and unused. Not even a crumpled grocery receipt on the floorboards.

"Fuck."

Returning his attention to the Outback, he thought about kicking the shatterproof windshield in, but didn't want to hurt anyone inside. He ran to his cruiser and fished a crowbar out of the trunk, hurried back to the vehicle, and levered the windshield free on one side. He used his hands to wrench it loose enough that there was space to shine his flashlight into the interior.

He steeled himself for horror. Father impaled by the steering column. Mother with her brains splashed over the glove box. A child or children in back, bodies broken and mangled. A baby in a car seat with—

It was empty.

"Oh thank Christ."

No one inside at all, though here at least there were signs of occupation: a Starbucks cup settled on the passenger window with lipstick smudged on one side, a purse with its contents scattered everywhere, a paperback bestseller with its leaves spread in the wheel well.

So where were they? He turned in a slow circle, looking first up and down the highway, sure that they must be somewhere nearby on the roadside. The road ahead continued for about half a mile before it bent to the right and disappeared behind the mountain. He could see no one there. He turned and walked to end of his own car, putting the headlights behind him, and

looked along the road there in case he'd missed them as he drove up. It was darker on this side, but still—nothing.

The woods loomed on one side of the highway. On the other, a cliff fell into a gulf of open space, where an endless range of forested mountains rolled into the distances. Wind whispered through the trees. Though it was early summer, the night was chilly and he wished for a jacket. He took a few steps off the side of the road, onto the soft shoulder, and trained his flashlight over the earth, looking for signs of passage.

Everything looked stark, black and white. He hadn't been out hunting in fifteen years; he wouldn't know tracks if he saw them, not anymore. He had the curious feeling that he was watching a movie of himself, and the thought of being observed at this futile investigation made him ashamed.

"Fuck this," he said to whomever might be watching.

Should he get in the car and drive ahead, looking for the survivors? What if he went in the wrong direction? What if they went into the woods, and he was driving away as they bled to death?

He shone his light into the tree line. It lit the oak trees directly before him and disappeared into a primordial darkness beyond.

A voice floated out from that darkness. Distant, high-pitched, and small. A child.

He couldn't make out any words.

"My name is Trooper Vicks! Stay where you are! I'm coming to help you!"

He cast another wary look at the station wagon behind him, troubled by its presence. It looked somehow familiar. Maybe its driver had already started into the trees, drawn by the same voice.

This is what you're here for, you goddamn coward, Vicks thought to himself; he stepped off the pavement and into the woods.

As soon as he passed the first trees, he found himself on an

incline. The ground was soft under his feet, damp from the recent rains. The clean scent of the woods—the varieties of oak, the moss clinging to bark and stone, the soil breaking underneath his boots, the rainwater pooled in logs and roots—filled his lungs, and he was reminded of the hunting trips he would take in these same mountains with his older brother and his dad, spending days with tents and rifles, building fires, telling stories, staring for long hours into the green stillness as they waited for a deer to step into the killing zone.

Someone out there was waiting for him now, needing his help.

"If you can hear me, call out again so I can find you!"

He stopped, awaiting a response. Again, nothing but the sounds of the woods at night, though this time they surrounded him. Crickets, small critters in the underbrush, the rustle of leaves in the high branches. These sounds were a lullaby for him once.

"Can you hear me? Call out if you can hear me!"

After another minute without a response, he continued forward.

The call couldn't have come from too far; if someone was injured or simply afraid, they'd stay near the road. The road meant safety. The road meant help. Vicks hastened deeper into the woods, calling out, pointing the beam of his light through the trees, making himself as conspicuous as he could.

Finally, he heard a voice. It was unmistakably a man's voice, coming from somewhere to his left.

"Here!" it called.

For a moment, Vicks paused. He was sure it was not the same person. The other had been a child, almost certainly a child, and it had come from farther up the mountain. The urge to ignore the adult and keep going to the child was primeval.

"Over here, please!" the man called again.

Vicks turned to his left and moved toward the voice, his feet

sliding on the sloped earth. Through the trees he made out a shape: small, dark, and hunched over, like a man curled into a fetal position.

"Just hold still," Vicks said. "Here I come. Why the hell'd you all go running off into the trees?"

"I did it! I'm so sorry! I did it!"

The man was curled up on the ground, his back to him. He wore a bright orange hunter's vest, camo clothing underneath, hiking boots. His hand was held over the side of his face and it looked odd, as though it had been broken. "Help me," he said. "Oh no, oh no."

"Are you hurt?" Vicks touched his shoulder.

The man straightened to a sitting position—something seemed wrong with his leg, it was bent in the wrong place—and then he stood, unfolding in segments, rising over Vicks's head, six feet, ten feet, twelve . . .

A shutter fell in Vicks's brain and he no longer tried to understand what he was seeing. The higher functions went dark and the lizard brain took panicked control. Vicks ran. He did not run back to the road, or away from the road, or in any particular direction at all. He simply accelerated away from this impossible thing as fast as he could, impervious to the branches snapped away by his face and his body, unaware of ricocheting off trees, blind to any purpose but flight.

After a time—probably only a few minutes, but the stitch in his side and his weakened muscles insisted it must have been so much longer than that—he put a hand against the bark of a maple and leaned over, heaving for breath. He looked behind him, the flashlight's beam splintering through the foliage, sending shadows leaping and twirling through the canopies. He strained to hear anything over the wheeze of his own breath.

Nothing but the normal sounds of the forest at night. Surely

that thing would have stilled the crickets into silence. Surely the whole forest would have trembled in quiet dread.

But no. The night wood sang its little songs to itself, peeping and cheeping under the stars.

Transferring the flashlight to his left hand, he placed his right on the butt of his sidearm, ready to draw. Only the awareness of other people out here—one of them likely a child—prevented him from pulling it free and aiming into the darkness.

He waited. Thirty seconds, a minute. Two.

Nothing.

How long ago had he called for assistance? Was it too soon to expect them out here? Probably. He was several dark, winding miles from town.

He toggled the radio affixed to his shirt.

"Dispatch, this is Vicks. Add an 11-99. May have a hostile on-site. Over."

"Say again, Vicks, did you say a 'hostile site,' over?"

"No, I said there's a *hostile on-site.* Send me some goddamn backup! Over!"

A quiet sound came over the radio, breaking up in a spurt of static. Did that motherfucker just laugh at him?

"Do you copy, dispatch?"

"I copy. Help is on the way. Hold tight, Vicks. Over and out."

"Fucking dick," Vicks muttered. He turned from his vigil and looked back upslope, where he thought he'd heard the child's shout come from before. He made his way up there, suddenly less eager to call out.

As he pushed forward a single point of reason in his mind reminded him, with growing insistence, that he was putting distance between himself and the road, where help would be arriving any minute. The tall man (*not a tall man, something else, something else*), if it was anything more than a trick of his imagination, was

out there somewhere, between him and the road. An icy sweat trickled from his hairline.

But there was a child. Maybe with her parents.

(*Why would they be so far from the scene of the accident?*)

It was his duty to go see. That's why he took this job. That's what he was here for. He was the light in the dark. He was the strength from on high. He had to go.

He hazarded a quiet call. "Hello? Tell me where you are. Help me find you."

The distant hiss of tires on pavement made him stop and turn. Through the trees he saw headlights approaching. He stood straight, ready to break for the road to greet them, but they swept past and disappeared around a bend, not even slowing.

An unreasoning sense of despair threatened to take him, but he shook it off with shame.

You're a goddamn cop. The shadows made you see something that isn't there. Do your job, you little bitch.

An echo from his brother, on the last hunting trip: *you little bitch.*

Once upon a time, Vicks had been afraid of the dark. A fact his older brother, an authoritative twelve years old, had ruthlessly exploited, especially that last trip, the one where their father had had his bad night. A stupid thought to come to the surface now.

He continued to creep up the slope. He strained to listen for any sign of activity, ahead or behind. The girl or the tall man, the impossible man. Belatedly it occurred to him that the tall man was why the girl and her parents had left the site of the accident. They were fleeing.

He tried to move quietly but each footfall crunched leaves and twigs beneath his weight, announcing his location. He turned again, walking backward briefly, alert for any signs of the tall man.

That's all he was. Just tall, maybe even abnormally tall, like a basketball player. Pushing seven feet, sure. In the uncertain light that would be easy to misread as something unnatural. He took comfort in the idea that it gave his pursuer a disadvantage. It would be harder for him to stay hidden.

The woods were still. Another car whispered by below, not stopping. He couldn't see the headlights this time.

A whimper from farther up the mountain. Close. Definitely a young girl.

"I'm coming. My name is Terry. I'm a policeman. I'm here to help you. Okay? Are you with your parents?"

Another echo from the past.

Where's your parents?

Not a cop, but a hunter. A fat old man—he'd seemed old at the time but he was probably only in his forties, Vicks thought uselessly—standing twenty yards away from him, a rifle held across his chest as the rising sun spread its light through the trees behind him.

What are you doing out here? Where's your parents?

Vicks, nine years old, ran to him, relief and terror flooding his body, making it impossible to respond. The hunter dropped to one knee and set his rifle down carefully, and received the strange, terrified little boy into his arms.

Hey, pal. Hey, it's okay. He held him by the shoulders at arm's length, meeting his eyes. *Are you okay, son? Was there an accident?*

Terry could only cry. He wanted to tell about Robbie and his dad but he couldn't get the words out.

The hunter rose to his feet, holding Terry in one arm, and called behind him. *Sam! Over here! I think there's been an accident!* And then, under his breath, *Oh shit oh shit.*

Focus, Vicks thought. *Fucking focus.*

He continued on, the slope getting steeper. He trained the

light on the ground, looking for solid places to put his feet. It would be easy to miss a step and go sliding halfway back down. A root here, a rock there, a stump, a ridge. Plenty of footholds, he just had to keep his wits about him.

Once, he'd climbed through these woods and up these slopes like a billy goat. But it had been a long time since he'd come back into the wilds. He never did develop a taste for hunting.

The top of the mountain peaked a good distance above him, several hundred yards at least. The forest canopy made a black ridge against the stars, their branches shifting in the chilly wind. The trees whispered to each other, night animals shuffled and darted.

A sharp snap sounded behind him—a big branch cracking beneath something heavy. A bear, maybe. But the bears should be sleeping. Everything good and holy should be sleeping.

He took his gun out of its holster and trained it on the woods behind him. He played the light back and forth, but that only made the shadows leap and twirl. Movement everywhere.

"You come out where I can see you," he said. "I swear to God I will shoot your ass if you keep fucking around."

He steadied the light. It illuminated a few trees, but accentuated the darkness around them. The woods were quiet. Mostly.

"Fuck this," he whispered, and toggled his radio. "Dispatch, this is Vicks. Where the hell is my backup, over?"

A wash of static.

"Dispatch, do you copy?"

A voice swam up through the white noise. "Who are you talking to?"

Vicks stared at the radio. "Andy, are you drunk? This is Vicks, goddamn it. Have you sent backup to my location? Over."

The voice laughed. He couldn't tell if it belonged to a man or a woman. "Who are you calling, baby? Who are you calling?"

A small, weak sound slipped out as he dropped the receiver and backed farther up the hill, all his attention concentrated on the crowded darkness below. He couldn't see his car anymore, even though he'd left the lights on. He couldn't see the road at all.

That laughter squatted in the middle of his brain and sounded again and again on a hideous loop. It didn't sound like Andy. He didn't recognize the voice.

A root connected with his heel and he fell backward, banging his shoulder on a tree and knocking both the flashlight and the sidearm from his hands.

His brother had laughed, too. It was a high, eerie laugh, and it upset Terry because he knew his brother was scared.

What's wrong with Dad? Terry had said, and Robbie had laughed his scary laugh. *It's not funny!*

Dad's crying because he has to leave you here tonight, Robbie said. *He doesn't want to but Mom's making him.*

What? That's not true!

Yes it is. You know how they're yelling about money all the time. They can't afford to keep you. You eat too much. You want too much. You're making us all broke.

No I'm not! I'll stop, I promise!

It's too late. And now he's taking you to the secret night.

Terry's blood froze. His brother had told him about the secret night before, when they stayed up too late and whispered to each other after the lights were off. He didn't like to hear about the secret night but sometimes he couldn't help it, and he asked Robbie to tell him more.

The secret night was the reason you had to be in bed and under the covers before it got too late, and why it was a good idea to have a night-light on. You could only get to it through a door, and the door moved all the time. Sometimes people got through it on purpose, but mostly it was by accident. It didn't

even look like a door. It looked like nothing at all, so you didn't even know you were through it until it was too late. And once you were through it you could never get out again.

"Help me!"

It was the girl. He saw her at last: a flash of white clothing ducking between the dark trees. He scrambled to his feet, scanning the ground for the flashlight and the gun. He couldn't find them. The flashlight must have been turned off or broken when he dropped it; losing the gun would spell real trouble. No time for it now, though.

"Stay put!" he called, and climbed up, having to use all fours to keep his balance on the gradient.

Several yards behind him he heard a male voice ask, as though speaking to itself, "Who are you calling?" It giggled, and asked the question again, this time sounding farther away. "Who are you calling?"

After another minute of climbing, he was running short of breath. He'd torn the skin on the palm of one hand, and ripped the knees on his trousers. But there she was at last. A young girl dressed in a white dress, something simple and elegant her parents had picked out for her, too light for these nighttime temperatures. She looked five or six. Her hair was long and straight, pale blond that seemed to cast light in a little nimbus. She was standing about ten feet away, watching him.

"Please, stay there! I'm here to help you." Vicks risked a glance behind him for the tall man, but he was nowhere in sight.

"I'm lost," the little girl said.

"Where are your parents? Were you in a car accident?"

Don't overwhelm her with questions, he told himself.

"They're back here. I think they're shot."

"Okay." The ground had leveled off a bit and he was able to walk on his feet now. The sounds of the woods at night were all

around him: the crickets, the slow tromping of small animals, the distant, hideous shriek of a coyote.

The girl fell backward, but stopped before she hit the ground; she looked as though someone invisible held her by the shoulders, and then started dragging her. The heels of her bare feet bounced over the earth and rocks, over exposed roots. "Help me," she said with a calm that raised gooseflesh on his arms.

He charged after her, knowing full well something was terribly wrong, but unable to watch a child being dragged into the darkness without acting.

He stopped only when her body left the ground, lifting into the air and hovering three or four feet over the earth as she continued to retreat, pulled through the branches of trees, asking for help as though she were reading cue cards in a school play.

His hand went for his sidearm, but of course it wasn't there. It was buried in leaves somewhere down the mountain.

She dangled there for a moment, and then something behind her moved. Something huge. A black gulf opened, and Vicks could only understand it as a throat. The child suspended between open jaws, barely discernible in the dark of the woods.

Like a lure, he thought crazily, and laughed out loud. An unhinged, scary laugh, like his brother's laugh all those years ago.

He's taking you to the secret night.

Vicks turned and ran. The path was steep and he immediately lost his footing and tumbled down the mountainside, slamming into trees and bouncing hard off rocks and exposed roots, his body reaching a velocity he knew would be fatal if his head collided with the trunk of a tree but he didn't care, faster was better; he could hear it pursuing, breaking branches and snapping trunks as it charged after him, he could feel its hot breath on his body, hear the child-lure pleading for help, its voice coming

not from its lips but from the gaping throat behind it, like some hunter's game call.

The radio toggled on and the static whine shrieked in the night, and Andy's voice shrilled out, "*Who are you calling, Terry? WHO ARE YOU CALLING?*"

He slammed into the trunk of a maple, bringing his fall to an abrupt halt. Pain flashed in his ribs and rippled out to his whole body. He tasted blood. He tried to pull in a breath but his lungs hitched halfway through. His ribs were cracked, maybe broken. He wrapped his right arm around his chest; a sob escaped him, but it hurt too much to repeat.

He saw a beam of light a dozen or so yards away, slightly above his position: the flashlight. So his gun must be nearby, too.

But then he saw what looked like a tree walking a little beyond it, and he knew the tall man was looking for him still, humming a happy little tune.

Vicks got to his feet and kept sliding down the hill, able to guide his trajectory a little more easily now, and soon he saw the flashing blue lights of the Dodge Charger, a pulsing lighthouse in the seething darkness.

He wept.

Vicks clambered down the last few feet, and soon his boots were on pavement again. The mountain rose behind him, and the wrecked cars were still there, though the station wagon looked different in the wash of his cruiser's headlights. It looked less specific, less distinct; in fact now he couldn't be sure it was a station wagon at all. Just a nondescript four-door, with small tendrils like taproots growing from one of its fenders, for all the world like a fringe of hair. And then it moved sideways, a few squalling inches toward the edge of the forest.

"No," Vicks said, and edged toward his cruiser. The blue

lights were playing all over the cars, the road, the woods, he must have misunderstood.

It moved again, dragging several feet before it stopped. Long roots and vines reached from its undercarriage and disappeared in the woods.

A lure, he thought again, and this time he couldn't stop laughing, no matter how much it hurt. He got into the cruiser and turned it around, gunned the engine down the road, giggling at first, then laughing hysterically through the rising pain.

Above him the stars pinwheeled in a bewildering, madcap dance, flaring and arcing and sizzling in the dark.

● ○

Two days later they found the owner of the Outback, a middle-aged woman who'd crawled from the vehicle and died of head trauma on the side of the road several hundred feet beyond where he'd reported the Chevy station wagon to be. If he'd only kept walking along the road, instead of running into the woods, he might have saved her. Probably not. But maybe.

Of the station wagon there was no trace. No tire marks on the road, no leaked oil, not even any paint left on the side of the Outback where it had apparently been hit. Vicks asked them to check the woods for signs it might have driven (*been pulled*) off-road. This earned him a few skeptical looks, but they checked, and found nothing.

Nor, of course, was there evidence of anything else, save the trampled path he'd made on his climb, and again on his graceless descent.

Andy, who had worked dispatch that night, reported that he had never called in a request for assistance, and indeed had not immediately responded to routine prompts. A transcript of his interactions that night backed him up.

Between that, and losing his gun, he was temporarily suspended from duty until he could be cleared by a review board and a psychiatrist.

The psychiatrist was a man called Dennis Waite. He was older than Vicks, but not by much. Maybe mid-thirties, with a thin beard to affect some gravitas. Not old enough to command respect, or to fool Vicks into thinking he had anything more to offer than some stale ideas he'd read in a book. His office was in a strip mall. Its interior was pale and stark. There were no windows; you couldn't tell if it was night or day outside. This, at least, was reassuring.

"What do you think really happened?" the doctor asked. Vicks had only told him about seeing the little girl, and how she might have been an illusion. A trick of the mind, who knows what. He did not and would not say anything beyond that.

"I don't know," he said. "There's no explanation for what I saw."

"There's always an explanation."

Vicks nodded. He needed that to be true.

He found himself talking about his dad. How did they get onto this subject? He must have let his guard down.

"So your dad had a breakdown that night?"

"I guess."

"What happened?"

"He took us out hunting. Me and Rob. And then when we were setting up the tent, he just started crying."

"About what?" Dr. Waite was sitting behind his desk, leaning back in his chair with his hands behind his head. He was probably just trying to be comfortable but he looked like a perp.

"He didn't fucking say. Okay? That's not how he was."

"But he was the sort who cried in front of his children?"

". . . No."

"It must have been upsetting."

You little bitch.

"It was scary, man. Rob didn't exactly help."

"What do you mean? What did he do?"

Vicks didn't want to talk anymore. The lack of windows, comforting such a short while ago, was starting to bother him. How long had he been talking to this guy? He couldn't shake the feeling that night had fallen outside. He knew darkness had weight. He could feel it straining the building's foundations.

"Terry? What did your brother do that wasn't a help?"

"Oh, you know, nothing serious. Big brother stuff."

"Like what?"

"What time is it, anyway?"

Dr. Waite looked at the clock on the wall, making no mention that it was in full view of them both. "Three forty. We still have some time."

"P.M., right?" Vicks said, and laughed weakly, to show that he was just joking.

"That's right," Waite said, as if it were a perfectly reasonable question. "Three forty in the afternoon."

"He, uh, he told me that Dad was taking me out into the woods to get rid of me. He was taking me to the secret night."

Waite sat forward. "What's the secret night?"

Vicks laughed but wouldn't meet his eyes. "Just dumb kid stuff. It's, like, the night behind the night. You step through a kind of doorway and you're in the night that never ends. It was a thing we invented to scare ourselves."

"That's a cruel thing to say to a little boy."

"I guess. Whatever."

"Is that what you think happened to your father?"

Vicks blinked. "What do you mean?"

"Did he go into the secret night? Is that why he did what he did?" He picked up a paper from a stack on his desk. "You say

your father brought you out on this camping trip, but your file tells me you were raised by a single mother. Your dad was never a part of your life." He put the paper back down. "He left your family when you were still a baby."

"He came back. He tried to make things better."

"Your mother says he kidnapped you and your brother. You were missing for three days."

"That's bullshit. She knew where we were."

"I'm only reading what it says." He paused, and gestured to a phone on his desk that spilled a cold smoke along the desk and to the floor. When Vicks looked at it, all sound vanished; there was only the absolute silence of the gulf beyond life. When he looked back up at Waite, the phone seemed to vanish and the sounds of the world returned.

"If I called Robert," Waite said, "would he say the same thing?"

"What? Why the fuck would you say that?"

He spread his hands. "It's just a what-if." When Vicks didn't respond, Waite said, "We can leave it for now."

The session ended shortly afterward. Waite shook Vicks's hand and told him he would clear him for a return to duty but would like to see him again on a regular basis. Vicks deflected.

He left Waite's office and walked down the short corridor to the glass door that opened onto the parking lot. It was dark outside. A thin moon burned in the sky.

"What the fuck," Vicks whispered. He stepped outside.

The parking lot was mostly empty, save a few old cars that probably never moved anymore. All the other shop fronts were closed. A few streetlamps shed soft white curtains of light.

He couldn't remember how he'd gotten here. Hadn't he driven his car? He must have. In any case, he needed a ride. He took out his cell phone and held it to his ear.

A hand fell on his shoulder. He turned and there was Waite, standing beside him.

"Who are you calling?" he said. His voice sounded different outside of his office.

"I don't know how to get home," Vicks said absently.

"Come on. I'll give you a ride."

• ◦

Vicks lived in a small second-floor apartment in the city. The building was not exactly a slum, but give it five more years. He lived alone except for his cat, an orange-furred layabout called the Brick. He'd found the Brick rooting through a dumpster one week after finishing the academy, and had taken him in as a kind of celebration.

"Things are going to get better for the both of us," he'd said. The Brick seemed to agree. In the three years since, the two of them had formed a bond based on respect and a mutual trust that the other would continue behaving as he had before. A good routine was the next best thing to love.

Vicks fell back onto the couch and made a space for his feet on the coffee table, pushing aside some unread mail, some drinking glasses, an opened box of Pop-Tarts. He turned on his laptop and looked at the news.

A local story held that they'd found the missing state trooper's cruiser on the side of a mountainous stretch of US 242. It seemed to have collided with a Subaru Outback carrying a woman and her granddaughter.

"What do you make of that, Brick? Who was that poor bastard? Crazy stuff."

Brick lay in a cocoon at the end of the couch. He would emerge from it as something new and astonishing. The cocoon

flexed, slowly and steadily. The movement seemed disturbingly sexual to Vicks, so he looked away. "That's fucked up," he said mildly.

A phone started to ring. It was hanging in the kitchen. The old-fashioned kind, the ones that hung on the wall and had a receiver connected by a cord. When he looked at it, it went silent. Everything went silent. Smoke fell from it like water, gathering on the floor.

His brother stepped out of the kitchen. He was twelve years old, with a large hole in his chest—an exit wound made by a rifle's bullet. He lifted the receiver and held it to his ear. Then he held it out to Vicks.

"It's Dad."

Vicks shook his head. He looked back at the laptop screen, but it had gone dark. He looked toward the window. The blinds were closed, but they rippled as though a wind blew against them. The cat made a heavy, wet sound from inside his cocoon.

He accepted the phone and brought it to his ear.

"Hello?"

His own voice came back to him. He sounded like he'd been crying. He sounded very young. "I can't get out," he said. "I'm lost. Please help me."

Vicks nodded, and hung up the phone. He went to the window and raised the blinds. Outside, the night filled the whole world. Dark, burning stars. Shapes moving below, shapes without form, wriggling masses. Cocoons ready to split. A weight from above, stupendous and implacable.

There were no roads.

Surely somebody would come to help. Surely somebody out there, somewhere, carried some light.

About the Authors

Nathan Ballingrud is the author of *The Strange*, *Wounds*, *North American Lake Monsters*, and most recently *Crypt of the Moon Spider* and *Cathedral of the Drowned*. He's twice won the Shirley Jackson Award and has been short-listed for the World Fantasy, British Fantasy, Locus, and Bram Stoker awards. His work has been adapted for both film and television. He lives in Asheville, North Carolina.

Pat Cadigan has won the Locus Award, the Hugo Award, the Seiun Award, the Scribe Award, and the Arthur C. Clarke Award. She lives in London.

Dan Chaon's most recent book is *Sleepwalk* (2022). He is the author of six previous books, including *Ill Will*, a national bestseller, named one of the ten best books of 2017 by *Publishers Weekly*, and a nominee for the Shirley Jackson Award. Other works include the short story collection *Stay Awake* (2012), a finalist for the Story Prize; the national bestseller *Await Your Reply*; and *Among the Missing*, a finalist for the National Book Award. Chaon lives in Cleveland, Ohio.

Clay McLeod Chapman writes books, comic books, and YA/middle-grade books, as well as for film and television. His most recent novel is *Wake Up and Open Your Eyes*. You can find him at www.claymcleodchapman.com.

Born in England and raised in Toronto, Canada, **Gemma Files** has been an award-winning horror author for almost thirty years. She is probably best known for her novel *Experimental Film*, for which she won both the Shirley Jackson Award and the Sunburst Award, and her Bram Stoker Award–winning short story collections *In That Endlessness, Our End* and *Blood from the Air* (both from Grimscribe). Her next collection, *Little Horn: Stories*, will be released in 2025 by Shortwave Publishing.

Stephen Graham Jones is the *New York Times* bestselling author of some thirty-five novels and collections, novellas and comic books. Most recent are the comics *Earthdivers* and *True Believers* and the novels *The Angel of Indian Lake, I Was a Teenage Slasher*, and *The Buffalo Hunter Hunter.* Stephen lives and teaches in Boulder, Colorado.

Eric LaRocca is a three-time Bram Stoker Award finalist and Splatterpunk Award winner. He was named by *Esquire* as one of the "Writers Shaping Horror's Next Golden Age" and praised by *Locus* as "one of strongest and most unique voices in contemporary horror fiction." LaRocca's notable works include *Things Have Gotten Worse Since We Last Spoke, Everything the Darkness Eats*, and *The Trees Grew Because I Bled There: Collected Stories*. He currently resides in Boston, Massachusetts, with his partner.

Josh Malerman is the *New York Times* bestselling author of *Bird Box* and *Incidents Around the House*. He's also one of two singer-songwriters in the Detroit band the High Strung, whose song "The Luck You Got" can be heard as the theme song to the Showtime show *Shameless*. He wrote some dozen novels in

the passenger seat of the band's van while touring the country before publishing *Bird Box,* his first published work. He also filmed a documentary capturing the writing of a novel, from idea to finished first draft. Malerman lives in the Detroit area with his fiancée, the painter-musician Allison Laakko.

Benjamin Percy is the author of seven novels—most recently *The Sky Vault* (William Morrow, 2023)—three story collections, and a book of essays. He's been writing *Wolverine* for Marvel Comics since 2017. His fiction and nonfiction have been published in *Esquire, GQ, Time, Men's Journal, Outside, The New York Times, The Wall Street Journal, Cemetery Dance,* and *The Paris Review*. His honors include the Whiting Award, the Plimpton Prize, an NEA Fellowship, a McKnight Fellowship, the iHeartRadio Award for Best Scripted Podcast, and inclusion in *The Best American Short Stories.*